LON CHANEY
AS
THE MAN WHO LAUGHS

Books by
Philip J. Riley

CLASSIC HORROR FILMS
Frankenstein, the original 1931 shooting script
Bride of Frankenstein, the original 1935 shooting script
Son of Frankenstein, the original 1939 shooting script
Ghost of Frankenstein, the original 1942 shooting script
Frankenstein Meets the Wolf Man, the original 1943 shooting script
House of Frankenstein, the original 1944 shooting script
The Mummy, the original 1932 shooting script
The Mummy's Curse the original 1944 shooting script (as Editor in Chief)
The Wolf Man, the original 1941 shooting script
Dracula, the original 1931 shooting script
House of Dracula, the original 1945 shooting script

CLASSIC COMEDY FILMS
Abbott & Costello Meet Frankenstein, the original 1948 shooting script

CLASSIC SCIENCE FICTION
This Island Earth, the original 1955 shooting script
The Creature from the Black Lagoon, the original 1953 shooting script (editor-in-chief)

THE ACKERMAN ARCHIVES SERIES - LOST FILMS
The Reconstruction of London After Midnight, the original 1927 shooting script
The Reconstruction of A Blind Bargain, the original 1922 shooting script
The Reconstruction of The Hunchback of Notre Dame, the original 1923 shooting script

CLASSIC SILENT FILMS
The Reconstruction of The Phantom of the Opera, the original 1925 shooting script
The Reconstruction of "London After Midnight" the original 1927 hooting script (2nd edition)

FILMONSTER SERIES - LOST SCRIPTS
James Whale's Dracula's Daughter, 1934
Cagliostro, The King of the Dead, 1932
Wolf Man vs. Dracula 1944
Lon Chaney as Dracula/Nosferatu
Robert Florey's Frankenstein 1931
Frankenstein - A play, 1931 (editor)
War Eagles (as editor)
Karloff as The Invisible Man 1932

AS EDITOR
Countess Dracula by Carroll Borland
My Hollywood, when both of us were young by Patsy Ruth Miller
Mr. Technicolor - Herbert Kalmus
Famous Monster of Filmland #2 by Forrest J Ackerman

FILM DOCUMENTARIES
A Thousand Faces - as contributor (Photoplay Productions)
Universal Horrors - as contributor (Photoplay Productions)

Mr. Riley has also contributed to 12 film related books by various authors
as well as numerous magazine articles and received the Count Dracula Society Award
and was inducted into Universal's Horror Hall of Fame and
won the Halloween Book Festival 2011 award in the horror category

LON CHANEY
AS
THE MAN WHO LAUGHS

An Alternate History for Classic Film Monsters

By

Philip J. Riley

Hollywood Publishing Archives

BearManor Media

BearManor Media
P.O. Box 1129
Duncan, OK 73534-1129

Phone: 580-252-3547
Fax: 814-690-1559

www.bearmanormedia.com

Cover Art - ©2012 By Paul Spatola.
 Since none of the scripts in this series
were thought to exist and were never produced, we have created mock-up posters in the vintage style of the period.
Lon Chaney's face replaced Conrad Veidt's in the image of the actual 1928 one sheet - by fantasy artist Paul Spatola
All photographs are from the Author's collection, unless credited in photo captions
Certain treatments were reset in LoveLetter font since the microfilm was not clear enough.

"Lon Chaney, A portrait of the Man Behind a Thousand Faces" by Adela Rogers St. Johns, first appeared
in Liberty Magazine - May 2-May 30th, 1931.

Note: You will notice a change in the size of the type on some pages. The reason for this is that most of the early
Universal scripts were printed on 8.5x13 legal size paper and needed to be reduced to fit on this books 8.25x11
paper size.

The Author would like to thank the following individuals who contributed and helped make this series possible.
Carl Laemmle Jr., R.C.Sherriff, Stanley Bergerman, Gloria Holden, Jane Wyatt, Otto Kruger, Marcel Delgado,
Robert Florey, Paul Ivano (Cinematographer), Paul Malvern (producer), Elsa Lanchester, Merion C Cooper, Patric
Leroux, Bette Davis, Bela G. Lugosi, Technicolor Corporation, John Balderston III, Loeb and Loeb Attorneys,
David Stanley Horsley ASC, Sara Karloff, Suzanne Garguilo

Author's Note: I interviewed the producers, directors, stars, cast and crew in the early to late 1970s. They were
recalling events that happened 35-45 years previous and sometimes memory fades or events are recalled from their
perspective point of view.

First Edition
10 9 8 7 6 5 4 3 2 1

The purpose of this series is the preservation of the art of writing for the screen. Rare books have long been a
source of enjoyment and an investment for the serious collector, and even in limited editions there are thousands
printed. Scripts, however, numbered only 50 at the most. In the history of American Literature, the screenwriter
was being lost in time. It is my hope that my efforts bring about a renewed history and preservation of a great
American Literary form, The Screenplay, by preserving them for study by future generations.

Mary Philbin and Conrad Veidt in the final 1928 release

Dedicated to Ray Bradbury, who was looking forward to this book.

Lon Chaney as the vampire in London After Midnight - MGM 1927
The wire holding the upper lips back can be seen in the right corner of his mouth.

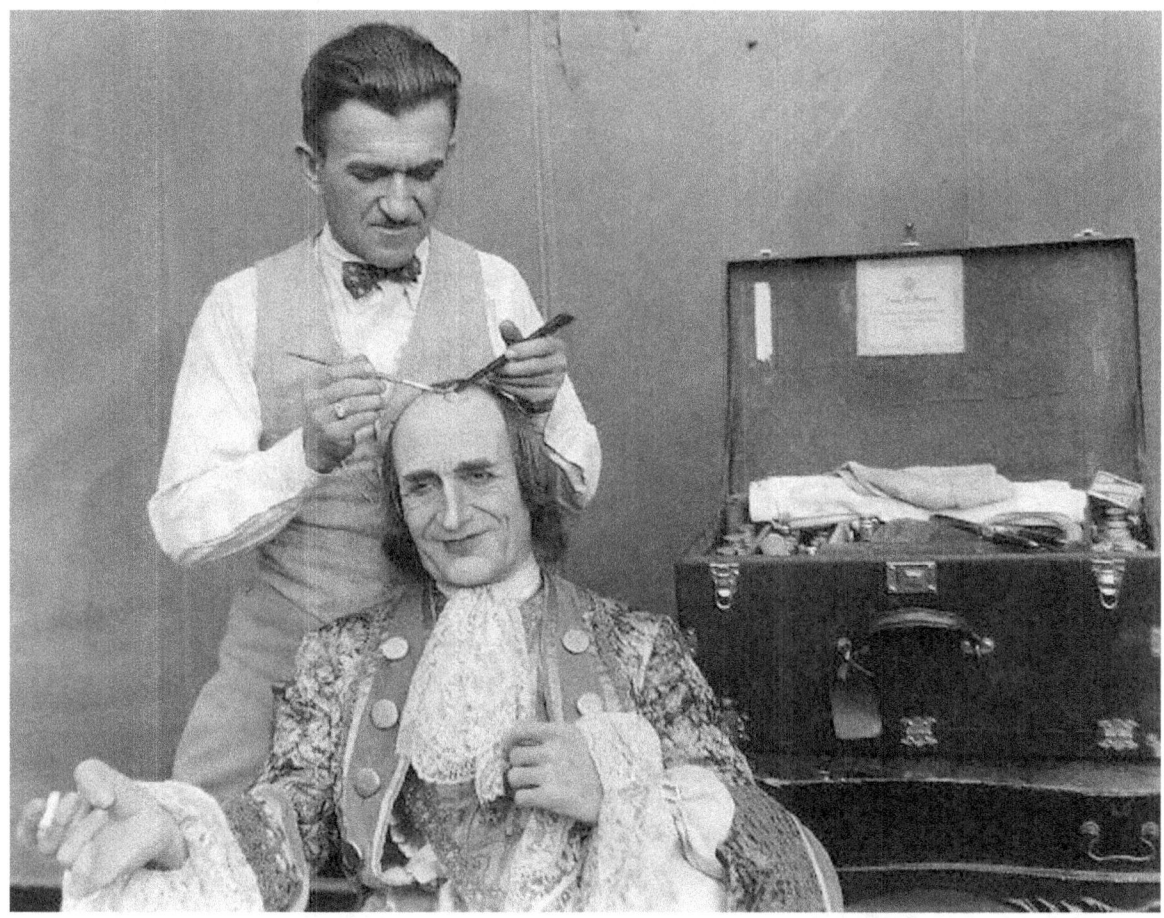

Jack Pierce applying his makeup to Brandon Hurst, Barkilphedro in the 1928 film

I discovered Lon Chaney was scheduled to start production on *The Man Who Laughs* when I was researching my book on *The Phantom of the Opera* at Universal Studio's Archives. Ernest Goodman from Universal legal Department had secured for me, Lon Chaney's legal file from Loeb and Loeb, Universal's lawyers at the time. In those files was an unfinished contract for the film which included a note asking if Chaney was to play a dual role: Ursus, the old philosopher, and Gwynplaine, The Laughing Man, whose face was disfigured into a permanent grin by outlaw gypsies, who bought and sold these children to travelling shows as freaks or side show attractions.

"Uncle" Carl Laemmle Senior, satisfied with the commercial and financial success of *The Hunchback of Notre Dame* had taken one of his many vacations to his homeland, Germany, secure in the knowledge that he would get some of his money back for the expensive Hunchback sets that Irving Thalberg, the studio general manager had spent, by producing another picture based on a Victor Hugo novel, could use those same sets.

The idea for *The Man Who Laughs* came from Isadore Bernstein

Bernstein is best remembered today as a screenwriter; having written over 60 titles from 1914 to 1938. Among the title is the 1918 *Tarzan of the Apes*. His association with the Laemmle family went back to the days when the office was in Chicago and later New York City.

When Carl Laemmle bought what is now Universal City, he sent Bernstein out to California as Studio Manager during the construction of his new west coast studio.

With the tremendous success of *The Hunchback of Notre Dame*, 1923, starring Lon Chaney, Laemmle announced to his exhibitors that Chaney was signed for a one picture contract, which at that time was not yet named.

In Laemmle's mind Bernstein's suggestion of *The Man Who Laughs* was perfect. He could re-use the expensive *Hunchback* sets and with the name of Victor Hugo again, it would be a sure hit. So he authorized the writing of the scripts and treatments so he could review them when he returned to Universal City.

On the following few pages you can view part of the legal file on Chaney's proposed The Man Who Laughs" from Loeb, Walker and Loeb attorneys:

A publicity portrait of Lon Chaney - taken around the time Universal had "The Man Who Laughs" planned for him.

Client _Universal_ Date _4-15_ 1924

Re _Lon Chaney_

Time consumed

Assigned from _U&C_ Assigned to

Nature of services _$2500 wk_ Star in "The Man Who Laughs" by Victor Hugo — or any story we may designate. Starts betw July 15 & July 28 — exact date To be designated by us. 8 wks guarantee. Make-up 3 days — not later than June 25, 1924

LOEB, WALKER & LOEB—SERVICE RECORD

it being understood that should the artist render services in the photoplay "The Man Who Laughs", he will portray the role of "Gwynplaine."

April 18th, 1924.

Universal Pictures Corporation,
Universal City, California.

Gentlemen:-   <u>Attention Mr. Bernheim.</u>

We are enclosing herewith three copies
of the proposed agreement with Lon Chaney.

Will you be good enough to give special
attention to the examination of this contract in order to ascertain whether or not it fully complies with the understanding
between yourselves and Mr. Chaney. Your special attention is
called to paragraph "18" of the within contract.

You will, of course, notice that the
within contract is somewhat longer than the contract which Chaney
had for "The Hunchback"; but in view of the fact that some difficulties were encountered in the production of that picture, we
have deemed it advisable to include in the within contract all
possible precautions.

While we do not know whether or not you
desire to carry insurance on Chaney during the period of production, we have included a clause allowing you to do so and requiring
Chaney to submit to the usual examinations for that purpose.

Very truly yours,

of Loeb, Walker and Loeb.

GWC:N.
ENC.3.

June 26th, 1924.

Re: Lon Chaney.

Mr. Julius Bernheim,
Universal Pictures Corporation,
Universal City, California.

My dear Julius:-

In accordance with our telephone con-
versation, I have prepared and am enclosing an amendment to the
Chaney contract which extends the term to October 1st, 1924. If
you think that you will need a further extension, please 'phone
me and I will be glad to dictate an additional clause over the
telephone, extending the time still further.   The within amendment should be signed by you and by Chaney and should be pasted
on the original contract, directly above paragraph "18" thereof.

Very truly yours,

GWC:RKN.
ENC.

of Loeb, Walker and Loeb.

11

Lon Chaney as The Phantom of the Opera, the production that replaced "The Man Who Laughs"

Clarence Brown - Universal's choice as director

Ernest Torrence was suggested to portray Ursus if Chaney decided
not to play duel roles of Ursus and Gwynplaine

Carl Laemmle Sr. left for Germany thinking all was well with the
production - But he returned to find Universal in chaos

Conrad Veidt who played Gwynplaine when the film was finally
produced in 1928

Mary Philbin as Dea - She finally starred in the film when Universal finally produced it in 1928

Carl Laemmle was very pleased at the reaction that Universal had secured a "one picture" deal, to his distributors and exhibitors in Chicago. Things changed when he arrived back at Universal City.

He gathered his staff around him and was pleased when he was shown Isadore Bernstein's synopsis, treatment and the first draft script by Alexander. He would surely be getting his money's worth, not only with the combined names of Victor Hugo and Lon Chaney, but he could take advantage of the existing costumes and sets from *The Hunchback of Notre Dame.*

Then came the storm. Irving Thalberg had no intention of marrying his daughter Rosebelle, and he announced that he was going to work for the newly formed Metro-Goldwyn company (Within the year, Louis B. Mayer's name was added to the new studio in Culver City - named M.G.M.). And he took Lon Chaney with him!

But he knew that Chaney would honor his contract with Universal and he asked his staff for the "Rights Agreement" for *The Man Who Laughs.* Nobody had secured the rights! Fortunately Laemmle had met Gaston Leroux, French Author and film maker himself, and he secured the rights to Leroux's *The Phantom of the Opera.*

CLAIRE WINDSOR

Claire Windsor - Bernstein's choice for Josiana

Norman Kerry was set to play Lord David (Dirry-Moir)

14

Carl Laemmle Sr. and Gaston Leroux, author of The Phantom of the Opera withe the actual Paris Opera in the background.

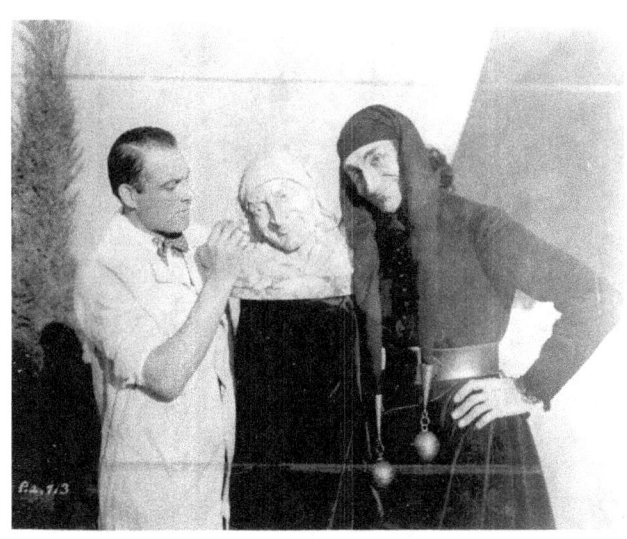

Barkilphedro, Brandon Hurst, poses in his Jester's costume

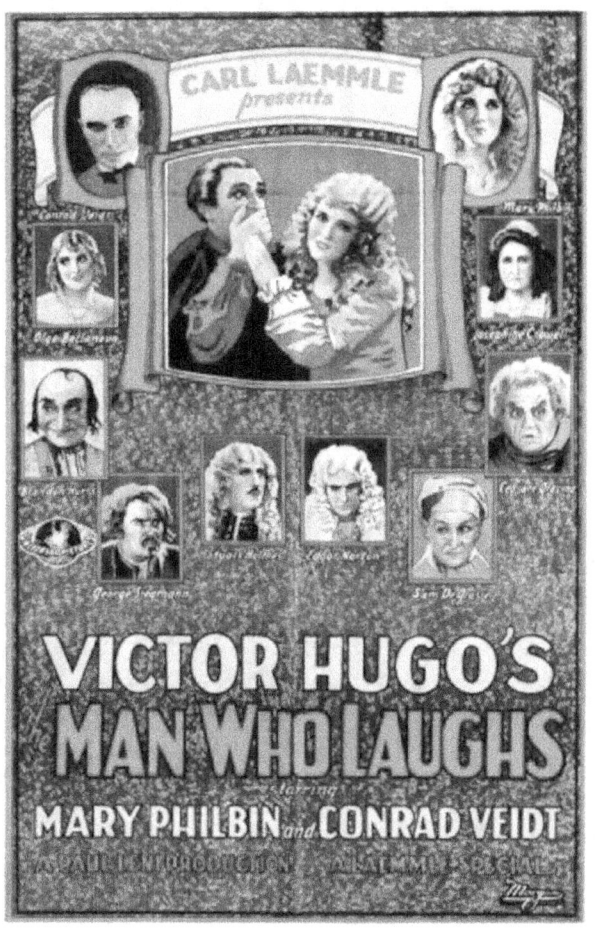

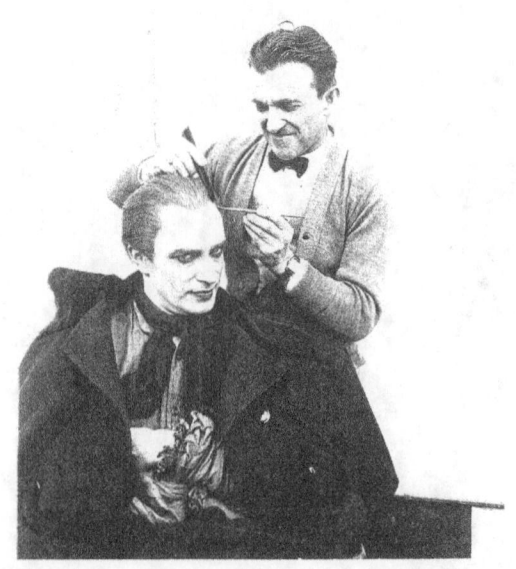

Jack Pierce applies his make-up to Conrad Veidt

Universal finally bought the rights to *The Man Who Laughs* from the *Société Générale de Films* for $35,000 on December 27, 1926 and it was eventually made with Conrad Veidt in the role intended for Chaney, with Paul Leni as director and Mary Philbin as Dea as originally intended in 1924. It was released in 1928 with orchestral sound discs and sound effects. (It is available on DVD with the original soundtrack recordings from Kino-Lorber video.)

The script included in this volume was the only full script from the period where the film was considered a Lon Chaney vehicle. All other scripts were dated after April of 1927 and half of them were in German.

Conrad Veidt as Cesare, in his somnambulist coffin - from The Cabinet of Dr. Calagari 1919 , the film which associated him with bizarre movies- . Werner Krauss (Dr. Caligari) to the left

16

Vintage German Poster - since all the principals in the 1928 release, even the scripts were in German.

Isadore Bernstein,26 November 1876 – 19 October 1944)
Universal Studio Manager, Writer, Producer after Thalberg departed to join MGM - "The Man Who Laughs" was his project and he
wanted it to star Lon Chaney in 1924

THE MAN WHO LAUGHS

By Victor Hugo

Adaptation and Continuity

By Isadore Bernstein

Titles by Victor Hugo

C A S T

"T H E   M A N   W H O   L A U G H S"

PROLOGUE:

GWYNPLAINE - as a boy of ten
LEADER OF COMPRACHICOS - a philosopher and
conscience of band, (Part.)
CAPTAIN OF VESSEL (Bit)
DEAD WOMAN (Bit)
DEA - as an infant (Bit)
Band of Comprachicos and crew

LON CHANEY-URSUS: Gruff, cynical, tender-hearted, whimsical
philosopher (Character lead)
HOME: a wolf - almost human

MAIN STORY:

DUCHESS JOSIANA - haughty, passionate, abandoned,
daring, always seeking new thrills; not
modern vamp; (Heavy)
LORD DAVID: The same ; polished, superior, arrogant
(Second lead.)
TOM JIM JACK: individual - reckless, hot-headed
boisterous (Character)

QUEEN ANNE: Middle-aged, unprepossessing, jealous
(Character-heavy)

BARKILPHEDRO: A servile, envious, crawling creature:
ambitious and heartless. (Heavy)

Gentlemen and ladies of court, pages
servants, etc.
GWYNPLAINE - the man; a tragic mask; wonderful
hideous, distorted face, fine character
(Character lead)

LON CHANEY:

URSUS - 15 years older than in prologue; less
bitter, more loveable and loving. (Character lead)
DEA - the woman, gentle, innocent, spirituelled
(Ingenue lead)

MARY PHILBIN suggested.

MASTER NICLESS, inn-keeper (Comedy part)
BOOB ASSISTANT at inn (Comedy part)
VENUS AND PHOEBE: Ursus maids-of-all work (Comedy parts

Audience and show-men

THE WAPENTAKE: A forbidding, sinister officer of
the law (Bit)

Officer of Quorum and soldiers.

20

ADAPTATION

By -

ISADORE BERNSTEIN

"THE MAN WHO LAUGHS"

CAST OF MAIN CHARACTERS

GWYNPLAINE:
            :- - - - - - - - - - - -LON CHANEY
URSUS   :

LORD DAVID - - - - - - - - - - - NORMAN KERRY

BARKILPHEDRO   - - - - - - - - CAESAR GRAVINI

DEA   - - - - - - - - - - - - -MARY PHILBIN

JOSIANA - - - - - - - - - - - - CLAIRE WINDSOR

ADAPTATION

By -

ISADORE BERNSTEIN

THE MAN WHO LAUGHS

By

Victor Hugo

Synopsis:

Foreword

Hugo has taken for the setting of this fascinating tale, the "merrie" old England of the late seventeenth century - nearly three hundred years ago - a period when the all - powerful nobles gaily and heedlessly trampled upon the defenseless common people.

And for the basis of the story he has chosen the horrible practices of the Comprachicos, who for the purpose of furnishing clowns and jesters, engage in the curious and abominable art of disfiguring and distorting innocent little children, that they might develope into amusingly hideous monstrosities, for the enter- tainment of the idle aristocracy.

These Comprachicos bargained in human beings, buying the raw material and selling the finished product, with no care for the suffering involved. Their questionable business was long countenanced, not only because it catered to the grotesque fancy of the pleasure-loving nobility, but also furnished a convenient means for disposing of individuals who promised to interfere with the ambitions and intrigues of princes. Undesirables need not be crudely killed, when they could be artistically defaced beyond re- cognition, and so effaced.

The men engaged in this nefarious profession were honest rascals of all nationalities, and they did a flourishing trade until, during the reign of William III, measures were taken to disperse the malefactors. Then, every wandering band with a child was under suspicion, and the terrorized Comprachicos sought to rid themselves of their menacing human merchandise as best they could.

(Foreword is explanatory - practices of Comprachicos will not be shown in picture.)

During the terrible winter of 1689, notable for its intense
severity, travellers along the English countryside might have observed
a strange pair (a partnership only to be conceived by the extraordinary
imagination of a Hugo*) - a man and a wolf - drawing together in double
harness a curious van, house and vehicle in one.

The owner of this van was URSUS, Doctor and Philosopher, Juggler
and Ventriloquist, Scholar, Poet, Fortune-Teller, whose great business
was to hate the human race. He ministered to the sick and needy that
they might live and suffer.

Ursus had taught his only friend and companion, HOMO, the wolf,
to stand upright, to retrain his rage into sulkiness, to growl instead
of howling. And, on his part, the wolf had taught the man what he knew:
to do without a roof, without bread and fire; to prefer hunger in the
woods to slavery in a place. Never did the wolf bite; the man did now
and then.

So these two mountebanks journeyed from village to village gain-
in a precarious existence from the curiosity and necessity of simple folk.

Toward nightfall of an icy winter's day, with a storm in the
offing, another company of wanderers were making hasty preparations for
departure in a little vessel moored in a sequestered bay along the
English coast. The waning daylight was obscured by a chilling fog, and
nature seemed to be conspiring with them in their apparent attempt at
secrecy. The company of not more than ten, with their baggage, crowded
the capacity of the tiny craft. Besides the captain and his crew, the
passengers comprised a band of various foreigners, at the head of which
was an old man whose costume and bearing indicated the doctor or philosopher.

The last and least of this refugee company was a boy of about
ten, with bare feet, wrapped in a sailor's jacket, descending to his
knees. The boy appeared to be attached to no one in particular, but
rather to be the slave of all.

When the last chest had been carried on deck, the child was
crowded off the gangway by the hurrying sailors, and the vessel cast
off, leaving the boy alone on shore.

The deserted child, offered no protest, but stood watching the
boat out of the inlet; then started up the steep, frozen path leading
from the water to the cliffs above

Clambering precariously to the top, he beheld a vast frozen
plain, with no sign of habitation; and looking seaward, watched the one
venturing ship, disappear.

There he stood, utterly alone - between a deserted land and a deserted ocean.

Then, drawing his jacket about him, he set out across the plain, courageously facing the Unknown.

****

The little vessel, running into the storm, was encountering difficulties. The captain was occupied by the sea; the doctor (the leader of the band) by the sky. The other passengers, not free from danger of the law, were brutally gay.

The doctor, observing an alarming blue 'snow cloud' called the skipper's attention, asking him what he saw. The skipper replied: "A blue spot - a niche in heaven." To which the doctor retorted: "For those who go to heaven; for those who go elsewhere, it is another affair. Every minute the fatal hours draws nearer. The will of heaven is about to be manifested."

****

After travelling some distance, the boy came upon a horrible object, enormous in the gloom- a ghastly form hanging from a gibbet.

Wonderingly the child gazed upon the apparition, until his numb little body, succumbing to the temper of the cold, was about to sink into eternal sleep; when the Thing above him moved, swayed by the wind; and the boy ran frantically into the night.

After a time, finding that he was not pursued by the spectre, and warmed by his activity, the little fellow again pushed onward, seeking shelter.

****

As the storm grew in intensity, while the captain cursed the doctor prophesied: "Death is in the east. If tonight, out at sea, we hear the sound of a bell, the ship is lost." The snow fell, the wind shrieked, while the band, in wild disorder, cried out: "We are free - free!"

"Silence!" commanded the doctor. Then thru the darkness the tolling of a bell - tolling from the ocean. They were between the danger signal and the breakers, being driven on the rocks.

****

Stumbling thru the snow, worn and bruised with stones, the lad heard a faint cry, and digging under a mound of snow, he discovered a dead woman, with a babe at her cold breast, a little girl, not a year old. He took up the child, who snuggled to him, comforted, and wrapping her in his jacket, trudged bravely on.

****

24

The little ship had narrowly escaped crashing on the
rocks, and the storm abating, lay in calm waters, when the
hold was discovered half full of water. With no means of
locating the leak, no pump, one small boat in which to make
their escape, shut in by encompassing snow, the exhausted
and terrified company waited for the dawn, and possible
deliverance. Under the falling snow, beads were counted,
prayers mumbled.

****

Finally the boy reached a dark and silent village,
where he knocked again and again at the doors of sleeping
and selfish burghers, but in vain. He felt the coldness of
man more terribly than the coldness of the night.

****

As the water rose in the hold, slowly but inexorably,
baggage and treasure where thrown over to lighten the ship.
They had exhausted their last expedient.

"Is there anything else we can throw overboard?"

"Kneel down!" commanded the doctor. "Let us throw
our crimes into the sea! Let us think no more of safety - let
us think of salvation! If the child we abandoned is alive,
let us come to his aid with prayer, if he is dead, let us
seek his forgiveness."

****

Despairing of succor, the boy had reached the edge
of the village, when, in the distance, he glimpsed a dim
light, and under his burden, the sleeping child, staggered
toward it.

****

Hastily, for the ship had not long to survive, the
doctor wrote upon parchment a message, which was signed by
the passengers and crew and sealed in a wicker-covered flask
bearing the name of one of their imprisoned comrades,
"Hardquanonne." Then it was committed to the ocean.

Kneeling in prayer, the sinners went to their doom.
The snow fell upon silent seas.
One thing alone floated - the flask with the message.

****

In answer to the boy's piteous appeal for shelter,
Homo growled, and Ursus growled, but finally admitted the
way-farer into the caravan.

25

The boy placed the bundle wrapped in his jacket, on
a chest, while Ursus searched for dry clothes. He rubbed the
half-frozen lad and put on him an old shirt and knitted
jacket. Grumbling that he would have to go without dinner,
he had prepared for himself, he placed food on the table
before the lad, who devoured it avidly. Ursus meanwhile,
complaining, "Gobble it up! Fatten at my expense! Fat
away, ill-born boy!"

Just as Ursus was about to drink the milk - all that
was left of his supper - he heard the babe crying. Unrolling
the bundle he exclaimed: "Another beggar!" and attaching a
sponge to the milk bottle, he put it in the babe's mouth.
"Suck, you little wretch."

His ravenous appetite somewhat appeased the boy
lifted a tearful voice to Ursus: "But you will have nothing."
"Eat! Eat it all up!" snorted Ursus, "Or I will kick you
out - both of you!" Then he returned to grumbling: "Not
a half-penny! And bundles which set to howling! I open
them and find beggars inside! Is that fair? And to think,
if I had not been eaten up by creatures of this kind for
the last thirty years, I would be rich!"

When the boy had finished eating and Ursus had heard
his story, he turned to Homo, gently licking the hand of the
sleeping infant. "Well, done Homo. I shall be your father,
your uncle. Adoption; it is settled - Homo is willing."

****

Ursus has all this time been too much occupied with
his angry grumblings and his kindly ministrations to give
the boy any close personal observation. But as he tucked
him away fro the night under a huge bearskin beside the
sleeping babe, the rays of the lantern fell upon the boy's
face.

"What are you laughing at? demanded Ursus in surprise.

"I am not laughing," the boy replied.

"Then you are frightful," commented Ursus. "Do not
laugh any more!"
Seizing the child in a grasp which would have been
furious if it had not been full of pity, Ursus demanded
roughly, "Who did this to you?"
"I have always been thus," responded the boy.
Ursus pondered: "It might not be so wholesome to inquire
too deeply into a case of this kind. Laugh away my boy."
The girl child, disturbed, opened her eyes, which reflected the lantern's ray like two mirrors.

"See," said Ursus, "She is blind."

(First five paragraphs explanatory - story as pictured starts
with sixth)

MAIN STORY

In the London of those days there was a tradition.
That tradition was Lord Clancharlie, who had sworn allegiance
to the Great Commoner, Cromwell, and, after Cromwell's fall
had remained loyal to his ideals. Scorned by the Royalist
peers as a mad-man, Lord Clancharlie left England, to live in
exile in Switzerland, where, it was rumored, he had married.

Now Lord Clancharlie had a natural son, LORD DAVID ,
a favorite at court, handsome, reckless, eloquent, courteous
and diplomatic, a perfect type of the English gentleman. His
mother had left him an income, sufficient - almost - to main-
tain his extravagances.

Lord David aspired to the peerage, and his service
to King James inclined his Majesty to grant Lord David's desire,
if he could do so without creating a peerage - a serious undertaking.

Fortune favored Lord David in the death of Lord
Clancharlie, the exile. It was reported that Lord Clancharlie's
wife also had died giving birth to a son, as beautiful as the
day. But this was only rumor, not fact, and King James put an
end to it, by declaring Lord David his sole heir - in default of
issue, and by his royal pleasure - of Lord Clancharlie, Lord
David's natural father.

This on the sole condition that, when she attained
marriageable age, Lord David should wed a girl, then in her
cradle, whom the King had, for personal reasons, created a
duchess - the DUCHESS JOSIANA. To this little duchess, the
king granted the peerage of Clancharlie; the peer to be her
husband.

About the year 1706, although Lady Josiana was twenty-
three and Lord David forty-four, they were not yet married.
She wanted to be free: he wanted to remain young. Josiana
admired Lord David, his horses, his dogs, his gaming, his
mistresses. Lord David bowed down before Josiana's resplendent
beauty, her hauteur and her audacity. They did not love -
they flirted.

Josiana was "the flesh", a rosy, voluptuous, witty,
daring. She had neither lovers not chastity, she appeared to
be yielding, but she was unapproachable, she thought little
of her reputation, much to her glory. What is frailty in
a plebeian, is frolic in a duchess; and Josiana was, almost
a queen.

Lord David affected, among other eccentricities, such as wearing cowhide boots and his own hair (a daring departure in a world of wigs) a passion for out-of-door shows of popular nature, circuses, fairs, and the like; and frequented the low taverns and haunts of London, where he used to dress as a sailer. There he mixed freely with the lower classes and was known as TOM JIM JACK.

Josiana, not to be outdone in defying conventions, rode a man's saddle, and went about unattended wherever her fancy led her.

QUEEN ANNE, the reigning sovereign of England, an unprepossessing woman of past forty, bare a grudge against her sister, the Duchess Josiana, first, because Josiana was young and beautiful, second, because she was betrothed to the dashing Lord David, whom Anne coveted for her devoted slave, if not her lover. She resented, too, the fact that her father, King James, had also been the natural father of Josiana, and had made her a duchess. Nevertheless, Anne tolerated Josiana's presence at court. Josiana's brilliant mind was more than a match for Anne's dull wit, and Anne saw no way of disposing of her.

Josiana was good-natured and generous after her fashion, and had attached to her household, among other hangeron's, an indignant scholar - BARKILPHEDRO - a servile, envious creature; a worm seeking an underground fortune, crawling toward power.

Josiana rather fancied this man of poverty and wit. She was kind to him, sometimes she even spoke to him and he became sort of a constant attendant, having access to her private rooms, even to her bed chamber. Through Josiana's influence, Barkilphedro had been appointed Flotsam Officer in the Admiralty Department, whose duty it was to examine and report upon objects cast up by the sea.

But though he had Josiana's entire confidence, Barkilphedro acted as a spy, reporting her doings to Lord David and the Queen. He hated for hate's sake and Josiana offered a target for his malice by bestowing favors upon him, while he, a scholar and man of talents, had to bow and grimace before her. He longed to humiliate the haughty duchess, who, disdainful of all danger, hardly knew that such a contemptible creature existed. Josiana could not be struck in the heart; her weakness lay in her pride, as Barkilphedro well knew; and he waited an opportunity to drag her proud spirit in the dust.

****

When Ursus gave shelter to the waif, Gwynplaine,
he entertained an angel of good fortune unawares. Grown
to man's estate, Gwynplaine had the form of an Adonis, but
the face of a monster - a comical monster, with a fixed
infectious grin. Year by year, with the growth of Gwynplaine's person and ugliness, their fortunes had bettered.

The van had been enlarged and decorated and provided
with a stage, upon which Ursus, Gwynplaine, the blind girl
Dea, and Homo, the wolf, gave performances. Whenever,
Gwynplaine, the mountebank, appeared, the audience held its
sides. The fame of "The Man Who Laughs" was carried far and
wide, and the pennies poured into Ursus' box.

Ursus had acquired two servants, gypsy girls. "We
are a wandering temple", he declared, and named them Phoebe
and Venus. Phoebe cooked, Venus scrubbed the temple, and
before the show, arrayed as goddesses, they blew on
trumpets. Ursus had composed for the performance an interlude which he called "Chaos Vanquished", in which Gwynplaine
appeared as the man, Dea the angel vision, Ursus as the
bear, and Homo as the Wolf. In this interlude, Man, cast
down, hears the angelic voice imploring him in song to
cast off his yoke, and answers in song: "Thou art soul -
I am heart." But when Gwynplaine lifted his head, disclosing his face, sentiment gave way to humor; the audience
roared, and Gwynplaine was recalled, again and again.

Whatever emotion Gwynplaine might feel, it was waked
by eternal, implacable hilarity. Behind the laugh, however,
there was a soul, which no one knew so well as blind Dea.
This beautiful and spirituelle girl wore a veil - the
dark, statuesque youth, a mask, his face. Dea, seeing not
his face, but beholding his soul, called him beautiful. She
worshipped him, he adored her, and Ursus, his bitterness
assuaged by his paternal love of the spirit, for Gwynplaine,
forebore to take advantage of Dea's infirmity, feeling
that she would not love him if she could see him as he was.

But Gwynplaine's face was his fortune, and he
gloried in its possession. He would not have changed faces
with Apollo. Was it not the means of caring for Dea?

These two, Gwynplaine and Dea, isolated my mis-
fortune, from their fellows, found happiness in each other.
Only one thing disturbed Gwynplaine's peace, the tragic
suffering of the poor and unfortunate. He longed to help
them, but was powerless. Ursus advised Gwynplaine to leave
the horizon alone. "You are the pickpocket of happiness,
my boy. The man who is happy by right is the lord. There
are coaches in the world; my lord is inside; the people
are under the wheels, the philosopher gets out of the way.
Stand aside and let them pass."

The Green Box, as the caravan was called, had never frequented cities, but the fame of "The Man Who Laughs" had extended so far that Ursus finally decided to go to London.

****

One evening, a man clad in a sailer's jacket, passing thru Southwark, London, a district near old London Bridge, caught the beginning of a strange, discourse, and stopped to listen:

"Men and women of London, here I am! I cordially wish you the joy of being English. You are a great people! Your fisticuffs are even better than your sword-thrusts. I mention this to your glory - I whom am neither English nor human, having the humour to be a bear———"

The listener, intrigued by what he had heard, entered the courtyard of Tadcaster Inn, paying the customary penny for admittance to the show, and beheld on the platform of a caravan an old man dressed in a bear skin - a young man like a mask, a blind girl and a wolf. "Gracious heaven", he cried, "What delightful people!

The merry-Andrews and mountebanks of the adjacent fair grounds were astounded and indignant at the amazing success of "The Man Who Laughs" and tried to break up the show. But Ton Jim Jack, who loved a good fight, routed the intruders, thus earning the gratitude of Ursus and his company: and a friendship sprang up between the laughing man and the stranger, who, though dressed like the common people, yet had an air of authority, and, admiring, applauding, swearing, shouting, joking, was always ready to blacken an eye or pay for a bottle.

The jealousy and envy of the competitive showmen caused them to appeal to certain persons of influence, and complaints were lodged against him. (Ursus) He was teaching the populace things they had no right to know, his sinful show was drawing people away from the churches, he was harboring an outlaw - the wolf. No definite action was taken against the show, but Ursus dreaded the outcome.

Another matter troubled him; Gwynplaine, stirred by Ursus's cynical philosophy and his observations of wretched social conditions, had recklessly remarked to Master Nicless, the inn-keeper, a boot-licking, law-abiding citizen - upon "the parasitical magnificence of the throne." A desitious speech! L'ese Majeste! Ursus was alarmed. Men had been sent to the gallows for less. He rebuked Gwynplaine. Then, terror-stricken, pointed out a man in black rod. "The wapentake - a terrible officer! When he touches you with his rod, all is over, you have to follow him." "Whither?" inquired Gwynplaine. "Wherever he likes," replied Ursus. "And if you resist?" "You are hanged." But the wapentake passed them by.

On an evening, just as the curtain rose upon "Chaos Vanquished," Ursus, glancing over his audience, observed that the erstwhile empty compartment for nobility was occupied - by a lady - alone.

She shone, she radiated, blotting out the others, even Tom Jim Jack was lost in the numbus of this dazzling creature. But tho she might, at a distance, appear to be a goddess, to those near her, she was all woman, perchance too much woman. To Gwynplaine she was a vision. He did not know that there were fleashly phantoms called vampires.

Behind the lady, at a respectful distance, stood a page, clad in scarlet with a plumed cap, indicating attendance upon a very great lady.

The lady watched Gwynplaine - but she laughed not.

At the close of the performance they saw her carried away in a splendid coach; Master Nicless informed them that she was a duchess, and, most amazing of all, Tom Jim Jack had gone away with her.

To Gwynplaine, Josiana was a revelation. He had seen the shadow in the women of the populace, the soul in Dea. Never before had he seen Woman, in the flesh. Josiana, with her warm skin, hinting at passionate blood, her seductive outlines, the half-revealed nudity of her attire, an ineradicable coquetry; was a promise to the senses and a menace to the mind. The mystery of sex had been revealed to Gwynplaine, and he felt for this woman, a strange, inexpressible longing. His dreams of Josiana scarcely touched Dea, who reigned in his soul. Still there was conflict within him - the conflict of the spiritual with the sexual. After a sleepless night, at length the angel of darkness was overthrown, and Gwynplaine suddenly thought no more of the unknown woman.

Neither Tom Jim Jack nor Josiana returned. But after her visit, complaints against the van-show vanished.

Gwynplaine's devotion to Dea increased. But to adore each other in shadows was not enough now. Troubled by an awakening desire, Gwynplaine walked out alone one spring evening, thinking of Dea as a man thinks of a woman, and re-proaching himself for this. He felt a yearning for the flesh - and Dea was not of the flesh.

Reeling under the influence of his desire, of the night, of spring, Gwynplaine walked on, his head bent, his hands clasped behind him. Suddenly he felt something slipped between his fingers, and turning quickly, he found in his hand a letter, in front of him, the duchess' page. Before he could utter an exclaimation of surprise, the page announced: "At this hour tomorrow, be at the corner of London Bridge. I will be there to conduct you - "Whither?" demanded Gwynplaine. "Where you are expected", and the page was gone.

Like a somnambulist, Gwynplaine returned to the inn, and standing in the light from the half-opened door, examined the envelope addressed "To Gwynplaine." He broke the seal and read:

"You are hideous; I am beautiful. You are a player; I am a duchess. I am the highest; you are the lowest. I love you! I desire you! Come!

Gwynplaine feared he was mad - then feared he was sane. A woman desired him. Incredible! A woman who had seen his face - a duchess! She dwelt in a regal region where she could take a prince - and she had chosen a mountebank. Gwynplaine was flattered. In his vanity as a monster; he was loved for his deformity. Still he detected a shadow which hung over this brightness. Should he go? "Yes," cried the flesh; "No", said the soul.

Finally Gwynplaine stole back to the van, and without undressing, laid his head on the pillow, but not to sleep. Storm raged within him, and had not abated when the day broke. Then he heard Dea's gentle voice; saw her standing in unconscious serenity; and was calm.

****

Gwynplaine, Dea and Ursus breakfasted together in the van, the lovers babbling sweet nonsense; they were all in all to each other. Ursus, the cynic, warned them, though he reveled in their happiness: "You are happy, that's a crime. Take care!" He complained, with assumed annoyance: "I'm no duenna, to watch lovers billing and cooing. I'm tired of it all; you may both go to the devil."

Here, Homo, lying at their feet, growled. "Be still, Homo," commanded Ursus. "I don't blame you for being in a bad humor, too, but be a philosopher."

The wolf, disregarding his master's command, sat up looking toward the door, and showing his teeth.

Dea, who had just tasted her cup of tea and handed it to Gwynplaine - a part of their lover's play -sat wrapt in happy meditation. Ursus was attempting to quiet Homo. Only Gwynplaine, looking up from his cup, beheld the terrible apparition.

A man in black, with a hood, in his hand an iron staff.

Leaning over, Gwynplaine whispered to Ursus, "The wapentake.!"

32

The man stretched out his right arm over the radiant
Dea, and touched Gwynplaine on the shoulder with his staff.
Gwynplaine sat petrified, as though he had been struck a
violent blow. Why he had been summoned, Gwynplaine had no
idea. But Ursus remembered tremblingly the complaint
against the show, and Gwynplaine's seditious utterances.
Both were silent. Dea was smiling. Then Gwynplaine at a
commanding gesture, rose and followed the wapentake. As he
passed out of the van, Ursus whispered, "On your life, do
not speak until you are questioned."

Gwynplaine followed the officer thru the courtyard as
though he were being dragged by an invisible chain. Master
Nicless imperiously silenced the cries of Phoebe and Venus
and servilely stood aside, while his foolish chore-boy gaped
open-mouthed, at the majesty of the law.

Gaining the street, Gwynplaine, wrapping his cloak
around him like a shroud, marched between two ranks of men.

The few curious idlers were restrained by law from
following. But Ursus, fearing for himself, yet still more fear-ful concerning
the fate of Gwynplaine, leaving word that Dea
was not to be told what had happened; braved the law, and
crept after the procession, at a distance, like a frightened
hare. Trying vainly to assure himself that Gwynplaine's arrest
was not a serious affair, Ursus followed from street to street,
until the cortege entered a little lande, leading to a high
wall, with narrow barred loopholes and a forbidding door with
a heavy knocker. The officer lifted the knocker and struck
three times, calling: "By order of her Majesty!" The door
swung back and the officer with his entourage entered. It
was the "Gate of Punishment" by which Gwynplaine had been
taken into old Southwark Prison.

****

When Gwynplaine heard the gate close, he trembled.
He was in a narrow, dark corridor, which wound torturously
and grew darker and darker as they proceeded, for they halted,
and the officer struck against an iron door which resounded
like a gong, and raised for their entrance.

****

Gwynplaine found himself standing at the top of a
flight of steep stone steps, looking down into a dungeon
lighted dimly by a lamp suspended from the ceiling. And below
the lamp, he beheld a man chained, in torture. The man looked
like a corpse, but was still alive.

(The torture can be merely suggested, or out altogether.)

Near the chained man was a great seat, on either side
of which stood a man in black robe, and on the seat an old
man in a red robe, motionless and ominous - holding a bunch
of roses.

(The roses indicated a magistrate.)

Gwynplaine stood, haggard and trembling, until the
officer touched him on the shoulder. Then he descended.

A voice from the shadow commanded Gwynplaine to approach and the officer informed him that he was before the
sheriff.

The sheriff addressed the man in chains, warning him
that this was his last chance to confess; if he did not, he
would be left alone in the dungeon to die; if he did confess
he would be merely hanged. After drawing a frightful picture
of the consequences, the sheriff begged! "Have pity on yourself. Give way to justice. Open your eyes and see if you
recognise this man."

Gwynplaine was pushed forward beside the chained man,
who made no sign. Then the officer turned the head of the
man toward Gwynplaine and raised his eyelids with his fingers.
The man, glimpsing Gwynplaine, raised his head involuntarily,
and gazed at him quiveringly: "Tis he - 'tis he!" he exclaimed,
then fell back.

Gwynplaine, terrified, protested - "It is not true -
it was not me! I do not know the man - he cannot know me!
I am innocent! I demand my liberty! You have before you
only a poor mountebank, "The Man Who Laughs."

I have before me, replied the sheriff, "Lord Fermain
Clancharlie, a peer of England." Rising and offering his
chair to Gwynplaine, he added: "Will your lordship deign to
seat yourself.?"

Gwynplaine, uncomprehending, looked behind him to see
who had been addressed. The officer placed him on the
chair. Then the sheriff drew from a pile of papers on a
table a yellowed parchment and read the confession of the ship-
wrecked Comprachicos:

****

The legitimate heir of Lord Linnaeus Clancharlie had
been sold at the age of two years, by order of King James;
mutilated and disfigured by one Hardquanonne, who stamped on
the child's face an everlasting laugh. The child answers to
the dame of Gwynplaine. Hardquanonne was imprisoned in a
dungeon of Chatham. The Comprachicos had been sworn to secrecy;
but having nothing more to hope from man, and everything to
fear from God, they now confessed to their crime, and
attached their signatures.

Then Gwynplaine remembered the band of men who had abandoned him.

The sheriff produced the flask in which the confession had been set afloat, on which, though it had been buffeted by the sea for fifteen years, the name of Hardquanonne, woven through the wicker cover in red reed, was still decipherable.

The prisoner, addressed by the sheriff, responded: "I swore to keep the secret; I have kept it as long as I could. Men of dark lives are faithful, and hell has its honor." Then turning toward Gwynplaine, he regarded him with devilish satisfaction: "We did it - the King by his will - I by my art. Now laugh forever!" and he began to laugh wildly.

The sheriff pronounced sentence of hanging upon Hardquanonne and commanded him to that Her Majesty for ending his torture. The executioner's assistant released the man. The sheriff commanded him to rise. But he was dead.

"'Tis of little consequence," commented the sheriff. "After confession, life or death is a mere formality." And ordered the dead man to be buried that night in the cemetery opposite the jail.

A man whom Gwynplaine had not before observed glided from behind a pillar, and presented himself; Barkilphedro , an officer of the Admiralty, to whom the flask had been brought, and by him unsealed and reported to the Queen. He informed Gwynplaine that he was a peer, equal to a prince; and that he was about to wed a duchess, the daughter of a King.

At this culminating shock, Gwynplaine fainted.

Barkilphedro had managed the whole affair, which had been kept a secret. The Queen was well pleased with a hideous husband for her sister, and Lord David free. Both Lady Josiana and Lord David had been summoned to receive her Majesty's commands. Barkilphedro was triumphant - he was about to satisfy his hate. And to advance his fortunes as well. Lord David owed him nothing - Lord Clancharlie - everything. He was going to have a lord of his own, a lord who would be his creature.

Ursus remained watching, without reason and without hope, long after Gwynplaine had been swallowed up by the maw of the prison. He stood gazing blankly at the two black walls on either side of the alley, on the prison, the other the cemetery.

At length he turned and retraced his steps, murmuring: "So much the better; the worthless fellow, the seditious rascal; he is in prison, just where he should be, and I am well rid of him - and Dea, too, she will do without him, and Homo and I shall be comfortable again."

Ursus returned, muttering, to the van, where he found Dea asleep, and Phoebe and Venus waiting. He ordered them to pack up the props and costumes; there would be no performance; he would inform Dea of Gwynplaine's fate when she awoke.

Dea, awakening, feared she had overslept, and commanded the maids to dress her quickly for the show. Ursus, meeting her ineffable, pleading look, suddenly ordered the maids to hurry, the show was about to begin.

Then followed a strange performance: Phoebe and Venus were instructed to beat upon their cymbals and blow their trumpets; the inn-keeper and his foolish assistant were persuaded with generous tips to make a racket, and Ursus, using his power of ventriloquism, imitated Gwynplaine and the audience; the hum of conversation, the wailing of children, barking of dogs. The tumult and confusion of a crowd prevailed, while Ursus and Dea played to empty seats; all the while Ursus kept up a running fire of repartee with the imaginary crowed. "I have one merit," retorted Ursus to a jobe, "a dry eye, I have never wept," - and brushed a tear from his cheek.

The curtain closed at the end of the performance and Ursus, taking off his wig, wiped his forehead, exhausted. But his wit had not been equal to Dea's intuition. She confronted him, imploring; "Where is Gwynplaine?"

While Ursus hesitated, not knowing what to replay, Master Nicless called him out. Someone had knocked at the inn, said nothing, and left Gwynplaine's hat and jacket. Ursus touched the garments lovingly, and sorrowfully; then rushed away.

Without conscious purpose, his feet led him involuntarily toward the prison. Just as he entered the deserted alley, he heard a bell tolling. The gates of the prison opened; a torch flowed; and a cortege issued, carrying a bier, crossed and entered the cemetery.

"He is dead! cried Ursus. "They have killed him! Gwynplaine, my child - my son!"

Ursus mourned before the prison, heedless of the passing
hours. Dawn broke and he rose and crept back to the inn.

Master Nicless, disturbed by the scandal which had
fallen upon his former respectable hostelry, was wondering how
he could get rid of Ursus, when he heard a knock; an imperious
knock of the Law. Trembling, Master Nicless admitted an
officer and Barkilphedro, he inquired for Ursus. "Your honor",
answered the shaking inn-keeper, "There he comes."

Ursus started. The police again! The officer fixed
Ursus with the stern eye of the law: "You have a wolf -
a misdemeanor! Tomorrow, by this hour, you and your wolf must
have left England, if not, the wolf will be killed and you will
go to prison!"

Ursus stood, stunned and grieved by this summary demand.
Master Nicless, anxious to facilitate Ursus' departure,
suggested that he could take ship at once for the continent,
his van and horses could be sold to a neighboring showman. The
officer remarked that he would soon require them, for all of
the showmen were to depart that day; the honorable gentleman
Barkilphedro, had brought orders that the fair grounds were to
be swept clean.

"Honorable Judge," implored Ursus; "I will go away
but I have a comrade whom I cannot leave behind - Gwynplaine."
"Gwynplaine is dead," announced Barkilphedro. Ursus' last
faint hope was extinguished; he bent his head. Barkilphedro
touched his arm and presented him with ten guineas (of the two
thousand) sent by a friend who wished him well. Then he departed.

The cringing inn-keeper protested to the officer that
with the removal of Ursus and Home, his house would be without
reproach and begged him to withdraw his man. Whereupon Master
Nicless was taken into custody for harboring, vagabonds,
with his boob boy as accomplice; and the inn ordered condemned
and closed.
                    ****

Gwynplaine's first conscious thought when he woke
late in the morning, was of Dea. He was filled with remorse
for his vain-glorious dreams and neglect of his dear ones. To
think that he had sent them money, when it was himself they
wanted. This was his house - he was master - he would go to
them!

He raised a curtain of tapestry and rushed into a
corridor, which led to another corridor, and then another.
What doors opened upon these corridors were locked. Along
the way, a statue in a niche, a painting, a priceless tapestry,
indicated luxury. But Gwynplaine passed them heedless,
seeking an exit and finding none. It was a labyrinth. He
ran on and on calling, "Dea - Dea!"
Near the end of a passage, closed by a curtain a
sound like dropping water arrested Gwynplaine's attention.
He pushed the curtain aside and stopped, spell-bound.
                    ****

When Gwynplaine came to himself, he was in a great
chamber, richly furnished and lighted by tapers, thru the
windows of which he glimpsed glorious gardens, fountains,
and statuary gleaming in the moonlight. He was clad in
princely garments.

Barkilphedro, bowing low before Gwynplaine, informed
him that he was in his own palace, and recounted impressively
Lord Clancharlie's position and privileges, lands, vassals,
and wealth; to all of which Gwynplaine listed in a stupor.

Finally Barkilphedro presented him with a casket containing two thousand guineas, which the Queen had sent for
his present wants.

Suddenly Gwynplaine remembered the dear ones he had
left behind. This fortune he would give to Ursus; he would
take it himself. But Barkilphedro declared this to be impossible; Gwynplaine was far from London at his court resi-
dence near the royal castle of Windsor; and, Barkilphedro
insinuated, should Gwynplaine attempt to leave at present, he
would find himself a prisoner. He would be obliged to remain
until the morrow, when he would take his seat in the House of
Lords. However, a man could not be made a peer of England
without his own consent.

"My lord, will you be a peer of England - yes or no?
This is a decisive moment. Destiny never opens one door with-
out shutting another; a step back is impossible. My lord,
Gwynplaine is dead - - do you understand?"

"Yes, replied Gwynplaine. "But you will take the
money to Ursus, my father, and tell him I am in no danger.
Go - at once!" Barkilphedro took the casket and bowed himself
out.

****

Left to himself, freed from anxiety concerning his
friends, and with Barkilphedro's words ringing in his ears;
Gwynplaine began to realize the grandeur of his estate.

"I was below; now I am on high! I shall have a
scarlet robe and a coronet; carriages, palaces, millions of
money. I may pluck the stars from heaven - I am a lord!"

In the excess of his wild emotion, suffering from
lack of sleep and food, Gwynplaine was suddenly overcome by
exhaustion, and sank upon a couch, into a deep sleep

****

Before Gwynplaine was a spacious room of rose-colored marble, in the center of which was a bath from which rose a sparkling fountain. Across this room and opening from it, he glimpsed a boudoir, through a curtain of silver tissue.

There a woman stood, naked, before a large mirror, her back toward the bath. She caught up a silken robe from the bed, and slipping it on, turned and came thru the transparent curtain. It was the duchess; the only woman who had seen Gwynplaine and desired him! He thought he had banished her remembrance but his breath came quickly. He tried to fly, but was held by a fearful fascination.

Josiana gazed at Gwynplaine in momentary astonishment, but without embarrassment; "Why it is Gwynplaine!" And with a spring like a panther, she threw herself passionately upon him. Then holding him off, she scrutinized him. Both were fascinated, he by her beauty and she by his ugliness. Gwynplaine was speechless, but Josiana overwhelmed him with a torrent of words; "How clever of you, to discover I had left London and to follow me! How did you get in, tell me? No, don't tell me; you have a right to enter like the gods - you are my lover! The master of my dreams! You shall be mine!

She sank to a couch, drawing him down beside her. "Here's a love affair that will be a blow to my family, the Stuarts," she mused. Then clasping the resisting, yet yielding Gwynplaine to her breast, she cried with a consuming passion: "I love you! I give myself to you, pure as a burning ember! Take me! and she bit him with a kiss.

Poor Gwynplaine was only human - but fate delivered him from this terrible temptation. A bell rang, and Josiana turned impatiently a silver panel opened, disclosing a letter on a golden salver. Josiana reached out and took the letter, still keeping her arm about Gwynplaine's neck. She broke the Royal Seal and handed the message to Gwynplaine, commanding him to read:

The message from the Queen acquainted Josiana with the discovery of Gwynplaine as Lord Clancharlie, and decreed that Josiana should marry him, instead of Lord David.

As Gwynplaine finished, wonderingly, Josiana snatched the letter from him, glanced at it, then turning to Gwynplaine coldly she commanded: "Be gone!" Gwynplaine stood confused and Josiana repeated scornfully: "Since you are my husband, be gone! This is my lover's place! I hate you!"

Gwynplaine, awakening as from an evil dream, and without another glance at Josiana, crossed to the curtain and went out.

Josiana then entered her boudoir, and sitting at a gilded desk wrote defiantly across the bottom of the Queen's message: "Madam: The arrangement will suit me just as well- I can have Lord David for my lover!:
****

In the corridor Gwynplaine encountered another
visitor, and from their lips issued a double exclamation:
"Gwynplaine!" "Tom Jim Jack!" After a series of mis-
understandings, in which Gwynplaine challenged Lord David
who replied that he could only fight an equal, Gwynplaine
announces himself as Lord Clancharlie. David laughed. "The
name of the man who is to win Josiana! I forgive you -
because we are both her lovers." Then Barkilphedro silently
appeared, bowing low, - he had come to escort Lord Clancharlie
to Parliament.

Gwynplaine pictured to himself his splendid entrance
into the House of Lords. He would appear as a torch bearer
to show them the truth; and as a sword-bearer, to show them
justice! They would applaud - it would be grand!

But after being installed in his position as peer,
he was smuggled, rather than ushered into the great hall.
The face of the new lord might cause a sensation; the dignity
of the House must not be disturbed. Therefor, Gwynplaine,
wearing a broad-brimmed hat which shaded his face, was taken
in, between two short-sighted old sponsors, and seated in an
obscure corner of the duke's bench, before scarcely any of the
lords had arrived.

At this time, the news of the discovery of Lord
Clancharlie's legitimate heir had only begun to be noised
about, but it was brought into the House by some of the later
arrivals; and gossip on the benches concerning more trivial
matters gave way before this amazing sensation. In the dark-
pannelled old hall, lighted by candles - for it was an evening
session - it was difficult for the lords to get a good look
at the new peer, whose face was in shadow.

Then the hall was further illuminated by high candelabras
placed on either side of the throne; the buzz of conversation
ceased and the session began. Gwynplaine, sitting in shadow,
still escaped notice.

After the presentation of the Commons to the House,
bills were read by the clerk, the first a proposal to increase
the annual income of the Prince-Consort. It was understood
that the bill was to be passed, and the peers voted, in the
order of their station: "Content". But when the name of Lord
Fermain Clancharlie was called, Gwynplaine rose and voted, "Non-
content."

Every face turned toward him and standing out in the reflection of the candelabra, his face was then first exposed to
view. Gwynplaine, by an heroic effort which he could exert in
extremity, so controlled his features as to obliterate for the
moment, the ghastly and fatal grin. Now his countenance was
terrible, forbidding, majestic. He plunged desperately into
the subject nearest his heart; his message to the lords concerning the wrongs of the common people.

"My lords, I bring you news - news of the existence of
mankind! I am come to warn you - to impeach your happiness. It
is fashioned out of the misery of your neighbors. I come from
beneath the pressure of your feet. Oh, you who are masters, do
you know the wrong you are doing?"

A hush had fallen upon the august body of peers.
Gwynplaine held them spell-bound with his burning words. Then,
seized by sudden emotion, a sob rose in his throat, he lost
control of his facial muscles, and his face relapsed into a
grinning mask.

The effect upon his audience is instantaneous. A
cloud of awe had hung over the assembly, it broke into delight.
Mad merriment took the whole House. It was a cruel laughter.
A volley of taunting exlaimations assailed Gwynplaine, like
bright wounding hailstones. Bravo, Gwynplaine! Good,
pantaleon!
    Vainly Gwynplaine tried to recapture his audience.
He told them the story of his sufferings, he appeals to them.
But they would not take him seriously, they returned ridicule
and insults. Then Gwynplaine turned against the haughty peers
forever, and prophesied their doom:

"This laugh - placed on my face by a king - expresses
hate, rage, despair - the desoltation of mankind! The people
are as I am. Today, you oppress them, but the hour will come
when they shall break your oppression. Behold the coming of
the people, the ascent of mankind, the beginning of the end,
the red dawn of catastrophe! All these things are in this
laugh of mine, at which you laugh today.

But they heeded not his warning, they roared with
laughter. The tumult was so great that the session was ad-
journed by the Lord Chancellor.

Gwynplaine, broken and defeated, sank to his seat and
fell into a reverie. When he awoke from his mournfull dream,
the House was deserted and the lights were being extinguished.
Gwynplaine replaces his hat and went out.

                    ****

In the vestibule he found Lord David, challenging
the whole House of Lords for the insult offered to himself -
through his half-brother, Lord Clancharlie.

Gwynplaine listened, then came forward, to him he had
hitherto known as Tom Jim Jack. "I thank you," he said, "But
this is my business."

Lord David drew back; "Oh it is you! In your speech
you spoke of a woman, who, after having loved Lord Linneaus
Clancharlie, loved Charles II. Sir, you insulted my mother."

"Your mother! exclaimed Gwynplaine. "In that case,
we are ——"

"Brothers", answered Lord David; and struck Gwynplaine across the face. "So that makes us equal - we can fight. Tomorrow we will cut each other's throats."

****

At midnight, a man richly apparelled, crossed London Bridge, in hot haste, and struck into Southwark. The watchman, beholding him, remarked: "It is a Lord, walking for a wager." But he was mistaken. It was Gwynplaine, the commoner, escaping from the cruelty of the Lords; returning to his own people, seeking those who loved him."

And he found the fair-grounds deserted; the inn dark and tenant-less, the van gone. Then he wandered wildly, and at last came again to London Bridge, where he stood leaning against the parapet, looking down into the dark waters beneath.

He saw nothing of the quay below and the little vessel making ready to sail. He heard the cruel laughter of the peers, felt the blow given to him by his own brother, was filled with the infinite desolation of lost love. The words of Barkilphedro whispered to him, "Destiny never opens one door without closing another." All was over. The final shadows gathered around him. The somber river, which had been the last refuge of countless others whom life had broken and bereft of the desire to live, alone welcomed him.

Taking off his coat and hat, he wrote on a scrap of paper. "I depart. Let my brother David take my place, and may he be happy." Signed: "Fermain Clancharlie, Peer of England." Then weighting them with a stone, he put his foot in a hole in the masonry of the parapet, drew himself to the edge, clasped his hands behind him and leaned over. "So be it!"

At this crucial moment, a rough tongue licked his hands. He shuddered and turned around. Behind him was Homo.

****

On the little vessel, ready to sail for Holland, stood the dilapidated body of the old van, and upon a mattress lay Dea, consumed by fever. Ursus, bending over her, feared that the slightest shock might be her end. As Gwynplaine led by Home, reached the ship, he heard Ursus voicing his fears for Dea, and waited, not daring to make known his presence.

The delirious girl, fancying the show was beginning, rose, despite Ursus' protests, and went through her part. When she had sung her song to Gwynplaine, he sang his response. Dea thought him a spirit, to whom she was being reunited through death.

Ursus, too astonished for words, watching Gwynplaine
take Dea in his arms, soothing her, assuring her that he was
not a spirit, but very human, that nothing should part them
again, that they would marry and be happy together. Ursus,
delighted, murmured that he was as great a fool as if he were
in love himself - he is in love - with them both, a parasite
of their happiness.

****

With the dawn, the vessel cast off and drifted down
the shining river, bearing Gwynplaine and those he loved to
an alien land, away from riches and greatness and power, toward
the promise of joy and peace.

T H E   E N D

Summary

"T H E   M A N   W H O   L A U G H S"

"The Man Who Laughs" is a tremendous story, It has everything essential for a big, appealing, popular, artistically and
financially successful production. It is particularly rich in
human interest and melodrama, which never fail to draw the crowd.

It is as great dramatically and picturesquely as "The
Hunchback of Notre Dame" more pleasing and entertaining.

It will cost only a quarter as much to produce as "The
Hunchback."

There is nothing which may appear censurable in this story
which cannot be easily avoided; The illegitimate origin of Lord
Davis and of Josiana may be only hinted at, or passed over, the
details of torture may be suggested, or out, and the prisoner shown
standing chained, the glimpse of the duchess naked, can be so veiled
by the curtain and shot at such a distance as not to offend the
chaste and virtuous. It would be a shame to sacrifice this scene,
if we can possibly get by with it, for it accentuates the degree of
temptation which Gwynplaine has to resist and from which he is delivered, and increase the dramatic intensity of this scene.

The picture will run to 12 reels, if the full story is told;
but it might be reduced to 10 reels without vitiating the plot
and characterization, if skillfully directed and edited.

The cost of the production is estimated at less than
$250,000; provided every set is standing before the company and
players are put on salary.

The preliminary work on the continuity has been done; it
will take approximately 4 weeks to finish it in a satisfactory
manner. It is recommended that Mr. Chaney and the director con-
sult with Mr. Bernstein on the continuity while it is being
written, so that no changes will be necessary after it is completed.

Clarence Brown is recommended to direct this picture,
because of his splendid work on his previous productions, especially,
in the handling of effective detail, which is especially desir-
able to create the right atmosphere for this story. No other
director, aside from Maurice Tourneur, could direct this particular
picture so well.

The love interest in this story is far greater than that
in "The Merry-Go-Round, which owed its success largely to the
simple and beautiful love affair between Agnes and Bartholomew.
Here we have a more unusual and appealing love motif in the ador-

ation of the blind girl, who worships a man; to the world a
laughing monstrosity, but to her a beautiful soul. And the
man responding with an unselfish affection and devotion,
keeping their love pure and spiritual, at the expense of his
sexual desires; refusing to take advantage of the girl's
blindness because he feels she would not love him if she could
see his face.

This is the biggest opportunity which Lon Chaney has
ever had. It offers a wide scope for his versatile genius
for characterization, by affording him two distinct roles;
that of Gwynplaine, the tragic-comic youth; and Ursus, the
whimsical old philosopher.

The part of Gwynplaine, despite his laughing mask, is not
so grotesque as Quasimodo in "The Hunchback," the combined
names of Victor Hugo and Lon Chaney should have great publicity
value and drawing power.

Mary Philbin, playing the part of the blind girl, Dea,
would certainly add to the success of the picture.

Paul Kohner Brandon Hurst Mary Philbin Cesare Gravini Carl Laemmle Paul Leni

March 18, 1924

To Mr. Bernstein   From Hugh Moffen

I have your note asking me to read immediately synopsis treatment
by Mr. Bernstein of Victor Hugo's story "The Man Who Laughed", asking
my opinion as to whether or not I think it would be a good Super-Jewel.

My opinion is that the story is excellent material for a Super-
jewel, and I recommend its production.

For what I consider the betterment of the story treatment, as so
well outlined by Mr. Bernstein. I add the following notes as suggestions,
to be acted upon or not as it seems fit, by the powers that be.

It might be better showmanship to use the original title in French,
"L'Homme qui Rire." Victor Hugo's Les Miserables" was done under its
French title, and very likely gained prestige thereby.

It would be perfectly possible, I am sure, to eliminate the illi-
gitimacy out of the story, by asking Lord David a detached nobleman with
a propensity for mingling with the common people. The fact that he and
Gwynplaine are natural brothers means nothing to the story. Lord David
could just as well be a clean common sympathetic character, and
of the story, except for human weaknesses. Would prefer to have him
make a mild attempt to win the blind girl by way of menace, but not carry
it too far.

Lady Josiana, need not be shown as a harlot, but merely a capricious
woman with a propensity for doing the opposite of what she is expected
to do or commanded to do. I would show as her reason for going to the
show at the fair grounds, that she was in love with Lord David and following him there using a visapi, as ladies did in those days when they
did not wish to be recognized in public. Seeing Lord David flirting with
Dea, the blind girl, she could retaliate upon him by pretending to be in
love with the Laughing Man, in a state of pique.

The characters of Lord David and Josiana are not clearly disposed
of, either in Victor Hugo's book or in Mr. Bernstein's adaptation. I
would suggest that shortly after she breaks matters off with the Laughing
Man, that she and Lord David become reconciled and secretly marry, or
be married with public pomp, as it best works out.

The ending seems tame, both in the book and in the adaptation.
I feel that it needs a bigger dramatic climax, and I suggest the following.

Break up Gwynplaine's long denunciation with out-breaks to Dea and
her guardian, departing from the show grounds, with the show property.
In the book Gwynplaine's denunciation in the parliament is twenty pages
long and it would have to be broken up in some such manner as this.
Would build up on his denunciation until some young lord in the
house came down on the floor, and faced Gwynplaine and challenges him, or
attacks him. This precipitates a sword fight, showing Gwynplaine defending
himself against the young lord and others who come to his assistance, so
that our hero is pitted against a number of men, perhaps using a sword

that is slipped to him by Lord David, who is in the assemblage. Would show Lord David as a good sport in this respect, and inclined to help Gwynplaine get out of the fix in which he finds himself.

After a sensational sword fight, during which there are cries of treason, would have Gwynplaine back steadily toward on of the small doors near the throne and make a getaway. Pursued by lords and guards he makes his way through passages up to one of the towers of the parliament house, probably the Big Ben Tower, on the Thames side.

From the top of the parliament house tower would have Gwynplaine make a high dive into the Thames, as his only means of escape. Would cut out the London Bridge episode and have him swim across the Thames, pursued by men in boats.

Then I would bring Gwynplaine to the deserted fair grounds, like a hunted animal, and cut back to pursuers for menace and suspense. Would have the wolf come to him at the deserted fair grounds and lead him to the boat where Dea and her guardian are about to embark.

Instead of making this a full rigged ship, would make it a raft or small sail boat to keep down expense.

In conclusion I wish to say that the love between the blind girl and The Laughing Man is a very beautiful thing, more beautiful than the love affair in "The Merry Go Round." The happy ending which Mr. Bernstein has put on the story is far preferable to the unhappy ending in Victor Hugo's novel. There is lots of power and color in this story and it is really Super-jewel material.

Another change that I would suggest would be that the villain, Barkilphedro,meet with some punishment for his misdeeds This might probably occur by receiving a sword thrust through a tapestry or curtain during the big fight in the parliament house, where he might be gloating over the turmoil that he has brought about.

Not knowing the actor whose name is Gravini whom you have suggested for the part of Barkilphedro, I suggest as an alternative Wallace. For the part of Ursus, I noticed that you have it doubled for Lon Chaney. I cannot see where doubling the part is going to enhance the value of the production. For the part of Ursus, I suggest Ernest Torrence, or Tully Marshall. For the part of Josiana, a vamp girl, somebody more typical than Clara Windsor might be suggested, In my opinion. Your suggestions of Lon Chaney as Gwynplaine, Norman Kerry as Lord David, and Mary Philbin as Dea are excellent, they could not be better.

SETS   AND   LOCATIONS

"T H E   M A N   W H O   L A U G H S"

EXTERIORS	INTERIORS
INLET-HARBOR	VAN
SHIP	DUCHESS' BOUDOIR AND BATH
PATH FROM HARBOR TO CLIFFS; PLAIN	*DUNGEON
*INN - MARKET PLACE - FAIR GROUNDS	CLANCHARLIE'S BED CHAMBER
ENTRANCE TO PRISON	CORRIDORS OF PALACE
ENTRANCE TO CEMETERY	HALL- HOUSE OF LORDS
PARAPET - END OF LONDON BRIDGE	VESTIBULE OUTSIDE HALL - H O L
QUAY AND SHIP	Sets starred are standing on lot.

Only a very small boat necessary for ship scenes in
prologue; a good-sized fishing boat might answer; close shots
in cheap tank set. Same boat to be used for last sequence.

The storm at sea could be taken at Laguna effectively.
Mr. Bernstein has a clever device for producing a snow storm on
the ship. with light or heavy fall of snow, any velocity of wind;
at very little costs.

The van can be constructed cheaply on any wagon, built
open at top, for both exteriors and interiers.

Entrances to prison and cemetery, walls with doors;
jail entrance on lot might be used.
Only the end of London Bridge need be shown, and small
section of quay.

The corridors of palace are fragments, with bits of
statuary, etc.

Vestibule, House of Lords, a side lot.

MAIN SETS:

Queen's ante-chamber need not be an elaborate set; a
room with decorated walls (tapestry), furnished with chairs, where
people await audience. All business connected with the queen
could be shot in such a set. If any private scenes are required
with her, a side set, supposedly opening from ante-chamber, would
answer.

Lord Clancharlie's bed-chamber must show evidence of
the luxury into which he has been suddenly thrust - to get his reaction.

Josiana's bath and boudoir will be the magnificent set;
marble walls, bath and fountain; boudoir only a fragment opening
off bath.

Hall - House of Lords will not be such an ambitious set
as suggested by name. At the period of this story, before the
building of Westminster, parliament convened in the baronial hall
of an old castle; the setting would be old, crude, simple.

The town square - the biggest and most expensive set
for the production - (which would include the fair grounds) we
already have in "The Hunchback" set. At a cost of less than
$10,000, the fronts of the houses can be changed so that they will
bear no resemblance to the former set, a be available for this
picture.

The "Hunchback" sets were used extensively in the production. Above, the Tadcaster Inn, where Gwynplaine performs his "Laughing Man" show with Dea, Ursus and Homo, the wolf

Detail of Plot Elements

"T H E M A N W H O L A U G H S"

****

COLOR AND ATMOSPHERE:

Curious house-van, drawn by man and wolf
Ancient craft, with figurehead
Gibbet, with hanging figure
Queen's court
Old English town, market place, fair grounds and
primitive shows
Dungeon-torture room of ancient prison
Entrance of prison and cemetery.
Splendid bits of Italian palace; glimpses of gorgeous gardens
Magnificent marble bath with fountain.
Stately, somber old hall, House of Lords, ancient setting
Old London Bridge and quay

SPECTACLE:

Shipwreck and snow storm at sea

ROMANCE:

Spiritual love between Gwynplaine and Dea, adoration of
blind girl for disfigured youth, and his tender con-
sideration for her.

SEX LURE:

Strange infatuation of voluptuous beauty, Josiana, for
the laughing monstrosity, Gwynplaine, her sensual influence upon him, her attempt to lure and seduce him,
his discovery of her seductive naked figure behind gauss
curtain; her tigerlike wooing of him, his temptation when
she offers herself to him with a passionate kiss.

INTRIGUE:

Conspiracy of Barkilphedro and Queen to humiliate
Josiana, leading to discovery of Gwynplaine and his
elevation to peerage, to the end that their jealousy
and revenge may be satisfied by marrying Josiana to
a monster.

HUMAN INTEREST:

Saving of lost children from storm by Ursus, and their
adoption. Paternal affection of Ursus for Gwynplaine
and Dea. Ursus' attempt to keep Gwynplaine's absence
from Dea, by presenting play to empty benches.

PATHOS:

Gwynplaine's pity for the unfortunate; tragic types
in crowd. Ursus' grief at supposed death of Gwynplaine;
when his garments are returned from prison, and when
Ursus thinks he sees him buried.

Ursus' distress at being banished from England.
Gwynplaine, crushed by ridicule of Lords; hurt by his
brother's blow; heartbroken when he finds Ursus and
Dea gone.
Gwynplaine's culminating misery, when he decides to end
it all.
Dea's suffering and desire to die when Gwynplaine is
taken from her.

COMEDY

        To be delivered from

                Cowardly, obsequious inn-keeper and boob boy
                Venus, who cooks, and Phoebe, who scrubs
                Tom Jim Jack, the roisterer
                Ursus; his whimsical philosophy; his habit of
                talking to himself and to the wolf.

DRAMATIC SITUATIONS:
MYSTERY AND SUSPENSE:

                Desertion of boy by Comprachicos
                Comprachicos hear death-knell in tolling bell
                Consternation of Comprachicos when ship is discovered
                sinking.
                Repentance and prayers of Comprachicos, who commit
                confession to sea.
                Drowning of Comprachicos, kneeling in prayer
                Boy confronted by Gibbet
                Discovery of dead woman and babe

                Tom Jim Jack discovers Ursus and company
                Fight of Tom Jim Jack and Gwynplaine, to eject
                intruders.
                Discovery of duchess in box at play
                Gwynplaine receives Josiana's letter
                Gwynplaine summoned by wapentake. Gwynplaine enters prison
                Gwynplaine enters dungeon, witnesses torture of
                Hardquanonne
                Reading of confession of Comprachicos
                Gwynplaine hailed as Lord Clancharlie - faints
                Gwynplaine awakes in palace-prison, threatened with
                extinction by Barkilphedro, forced to make decision.
                Gwynplaine intoxicated by realization of his power as
                a Lord
                Ursus watches burial cortege; thinks Gwynplaine dead;
                wild with grief
                Gwynplaine attempts to escape from palace
                Bwynplaine discovers Josiana, nude, at bath

Josiana attempts to seduce Gwynplaine
Arrival of Queen's message
Josiana's infatuation turns to hate; she dismisses
Gwynplaine, defies Queen
Gwynplaine encounters Lor David in palace
Ursus banished from England, threatened with
imprisonment; informed that Gwynplaine is dead
Gwynplaine votes in opposition to Lords

House of Lords addressed impressively by Gwynplaine
Gwynplaine loses control of his face
Gwynplaine mocked and insulted by Lords -
prophsizes their destruction
Lord David challenges and strikes Gwynplaine
Gwynplaine finds inn deserted, van gone
Gwynplaine on verge of suicide - prevented by Homo,
the wolf
Dea, delirious, goes thru her part in play
Gwynplaine appears, as one arisen from the dead.

This is the end of Isadore Bernstein's contribution to the writing of The Man Who Laughs.   You will notice slight changes in spacing and punctuation in various sections of the script by J. Grubb Alexander, based on the treatment by Bernstein - This is due to different typist being assigned selected scenes to type in order to complete the script that much faster. This was a typical practice on all the scripts in this series- Editor

Set Still showing the Comprachico's escape boat - Note wind machines in foreground.

THE MAN WHO LAUGHS

Adapted from

Victor Hugo's Novel

****

Adaptation and Screen Play

by

J. Grubb Alexander

Story Supervision

BELA SEKELY

****

FADE IN:

TITLE   SEVENTEENTH CENTURY ENGLAND --
                         IN THE REIGN OF HIS ROYAL MAJESTY
                         KING JAMES II

LAP DISSOLVE OUT AND INTO:

TITLE: A STORMY WINTER NIGHT ALONG THE ROCKBOUND
                         COAST

FADE OUT.

FADE IN:

1   EXT. ROCKY SHORELINE. NIGHT SEQUENCE

MED. LONG SHOT of the comprachico's ship, another
shore. A steady stream of comprachico are hurrying
across the glangplank. It is windy and starting to

                              (CONTINUED)

55

1   (CONTINUED)

DOUBLE EXPOSE OVER SCENE A PARLIAMENTARY EDICT, ON
PARCHMENT, WHICH STATES THE FOLLOWING.

> The comprachicos, being gypsy bands
> of vagabonds and kidnappers;
>
> And being further, buyers and sellers
> of children and being versed in
> certain unlawful surgical arts, whereby
> they transform these stolen children
> into clowns and jesters, by sculpturing
> the living flesh of their faces and
> bodies into monstrosities;
>
> Therefore, these comprachicos are
> hereby banished from England, under
> pain of death.
>
> (Signed by the Great Seal of England)
> (and under the head of Parliament   )
>
> James R.

As this double exposed edict gets clearer, it fills the
screen, so that it is readable. (At this point, can be
inserted the foreign translation of this edict where
necessary) Then the edict dissolves slowly out, as the
Comprachicos are again seen, boarding their ship. The
last stragglers hurry across the gangplank.

2   EXT ROCKY HEADLAND

MED. SHOT of GANGPLANK FROM ABOVE. In this closer shot, the
last stragglers hurry aboard. Then a man and an old hag-like
woman start up the gangplank from the ship, dragging a little
boy between them. He is about ten years old, and his face
is not clearly seen. They hurry him aboard, with nervous
looks behind them, as though they were fearful of something.

3.   EXT. SHIP

MED. SHOT OF DECK, as the other comprachicos and all
make ready to embark. Everything is bustle and haste as
they watch the storm clouds gather.

4   EXT. SHIP

CLOSEUP AT WARF of a sailor's hands as he pulls the ropes
that lead to the sail block.

5   EXT. SHIP

CLOSEUP OF MATE, as the gales start up and gather the
force of the sharp storm wind. Snowflakes swirl through
picture.

6.   INT. DECK CABIN

CLOSE SHOT OF DR. HARDQUANONNE, as he sits over a cabin
table. The camera shoots down upon his bent shoulders
and head, as he pours over an old parchment. His back
is to camera, and the shot comes forward until we can see
the parchment in the light of the cabin lamp. It is the
parchment which states that Gwynplaine was mutilated by
order of the King, but before we can read it, the shadow
of Hardiquanone's head moves back and forth across it
as the lamp starts to swing, swing to the rolling of the
ship caused by the wind in the sails. Hardquanonne looks
up with a start.

7   INT. DECK CABIN

CLOSEUP OF THE CABIN LAMP as it swings violently back and
forth, to the roll of the ship.

TITLE   THE COMPRACHICO SURGEON, DR. HARDQUANONNE.

8   INT. DECK CABIN

            MED. CLOSE SHOT of Hardquanonne. In realization that the
            ship is getting underway, he puts the parchment away
            within his jacket very carefully. Then he hurries out
            of the cabin thru door behind him.

9   EXT. SHIP

            MED. CLOSE SHOT of deck cabin doorway. As scene cuts in,
            Hardquanonne comes out of the cabin in a rush of wind and
            closes door after him. He looks around and then his gaze
            centers suddenly on something out of picture.

10.   EXT. SHIP

            CLOSEUP OF HARDQUANONNE. getting a good study of his
            face, and the sudden surprise and anger upon it, as he
            looks out of picture.

11   EXT. ROCKY HEADLAND

            MED. SHOT FROM THE SHIP GANGPLANK TOWARD SHORE
            as scene cuts in, the gangplank is being pulled in, and
            the little figure of the boy stands out clearly in the
            snowy background, a lonely little figure on the rocky
            coast. The man and woman who took him ashore are
            helping with the gangplank.

12   EXT. SHIP

            CLOSE HOT OF HARDQUANONNE, as he sees the boy, and the
            gangplank being pulled in. He hurries from picture in an
            angry mood.

13   EXT. SHIP

            MED. SHOT of group near gangplank. As scene cuts in, they
            finish pulling in the gangplank. The man and old woman are
            in scene. Hardquanonne dashes into picture, and points
            off to the shore, ordering the gangplank put out again. The
            sailor's hesitate, and then other comprachicos enter
            picture and crowd around Hardquanonne.

14   EXT. SHIP

            CLOSEUP OF HARDQUANONNE. He glares around him in a rage,
            and gives crisp orders.

TITLE   "The gangplank! Bring back that boy!"

            BACK: He finishes title, as though he expected to be obeyed.

15   EXT. SHIP.

            MED. CLOSE SHOT of the comprachicos surrounding Hardquanonne.
            They murmur together, and shake their heads. The man and
            old woman who took the boy ashore crowd into picture. Then
            Hardquanonne enters picture, and orders them sternly,
            pointing off. He starts past them, but they block his way.

16   EXT. SHIP.

            CLOSEUP OF THE COMPRACHICOS who took the boy ashore, with
            the old woman. He talks sullenly

TITLE   "We will have no victims aboard this
                            ship, to convict us of our trade.

            BACK: He finishes title, in a stubborn manner, as though
            his mind was made up.

17   EXT. SHIP

            CLOSEUP OF HARDQUANONNE. He answers quickly.

TITLE   "But this boy means money and
                            safety!"

            BACK he finishes title convincingly.

18   EXT. SHIP.

            MED SHOT OF HARDQUANONNE AND COMPRACHICOS. He starts
            past them, thinking that his words will convince them,
            But they block his way with angry murmurs, and begin to
            force him back from the gangplank and the railing.
            He struggles against their numbers, but the weight of
            them forces him to yield to their will, and inch by
            inch, he is forced back.

19   EXT. SHIP

            CLOSEUP OF HARDQUANONNE as he fights vainly, and is
            slowly forced back through picture. He shouts:

TITLE   "He is of noble birth!"

            BACK: He finishes title and looks around, but still he is
            pushed thru picture. He tries stronger and shouts again.

TIT:E   "I have the written proof!"

            BACK: He finishes title, but still he is pushed backward
            along the deck, as the camera follows him. He shouts
            louder, trying to convince these people.

TITLE   "With the King's own hand, upon a
                         parchment!"

            BACK: He finishes title as he is pushed along, and then
            frantically shouts out the secret.

TITLE   "He is the son of Lord Clancharlie!
                         A Peer of England!"

20   EXT. SHIP

            MED. SHOT OF COMPRACHICOS as they crowd Hardquanonne back
            along the deck. As scene cuts in, he is finishing the
            last title. But it makes no impression upon them, as they
            check his progress toward the rail.

20-23   NOTE: HARDQUANONNE loses in his efforts and the ship sails
               into the stormy night, leaving the little boy alone in the
               bleak rocky shore in the snow. (Copy last draft)

               CUT TO: INT. CASTLE KING's BEDROOM

24   INT.

               SEMI CLOSE SHOT OF PATRON SAINT. As scene cuts in,
               the saint revolves as if on a pivot, disclosing an
               opening in the wall. Barkilphedro enters, and the
               patron saint revolves back into place. He is the
               Jester of James II, and dressed in dark tights.
               He carries a Jester's stick, whose head is a symbol
               of his character.

TITLE   BARKILPHEDRO, THE JESTER OF HIS
                         ROYAL MAJESTY, KING JAMES II....

               BACK: Barkilphedro makes a little bow of mockery - a fool's
               bow - to the King out of picture.

TITLE   ...HE MIGHT WELL HAVE BEEN THE
                         JESTER AT THE COURT OF HELL.

               BACK: The fool's grin fades from Barkilphedro's face into
               an expression of nasty grimace. He starts from picture
               toward the King's bed.

25.   INT. KING'S BEDROOM.

               MED. CLOSE SHOT. King's bed. Barkilphedro enters picture
               and whispers to the sleeping King. The King does not
               awake. Barkilphedro looks down at him with a glance of
               malice. He whispers again, nudging the King with his
               Jester's stick. The King only stirs restlessly.
               Barkilphedro leans closer and whispers louder.

TITLE: "Lord Clancharlie is captured!"

               BACK: As Barkilphedro finishes the title, the King sits
               up, wide awake. He questions Barkilphedro in a fanatical
               manner, as though this were the greatest dream of his
               life. Then he starts from picture quickly and Barkilphedro
               follows him.-

26   INT. KING'S BEDROOM

            MED. CLOSE SHOT. Of the moveable patron saint. The King
            enters picture, sot stopping to change his clothes. The
            patron saint moves aside, and the King hurries into the
            secret passageway, followed by Barkilphedro. The patron
            saint swings back into place.

27   INT. SECRET CORRIDOR

            MED. SHOT. The King starts down the corridor as Barkilphedro
            takes the candle from the wall bracket and follows after him.

            THE CAMERA MOVES ALONG WITH THE KING and BARKILPHEDRO. They
            walk down the corridor's length to a door at the end. The
            King opens the door and passes through. Barkilphedro places
            the candle in wall bracket and follows through the door after
            the King.

28   INT. KING'S PRIVATE CHAMBER

            MED. SHOT. As scene cuts in, Lord Clancharlie is discovered
            standing near the entrance door. Behind him are two hench-
            men of the King. Lord Clancharlie is ironed and shackled. He
            looks off, proud not unafraid, as the King enters picture with
            an air of great satisfacton.

TITLE   "So at last, the rebel Lord Clancharlie
                            has dared to return from exile."

            BACK: He finishes title and continues to look into the eyes
            of Clancharlie, with a malicious gaze. Clancharlie does not
            flinch. The King steps toward him and looks to see that the
            irons are secure. Then he waves aside the guards, gives
            Clancharlie another look, and turns his back upon him, walking
            from picture.

29   INT. KING'S PRIVATE CHAMBER

MED. FULL SHOT. as scene cuts in, the King is walking
toward his great thrown chair. Barkilphedro is standing
as before near the entrance door, with the guards backed
away from him. The King turns and beckons Clancharlie
closer. Clancharlie scuttles forward, and the King stops
him, turning and seating himself in the throne chair.
There is a tableau so the King watches Clancharlie silently,
like a great cat before a kill. Lor Clancharlie is standing
before the King's throne chair.

30   INT. KING'S PRIVATE CHAMBER.

SEMI CLOSE SHOT of LORD CLANCHARLIE. The King leans
forward into picture, with a triumphant air of utter
hatred. He talks.

TITLE   "The years have not dulled our memory
                         nor the Executioner's axe."

BACK: He finishes title, but Lord Clancharlie is not even
perturbed. He is even defiant. The King flares up, as
he notes that he is making no impression upon this men he
wants to hurt.

31   INT. KING'S PRIVATE CHAMBER

CLOSE SHOT OF THE KING'S CHAIR. The King leans back into
picture, very angry. His revenge is losing its
sweetness. Barkilphedro leans into picture, toward
the King, and whispers a suggestion with a diabolical
grin. The King's eyes narrow, and he leans forward and
talks with cruel air.

TITLE   "Or, since you once refused to kiss
                         our hand, you shall kiss the IRON LADY
                         instead."

BACK: The King finishes title, and watches for its effect.

32:          INT. KING'S PRIVATE CHAMBER

CLOSEUP of Lord Clancharlie. He looks off and takes his
new sentence of the King without a tremor. He shrugs his
shoulders as though it made no difference to him. He talks
in proud defiance.

TITLE: "I can expect no mercy from the King
who stole my baby son from me."

BACK: He finishes with a calm lifting of his head, so
that even the shock of this memory will not be apparent.

33   INT. KING'S PRIVATE CHAMBER

SEMI CLOSE SHOT of the King and Lord Clancharlie. Lord
Clancharlie's indifference angers the King. This man is
robbing him of his revenge. He talks in a last effort
to sting the feelings of this proud prisoner.

TITLE: "Suppose that, by our grace, your
son were still alive."

BACK: He finishes title and Lord Clancharlie takes it with
a shocked expression. The thought jars him from his pose of
indifference. A look of wild hope dawns upon his face, so
he leans toward the King and asks him if this is really true.
The King nods and plays with him. He pleads with the King to
allow him just one word with his boy. The King allows him to
proceed until he is figuratively grovelling at his feet. The
King's revenge is taking on sweetness, and he talks to give
Clancharlie the final thrust to break his heart.

TITLE: "You would not know your own child now,
my lord. We sold him to the comprachicos."

CUT FROM TITLE TO FOLLOWING SCENE

34   INT. KING'S PRIVATE CHAMBER

            LARGE CLOSEUP of Lord Clancharlie. He looks off and an
            expression of utter horror dawns upon his face. He repeats
            the word, as the following title dissolves over scene:

TITLE: "Comprachicos!"

            BACK: There is an awful terror in his gaze as though the
            mere mention of the word conjured up fearful visions.

35   INT. KING'S PRIVATE CHAMBER

            CLOSE UP BARKILPHEDRO. He looks out of picture toward the
            King, and pulls back his mouth with his fingers into an imi-
            tation of Gwynplaine's smile. There is a suggestive gleam
            of meaning in his eyes and action.

36   INT. KING'S PRIVATE CHAMBER

            CLOSEUP OF KING. Je gets Barkilphedro's look, and laughs
            with a cruel air. Then he turns toward Lord Clancharlie
            out of picture. He talks as though he were digging his
            knife of revenge in deeper.

TITLE: "By our command, their butcher, Hardquanonne,
                        carved a grin upon his face - to laugh forever
                        at his fool of a father, who dared defy the King."

            BACK: The King finishes title. It is his crowning bolt of
            torture.

37   INT. KING'S PRIVATE CHAMBER

MED. SHOT of Lord Clancharlie. He takes the title with a
gasp of horror, and leans backward, as though having been
struck with a mallet. Then he stops, and a transition
comes over him. He becomes a wild man, and starts forward
to kill the King. He tries to run, but his chains hold
him back, and he lifts his manacled arms as though he were
trying with all his strength to break the chains and crush
the King beneath them.

38   INT. KING'S PRIVATE CHAMBER

MED. FULL SHOT. As Clancharlie makes for the King, the
Kings gets up from his throne chair in a startled manner.
He backs quickly toward the tapestry-hung wall behind
him, and Barkilphedro follows him.

39   INT. KING'S PRIVATE CHAMBER

MED. CLOSE SHOT toward tapestry-hung wall.
The King backs into picture and Barkilphedro follows him,
pulling aside the tapestry and disclosing the entrance
to the secret corridor. As the King starts through, he
shouts off to the henchmen:

TITLE: "Too - - the iron - - l - a -d - y !"

CUT FROM TITLE TO FOLLOWING SCENE

40   INT. SECRET CORRIDOR

MED. REVERSE SHOT against the tapestry-covered entrance.
As seen cuts in, the forms of the King and Barkilphedro's
hand are seen in the half-open entrance-way. Then Barkilphedro's
hand closes the curtain in front of the King and Himself.
The scene is black for a few feet. Then a little figure
dissolves slowly into picture as though it were very far away.
As it comes toward camera with a lightning-like rush of speed
we see that it is the iron Lady. It stands beneath the rays
of a lantern of a dungeon and steps in a close shot, with
foreground enough for outlines. The hands of the two executioners
reach into picture and upon the instrument of torture. Then
Lord Clancharlie steps up into it and the Iron Lady starts to
close upon him.

41   INT. DUNGEON

LARGE CLOSEUP of Lord Clancharlie's head against the background
of the Iron Lady. He calls, crying out to his lost son. He
does not fear the death that is coming to him - only thinks of
the terrible predicament of his little boy, who has been mutil-
lated into a laughing mask by the comprachicos.

TITLE: "Son! My poor little son!"

BACK: He finishes title in an agonized manner as the Iron
Lady starts to close around him.

LAP DISSOLVE OUT AND INTO:

42   EXT. ROCKY HEADLAND. NIGHT SEQUENCE CONTINUED

MED. LONG SHOT of the boy, Gwynplaine. As scene transposes
in, his lonely little figure is seen as he trudges along through
the snowstorm. He comes toward camera out of the desolate
waste.

43   EXT. ROCKY HEADLAND

CLOSE SHOT of Gwynplaine. As the camera follows him along.
The collar of his sailer's vest is turned up high about his
ears, and we do not see the laugh upon his face. He stumbles
over a hidden rock and lifts his foot with the pain of the
contact. Then he starts forward again. His feet are now moving
like clockwork - just mechanism. Then he stops. He shivers
pitifully, and forges out again with his head bent before the
storm.

44   EXT. ROCKY HEADLAND

MED⬛ CLOSE SHOT of gibbet. It is dimply distinguishable in the
storm. The tarred figure of a hanged man dangles from the gibbet
by a chain around his neck. The figure jumps around in the
wind as the snows swirls past. Several ravens are flying around
the gibbet, while others are perched on top of it, waiting for
the dead figure to stop oscillating, so that they can pounce
upon it. Gwynplaine enters picture with his head bent before
the storm. He approaches the gibbet without noticing where
he is going, nor that he is walking directly toward it.

45   EXT. ROCKY HEADLAND

CLOSE SHOT of Gwynplaine. He walks toward camera with head
bowed, before the storm, when the feet of the tarred man upon the
gibbet, swing through picture. They almost kick Gwynplaine and
he instinctively stops and ducks his head as the feet pass out
of picture in an arc. He looks up in a frightened manner as he
sees the gibbet out of picture.

46   EXT. ROCKY HEADLAND

            CLOSE SHOT of the gibbet. This shot is looking straight up
            at the gibbet as though seen from Gwynplaine's angle. The
            gibbet and the man that hangs from it are shadowy ghost-like
            figures in the storm. The feet are very big and the figure
            oscillates weirdly in the snow. It looks like a crazy looking
            scarecrow. The ravens above it stand out clearly against the
            snow.

47   EXT. ROCKY HEADLAND

            MED. CLOSE SHOT of gibbet. Gwynplaine is looking at this
            apparition of horror with a frightened air. Then he manages
            to pull his gaze from the figure and make his feet move in his
            terror. He runs away from the gibbet over the rough, snow-clad
            country.

48   EXT. ROCKY HEADLAND

            MED. CLOSE SHOT of rocky slope in the uneven ground. As scene
            cuts in, several small boulders roll down the slope past camera.
            Gwynplaine follows them through picture as he slides down upon
            the icy surface, losing his footing in his haste. He comes to
            a stop in foreground at the bottom of the dealivity. Bruised
            and shivering, he looks back and listens through the storm.

49.   EXT. ROCKY HEADLAND

            MATTED CLOSEUP of the gibbet. Getting only the top of the
            gibbet, with the chain dangling out of picture. The ravens
            move around as if croaking, and the chain creaks back and forth -
            as the dead figure pulls on it out of scene.

50   EXT. ROCKY HEADLAND

MATTED CLOSEUP of the past of the gibbet, with only the feet
and legs of the dead figure showing. They bang against the
post as though the feet were kicking it.

81   EXT. ROCKY HEADLAND

MED. CLOSE SHOT of Gwynplaine. He listens, trying to conquer
the fear within him. Then he crawls to his feet and turns to
start onward. As he takes a step, he looks out of picture as
through his gaze caught something of interest, something that
further increased his fear.

52   EXT. ROCKY HEADLAND

CLOSE SHOT of two ravens, as they walk across picture as though
crossing Gwynplaine's path ahead of him. Two other ravens
follow them as though there were something drawing them.

53   EXT. ROCKY HEADLAND

CLOSE SHOT of Gwynplaine. He looks off and his eyes follow
the progress of the ravens. Then they center upon some object
ahead of him. He fathers courage and starts out of picture
slowly

54   EXT. ROCKY HEADLAND

            MED. SHOT toward the base of a little cliff. In the snow at
            the base of it, the form of a woman is lying. She is half
            buried in the snow, and a baby is upon her breast, but not seen
            in this longer shot. The ravens are seen as they walk toward
            the shape in the snow.

55   EXT. ROCKY HEADLAND

            SEMI CLOSE SHOT of the dead mother and the baby, Dea. The
            ravens fly out of picture, and Gwynplaine leans down in the snow
            to see what the figure is. He reaches forth his hand at the cheek of
            the woman's face. Then he craws back his hand at the shock of
            its coldness, in realization that she is dead. He sees the baby
            and picks it up from the woman's arms. He stands upright with
            the baby.

56   EXT. ROCKY HEADLAND

            CLOSE SHOT of Gwynplaine. He holds the little baby to him and
            ascertains that it is alive. He feels the baby's hand and sees
            how old it is. Then he unbuttons his sailer's vest, which is
            much too large for him. He puts the baby beneath it and buttons
            the vest up again, wrapping the baby up warmly. Then he turns
            away and starts from picture.

57   EXT. ROCKY HEADLAND

            MED. LONG SHOT. In background, a high and dangerous looking
            natural bridge is seen, as described in Victor Hugo's book. Like
            a long backbone of granite. Gwynplaine enters picture. He
            trudges away toward background over the treacherous causeway.
            He slip again and again as he climbs the sloping bridge of rock
            a small, pitifully lonely figure in the snowstorm.

58   EXT. ROCKY HEADLAND

CLOSE SHOT of a precipitous fissure in the causeway. It is
about three feet across. As scene cuts in, Gwynplaine enters
picture and walks to the edge. He looks down into the black
depths, holds the baby closely to him and jumps across. He
struggles on the opposite side and manages to gain a footing.
Then he starts again onward.

59   EXT. ROCKY HEADLAND

CLOSE SHOT. As scene cuts in, Gwynplaine's bare feet are seen
as he trudges along through the snow. He walks out of picture,
leaving behind him the imprint of his little footprints in the
snow. The camera moves along, traveling the zig-zag path of
little bare footprints in the snow.

LAP DISSOLVE OUT AND INTO:

60   EXT. VILLAGE OUTSKIRTS

CLOSE SHOT of Gwynplaine's feet. He walks along, as the
camera follows him. His steps are very weary, as though
he were very nearly on the point of giving up. Then suddenly
his footsteps quicken as though with hope. They get faster
and faster, as he hurries over the snow.

61   EXT. VILLAGE

MED. LONG SHOT. This is a glass shot of a little English
village, which shows up through the snowstorm in the background.
In foreground, the small figure of Gwynplaine can bee seen, as
he hurries toward this haven over the snow.

LAP DISSOLVE OUT AND INTO:

61   EXT. VILLAGE STREET

            MED. CLOSE SHOT of a house. As scene transposes in, Gwynplaine
            enters picture as he hurries along. He stops as he sees a
            figure in the doorway of the house. It is the town beadle,
            very pompous and imposing looking fellow, covered in full
            regalia despite the storm. The beadle is sleeping in the
            protection of the doorway.

63   EXT. VILLAGE STREET.

            CLOSE SHOT of Gwynplaine. He holds the little baby in this
            full figure shot and puts one foot against the other, hesita-
            tingly, as he wiggles his frozen toes stiffly, and tries to
            warm them. His laugh is not seen, nor has it been seen, up to
            this point. He starts forward, and then hesitates as though
            he were afraid of the officer of the law.

64   EXT. VILLAGE STREET

            CLOSE SHOT of the beadle, as he sleeps in the doorway.
            His snoring and puffing blows his beard out in the wintry
            air in a startling manner. Beside him is a big, ugly-looking
            club. His lantern is sitting on the stone doorsill.

68   EXT. VILLAGE STREET

            MED. CLOSE SHOT of house. Gwynplaine looks at the imposing
            figure of the beadle in awe, and starts out of picture with quickened
            steps.

66   EXT. VILLAGE STREET

            MED. CLOSE SHOT along a low wall. Gwynplaine enters picture
            and walks toward a little ray of light that extends from behind
            the wall, where the wall turns in background. The camera follows
            him and stops at the turn, as Gwynplaine steps to see where the
            light is coming from. As the camera shifts its angle around the
            corner of the wall, Ursus' van is seen at the end of a short
            alleyway. A light shines out from the little window in the
            rear. A light shines out from the little window in the
            rear. Homo, the trained wolf, is chained to the rear wheel
            of the van. Gwynplaine gets up his courage at the cheery glow
            of the light and starts toward the van.

67   EXT. URSUS'S VAN

            MED. CLOSE SHOT of the rear of the van. Homo gets up and
            bares his teeth as Gwynplaine enters picture. Gwynplaine steps
            back and then sees that Homo is chained. Then he starts around
            him toward the van door. As he does so, Homo jumps forward
            on his chain and growls at him. Gwynplaine stops, and the little
            window in the door opens, as Ursus looks out to see what is the
            matter.

68   EXT. URSUS'S VAN

            CLOSEUP of window. Ursus looks around, and his gaze centers
            upon Gwynplaine out of picture. He squints down at the small
            boy and talks in a surly manner.

TITLE: "Who comes to the door of Ursus, the
                            philosopher, at this time of night?"

            CUT FROM TITLE TO FOLLOWING SCENE:

69   EXT. URSUS' VAN

        CLOSEUP of Gwynplaine. He looks up toward the face of
        Ursus out of picture, but the shot is angled so that his
        laughing mouth is not seen as he speaks title.

TITLE: "I am Gwynplaine."

        BACK: He finishes title with a hopeful air, waiting for an
        invitation to enter the warm van. He shivers and holds the
        little baby closer to him beneath his coat, so that it cannot
        be seen as a baby in the shot.

70   EXT. URSUS VAN

        CLOSEUP of Home. The dog-like wolf strains at his chains
        and growls loudly in a ferocious manner.

71   EXT. URSUS VAN

            CLOSEUP of Ursus, as he leans further out the little window.
            He studies the little boy with a quizzical glance, and then
            looks down toward Homo. He talks commandingly to the wolf:

TITLE: "Be quiet, Homo! A knave who dares
                                disobey the king's curfew does not
                                fear your wolfly growl."

            BACK: He finishes title in a dry manner, as he looks again
            in the direction of Gwynplaine and beckons to him with his
            head that he can come in, and get warm.

72   EXT. URSUS VAN

            MED. SHOT of the rear of van. As scene cuts in, Homo slinks
            back to his place beside the wheel obediently. Gwynplaine
            approaches the door and it opens, as Ursus lets down two little
            steps and bids Gwynplaine enter.

73   INT. URSUS VAN

            MED. FULL SHOT. As scene cuts in, Gwynplaine enters thru
            the door. Ursus watches him as he passes inside. Gwynplaine
            shivers pitifully, and Ursus leans out the door and scoops up
            several handfuls of snow. He closes the door, and puts the
            snow in a bowl. Then he beckons Gwynplaine to come nearer
            and to feed himself. Ursus pokes up the fire and rubs Gwyn-
            plaine's cold feet with the snow. But Gwynplaine is seated
            in the shadow, with his head out of range of the lighted lantern,
            which illuminates the little van. His face is not seen clearly
            by Ursus or the audience.

74   EXT. VILLAGE STREET

MED. CLOSE SHOT of the beadle. He is waking up and looking
around him, having been roused by Homo's barks and growls. He
gets up, looking at the hour, and stretches himself to his full
height. As he starts forward, he looks down at his feet and
stops short. He bends over and holds down his lantern toward
the snow.

75   EXT. VILLAGE STREET

CLOSEUP of Gwynplaine's footprints in the snow. They are
illuminated by the beadle's lamp. He lowers it into picture
and looks at them more closely.

76   EXT. VILLAGE STREET

MED. CLOSE SHOT of the beadle. He straightens up slowly
with an air of great importance. Here is work to be done in
keeping with his great official position. Some rascal is
abroad and breaking the King's curfew. With a stern face, he
starts out of picture, holding the lantern toward the ground
and following the trail of Gwynplaine's little footprints in
the snow.

77   INT. URSUS VAN

MED. SHOT Ursus is busy at the stove. He pulls an iron bowl
nearer to the heat, and stirs some porridge to feed the wander-
er. His back is to Gwynplaine, as Gwynplaine continues to
bathe his bare feet with the snow. Suddenly Gwynplaine starts
to take the baby from beneath his coat. The baby cries. Ursus
turns quickly and looks down at the baby with a start of surprise. He takes the baby from Gwynplaine. He looks at it and
holds it gingerly, questioning Gwynplaine. Gwynplaine shakes
his head, that he doesn't know who the baby is. He pantomimes
how he found it while Ursus turns away from him with a wry
grimace of distaste for the situation.

78   INT. URSUS VAN

CLOSEUP of Gwynplaine. He starts to take off his sailor's vest
as he becomes warmer. Now his face is seen for the first time,
but he is partially in shadow, and the full effect of the laugh
is not yet evident.

79   INT. URSUS VAN

CLOSE SHOT of Ursus. His back is still to camera, as scene cuts
in. He turns, still holding the baby in his arms, and looks
toward Gwynplaine. Ursus talks, a bit out of humor.

TITLE   "Stop laughing!"

CUT FROM TITLE TO FOLLOWING SCENE:

80   INT. URSUS VAN

CLOSEUP of Gwynplaine. His laugh is visible in the dim light
from the stove, but it does not stand out yet in all its clarity.
He answers quickly, with a shake of his head.

TITLE   "I am not laughing!"

BACK: He finishes title, with a look off toward Ursus.

81   INT. URSUS VAN

MED SHOT. Ursus turns impatiently toward Gwynplaine, and gives
him another sharp look, wondering why he is lying like this.
He grasps the lantern from its hook and starts toward Gwynplaine, still holding the baby clumsily.

82   INT. URSUS VAN

CLOSE SHOT of Gwynplaine. As scene cuts in, he is in partial
shadow as before. Then the light starts to break upon his face,
as though Ursus were approaching with the lantern. His face
is seem clearly, for the first time. The audience now sees
his horrible laugh and distorted visage. Then Ursus leans into picture with the lantern and looks at Gwynplaine's face in
awe. Sudden understanding is registered upon the old man's
face and he nods his head as he murmurs in plain pantomime,
"Comprachicos' work."

83   EXT. URSUS VAN

MED. CLOSE SHOT of the rear of the van. As scene cuts in
the beadle enters picture with his lantern, as he follows
Gwynplaine's footprints laboriously up to the door. He knocks
loudly with his staff, as Homo, the wolf, jumps at him.

84   INT. URSUS VAN

MED. SHOT. Ursus turns quickly from Gwynplaine, as he hears
the noise at his door. Then he puts the lantern back upon its
back and tiptoes to the door, telling Gwynplaine to be quiet.
Ursus hold the baby in an awkward manner and manages to peer
out the window cautiously. He turns with a startled look as
he recognises the beadle. He starts from the door quickly
and tells Gwynplaine to do as he says. He walks to the chest,
which serves as his bed, and lifts the lid, motioning Gwynplaine to hide inside.

85   EXT. URSUS VAN

CLOSE SHOT of beadle at the door. He strikes out below him
at Homo, as the wolf snarls and jumps into picture on his chain.
Then the beadle pounds again upon the door, demanding admittance in the name of the law.

86   INT. URSUS VAN

MED. SHOT. As scene cuts in, Gwynplaine has disappeared into
the chest. Ursus looks at the baby a moment, wondering what
he shall do with it. The he quickly holds it behind him in
a dexterous manner, and walks toward the door. He opens it,
and the beadle stomps in, with an important air. He looks
Ursus up and down with his lantern, but Ursus always keeps his
face toward him, and the baby behind him, then the beadle looks
around the floor and registers his dumbness by peering
into the most impossible places. He turns upon Ursus with a
severe look of chagrin. He questions him pompously.

87   INT. URSUS VAN

CLOSE SHOT of Ursus. He looks off, as he tries to keep the
baby hidden, and answers the beadle with a shake of his head.

TITLE: "No man has entered my door tonight - -
                          I give you my word."

BACK: He finishes title, with a meaning look under his eyebrows. Then he (the beatle) enters picture and leans toward
him. He tries to peer over his shoulder, but Ursus deftly
turns away. The beadle tries to peer around his back, but he
is too fat. Finally he doubles up quickly and peers thru
Ursus' crooked arm. He straightens up, and points toward
Ursus' back. Ursus produces the baby, with a sheepish look,
pantomiming that certainly this is not a man. The beadle
looks at the baby, as he weighs the matter carefully in his
mind. Then he looks around the van, and a great thought
strikes him. He talks as though passing judgement.

TITLE   "A baby and no wife! Such a magician
                          must leave town!

BACK: He finishes title and steps away from Ursus, in awe,
at such a situation. Ursus takes the command in good humor,
and with a wry grimace at the baby,

88   INT. URSUS VAN

MED CLOSE As scene cuts in, the beadle stalks out the door,
closing it after him. Ursus walks to it and bolts it after him.
He listens to his retreating footsteps.

89   INT. URSUS VAN

CLOSE SHOT of Chest, As scene cuts in, the lid opens cautiously, and Gwynplaine sticks his head up. Seeing the coast is
clear, he lifts the lid higher and starts to get out.

90   INT. URSUS VAN

MED. SHOT. Ursus walks in the door toward the stove, and talks
to Gwynplaine as Gwynplaine approaches him.

TITLE   "I pray for food, and I am sent two
                          extra mouths. And what a mouth you
                          have!"

BACK: He finishes the title, as he looks at Gwynplaine. Then
he turns and take the bowl from the stove. He hands it to
Gwynplaine, telling him to be careful and not burn his hand.
Gwynplaine takes it and the baby starts to cry. Ursus holds
her up, pantomiming that she shall look at Gwynplaine. He talks
to her.

TITLE   "Look at him, thou squalling bundle!
                          His face would make the King's
                          Executioner laugh!"

BACK: He finishes title, as he bounces the baby up and down on
his hands in front of Gwynplaine. But the baby doesn't seem to
see Gwynplaine. Ursus looks into the baby's eyes, and takes a
step, reaching for the lantern from its hook.

82

91   INT. URSUS VAN

            CLOSE SHOT of Ursus, as he holds the baby. He rings the
            lantern into the picture and passes it up and down in front
            of the baby's eyes, with the baby's back to the camera. A
            shocked look comes into Ursus' face and he talks off as
            if to Gwynplaine out of picture.

TITLE   "The snow has mercifully closed her
                            eyes, and she will never see your face.
                            She is blind!"

            CUT FROM TITLE TO FOLLOWING SCENE

92   INT. URSUS VAN

            MED. SHOT As Ursus finishes title, Gwynplaine looks at
            the bay in pity. He stops eating, from the bowl of porridge,
            and Ursus hands the baby to him. Gwynplaine sits on the
            chest and holds the little baby on his knee. He feeds it
            by dipping his finger in the porridge and sticking it in the
            baby's mouth. Ursus turns from him and takes a coat down
            from the peg on the wall. He closes the stove, dampening
            the fire, and hangs the lantern back upon the hook. Then
            he unbolts the door and steps out into the stormy night,
            to obey the order to get out of town. The door closes
            after him.

93   EXT. URSUS VAN

            MED. CLOSE SHOT. Ursus walks from the van door to the wolf,
            Homo. He unchains the wolf and Homo jumps up and paws him,
            licking his face in a friendly manner. Ursus pats his head
            and pantomimes that they are starting on their way. He
            starts around the van toward the front of it, and Homo trots
            behind him. Then, the van starts to turn in picture as
            Ursus walks back, turning the van around, as he walks between
            the shafts. He stops and drops the shafts to adjust the
            harness around Homo.

94   INT. URSUS VAN

MED. SHOT Gwynplaine finishes the porridge ravenously.
He licks the bowl clean and offers the last finger full of
the gravy to the baby on his lap. But the baby is quiet
and going to sleep against his shoulder. Gwynplaine picks
the baby tenderly up and places her tenderly upon the
bearskin rug on top of the chest. Then he walks on tiptoes
to the stove and puts the empty bowl back upon it. He
warms his little hands and rubs his eyes sleepily. He is
sore and tired. Painfully, he limps back to the chest
on his cut feet. He lies down beside the baby and pulls
the bearskin rung over them.

95   INT. URSUS VAN

CLOSE SHOT of Gwynplaine and the baby, Dea, as scene cuts
in, Gwynplaine closes his eyes, dropping off into the deep
sleep of exhaustion. The baby reaches up and grabs hold
of his ear, hanging onto it. Then the baby snuggles up
against the warmth of Gwynplaine's body, as the little arm
drops around his neck.

96   EXT. VILLAGE STREET

MED. SHOT, shooting along the wall that turns into the
alleyway where the van is encamped. As scene cuts in,
the little van rolls out of the alleyway. Ursus and
Homo are pulling it, side by side in the shafts. It turns
past camera and starts background thru the snowstorm,
with a steady crunch of the wheels through the snow,

97   EXT. VILLAGE OUTSIDE

CLOSEUP of the feet of Ursus and Homo, the wolf,
as they trudge along, side by side through the snow

TITLE   THROUGH EACH CHANGING SEASON -
                           CRUNCHING THE YEARS UNDER FOOT
                           IN SNOW IN RAIN, STORM AND
                           SUNSHINE

          FADE IN

98   EXT. FOREST GLADE.   DAY SEQUENCE

          CLOSE SHOT of the feet of Ursus and Homo, the wolf,
          an akeley shot as they walk along, pulling the van. Underneath
          their feet is a carpet of grass, and spring glowers stick up
          their heads thru the green surface.

          LAP DISSOLVE OUT AND INTO:

99   EXT. COUNTRY ROAD   START SEQUENCE

          CLOSE SHOT of the feet of a horse, and Gwynplaine. The horse
          is pulling the van and Gwynplaine is walking beside him.
          These feet and legs have replaced the feet of Ursus and Homo.
          It is raining. The caravan follows along, as the horse and
          Gwynplaine splash thru the water and mud.

100   EXT. COUNTRY ROAD

          MED. CLOSE SHOT of the van, as it is pulled through the rain-
          storm. Gwynplaine is walking beside the horse. He is not
          clearly seen in the shot. A light shines through the window
          in back of him.

TITLE   WITH GWYNPLAINE GROWN TO MANHOOD
                           THIS SCHOLAR OF THE LEARNED URSUS
                           HAS TURNED SOURCE FOR A LIVELIHOOD.

101   INT. URSUS'S VAN

CLOSE UP of Gwynplaine's make up articles. They are lying
upon a little shelf, and get over clearly that his occupation
that of a clown. A curious clown mask is leaning against
the wall.

102   EXT. COUNTRY ROAD

MED. CLOSE SHOT of Gwynplaine, as he walks along beside the
horse that pulls the van.

103   INT. URSUS'S VAN

CLOSEUP of makeup material as before. Dea's hand enters
picture, and with a sure touch feels toward the mask and
strokes it tenderly.

TITLE   THE BLIND SNOW CHILD, DEA, HAD FOUND
                         LIFE AND LIGHT IN GWYNPLAINE

104   INT. URSUS' VAN

CLOSE SHOT of Dea. She is sitting on a stool, and her hand
is still stroking Gwynplaine's mask on his makeup shelf.
This makeup shelf is on the wall of the little van. There is
a mirror above it. Dea's face is turned from camera, but
seen in the reflection in the mirror.

105   INT. URSUS' VAN

MED SHOT of rear partitioned enclosure. A curtain has been
put up which separates the little van into two compartments.
Ursus is seated near the fire, toasting his rheumatic shins.
He looks over at Dea. He watches her with Gwynplaine's mask,
and talks:

TITLE   "You live in a fairy world of an
                         imagination. How fortunate that you
                         cannot see."

BACK: He finishes title as he watches her. Beside him Homo
is sleeping. Dea turns toward Ursus as though at the sound
of his voice. She answers sweetly:

TITLE   "But everything is beautiful! It only
                         gets dark when Gwynplaine is not near me."

BACK: She finishes title and turns her head toward the front
of the van as though she is listening for some sound of
Gwynplaine.

105   EXT. COUNTRY ROAD.

MED. CLOSE SHOT of Gwynplaine as he walks along beside the
horse thru the mud and rain.

106   INT. URSUS' VAN

MED. SHOT of rear compartment. As scene cuts in, Ursus rises
stiffly and walks to Dea. He watches her with an understanding look and a glance toward the front of the van.

                                        (CONTINUED)

107   (CONTINUED)

TITLE   "You are still children, and luckily
                         love is blind. Go to bed now, and
                         pray that it remains so."

BACK: He finishes title, and she rises obediently. He pats
her hand with a rough tenderness. He loves these two children
he has adopted, but his philosophy makes his exterior gruff.
He leans over and kisses her hair tenderly above the forehead.
Then he pinches her cheek, pantomiming that she needs more
roses in them, and hurries her to bed. She exits thru the
curtain, and Ursus yawns and returns to his place beside the
fire.

108   EXT. COUNTRY ROAD

MED. CLOSE SHOT of Gwynplaine, as he walks beside the horse.
Behind him a little window in the front of the van opens, and
Dea calls out, as she appears in it. Gwynplaine backs toward
her. She puts her hand thru the window toward him.

109   EXT. COUNTRY ROAD

CLOSEUP of the window in the front of the van. Dea's hand
is extended thru the window. Then Gwynplaine's hand reaches
up and takes her hand in his with a tender brotherly air.

110   EXT. COUNTRY ROAD

MED. CLOSE SHOT of the van, as the Horse pulls it along.
Gwynplaine bids a tender good night to Dea, and Dea withdraws
her hand inside. The window closes, and Gwynplaine comes
forward again beside the horse.

111   EXT. COUNTRY ROAD

CLOSE SHOT of Gwynplaine's feet as he walks beside the horse.
They step along through the mud. The horse is slow and weary
in his motions. But there is a firmness and lightness to
Gwynplaine's feet despite the mud.

LAP DISSOLVE OUT AND INTO:

112   EXT. ANOTHER COUNTRY ROAD   DAY SEQUENCE

MED. CLOSE SHOT of the feet and forelegs to two horses, har-
nessed side by side. It is a summer day, and the country
road is spotted with woods. As scene transposes in,
these two strong horses are galloping over the road.

                              FADE OUT.

TITLE   TO PROSPERITY AND THE GREEN BOX
                          WITH GWYNPLAINE'S POPULARITY GROWING
                          BY LEAPS AND BOUNDS THRU THE COUNTRYSIDE.

FADE IN

113   INT. GREEN BOX STOCK   DAY SEQUENCE

          CLOSEUP of Ursus' hands. He rubs them together in a
          satisfied manner, as though he were pleased at something
          out of picture.

114   INT. GREEN BOX   STOCK

          MED. CLOSE SHOT shooting over the footlights of the stage,
          and straight into the upturned face of a small audience.
          As scene cuts in, the face of Gwynplaine, dressed in clown
          makeup and costume, is on the stage, with his back to camera.
          He jumps into the air, with a funny motion, finishing his
          set. The farmers and villagers, whose gaze up at him, laugh
          uproariously at this funny fellow.

115   EXT. GREEN BOX

          MED. LONG SHOT. As the scene cuts in, the curtain starts
          down over the stage, hiding the form of Gwynplaine. The show
          is over. The Green Box is standing in the background, that
          suggests a small country village. About twenty farmers and
          villagers are grouped in front of it. They turn and start for
          home, still laughing and in good humor.

117   EXT. GREEN BOX

       MED. CLOSE SHOT of a group of village dogs. They are standing
       in a group around Homo. They, too, are witnessing a show, as
       they look at his funny-looking dog. Homo turns away and
       steps into the Green Box. The show is over.

118   EXT. GREEN BOX

       CLOSEUP several of the villagers as they start for home.
       Only their faces are seen as they turn and whistle for
       their dogs.

119   EXT. GREEN BOX

       CLOSE SHOT of the village dogs. They turn, one by one
       as they hear their master whistle, and run out of picture.

120   EXT. GREEN BOX

       MED. CLOSE SHOT near the Green Box. The farmers and
       villagers are passing thru picture on their way home.
       They nudge each other and laugh about Gwynplaine. Stranger
       is standing and watching the passing throng of country folk.
       He is Hardquanonne but much changed in dreams and appearance.
       The last villager passes him, and he stands alone in scene.

121   EXT. GREEN BOX

       SEMI CLOSE SHOT of Hardquanonne. He turns his head toward
       the Green Box out of picture, and walks from picture, in the
       opposite direction to that taken by the villagers. His
       tread is stealthy.

122   INT. GREEN BOX   GWYNPLAINE'S ROOM

(This is the troupe's living quarters, in which Ursus and
Gwynplaine sleep. A door leads to the outside through the
rear of the van. An entryway leads from this room to Dea's
sleeping quarters in the front of the van. This entryway
passes a small kitchen. There is a door in the entryway
which leads to the stage. The stage occupies one side of
the van, while the living quarters occupy the other side,
running lengthwise.)

MED. SHOT Gwynplaine is seated at his makeup table. He
turns as Dea enters, followed by Ursus. Ursus is very much
excited, and looks at the two children, happily. He rubs
his hands together in a pleased manner and produces his
little leather bag in which he carries his money. He pours
the coins from it out into his hand, and shows the money to
Gwynplaine. Then he talks:

TITLE   "You are a big success. In London
                         you will be a bigger success."

BACK: He finishes title with a nod of conviction, and
hurries Dea and Gwynplaine, pantomiming that they must
be on their way. He walks to the rear door and exits.
Gwynplaine turns back to his makeup table. Dea pauses a
moment and touches the clown mask on his makeup table,
as it lies beside him. Gwynplaine looks up at her with a
worshipful gaze of tenderness. Then she turns with a
happy smile and walks to the entryway to go to her room.
Gwynplaine watches after her with a thoughtful air.
Then he turns toward his makeup table to take off his
makeup.

123   INT. GREEN BOX   GWYNPLAINE'S ROOM

CLOSE SHOT of window. As scene cuts in, the face of
Hardquanonne, as he lifts his head up into picture.
He looks inside and around furtively. Then he sees
Gwynplaine and watches through the window with a
cunning air.

124   INT. GREEN BOX GWYNPLAINE'S ROOM

CLOSE SHOT OF GWYNPLAINE, as he takes off his makeup.
Before his makeup mirror, beneath the clown makeup
the laugh still remains upon his face. There is a certain
sadness of heart in Gwynplaine's attitude as he pauses for
a moment and looks into the mirror at this laugh that cannot
be removed with the other makeup. He puts the thought aside
and turns away, to busy about his duties.

125   INT. GREEN BOX   GWYNPLAINE'S ROOM

CLOSE SHOT of window. Hardquanonne is looking thru, as
before. There is an air of keen satisfaction in his
expression, as he realizes that there is no mistake -
that this man must be the boy he operated upon years
before. A cunning pride is registered upon his face,
as he notes this wonderful smile that he has made.
He turns away from the window and disappears from
picture.

126   EXT. GREEN BOX

MED. CLOSE SHOT. Ursus is discovered as: he is harness-
ing the horses, preparatory to leaving the village. Homo
is beside him. Suddenly, Homo turns and growls, as he
looks out of picture. Ursus stops in his task and looks
in the direction of Homo's attention.

127   EXT. GREEN BOX

MED. CLOSE SHOT at end of Green Box. The side toward the
living quarters is around the corner, as scene cuts in,
Hardquanonne walks into picture, closing from the proximity
of the window. He looks off with a disarming smile, bows
politely, and starts out of picture.

128   EXT. GREEN BOX

             MED CLOSE SHOT OF URSUS. As scene cuts in, Ursus commands
             Homo to be quiet and Hardquanonne, pointing to the Green Box
             and indicating that he is a brother showman. He talks:

TITLE   "You have a wonderful clown.
                          He is worth a lot of money."

             BACK: Hardquanonne finishes title with an oily smile. Ursus
             takes this man's congratulations in a pleased manner. He beams
             at Hardquanonne, and thanks him profusely for mentioning his
             poor show, pantomiming that he is very glad - he likes it.
             He finishes and questions Hardquanonne politely, asking who he
             may be, that he takes such a friendly interest.

TITLE   "I too have a show - with a
                          five-legged cow."

             BACK: He finishes title, continuing to explain his
             business, and what a great attraction this cow is.

129   EXT. GREEN BOX

             CLOSE UP URSUS. He looks off in a pleased manner at meeting
             this engaging man, who seems so friendly. Then he talks
             questioningly:

TITLE   "You go to the London Fair?"

             BACK: He finishes title in an engaging manner

130   EXT. GREEN BOX

CLOSE UP HARDQUANONNE. He nods his head in answer to Ursus'
question, and talks with a suave smile:

TITLE
                "Of a surety, we will meet there.
                I will not forget your clown's
                laughing mask."

131   EXT. GREEN BOX

MED. CLOSE SHOT of Ursus and Hardquanonne. Ursus takes
Hardquanonne's title, and Hardquanonne bows deeply, bidding
goodbye to Ursus. Ursus bows also, taking leave of Hardquanonne, politely. Then Hardquanonne gathers his cloak
around him and walks from picture. Ursus looks after him, well
pleased with himself and his show.

132   INT. GREEN BOX.   STAGE

MED. SHOT. Gwynplaine is shifting scenery and clearing up
the stage. He is hurrying, and happy in his work. He slices
the wings across the stage into their places, so that the
front of the theatre can be folded up and the Green Box made
ready for travelling.

133   INT. GREEN BOX DEA'S DOOR

MED. CLOSE SHOT Dea is on, her makeup is off, and she is
endeavoring to change her costume. It, however, has become
caught. The ribbon which laces the dress up the back has become knotted. The bodice is partially off, however, and the
shoulder and bare arm is visible, disclosing a portion of
her bosom. She cannot unfasten the knot in the ribbon, and
gets up to seek help. Unconscious of her bare shoulder and arm
she walks sure-footedly to the entryway and exits.

134   INT. GREEN BOX

           MED. CLOSE SHOT, as Gwynplaine shoves a wing into place at
           the back of the stage. As he does so, the door opens, and
           Dea starts out, calling his name. Gwynplaine turns toward
           her, telling her that he is here. She comes toward him
           quickly, and he notes for the first time that she is partially
           disrobed.

135   INT. GREEN BOX.   STAGE

           MED. CLOSE SHOT of Gwynplaine. As Dea enters picture to him,
           he looks at her with a certain awe, as his eyes center upon
           her white shoulder and arm. She turns her back to him and
           indicates the knot in the ribbon. He starts to unloose it.
           But he cannot take his eyes from the whiteness of her skin. He
           suddenly becomes aware of her nearness -- that she is a woman.
           He becomes nervous, and bungles the knot. She snuggles back
           against him, so that he will have a better grasp at the ribbon.
           Her nearness only excites him further, but he succeeds in
           untying the ribbon. She smiles up at him over her shoulder
           and leans back against him comfortably. He looks down at her
           arm, and reaches his hand toward it. He strokes it, and his
           other arm creeps around her shoulder. She leans her head back,
           and in a burst of emotion he bends over and kisses the white-
           ness of her arm. At the contact he straightens up with a
           startled look. But instead of being angry, Dea pantomimes for
           him to repeat the act. Gwynplaine is very much flustered
           and instead of accepting her mute invitation he drops his arm
           from around her shoulder and steps away from her.

136   INT. GREEN BOX STAGE

           CLOSEUP of Dea. She is very still, and waiting for Gwynplaine
           to kiss her arm again. She has felt the thrill of his lips
           upon her flesh, and holds her arm forward with an innocent
           gesture, as though mutely repeating her request.

137   INT GREEN BOX STAGE - CLOSE SHOT

          of Gwynplaine. He turns toward camera and takes Dea's hand,
          as she thrusts her arm into picture. He looks down at it,
          and talks quickly, with a shake of his head:

TITLE: "You only ask this because you cannot see
                          me. Everyone else shrieks with laughter
                          or runs away."

          CUT FROM TITLE TO FOLLOWING SCENE:

138   INT GREEN BOX STAGE - MED CLOSE SHOT

          of Gwynplaine and Dea. Gwynplaine finishes title, and Dea
          drops her hand to her side with a little hurt expression.
          She talks in quick answer:

TITLE: "But why? Are you not my beautiful
                          Gwynplaine?"

          BACK: She finishes title and Gwynplaine looks at her with
          a look of disbelief. He looks away quickly, turning his
          face from her in realization of how her imagination is trick-
          ing her. He talks with a shake of his head.

TITLE: "I am really very horrible."

          BACK: He finishes title, and Dea takes it with a firm shake
          of her head. She approaches him, reaches out to locate him,
          and lays her hand upon his arm. Then she talks:

TITLE: "Story-teller! If you were really horrible
                          I would not love you - or want you to kiss me."

          BACK: She finishes title, and Gwynplaine looks at her,
          as her hand lies upon his arm. The desire to accept her
          love is great as she smiles sweetly up at him. He looks
          into Dea's beautiful face and sees the response to his
          emotion upon it. He reaches out and gathers her tenderly
          into his arms, yielding to his temptation. He holds her

138   CONTINUED

against him, and she lifts her face toward his. He bends
over, to kiss her on the mouth.

139   INT GREEN BOX STAGE - CLOSEUP

Of make-up mirror. It hangs against the theater wall in
the wings. As scene cuts in, the reflection of Gwynplaine's
face and Dea's are seen in the mirror. He is about to kiss
her. As his lips near hers, his eyes turn, as though
attracted subconsciously to his reflection in the mirror.
There is a tremendous contrast in the picture, with his
horrible laughing face so close to the sweet beauty of Dea's.
He stops short in his spot and looks in awe at the reflection,
which has almost the question of a vision.

140   INT GREEN BOX STAGE - SEMICLOSE SHOT

Of Gwynplaine and Dea angled in front of the mirror.
Gwynplaine quickly releases Dea and reaches over toward the
mirror, brushing it from the wall, as though the sight of
it made him angry. It falls to the floor. She senses
some change in him and talks toward him, in such a position
that her head as she stops with her back to camera, cuts
off the lower part of his face from view.

141   INT GREEN BOX STAGE - CLOSEUP

of the heads and shoulders of Gwynplaine and Dea. They are
in the same position as in previous scene. The back of her
head toward camera and hides the lower part of Gwynplaine's
face. As she looks upon him, his eyes register the agony
and hopelessness he feels. She believes him beautiful. He
cannot make her see the truth. Therefore to take her love
is imposed bliss. She reaches her arm up to his with a tender
motion and starts to entangle his neck. With an agonized
gaze down at her he gently lifts her arms from about his
neck and lowers them from picture

142   INT GREEN BOX   STAGE - MED CLOSE SHOT

Of door to entryway. As scene cuts in, the door opens
and Ursus enters with Homo. He stops as he looks off
and sees Gwynplaine and Dea. There is a wry grimace
registered upon his face, and he talks to Homo disgustedly.

TITLE: "Such calf-like billing and cooing is
                          tiresome! Some day we will marry them and
                          cure this happy love sickness."

BACK: He finishes title with a sly wink at Homo, and Homo
barks, wagging his tail. Then Ursus starts from picture.

143   INT GREEN BOX STAGE - MEDIUM SHOT

Toward Gwynplaine and Dea. Gwynplaine turns at Ursus'
approach and Homo runs up to him, wagging his tail.
Ursus' entrance has interrupted the tenseness of the scene.
Ursus hurries Gwynplaine, and tells Dea that she must go
to her room at once and finishes dressing. He is like an
old mother hen, and pulls Dea's dress up over her arms.
Then he hurries her along toward the door, scolding
Gwynplaine for keeping her out here on the stage. Ursus
sees the mirror on the floor and picks it up, places it
upon a small table against the wall. Then he follows
Dea through the door again, telling Gwynplaine to hurry -
that they are starting on their way. Gwynplaine watches
him exit and the door closes behind him. Homo remains with
Gwynplaine.

144   INT GREEN BOX   STAGE - MED CLOSE SHOT

Of Gwynplaine. He turns to resume his work and stops to
pet Homo, as Homo jumps up at him. He is standing beside
the little table. He looks down, his eyes drawn to the
little mirror which Ursus has placed upon the table.

145   INT. GREEN BOX STAGE

LARGE CLOSEUP of the mirror on the table. Gwynplaine's face
is seen in it, as he watches his reflection. His hand quickly
enters picture upon the mirror, and covers the half of the
reflection that shows his laughing mouth. Only his eyes are
seen. They register all suffering behind them, and fill with
tears at the realization of the laugh that smiles evilly between Dea and himself. As the tears overflow the lids, they
drop down into picture upon the back of his hand. Homo's head
tips into picture and licks the tears from Gwynplaine's hand
in a sympathetic manner.

146   INT. GREEN BOX GWYNPLAINE'S ROOM

CLOSEUP of Gwynplaine's makeup table. Upon the surface is
clearly registered his clown makeup material. The wig-like
skull-cap, clown's pig bladder, and clown mask are clearly
registered. The articles typify Gwynplaine and his life.

LAP DISSOLVE OUT AND INTO

147   INT. JOSIANA'S BEDROOM. DAY SEQUENCE

CLOSEUP of gorgeous dressing table. It is covered with
toilet luxuries from all over the world. The articles typify
a woman's boudoir and get over an atmosphere of great wealth.

TITLE   IT IS A FAR CRY FROM GREEN BOX TO PALACE-
                         BUT BY THE GRACE OF THE LATE KING JAMES II,
                         A CLOWN'S UNKNOWN BIRTHRIGHT NOW BELONGS TO
                         THE DEVIOUS JOSIANA

100

148   INT. JOSIANA'S BOUDOIR

CLOSE SHOT of bathing pool. This is the boudoir described
by Victor Hugo's book except for the mirrored walls, which are
impossible to shoot. An open archway connects with Josiana's
bedroom. Over the bathing pool, a fountain sprays a fine mist.
This mist forms a motion-like haze over the water.

As scene cuts in, the camera is shooting down at the water.
The Duchess Josiana is discovered on. Her head and shoulders
are visible. Her face is toward camera and she presents a
beautiful picture. She is immersed in the pool to her
shoulders. She starts to swim out of picture - or walk out
with her feet upon the bottom of the pool. Through the water,
her nude form can be just suggested and dimly outlined.

149   INT. JOSIANA'S BOUDOIR

CLOSEUP of a little trained baboon. He is in scarlet and
gold livery and is squatted on the edge of the pool looking
down into the water, as though watching the Duchess Josiana.
Water is splashed up into his face as though the Duchess were
wetting him for his scrutiny of her. The baboon turns and
runs quickly out of picture.

150   INT. JOSIANA'S BOUDOIR

MATTED CLOSE SHOT of the steps that lead out of the sunken
bath pool. As scene cuts in, the Duchess Josiana's bare
limbs start up the steps out of the water. The camera follows
her as she walks up the steps. But the shot is matted so
that it is cut just above her knees. She stops on the
pool's edge, and a silken robe enters picture as though put
around her by a servant. It closes around her bare limbs and
she starts out of picture.

LAP DISSOLVE OUT AND INTO:

151   INT. JOSIANA'S BOUDOIR

           CLOSEUP of Josiana's head and shoulders. As scene transposes
           in, she is registered as sitting before the gorgeous dressing
           table in her boudoir. The hands of a servant enter picture
           and pull back the robe from her shoulders. The robe falls
           below camera line and her shoulders are nude below the throat,
           giving the effect as though she were nude in the chair below
           the camera line. The hands of the woman servant perfume and
           message Josiana's body below the camera line, getting over
           the action by suggestion.

           LAP DISSOLVE OUT AND INTO:

152   INT. JOSIANA'S BOUDOIR

           CLOSE SHOT at the foot of Josiana's chair. The baboon is
           on in picture. As scene transposes in, the baboon pulls
           aside the silken robe, disclosing Josiana's bare limbs.
           Then he starts to put on Josiana's stockings as though
           trained to act in this capacity.

AN OLD ACQUAINTANCE STILL MANAGES TO MAKE HIMSELF
                      USEFUL AROUND THE COURT. AND QUEEN ANNE NOW SITS
                      UPON THE THRONE OF ENGLAND...

153   INT. JOSIANA'S HALLWAY

             MED. SHOT of door to Josiana's boudoir. As scene cuts in,
             Barkilphedro enters picture. He is recognizable as the
             Satanic jester of James II. He is dressed in a dark
             tight-fitting Jester's suit. He stops at the door and
             listens at it with a crafty expression. Then he knocks,
             waits a moment and enters the room.

154   INT. JOSIANA'S BOUDOIR

             MED. FULL SHOT Barkilphedro enters the hall door. Josiana
             is in front of dressing-table. She is dressed in a silken
             robe. She is admiring herself in the mirror. She turns
             toward Barkilphedro as he greets her with a bow. She turns
             languidly as Barkilphedro approaches her. She dismisses her
             servants, who start toward the bedroom archway.

155   INT. JOSIANA'S BOUDOIR

             MED. CLOSE SHOT of Josiana. She looks off as Barkilphedro
             enters picture. He bows before her and talks with a shrewd
             look which takes in all her beauty in one glance.

TITLE   "My Lord Dirry-Moir begs leave to
                         attend Your Grace at the Queen's
                         concert on the morrow."

             BACK: He finishes title and she sneers with an amused smile,

TITLE   "This sudden order of my betrothed
                         bespeaks a purpose. How much has
                         he lost at gaming this time?"

             BACK: She finishes title with a questioning look at
             Barkilphedro and seeking information from this willing spy.
             Barkilphedro grins up at her in a servile manner and answers
             quickly,

TITLE   "Enough for My Lord's creditors to toast the
                         day of his wedding to Your Grace."
                                                     (Continued)

                                103

155 Continued:

BACK: She takes the title with a little look of impatience.
Then she burst into a laugh as she thinks of the long wait
those creditors are going to have. Barkilphedro watches her
and his look changes to eager admiration.

156   INT. JOSIANA'S BOUDOIR

CLOSEUP of Josiana. She stops laughing and looks out of
picture, studying Barkilphedro. Then she talks with a
certain impatience.

TITLE   "These pretty courtiers and lords are
                         annoyingly alike. You are, at least
                         ugly enough to be interesting and
                         different."

BACK: She finishes title as she turns in her seat and
studies Barkilphedro out of picture.

157   INT. JOSIANA'S BOUDOIR

SEMI CLOSE SHOT of Josiana and Barkilphedro. He cannot help
but feel this woman's lure, and although he hates her and
plots against her, there is desire in his glance at her.
She talks condescendingly.

TITLE   "You may kiss my hand."

BACK: She finishes title and Barkilphedro looks up with a
fawning glance. He shakes his head and talks in answer to
her speech.

TITLE   "Ney, your feet befits me better, Your Grace."

BACK: He finishes title and bends down over her little foot.
She lifts the hem of her gown and he kisses her slipper with
the air of a worshipper at the shrine of a Goddess. Then she
gives him a brutal push with her feet, as if in sudden
disgust. The force of the impact against him pushes him out
of picture toward the pool, as though he had been kicked off
balance.

158   INT. JOSIANA'S BOUDOIR

           MED. CLOSE SHOT of pool. As scene cuts in, Barkilphedro
           topples into picture and falls into the pool with splash.
           With a look of supreme hatred, he come to the surface,
           grasps the steps and starts to climb out.

159   INT. JOSIANA'S BOUDOIR

           MED. SHOT getting the edge of the pool and Josiana at her
           dressing-table in background. As scene cuts in, she
           deliberately turns her back to the pool. Then she picks up
           an ostrich fan from the dressing-table and waves it back
           and forth across her face luxuriously. It is like the wagging
           of a panther's tail. Barkilphedro climbs out of the pool and
           shakes himself. He glances toward Josiana and as he sees she
           is not looking, a demonical look of hatred appears on his
           face. Carried away by his rage, he stealthily draws a dagger
           from his costume. Then with catlike steps, he starts toward
           the Duchess with his dagger held behind him.

160   INT. JOSIANA'S BOUDOIR

           MED. CLOSE SHOT of Josiana. Barkilphedro enters picture
           and pauses with his dagger gripped tightly behind him.
           Then Josiana turns toward him and immediately, Barkilphedro's
           manner changes. Again he is crafty and servile. He hides
           the dagger behind him as Josiana speaks in a commanding tone,

TITLE   "Tell My Lord Dirry-Moir that the
                           Queen's command are as boring to
                           me, as is the thought of my marriage
                           to him at this moment."

           BACK: She finishes title and turns away with an air of
           dismissal. Barkilphedro watches her a moment and then
           quickly walks from picture, keeping his dagger out of sight.

161   INT. JOSIANA'S HALLWAY

MED. CLOSE SHOT of Josiana's door. It opens and Barkilphedro slides out. He closes it behind him and his face
changes to a look of diabolical hatred. Stealthily, he
puts his dagger away and exits with an evil grin of
cunning.

                              FADE OUT...

TITLE

ALL ROADS LEAD TO LONDON –
WERE THE BAKER'S BOY MAY LAUGH
AT THE MOUNTEBANK'S FACE.

FADE IN

162   EXT. SOUTHWARK FAIR   DAY SEQUENCE

MED. LONG SHOT of a show. This is a show which exhibits
a five-legged cow. A big lurid poster proclaims this fact.
There is an open platform, up to which steeps lead. On the
platform a fenced enclosure looks down into a pit, where
the five-legged cow is being shown. Behind this show
and beside it, other shows are seen as a background.
A high wire walker and a show of Caucasian dancing girls.
This scene is crowded with merrymakers. They are composed
of the common people, and are laughing and enjoying
themselves in a boisterous manner. A great many of them
are entering the show that displays the five-legged cow.
Hardquanonne is the proprietor of this show, and is standing
in background on the platform, ushering the people into the
show. This scene is to give a general atmosphere of a portion
of the fair, while it centers upon Hardquanonne's show.

163   EXT. HARDQUANONNE'S SHOW

MED. CLOSE SHOT. Of the people as they surround the fenced-
in pit-like enclosure. They look down in awe and wonder.
The camera gives a good shot of their various expressions.
These people are supposedly looking at the five-legged cow,
which is not seen. Some girls and women giggle at the sight.
All are in a holiday mood.

164   EXT. HARDQUANONNE'S SHOW

MED. SHOT of the entire show, as Hardquanonne stands at the
entrance. Thru the crowd that passes the show, two gypsy
girls are marching. One blows a trumpet and the other drums
a drum, to attract attention to another show. The people
gather around them, and the gypsy girls throw handbills into
the crowd and move on out of picture, as the crowd picks up
the handbills and follow the gypsy girls, evidencing in the
actions that the show, which the gypsy girls are advertising
is very popular. The people start to come out of Hardquanonne's show and follow the others after the gypsies.

165   EXT. HARDQUANONNE'S SHOW

CLOSE SHOT of Hardquanonne. He picks up one of the
handbills that the gypsy girls threw into the crowd.
He reads it, with a thoughtful air.

INSERT: CLOSEUP of handbill, which states that
                           Gwynplaine, the greatest clown in all
                           Christendom, and known as the LAUGHING
                           MAN, may be seen in the courtyard of
                           the Tadcaster Inn. The show is start-
                           ing right away, and here is a sight
                           that no one can afford to miss.

BACK: Hardquanonne looks up from the handbill with a
shrewd look of satisfaction. He looks off and watches
the crowd.

166   EXT. HARDQUANONNE'S SHOW

MED. SHOT A reverse shot as though seen from Hardquanonne's
position. The people are milling around good-naturedly.
Another show composed of a funny little theatre, with a
group of acrobats, a fireeater, and a tattooed man, form
the background opposite to Hardquanonne's show. The gypsy
girls, with the trumpet and drum, are winding thru the crowd,
throwing their handbills. The people are reading the handbills and hurrying along to get to this show before it opens.
All are boisterous, some drunk and disorderly. The common
people of London are enjoying themselves without restraint.
Thru the crowd a well-dressed dandy is seen here and there,
with a cloak around him. Some of these are masked with funny
false-faces. They are gentlemen, seeing the sights. A
spirit of carnival is everywhere.

TITLE   WHILE QUEEN ANNE'S COURT MUST YAWN IN
                           BOREDOM AT TIRESOME ROYAL CONCERTS.

167   INT. PALACE SALON

           MED. FULL SHOT. This is a glass shot, with a patched in set
           to convey the idea of a huge salon in the Queen's palace.
           The Queen is seated in her throne-like chair. Surrounding
           her, is her Court. The ladies are seated, as are some of
           the gentlemen. The shot is grouped to show the magnificence
           of the atmosphere, and although the Court numbers nearly a
           hundred people, there is an atmosphere of lonesomeness to
           this crowd in this huge room. There is a vacant chair near
           the Queen. Upon this chair is the crest of a Duchess, with
           a coronet and an emblem below it. The ladies and
           gentlemen of the Court are sitting stiffly around Queen Anne
           as a small orchestre plays ponderously in the center of the
           huge salon.

168   INT. PALACE SALON

           CLOSE SHOT. The orchestre. They play without ceasing.
           It is evident by their actions that the music is very heavy.
           Evidently a symphony of some kind, or something from Bach.
           The idea conveyed by this scene is that of an orchestra which
           is so highbrow in its intent that the music is terrible.

169   INT. PALACE SALON

           MED. CLOSE SHOT. A portion of the court. A panned shot of
           the assemblage as the camera moves. All are very bored and
           stifle yawns with an effort. They are ill at ease, and
           trying to wear a brave front. Compelled to stay here and
           utterly miserable.

170   INT. PALACE SALON

           CLOSEUP of Queen Anne. Beside her is the vacant chair,
           with the crest of the Duchess upon it. The Queen looks at
           the empty chair with an impatient air. She turns her head
           and talks, calling someone out of picture.

TITLE   "My Lord Dirry-Moir."

           CUT FROM TITLE TO FOLLOWING SCENE

171   INT. PALACE SALON

CLOSE SHOT of Lord Dirry-Moir. He is seated in a chair
near the Queen. His attitude is one of unutterable
boredom. As scene cuts in, he turns his head and comes
to, quickly, as though pulling himself from a daze.
He arises and exits toward the Queen.

172   INT. PALACE SALON

MED. CLOSE SHOT of Queen Anne, with the Duchess' vacant
chair beside her. Lord Dirry-Moir enters picture from
behind the Queen's chair. He bows to her, as he leans
upon the empty chair. The Queen looks up at Lord Dirry-
Moir and talks indignantly.

TITLE
                "The Duchess Josiana's absence is becoming
                conspictuous. Her tardiness bespeaks
                deliberate intent to belittle us."

BACK: He finishes in the manner of the born Courtier. Every
thought and act but to please the Queen. The Queen looks at
him with a thoughtful air, and gives her consent to his
withdrawal, accepting his services. Dirry-Moir withdraws
from the Queen's presence, and she looks again at the empty
chair in an outraged manner.

173   INT. PALACE SALON

MED. CLOSE SHOT of Barkilphedro. He leans against a decor-
ative pillar, beneath a frieze of this palatial
room. He watches the court in front of him. His eyes take
in Dirry-Moir's progress to the door. There is a sneer on
his face. He erases it and exits from picture, with a
cunning, suave look. He still wears a dark-colored Jester's
suit,

174   INT. PALACE ANTEROOM

MED. FULL SHOT. This is the anteroom and reception room
which leads to the salon. There is a long French window
that leads to a ballustraded balcony. A door leads to the
salon, and another door opposite to a palace corridor,
As scene cuts in, several palace lackeys are on, in royal
livery. There are, also, three pages of the Queen's household present. These pages are beautiful golden-haired little
boys. The lackeys are amusing themselves at some game that
took the place of our modern crap-shooting. The little pages
are, also, interested in the game. The salon door opens
and Lord Dirry-Moir comes out. Immediately all the lackeys
run to their places and stiffen up like statues. The little
pages also line up stiffly.

175   INT. PALACE ANTEROOM

MED. CLOSE SHOT. The salon doorway. Lord Dirry-Moir is
closing the door after him. A transition comes over him
and his boredom drops from him. His relief at getting
away from the Queen's Court concert is tremendous. He even
stretches, and throws out his chest, at the feeling of
freedom. Then he looks off out of picture, and beckons to
the pages. The three pages run into picture, and Dirry-Moir
talks to them, as he takes out his purse.

TITLE   "Make immediate search for Her Grace,
                   the Duchess Josiana - in the usual places."

BACK: He finishes title with a broad wink at the pages, and
gives them each a coin from his purse. They bow stiffly
and turn from picture.

176   INT. PALACE ANTEROOM

MED. SHOT. The pages walk to the corridor doorway and exit,
as the lackeys stand aside stiffly. Lord Dirry-Moir walks
toward the balcony window with springy steps. He opens the
window and exits, closing it after him. The lackeys stand
stiffly at attention, as the window closes, they all hurry
again to their game, knowing Lord Dirry-Moir's habits, and
that they have nothing further to fear from him.

177   EXT. ANTEROOM BALCONY

MED. SHOT. This is a low ballustraded balcony, at a short
distance above the Palace Gardens. As scene cuts in, Lord
Dirry-Moir is breathing in the fresh air, and stretching his
arms after his long session at the concert. He leaps lightly
over the ballustrades to the garden below, and hurries away,
whistling cheerfully.

178   INT. PALACE SALON

MED. CLOSE SHOT. The Queen with Duchess Josiana's vacant
chair beside her. Barkilphedro is standing behind the
Queen's chair, and is whispering into Her Majesty's ear,

TITLE   "Mayhaps the Duchess Josiana again seeks -
                      diversion, according to Her Grace's taste."

BACK: He finishes title in a malicious, insinuating
manner. The Queen nods as she looks at the vacant chair.
Barkilphedro's words are like a sweet morsel which she
loves to roll under her tongue.

179   INT. PALACE SALON

CLOSEUP of Duchess Josiana's chair, with the crest and
coronet plainly visible in shot.

LAP DISSOLVE OUT AND INTO:

180   EXT. SOUTHWARK FAIR   DAY SEQUENCE

CLOSEUP of roundsbrat cup. On it is an exaggerated
burlesque of a crest:
                      A pig's head, with a crown on it, and the
                      head of Punch, with a harp on its hook.

IN THIS TRANSPOSED SCENE of the burlesque crest on the side
of the roundebout car, the car is moving and the camera
follows it - either from the car behind or in some feasible
manner. These roundebouts resemble the modern merry-go-round,
except that each car hung separately from overhead supports.
The camera tilts upwards, and widens the shot, getting the
Duchess Josiana seated in the car. She is dressed in old
clothes, dirty and worn. Like those of the London's scullery
maids. She is laughing boisterously, and her manner is
unrestrained and common. The shot widens getting the full
car, as it swings around. A tough-looking man is seated opposite to the Duchess Josiana. He is a distorted, gross type of
individual. He slaps the Duchess on the knee, and she
responds in kind.

181   EXT. SOUTHWARK FAIR

MED. LONG SHOT of roundabout, it whirls around and round,
its cars all filled with people. The boisterous crowd
pass in front of the show, and wait for their turn upon it.
Again we see the two gypsy girls, as they enter picture and
go thru the crowd, blowing their trumpets and beating upon
their drums to advertise Gwynplaine's show. The swing begins
to stop, and people crowd toward it.

182   EXT. SOUTHWARK FAIR

MED. SHOT of roundabout. A car swings into picture and stops.
It is filled with rough-looking characters. They laugh and
stagger out of picture. Other characters crowd into picture
and get into the swing, and it moves from picture. The next
car enters picture and stops. Duchess Josiana gets out,
followed by the big, rough man. People crowd into the
car, and the gypsies pass thru picture, throwing the handbills
that advertise Gwynplaine's show.

183   EXT. SOUTHWARK FAIR

MED. CLOSE SHOT of Duchess Josiana in the crowd. She catches
one of the handbills from the gypsy girls and reads it with
interest. If necessary, insert here a closeup of the handbill
which tells of Gwynplaine, as before. Duchess Josiana passes
out of picture, with the crowd, bound for this now, interesting
show. The big man follows her, trying to keep up with her
but other people here come between them.

184   EXT. TADCASTER INN

MED. SHOT toward entrance. A crowd of people are
going in, while others come out. Above the gateway
is a sign fastened beneath the sign of the Tadcaster
Inn. This sign indicates that Gwynplaine, the Laughing
Man, is to be seen here. The gypsy girls enter picture
and take up their positions on each side of the gateway,
advertising the show.

185   EXT. TADCASTER INN

MED. CLOSE SHOT of entranceway. The people pass out
past camera, laughing at the show they had seen. Above
their heads, and plainly seen, is the sign which advertises
Gwynplaine, the Laughing Man. Among the people coming out
is Lord Dirry-Moir. He has a cloak on, and a false-face,
with a funny-looking long nose, disguises his personality
as he passes camera, the Duchess Josiana passes into
picture on her way into the show.

186   EXT. TADCASTER INN

SEMI CLOSE SHOT of Lord Dirry-moir. He stops, as Duchess
Josiana passes close to him. He leans toward her, and
whispers into her ear.

TITLE   "Duchess Josiana! The Queen awaits your
                        presence in no uncertain humor."

BACK: The Duchess Josiana turns sharply, as she stops
and looks into the funny false-face of Lord Dirry-Moir.
He quickly pulls the mask from his face by the long nose.
She recognizes him with a start. He winks, and again
covers his face with the mask. Then he passes on out of
picture. She hesitates a moment, and looks after him with
an air of great annoyance. Discretion overcomes her desire
to ignore Lord Dirry-Moir's warning. She turns and walks
past camera away from the show.

                                     FADE OUT....

TITLE   THREE SYMPHONIES OF BACH LATER - -

FADE IN

187   INT. PALACE SALON.   DAY SEQUENCE

MED. CLOSE SHOT of the Queen. As scene fades in, the Queen's anger is mounting, as she gazes toward the empty chair of Duchess Josiana beside her. Barkilphedro is standing behind the Queen's chair, and watches her with a cunning glance.

188   INT. PALACE SALON

MED. CLOSE SHOT of orchestra. They stop playing in a weary manner.

190   INT. PALACE SALON

MED. SHOT of the court. The ladies and gentlemen are bored to the point of misery. They look hopefully toward the Queen. Each one awaits Her Majesty's indication that the concert is over. The Queen motions for the orchestra to continue, and the court sits back hopelessly.

190   PALACE SALON

           MED. CLOSE SHOT of orchestra. The orchestra leader bows and
           waves his baton, as the orchestra starts up playing again.
           It might give a comedy touch here, to use slow-motion
           photography.

191   INT. PALACE SALON

           SEMI CLOSE SHOT of the Queen. She leans back in her chair
           in a determined and stubborn manner, with a glance at the
           empty chair beside her. She is going to await the Duchess
           Josiana's arrival if it takes all afternoon. Barkilphedro
           leans into picture and whispers in the Queen's ear.

TITLE   "As Lord Dirry-Moir takes his betrothal
                           to the Duchess Josiana so lightly, -
                           mayhap search should be made for my Lord."

           BACK: He finishes title with a cunning look of meaning at
           the Queen. She takes it and then commands him to search
           for Lord David. Barkilphedro glides from picture, on his
           mission. The Queen glares at the empty chair beside her. Her
           indignation is mounting to rage.

192   INT. PALACE ANTEROOM

           MED. FULL SHOT. As seen cuts in Lord Dirry-Moir is entering
           thru the balcony window on his return from the Fair. The
           lackeys are standing at attention in their places. Lord Dirry-
           Moir's costume is the same as seen before in the palace salon -
           he has left his cloak and mask elsewhere. He steps and combs
           his wig, as though waiting for someone. The door to salon
           opens, and Barkilphedro comes out. He sees Lord Dirry-Moir
           and bows to him servilely.

193   INT. PALACE ANTEROOM

CLOSE SHOT of Barkilphedro. He is looking off at Lord
Dirry-Moir in the attitude of bowing. But his gaze is
appraising him shrewdly. He turns his hand in the opposite
direction, as though his interests were drawn across the room.

194   INT. PALACE ANTEROOM

MED. CLOSE SHOT of the door to outer corridor. As scene cuts
in, the lackeys are opening the door to admit someone. The
Duchess Josiana enters. She is a different Duchess - a
gorgeous sight, and her carriage is aristocratic in bearing,
in direct contrast to her former appearance. Her clothes,
however, are directly against the styles of the period. While
the Queen and the ladies of the Court wore gowns of the period-
think and puffy around the waist, this gown of Duchess Josiana's
shows her figure to advantage, and resembles more the mode of
Cleopatra.

195   INT. PALACE ANTEROOM

CLOSE SHOT of Lord Dirry-Moir. He looks off, with an air
of wonder and awe at the Duchess' appearance and dress. He
starts from picture, with a bow of courtly etiquette.

195   INT. PALACE ANTEROOM

Med. CLOSE SHOT of the Duchess Josiana. Lord Dirry-Moir
enters picture, and bows over the Duchess' hand. There is a
twinkle in his eye, but there is no indication that he has
seen her before this afternoon. Barkilphedro enters picture.
He looks at the Duchess and toward Lord Dirry-Moir. He talks
insinuatingly.

TITLE   "I see that your Lordship found
                         Her Grace."

BACK: Barkilphedro finishes title and bows his way out the
door past the Duchess and Lord Dirry-Moir. Lord Dirry-Moir
leads the Duchess toward camera out of picture. The lackeys
close the door behind them.

197   INT. PALACE ANTEROOM.

MED. CLOSE SHOT of door to salon. Lord David Dirry-Moir and
Duchess Josiana enter picture. At the door Lord David stops.
He leans toward the Duchess and talks, with a glance at her
gown:

TITLE   "You look beautiful, but to disobey
                         the Queen's edict in dress, in her
                         Majesty's present mood, is not wisdom."

BACK: Josiana take the title. She is pleased at the compliment
and answers with a haughty lift of her head:

TITLE   "The style is designed to hide the
                         Queen's fatness. I have nothing to
                         hide like Her Majesty.

BACK: She finishes title with fire, and Lord Dirry-Moir glances
out of corner of his eye at her. The doors start to open
before them, and they start into the salon.

196   INT. PALACE SALON

MED. CLOSE SHOT of the Queen as she sits in her chair, with
the Duchess Josiana's empty chair beside her. Queen Anne
turns her head. She looks off with a sudden stiffening of
her form, as she beholds the entrance of the Duchess Josiana
in her daring costume. Astonishment changes to outrageous
indignation, as she watches off, hardly believing her eyes.

199   INT. PALACE SALON

MED. SHOT of the assembled court. AN AKELEY SHOT as Josiana
walks part the courtiers and the ladies-in-waiting, in her
approach to the Queen. All greet her with the proper form
of etiquette. But the ladies, all dressed in the same
fashion as the Queen, glances at her in wide amazement and
disapproval. The gentlemen who can evade the eyes of the
other ladies look after Josiana in bold admiration. Josiana
knows she is the center of all eyes, and her poise is
perfect as she walks past the court on the arm of Lord Dirry-
Moir. The shot brings the camera to the Queen's chair, and
Josiana bends low in the proper courtesy before Her Majesty,
as Lord Dirry-Moir steps back, with a deep bow to the Queen.

200   INT. PALACE SALON

CLOSE SHOT of the Queen. She rises to her feet, and assumes
her full height. There is poise in her attitude and she is
a Queen. But she has been wounded deeply and her hatred is
blazing forth from her eyes. She talks:

TITLE   "The pleasure of your company is only
                        exceeded by your Grace's insulting
                        immodesty of dress."

BACK: She finishes title, having a hard time to control
herself, at this flagrant insult to her dignity before the
court,

201   INT. PALACE SALON

             CLOSE SHOT of Duchess Josiana. She straightens up, and
             courtesies again ironically. She is perfectly poised, and
             enjoying the situation immensely. It is a thrill to her.
             She looks around her with a demure look of helplessness,
             holding her dress about her as though to hide her shame,
             but only disclosing more clearly the lines of her figure.
             She talks with an innocent stare, around her.

TITLE   "Is there not a gentleman to rescue
                           me from my shame?"

             CUT FROM TITLE TO FOLLOWING SCENE:

202   INT. PALACE SALON

             MED. SHOT As josiana looks around in mock helplessness.
             Lord Dirry-Moir is standing behind her. The court is stand-
             ing, as is the Queen. The gentlemen of the court cannot keep
             their looks from ogling Josiana's figure, but the ladies of
             the court look toward her in stern disapproval. The Queen
             turns back upon Josiana, and deliberately walks toward the
             entrance. The court follows Her Majesty, the lackeys hold
             open the door, and they exit. The door closes and the Duchess
             Josiana is left alone in court with Lord Dirry-Moir.

203   INT. PALACE SALON

             MED. CLOSE SHOT of orchestra. The musicians are all standing
             in respectful attitudes, watching the Queen exit with sighs
             of relief. Hurriedly they collect their instruments together,
             and the stacks of music. Here also slow motion photography
             could be used to show how tired and weary this orchestra has
             become.

204   INT. PALACE SALON

       MED. CLOSE SHOT of Queen's chair. Duchess Josiana walks to
       the chair, with a light step, and perches herself upon the arm.
       The occurrence has left no impression upon her. Lord Dirry-
       Moir enters picture. He looks at her with a shake of his
       head, and talks seriously:

TITLE   "The Queen has always hated you.
                         For this insult to her dignity
                         she will have your life's blood."

       BACK: He finishes title, but Josiana merely shrugs her
       shoulders. She changes the subject and talks to Lord
       Dirry-Moir.

TITLE   "Tell me of this clown, Gwynplaine,
                         whom I failed to see at the fair. Is
                         he truly so monstrous - so grotesque?"

       BACK: She finishes title, and Lord Dirry-Moir tells her of
       this funny clown, mimicking him as Josiana listens, enthralled.

205   INT. JOSIANA'S BOUDOIR

       CLOSEUP of a silver tray upon a table. It is a tray for
       receiving notes and letters. Upon it are many letters of
       different shapes and sizes, all unopened, and all addressed
       to the Duchess Josiana, with her name plainly registered.
       Barkilphedro's hand enter picture and picks up one of
       the notes.

206   INT. JOSIANA'S BOUDOIR

MED. CLOSE SHOT. Barkilphedro is on in Josiana's boudoir.
He is in the act of picking a letter from the silver tray
as scene cuts in. A little colored page, dressed like a
small Sultan, is curled up on the floor beside the door, sound
asleep. Barkilphedro looks toward him and around the room
cautiously. Then he looks down at the letter and smells it.
He evidently knows the perfume, and throws it back upon the
tray. He picks up another letter and smells it. This he
also throws back upon the tray. He picks up a third letter,
and smells it. He smiles to himself, with an amused air, as
he looks down at this letter.

207   INT. JOSIANA'S BOUDOIR

CLOSEUP of Barkilphedro's hand, holding note. Behind the
note the hand of a senile old man dissolves into picture.
He is bewigged and painted like a dandy. He dissolves out,
and Barkilphedro throws the letter out of picture. He picks
up another letter into picture, and another fop fades in
behind it. This one is a simple looking young Dandy of the
court. All curled up and powdered like a woman. Barkilphedro
throws this letter away, as the head dissolves out. Then he
picks up a large letter, and holds it into picture.

208   INT. JOSIANA'S BOUDOIR

MED. CLOSE SHOT of Barkilphedro, angled in another direction,
so that it shows a dim impression of the boudoir back of
him. He is looking at the large letter in a puzzled manner.
He looks around cautiously. Then he deliberately opens the
letter in a deft manner, and reads it.

(Continued)

208 (Continued)

INSERT   CLOSEUP of letter. It is a long letter.
                            It is scrolled rapidly thru picture, as
                            though Barkilphedro were reading it
                            hurriedly. At each important piece of
                            information it stops, and the sentence
                            is readable. These sentences convey
                            the following thoughts:

                            Your Grace is the possessor of all the
                            estates of Lord Clancharlie.

                            Your mother made this possible by her
                            friendliness with our former sovereign
                            James II.

                            You are a rich woman - - I am a poor man.
                            But I hold certain information which proves
                            that the lost heir to Lord Clancharlie's
                            estates is not dead.

                            I beg leave to approach your Grace, so
                            that this information may be disposed of
                            to our mutual benefit.
                                    (Signed) Dr. Hardquanonne.

BACK: Barkilphedro looks up with a start. A cruel look of
satisfaction comes over his face. Deliberately he puts
the letter back in the envelope and hides the envelope in
his tunic. There is a diabolical look of cunning upon his
face, as he looks down at the tray of letters. Then he picks
up the false-face worn by Dirry-Moir at the fair. It evidences
the fact to the audience that Lord Dirry-Moir brought the
Duchess Josiana home. Beneath the mask is a little handbill.
Barkilphedro also picks this up and looks at the two articles
closely.

209   INT. JOSIANA'S BOUDOIR

CLOSEUP of Barkilphedro. He looks down at the articles in
his hands, with a thoughtful air, as though he were trying to
match some puzzle together from the past. A light dawns
upon him, and he grins to himself in an attempt to mimic the
grin of the Laughing Man that the comprachicos made of Lord
Clancharlie's son. His eyes glow with cunning satisfaction at
this tremendous secret that is almost within his grasp.

210   INT. JOSIANA'S BOUDOIR

CLOSEUP of Barkilphedro's hand. He holds the false-face with
the funny nose. This hangs from its string. The object of
interest is the handbill which advertises Gwynplaine, The
Laughing Man.

FADE OUT......................

211   EXT. TADCASTER INN - - NIGHT SEQUENCE

          CLOSE UP of the sign of the Inn. As scene cuts in, the
          hand of Gevicun, the Inn choreboy, is hanging a lighted
          lantern beside the sign. It rays illuminate the sign, and
          show clearly the placard which hangs to it. This placard
          advertises the fact that Gwynplaine, the famous Laughing
          Man is to be seen in the courtyard. Under this is the
          price of admission.

          LAP DISSOLVE OUT AND INTO:

212   EXT. TADCASTER INN - - COURTYARD

          MED. FULL SHOT. This courtyard is as described in Victor
          Hugo's book. On the three sides, the Inn is built around
          it. Against the other side - which is a well - the Green
          Box is standing. It forms a natural theatre, with the doors
          from the taproom facing the Green Box. Around the three
          sides of the hotel, the second story balcony forms a gal-
          lary. In the center of this and facing the Green Box, is
          a partitioned space for the nobility. In this box are
          some chairs from the Inn, and a grand armchair of yellow
          velvet for any great personage.

          As scene transposes in, the courtyard is filling with
          people. They eat pies, gingerbread - clatter together
          and jostle each other crudely - as they seek positions
          for good views. The side of the Green Box is down and the
          curtains closed over the stage. The footlights are not
          yet lit.

213   EXT. TADCASTER INN - COURTYARD

          MED. CLOSE SHOT of courtyard entranceway. The two gypsies
          with Ursus' show are beside the door. One drums upon her
          drum to attract attention that this is the entrance to the
          show in the courtyard. The other sits beside a barrel
          which has been fashioned into a rough ticket-office. The show
          is popular and a steady stream of characters are passing
          through, as they deposit the price of admission with the
          gypsy. Ursus is standing beside the entrance way, watching
          the people in satisfaction. He rubs his hands together
          at their great success.

214   EXT. TADCASTER INN - COURTYARD

MED. CLOSE SHOT of the Green Box. There is no sign of
activity. The curtain is down, and the form of Homo,
the wolf, is lying chained to the wheel. A little curtained, tent-like enclosure hides the rear of the van
from the public. It extends from the corner of the
stage toward the wall in back of the Green Box. There
is a dim light behind it. The shadow of a man is seen
upon this curtain. He is stooped over and not recog-
nizable.

215   EXT. TADCASTER INN - COURTYARD.

MED. CLOSE SHOT of the rear of Green Box behind the
curtained enclosure. In the light of a little lantern
that hangs over the rear door, Gwynplaine is discovered
seated upon the steps. The door is closed, and he is
stooped over, in an attitude of brooding, and despondency.
He is not made up for the show, outside of his costume.
His laugh is concealed by the manner in which his head
drops forward against his collar.

216   INT. GREEN BOX

MED. SHOT of rear compartment. As scene cuts in, Dea
enters from the entryway. She stands still a moment
listening, and then calls a bit anxiously.

TITLE   "Gwynplaine!   Gwynplaine!"

BACK: She finishes title, as she realizes that he is
not here. She comes forward and feels around the room
in a worried manner. She approaches his makeup table
and ascertains that he is not made up for the show as
yet. She herself is dressed for the performance. She
sits down to wait - with a tense expression of nervous
anxiety; her ears strain to catch the slightest sound of
his whereabouts.

217   EXT. TADCASTER INN - GWYNPLAINE.

MED. CLOSE SHOT of Gwynplaine. He looks up, as though
he has heard Dea's call. The sound causes an agonizing
interruption to his thoughts. He drops his head on his
hands, and hold his mouth more securely covered from
view. Then he gets up and turns toward the Green Box.

218   INT. GREEN BOX.

CLOSE SHOT of Dea. She looks up with her blind stare,
and listens, as though she hears Gwynplaine outside.
Then a happy smile is registered, as she turns her head
toward the door.

219   EXT. TADCASTER INN - - COURTYARD

CLOSEUP of steps of the Green Box. As scene cuts in,
Gwynplaine's feet enter picture - as he ascends steps.

220   INT. GREEN BOX

MED. SHOT OF REAR COMPARTMENT. It is Gwynplaine's step
that Dea has recognized, causing the smile upon her good
face. She gets up expectantly and turns toward the door
as Gwynplaine enters. He stops beside the door as he sees
her waiting.

221   INT. GREEN BOX

CLOSEUP of Dea. She looks off, with a look of happiness -
and waiting expectantly for him to greet her. She is a
picture of sweet purity, and yet a woman.

222   INT. GREEN BOX

CLOSE UP of Gwynplaine. He looks off - at this girl
whom he loves - and the great love he feels for her is
registered in his expression. With an instinctive
gesture, he half moves toward her, as if mutely
begging her to help him win the battle in his heart -
then he drops his head hopelessly, and starts from
picture,

223   INT. GREEN BOX.

MED. SHOT, Gwynplaine turns toward Dea as she approaches
him, a bit puzzled that he has not greeted her. There is
a look of yearning registered in his face as she approaches
close to him. She touches him on the arm and her look of
joy returns at the contact. She clings to his arm happily,
and pantomimes how glad she is that he has returned. In
a flood of words, she chatters on, asking where he has been,
and why he has left her alone so long. The scene is torture
for him and her touch acts like a spur to his desire for
her. He looks down at her with an expression of utter love
for this girl he wants as a wife and woman. She stands
motionless, and stops talking suddenly, as she realizes
that he has not answered her. She pantomimes, what is the
matter? Unable to stand her nearness and the contact of
her touch, without grasping her in his hungry arms, Gwynplaine turns abruptly from her and walks to his makeup
table. She turns and a hurt look is registered as she
listens to him walk away. She senses his deliberate
effort to avoid her touch and walks slowly toward him.

224   INT. GREEN BOX.

SEMI CLOSE SHOT of makeup table. Gwynplaine drops into
his chair beside it. Then Dea enters picture to him. He
takes off his mask and deliberately busies himself with
his makeup materials. He talks up to her in an effort to
be light and friendly, but there is a strained effort apparent behind his attempt at naturalness. He turns toward
the mirror as he pulls back the neck of his shirt. His
face is visible in the mirror. It confronts him, almost
like an apparition of evil, and he turns away quickly as
though startled. He seems uglier than ever. Dea talks
to him questioningly:

(CONTINUED)

224 (CONTINUED)

TITLE: "Why do you never help me
                                    with my makeup any more?"

BACK: She finishes title and Gwynplaine takes it. It
breaks the shock that the sight of his face has given him
and he turns toward her, away from the mirror, and answers
her.

TITLE: "I cannot trust my hands - the
                                    excitement of London has made
                                    me nervous and clumsy."

BACK: He finishes title in a strained manner, not
daring to look up toward her face, although he knows she
cannot see the lie on his lips. Dea is puzzled, and then
she talks with a sweet shake of her head as though she could
not understand.

TITLE: "But your touch is my heaven and
                                    lately you seem so far away from me."

BACK: She finishes with a little troubled air and reaches
out, grasping Gwynplaine's hand with a sure touch as it
lies on the makeup table. He tries to evade her touch,
but she finds his hand and clings to it. It is torture to
Gwynplaine, and he looks up at her in an attitude of hopeless love. A love so deep that it causes him agony.

225   INT. GREEN BOX.

           CLOSEUP of Gwynplaine's and Dea's hands on the makeup
           table. As scene cuts in, he gently withdraws his hand
           from beneath her grasp, and lifts it from picture.

226   INT. GREEN BOX

          CLOSEUP of Dea. She thrusts her hand into picture with
          a little hurt look. Gwynplaine's attitude puzzled her.
          She talks questioningly:

TITLE: "Ursus always talks of our marriage.
                    Maybe that is it - maybe you do not
                    love me enough to marry me?

          BACK: She finishes title with an anxious air as though
          she hoped this were not the case. But woman-like she
          is forced to ask it.

227   INT. GREEN BOX.

          CLOSEUP of Gwynplaine. He takes her title. There is a
          look of tender denial to her question and his eyes burn
          with his love for her. There is an enquiring look in
          them as he realizes that she has asked him, that she
          would be ready to marry him. He talks as he rises slowly
          to his feet:

TITLE: "You would marry me - - without
                    seeing me?"

          CUT FROM TITLE TO FOLLOWING SCENE.

225   INT. GREEN BOX.

          MED. SHOT of Gwynplaine and Dea. As scene cuts in, she takes
          his title as he looks up at her and finishes title as he
          rises to his feet. The answers him with a sweet smile of
          love:

TITLE: "I know you are beautiful
                    and I love you!"

          (CONTINUED)

130

228 (CONTINUED)

BACK: She finishes title and he take it. At first
there is hope in his gaze at her. Then he realizes her
blindness and drops his arms to his side. He looks at
her with a wistful yearning. His desire at this promise
of her love changes to tenderness. Slowly, he bends down
on one knee, and lifts the hem of her dress. He kisses it,
knowing that this piece of cloth cannot feel the imprint
of his horrible lips. She reaches out for him and touches
his head. She lays her head with a caressing touch upon
his head. Then the door opens and Ursus enters.

229   INT. GREEN BOX.

CLOSE SHOT of Ursus, he is excited, as he closes the
door behind him. He talks in a delighted manner.

TITLE: "A lady of the gentry just paid in coin
                    for the box in the gallery!"

BACK: He finishes title, and holds up the gold coin for
them to see. Then his look changes, as he takes in the
scene out of picture. He starts from picture.

230   INT. GREEN BOX.

MED. SHOT toward Gwynplaine and Dea. They have not even
noticed his entrance. Ursus approaches them with a knowing
smile. Then he coughs violently with a great show of
gruffness, and tells them both to get ready - that the
show is about to begin, and that Gwynplaine is not made up.
Gwynplaine gets to his feet, with a sheepish expression
and Dea exits into the entryway. Gwynplaine goes to his
makeup table and starts to make up, as Ursus gets out his
Punch and Judy dolls to prepare for his set. His back is
turned to Gwynplaine, and Gwynplaine drops his head in his
hands, yielding for a moment to his great suffering. He
stares at the floor silently, and Ursus looks toward him.
With a puzzled expression, Ursus approaches him.

231   INT. GREEN ROOM

SEMI CLOSE SHOT of Gwynplaine. He sits as before, with
his head in his hands, and looking and staring at the
floor. Ursus enters picture, and asks what is the
matter. Gwynplaine looks up, quickly and talks in answer
as he tries to hide the suffering that is reflected in
his eyes.

TITLE: "Dea is a woman -- and she loves me."

BACK: He finishes title with an air of agony and Ursus
raises his eyebrows in surprise, pantomiming that this
fact is surely nothing to weep about. He talks with
a shrug of his shoulders.

TITLE: "Dea is beautiful - and she has
                         never seen your face. You should
                         thank Heaven that she never will."

BACK: He finishes title and Gwynplaine takes it. Then
Gwynplaine answers with a hopeless expression of resig-
nation:

TITLE: "That is why I can never
                         love her - as a man."

BACK: He finishes title and turns abruptly to his makeup
table, starts to make up, as Ursus looks at him with a
comical expression of puzzled wonder. He turns and exits,
muttering to himself.

232   EXT. BALCONY BOX.

MED. SHOT. The Duchess Josiana is entering the box. Her
little colored page is with her. She seats herself in
the grand armchair of yellow velvet from the Inn. She
leans back against the chair and holds up her mask before
her face, as she watches over the railing. The little
page stands stiffly behind her.

233   EXT. SOUTHWARK PAIR.

MED. CLOSE SHOT of Hardquanonne. He stands on the platform
in front of his show. Two yeomen of the Queen's Guard
enter picture, and approach Hardquanonne. He looks at
them in amazement, not understanding their presence.
Before he has a chance to say anything, they make him
their prisoner, and arrest him. Hardquanonne is dazed,
and the two officials of the Queen's Guard hurry him out
of picture from the platform. The crowd gapes at him,
and laugh derisively. Many showmen have been arrested
before at these Fairs - most of them are fakers.

234   EXT. SOUTHWARK FAIR.

MED. CLOSE SHOT of Barkilphedro. He is standing in the
corner of a quiet alleyway. His eyes gleam with satisfaction as he wanders out of picture. He is cloaked and
his jester's suit is hidden from view. As he watches
the yeomen drag Hardquanonne into picture. Immediately
Barkilphedro points at him and pantomimes: "Search him!"
The yeomen search the struggling Hardquanonne, and produce
a packet from his innermost pocket. Barkilphedro snatches
it from them to look at it.

235   EXT. SOUTHWARK FAIR.

CLOSEUP of Barkilphedro. He opens the packet and quickly
unfolds an ancient piece of parchment. It is the same
parchment which we saw in the first sequence on the comprachico's boat. Quickly Barkilphedro scans it.

INSERT: CLOSEUP of parchment. It reads to the
                           effect that the son of Lord Clancharlie
                           has been mutilated, and his face carved
                           into a Laughing Mask by the comprachicos.
                           That he was kidnapped and sold to the
                           comprachicos, and the operation performed
                           by royal command. It is signed by the
                           King's seal, and JAMES II.

BACK: Barkilphedro looks up from the parchment with a
crafty look of triumph. He sticks it safely away in his
tunic. Then he steps from picture.

236   EXT. SOUTHWARK FAIR.

SEMI CLOSE SHOT of Hardquanonne. Barkilphedro steps into
picture and confronts the furious Hardquanonne. The hands
of the Yeomen hold Hardquanonne a prisoner in the picture.
Barkilphedro talks:

TITLE: "So the comprachico Dr. Hardquanonne, has
                       made a clown from his handiwork? How
                       unfortunate that I know the value of your
                       secret."

BACK: He finishes title, and Hardquanonne looks at him
in cold rage. Barkilphedro ignores the menace in
Hardquanonne's attitude and pushes his face forward as
he continues:

TITLE: "Does this laughing mountebank know
                       you carved him out of lordly flesh --
                       and that he is a peer of England?"

BACK: He finishes title, and Hardquanonne struggles with
his captors. Barkilphedro throws back his head and laughs
in a diabolical manner at him. Then the Yeoman drag Hardquanonne from picture, at a sign from Barkilphedro. Barkilphedro watches them off, and then quickly turns and
hurries out of picture in the opposite direction.

237   EXT. TADCASTER COURTYARD.

Med. SHOT of people in the first rows of the crowd. They
are restless and are evidently waiting for the main at-
traction, the Laughing Man. One bold individual shouts
toward the stage out of picture.

TITLE: GWYNPLAINE! Gwynplaine! Let
                     us see the Laughing Man!"

BACK: He finishes title and the others take up the cry.

238   EXT. TADCASTER COURTYARD

             MED. FULL SHOT. The crowd takes up the cry of the others,
             and wave their arms toward the stage, whistling and
             calling for Gwynplaine.

239   INT. GREEN BOX

             MED. CLOSE SHOT in the wings of the stage. Gwynplaine
             and Dea are waiting to go on for the show. He listens
             to the cries outside. He bows his head before the sound -
             this sound, which brings to his mind that he is only a
             clown, to be laughed at by others. Ursus enters picture
             behind them. He points off, and tells Gwynplaine to listen
             to the crowd; that it is wonderful. Gwynplaine lifts his
             head, now the actor. Ursus reaches over and starts to
             pull up the curtain.

240   INT. GREEN BOX.

             MED. SHOT across the stage from the wings, shooting over
             the footlights and getting the heads of a portion of the
             crowd in the audience. The curtain goes up, and Gwynplaine,
             now the mountebank, walks upon the stage to begin his act,
             followed by Dea.

241   EXT. TADCASTER COURTYARD.

             SEMI FULL SHOT of the crowd. The people break into roars
             of laughter as they see Gwynplaine. They crowd together
             toward stage and nudge each other. The laughing increases
             like a gale and in a moment, the crowd is shrieking and
             shouting with unrestrained merriment.

242   EXT. BALCONY BOX.

        MED. CLOSE SHOT as scene cuts in, the Duchess Josiana
        leans forward in her chair and looks over the railing
        toward the stage. She lowers her mask in her great
        interest. But she is nor laughing, instead her face is
        a picture of intense emotion, as though the sight of
        this laughing man thrilled her. Her eyes burn with a
        fierce fire, as she stares intently down toward the
        theatre over the railing.

243   EXT. BALCONY BOX.

        CLOSEUP of Josiana. She leans slowly into large closeup,
        as she looks down over the railing with her face uncov-
        ered. With a fascinated gaze and a stare that is hyp-
        notic in its influence her eyes focus, as her face comes
        closer and closer to the camera, until they nearly fill
        the screen.

244   EXT. TADCASTER COURTYARD

        MED. CLOSE SHOT of stage. Gwynplaine and Dea are
        in the midst of their act. He turns and hesitates a
        moment, as though he sensed Josiana's gaze at him.
        Then he continues the act, but his gaze remains in the
        same spot as he goes through his business, mechanically,
        his eyes drawn to Josiana's look in the balcony.

        LAP DISSOLVE OUT AND INTO:

245   EXT. TADCASTER COURTYARD.

        CLOSEUP of Gwynplaine on the stage. As scene transposes
        in, his head and shoulders fill the screen. His eyes
        are centered as though hypnotized by Josiana's look.
        He cannot take his look away from this woman. And he is
        all she sees upon the stage.

246   EXT. TADCASTER COURTYARD.

MED. FULL SHOT of the crowd and the balcony box, shooting
toward them, as if seen by Gwynplaine from the stage.
The faces of the crowd are seen upturned toward the stage.
It is a hilarious crowd, poking and shaking back and
forth; drunk with laughter. Above it, the form of Josiana
stands out, as she leans over the box rail. The crowd
starts out of focus and into blur of laughing faces.

LAP DISSOLVE OUT AND INTO:

247   EXT. BALCONY.

CLOSEUP of Duchess Josiana. As scene transposes in, her
head and shoulders fill the screen. Hers is the only
face that stands out thru the other faces, upturned toward
Gwynplaine. The face of this beautiful woman, who is not
laughing at him, is now the whole audience to Gwynplaine.

248   EXT. TADCASTER COURTYARD.

MED. CLOSE SHOT. As scene cuts in, Gwynplaine finishes
his set, and the curtain falls. The show is over. The
crowd applauds loudly, and starts to disperse. The people
laugh and nudge each other, as they make their way toward
the entrance.

249   EXT. BALCONY BOX.

MED. CLOSE SHOT. The Duchess Josiana straightens up in
her chair and rises. She beckons her page, and reaches in
her bag, drawing out a small pen. The page instantly
produces the usual writing material from his voluminous
trousers and holds it up, while the Duchess writes hastily
upon it. She puts the note in an envelope, seals it, and
addresses it. The page takes it, as she bids him hurry,
and exits quickly from the box. The Duchess Josiana
looks over the railing again with a speculative gaze, and
then quickly holds her mask in front of her face, as she
turns away and starts from the box.

250   EXT. TADCASTER COURTYARD

MED. CLOSE SHOT the curtained tent-like enclosure
that hides the rear of the Green Box. In background the
gypsy girls into scene, snuffing out the footlights. In
foreground, the figure of Barkilphedro is seen, as he
stands silently. His gaze is turned upward as though he
were watching the Duchess in the box. An amused sneer
overspreads his face.

251   INT. GREEN BOX.

MED. SHOT of rear compartment. Gwynplaine is on with
Ursus and Dea. Ursus is talking excitedly about the great
success of their show, and Dea has stopped a moment to
listen. Ursus slaps Gwynplaine on the back and talks
enthusiastically.

TITLE: "What a crowd! What a success! And a
                          grand lady in the gallery box -did
                          you see her?"

CUT FROM TITLE TO FOLLOWING SCENE:

252   INT GREEN BOX.

CLOSE SHOT of Gwynplaine. He takes Ursus' title and nods.
There is a certain preoccupied air about him, as though
he were dazed, and he talks with a certain excitement
registered.

TITLE: "I saw nothing else - and I also
                          saw that she did not laugh at me."

BACK: He finishes title and drops into his chair, at the
makeup table, in front of which he has been standing. He
looks at his face in the mirror as if he wished to see
how it were possible for anyone to look at him and not
laugh.

253   INT. GREEN BOX.

CLOSEUP of Dea. She looks off with her vague stare. She
senses something in Gwynplaine's attitude that she cannot
understand. It troubles her.

254   EXT. TADCASTER INN COURTYARD.

MED. CLOSE SHOT of the curtained enclosure, which hides
the rear of the Green Box. As scene cuts in, Barkilphedro
quickly steps back into the shadows and covers his face
with his cloak. Josiana's page enters picture with the
note from his mistress. He exits behind the curtained
enclosure. Barkilphedro looks after the little page,
and lowers his cloak from his face. He grins, in a
crafty manner - looks out of picture at the Duchess' box -
and then walks from picture with a look of diabolical
satisfaction upon his face.

255   INT. GREEN BOX.

MED. SHOT of rear room. Ursus turns toward the door, as
tho' he heard a knock upon it. Dea also listens, and
Gwynplaine gets up to see who it is. A knock at their
door is an unusual occurrence. Gwynplaine walks to the
door to open it.

256   EXT. TADCASTER COURTYARD.

MED. CLOSE SHOT of the rear of the Green Box. The little
page is waiting. The door opens, and Gwynplaine steps out
upon the top step. He looks down at the page in surprise.
The little colored boy stands on his tiptoes and hands up
the note to Gwynplaine. The page looks at Gwynplaine in
proud awe at being so close to this great clown. Then he
turns and runs quickly from picture. Gwynplaine looks down
at the note with an expression of wonder. He smells it,
and a pleased expression comes over his face. Then he opens
it and reads it by the light of the little lantern over the
door.   (CONTINUED)

256 Continued

INSERT: CLOSEUP of Duchess Josiana's note:

         To Gwynplaine:
          You are hideous. I am beautiful.
         You are a mountebank; I am a duchess.
         I am the highest; you are the lowest.
         I desire you! I love you! Come to me!
         My page will meet you at midnight at the
         corner of London Bridge, to conduct you
         to my house.

BACK: He looks up from the note with a look of awe.
Then Ursus appears in the doorway above him. Gwynplaine
quickly hides the letter in his jacket and turns,
entering the Green Box, and closing the door after him.

257   INT. GREEN BOX

MED. SHOT Gwynplaine walks silently to his makeup table.
Ursus questions him as to who visited him. Dea is anxious
and asks whether there is anything the matter. Gwynplaine
shakes his head to both that it is nothing of any importance.
Dea enters the curtained partition toward her compartment.
Ursus is not so easily fooled, and walks over toward Gwynplaine. Then he questions him closely, talking, insisting
that Gwynplaine tell him. Gwynplaine looks up and talks in
answer to Ursus' persistent questioning.

TITLE   "A woman who has seen my face wants
        to make love to me."

BACK: He finishes title and Ursus throws back his head in
an amused laugh. Gwynplaine assumes an air of defiance and
reaches into his pocket as if to hand the letter to Ursus,
to read for himself. He thinks better of it, and Ursus talks
with a quizzical look at Gwynplaine's face.

TITLE   "But you have not seen her face."

BACK: He finishes title and Gwynplaine looks away. He knows
it is the woman who looked at him. He feels this instinctively. But he says nothing, and turns toward his makeup table.
Ursus claps him on the shoulder and registers that he had
better stick to Dea, that he can see that she is very beautiful. Then Ursus turns away and walks out the door to settle
up with Master Nicless with his share of the admission money,

258   INT. GREEN BOX

SEMI CLOSE SHOT of Gwynplaine. He draws the note from
his pocket, now that he is all alone. He looks at it
again, and up at his face in the mirror. He looks off
toward the curtain, beyond which is Dea's compartment.
Then he looks at his face again in the mirror and at
the note. There is sudden hope in his face and a determination to see if this woman means what she says: If
she is the beautiful woman of the box, and if it is
possible for a woman to look at his face and still want
to love him. Quickly he lays the crumpled note upon his
makeup table and starts to take off his stage makeup.

                          FADE OUT.....

FADE IN

259   EXT. STEEPLE - NIGHT SEQUENCE - MED CLOSE SHOT

As seen fades in, an ancient steeple with a clock in it
is seen against the night sky. TROLLEY CAMERA QUICKLY
UP TO CLOSEUP of the steeple clock. It indicates twelve
o'clock. DOUBLE EXPOSURE OVER THIS SCENE, with the scene
still on: four other miniature steeples, one after the
other, and then five different bells of these steeples
dissolve into picture as they ring the midnight hour. Twelve
o'clock is striking in the five parishes of Southwark.

LAP DISSOLVE OUT AND INTO:

260   EXT. THAMES BRIDGE - MED CLOSE SHOT

As scene transposes in closely, a corner of the bridge's
parapet is seen, as the wall curves away from the shore.
A mist hangs over the Thames, hiding the background. A
lamp sheds it light dimly over the scene from an old-
fashioned lamp post. The Duchess' little colored page
is waiting silently.

261   EXT. THAMES BRIDGE - MED CLOSE SHOT

Of the old wall along the Thames. Behind it a mist hangs
over the river. Gwynplaine enters picture. He is holding
his cape or ulster close around his face, hiding his image.
He stops short as he sees the page out of picture. A
double cut here to the page, and back to Gwynplaine, might
be advisable. Gwynplaine hesitates. He turns, as if to
retrace his steps. Then he looks over the wall, as though
the noise of the water below drew his attention.

262   EXT THAMES RIVER - MED CLOSE SHOT

Of the surface of the water, as if seen from Gwynplaine's
position at the wall above. The water laps against a stone
abutment of the bridge. Then words take form, as if
formed from the froth of the restless waves. They form and
break and form and break again, always forming the same words
DEA, DEA, DEA.

263   EXT. THAMES BRIDGE - CLOSE SHOT

Of Gwynplaine's face as he stares down over the low wall
from the bridge above. His eyes are tortured, as he
watches his vision in the water which seems to call to him.

264   EXT. THAMES RIVER - MED CLOSE SHOT

Of the surface of the water as before. The last foamy
word that reflects Dea's name dissipates, and with a sudden
swirl of the water the following title dissolves in over
the waves, as if outlined in fiery foam:

TITLE: "But if a beautiful Duchess really loves you -
                          then Dea could love you, and you would not be
                          deceiving her. You must find out!"

BACK: The title is dissipated by the action of the waves,
and the water is dark under the light of the lamp above,
as before.

265   EXT. THAMES BRIDGE - MED CLOSE SHOT

Of Gwynplaine. He looks up from the water with a sudden
firm resolve. With firm steps he starts out of picture
toward the page.

266   EXT THAMES BRIDGE - MED CLOSE SHOT

Of Duchess' page. He is still waiting. Gwynplaine
enters picture and approaches him. Without a word, the
page starts out of the picture. Gwynplaine hesitates a
moment, and then follows after.

267   EXT. THAMES BRIDGE - MED CLOSE SHOT

Of portion of wall. The scene is shadowed. A figure is
standing watchfully and motionless. It is Barkilphedro.
He is registered rather by the impression of his outline
than by the distinct face of the man. Like an evil spirit
that hovers menacingly. He walks quickly from the picture
as his cloak sweeps after him in the misty air.

258   INT GREEN BOX - MED SHOT

On Dea's apartment. The scene is dark, only lightened by
the moonlight which shines in through the front window.
The two gypsy girls are asleep on their bed upon the floor.
Dea sits up in her bed and the shaft of moonlight hits
her face as she listens around her. There is a troubled
expression of anxiety upon her face as though some sixth
sense informed her of Gwynplaine's absence from the Green
Box. Slowly she gets up and reaches for a robe, pulling
it around her. Then she walks out of the compartment without awaking the sleeping gypsies. She walks sure-footedly.
The dark room makes no difference to her progress, as she is
blind. She exits through the curtain that leads across
the stage to the rear compartment.

259   INT. GREEN BOX - MED SHOT.

Of the rear compartment belonging to Gwynplaine and Ursus.
Gwynplaine's bed is, of course, empty. In the moonlight
the form of Ursus can be seen as he sleeps soundly upon
his couch. He wears a night-cap. The moonlight lights
the compartment dimly through the rear window in the door.
A shaft of moonlight brings out Gwynplaine's makeup table
clearly. The curtain parts in the entrance way to the
stage, and Dea enters. She walks into the compartment
and listens as she turns toward Gwynplaine's bed Then

(continued)

(269 continued)

she approaches his bed and feels it with her hands. She
ascertains that Gwynplaine is not there. She is frightened
and hurries toward Ursus' couch. She listens and hears his
snoring, but she does not awaken him. Then she walks to
Gwynplaine's chair and feels around it and the make-up
table. Her hand encounters no sign of Gwynplaine's presence.
She is becoming panic-stricken and gropes around her, on
the make-up table to try and find the mask he always wears
when he goes out. It is not there and she covers the
table thoroughly with her touch.

270   INT. GREEN BOX - CLOSEUP

Of the top of make-up table. Clearly seen in the moonlight
is the Duchess Josiana's note. It is crumpled and lying
among Gwynplaine's make-up materials. Dea's hand is searching the table vainly for the mask. Then her hand comes in
contact with the note. This is a strange article and she
instinctively grasps it.

271   INT GREEN BOX - MED SHOT

Dea grasps the note tightly and looks around her with an
anxious air. This unusual absence of Gwynplaine is causing
a great fear to come over her. With her only thought to
find Gwynplaine, she walks to the door and opens it. She
exits into the courtyard, still holding the Duchess' note in
her hand. Of course, she has no way of knowing what it is,
but with that sixth sense given to blind people from birth,
she intuitively feels that this strange piece of paper that
she found on Gwynplaine's makeup table, has something to
do with his absence.

272   EXT TADCASTER COURTYARD - MED SHOT

With the Green Box in the foreground and shooting toward the
Inn. The inn is in darkness and only the moonlight lights
up the courtyard. Dea comes sure-footedly down the steps
from the Green Box. Homo, the wolf, gets up but does not
bark as he recognizes her. He lies down again and Dea call
softly for Gwynplaine. Then she starts forward and step
by step, gropes her way around the courtyard toward background.
Her steps burry with her increasing nervousness as she receives
no response to her call. Around in a circle she gropes her

(continued)

(272 continued)

way, now stumbling over the flagstones. She approaches
camera and the Green Box. Her face wears an agonized
expression of great fear, and she holds her hand to her
heart as if it were difficult to breathe. She stops
helplessly beside the Green Box and turns round and round
as if she were in a dark maze. Then she leans against the
Green Box wheel with a gasp of pain as though she could not
get her breath.

273   EXT. TADCASTER INN COURTYARD - SEMI CLOSE SHOT

Of the Green Box wheel. Dea clasps her hand over her heart
and waits for the attack to leave her. She is faint and
weak. The attack passes and she sits down upon the ground
and leans her head back against the wheel. The sudden
fright and the attack from her heart was weakened her and
she sits motionless a moment with her face of purity upturned in the moonlight. Homo enters picture and lies
down close to her. Then he starts to lick her hand as it
lies in her lap.

274   EXT. TADCASTER INN COURTYARD - CLOSEUP

Of Dea's hand. It lies in her lap as she clasps the
Duchess Josiana's note in it, which she is still holding
subconsciously. Homo is licking her hand. At the warm-
ing touch she opens her hand and pets him as the crumpled
note is still retained in her grasp. Homo's comforting
nearness is a help as she silently waits for Gwynplaine's
return.

275   EXT. CORLEONE LODGE - MED CLOSE SHOT

Of gateway. Over the gateway is the name carved in stone
which designates that this is Corleone Lodge. The Duchess'
coach, with her crest upon its side, drives thru the
gateway as the great gate swings open to admit it. The
coach enters, and the gates close behind it with a clang.

276   INT MOVING COACH - MED SHOT

Gwynplaine is sitting back against the cushions. The
Duchess' page is seated opposite him. The rocking action
of the coach stops. As the vehicle comes to an abrupt
halt, it throws Gwynplaine off balance. He sits upright
and the door opens. A servant of Josiana's in livery,
sticks his head in the coach and hands Gwynplaine a blindfold. The servant bids him put it on. Gwynplaine does
so and the servant ties it tightly behind the head. Then
the servant takes his hand and leads him out of the coach.
The coach door closes after him.

277   INT. QUEEN'S SITTING ROOM - MED SHOT

Queen Anne is seated in a chair, while Barkilphedro is
entering her presence from the direction of the outer
door. He bows before her and takes the parchment which
he took from Hardquanonne from his pocket. He unfolds it
and hands it to the Queen. She takes it and starts to read
it, as Barkilphedro waits respectfully. The Queen looks
up with rather a puzzled air as she indicates what this
parchment means. It is not necessary to show an insert
of this parchment here, as the audience knows what it is.

278   INT. QUEEN'S SITTING ROOM - SEMI CLOSE SHOT

Of the Queen and Barkilphedro. Barkilphedro respectfully
enlightens Her Majesty.

TITLE: "I have discovered that this lost heir of
                          Lord Clancharlie is alive. He is Gwynplaine,
                          the famous Laughing Mountebank."

BACK: He finishes title and the Queen takes it in a
thoughtful manner. Barkilphedro explains further.

TITLE: "It means, Your Majesty, that the Duchess
                          Josiana's estates and peerage belong to this
                          clown by the law - that she is a pauper!"

BACK: He finishes, with a cunning look at the Queen, as he
imparts this information to her.

279   INT QUEEN'S SITTING ROOM - CLOSE SHOT

Of the Queen. She takes Barkilphedro's information with
a look of supreme satisfaction. Here is a way to hurt
this Duchess whom she hates. She talks, with the air of
a cat contemplating a mouse.

TITLE: "Tis a shame to hurt the dear Duchess
                         thusly, but our course is plain."

BACK: She finishes title, and Barkilphedro leans over the
back of her chair into picture. He whispers into the Queen's
ear some further information.

TITLE: "If it pleases Your Royal Majesty, this
                         Gwynplaine is expected in her Grace's
                         apartment this night."

BACK: He finishes title and the Queen takes it with a
triumphant expression. Barkilphedro whispers again, sug-
gesting more deviltry to the Queen. Her face brightens
and with a look of diabolical cunning, Barkilphedro withdraws his face from picture.

280   INT QUEEN'S SITTING ROOM - MED CLOSE SHOT

Of the Queen. Barkilphedro hurries to her desk and brings
writing materials to Her Majesty. He sips the pen and hands
it to her, and she writes with an expression of malicious
triumph. She signs her name, and Barkilphedro dusts it
for her, with the dusting powder. Barkilphedro returns the
writing materials to their place and the Queen rolls up the
parchment with a caressing touch, as though its feel pleases
her. Barkilphedro returns before Her Majesty. The Queen
hands him the parchment. She talks with a gracious air.

TITLE: "For this valuable service, we should reward you
                         Barkilphedro."

BACK: She finishes title, asking him what he would like.
Barkilphedro narrows his eyes shrewdly and answers, as
though he already has this reward framed in his mind for a
long time.

TITLE: "I would cease being a Jester - and this new
                         Lord Clancharlie will undoubtedly require a
                         Chief steward for his affairs.

                                         (continued)

148

(280 continued)

BACK: He finishes title, and the Queen nods, granting him
the position. Barkilphedro's eyes shine with satisfaction.
He bows deeply, and kisses the hem of the Queen's garment.
Then he turns and exits from her presence. The Queen looks
after him, and a smile of malicious triumph is registered
upon her face, as she thinks of the Duchess Josiana.

281   INT JOSIANA'S HALLWAY - MED SHOT

Of Josiana's boudoir door. As scene cuts in, Gwynplaine is
led into picture. He is still blindfolded. One of
Josiana's personal servants is conducting him. They stop
before the door. The servant opens it and leads Gwynplaine
thru it into the boudoir.

282   INT JOSIANA'S BOUDOIR - MED CLOSE SHOT

Of hallway door. Gwynplaine is led from the door toward
camera. The servant stops him in the foreground. Then
the servant rushes up and unties the blindfold, ripping
it from Gwynplaine's face. He still has his own mask on,
which covers his mouth. Gwynplaine is dazed and blinks
at the sudden bright light as it hits his eyes. The servant
withdraws and the door closes behind him. Instinctively
Gwynplaine turns his head as he listens to the door close.

283   INT JOSIANA'S BOUDOIR - CLOSEUP

Of Gwynplaine's head and shoulders. He turns toward camera
again from his look toward the door, and blinks his eyes,
trying to see his surroundings in a sudden glare which has
blinded him after the blindfold.

285   INT JOSIANA'S BOUDOIR - MED FULL SHOT

Shooting from Gwynplaine's position near the hall door.
As scene cuts in, the set is blurred, giving the impression
of a very bright light with the objects in the room indis-
tinguishable. Slowly the objects take form and stand out
with unusual clearness. The camera pans around the set and
(continued)

149

(284 continued)

stops at the bedroom archway. Through it, Josiana is seen
as she lies on her bed with closed eyes. She is clothed in
a transparent and flimsy garment, which show her figure as
much as censorship will permit, but enough to offer a striking figure of feminine allurement.

285   INT JOSIANA'S BOUDOIR - MED SHOT

Toward Gwynplaine. He looks off with a startled look of
wonder. His gaze is riveted on the form of this beautiful
woman. It is she; the beautiful woman he saw in the box.
He hesitates and then starts toward camera. He stops and
turns as if to retrace his steps toward the hall door.
Then he looks off again and slowly he starts forward. He
must be sure that this woman expects him, or he has not
accomplished his purpose in coming here. TROLLEY CAMERA
AHEAD OF HIM WITH AN AKELEY SHOT. He crosses the set toward
the bedroom archway. He stops and hesitates as he looks in,
hesitating to go further.

286   INT. JOSIANA'S BEDROOM - CLOSE SHOT

Of Josiana as she lies upon the bed with closed eyes. This
shot gets over Gwynplaine's view of her and accentuates
all of her beauty and charm.

287   INT JOSIANA'S BEDROOM - SEMI CLOSE SHOT

Of Gwynplaine as he stands in the bedroom archway, looking
at Josiana out of picture. His gaze is drawn to the lure of
this beautiful woman. He feels her voluptuous charm.
It is the first woman he has ever seen in this state.
He starts forward, drawn by the temptation of her nearness
AN AKELEY SHOT. Gwynplaine walks through the archway and
to the bed as the camera follows him. He stops and looks down
at Josiana with a confused and embarrassed look

288   INT JOSIANA'S BEDROOM - CLOSEUP

Of Josiana. She moves and purposely sticks her bare knees
out through the folds of her garment, showing a portion of
her bare limb. But she does not open her eyes.

289   INT JOSIANA'S BEDROOM - MED CLOSE SHOT

Of Gwynplaine as he stands beside Josiana. His gaze is
drawn suddenly to her bare limb as it peeps out from her
filmy garment. He feels as though he were trespassing
upon a view too intimate for his eyes. He turns away, but
he cannot take his eyes from this beautiful woman. Her
temptation is drawing him. He gathers courage and reaches
out toward her, touching her lightly. But she does not
awaken. Then, he becomes panicky; maybe he is not expected,
maybe he is intruding. Again he reaches out to try and
awaken her. This time his touch strays to her bare knee.
His hand is quickly withdrawn as though he had been burned,
and he draws back a step from the bed at the contact. He
turns, instinctively fighting the temptation within him.
But again his gaze is drawn toward Josiana. He turns away
and walks quickly from picture, away from the bed.

290   INT JOSIANA'S BOUDOIR - MED FULL SHOT

As scene cuts in, Gwynplaine slowly walks out of the bedroom
archway into the boudoir. He hesitates and looks back.
A DOUBLE EXPOSED VISION OF DEA PANS INTO PICTURE.
Gwynplaine turns and starts toward door to hall, with firm
steps, walking right through the vision of Dea as though
it conveyed his mental state. The vision of Dea remains on
in scene as Gwynplaine walks across the set toward the hall
door.

291   INT JOSIANA'S BEDROOM - CLOSE SHOT

Of Josiana. She opens her eyes and watches this man like
a spider watching a fly from the center of its web. Then
she turns her had upon the lace pillow and call off in a
seductive manner.

(continued)

(291 continued)

TITLE:
"Gwynplaine! I am not asleep
Come to me."

LAP DISSOLVE OUT AND INTO:

292   INT JOSIANA'S BOUDOIR - MED SHOT

Toward Gwynplaine. He is walking toward the door to hall
and the vision of Dea is still on. As scene cuts in, he
stops and turns at the sound of Josiana's title. The
vision of Dea fades out. Gwynplaine looks off as though
this sound had electrified him. He is expected here. This
beautiful woman has called his name. He is not too ugly
for her to want him here. He hesitates a moment and yields
to the temptation of this woman's lure. He starts back
toward camera, retracing his steps toward the bedroom
archway. AN AKELEY SHOT. As he walks across the boudoir
and enters the bedroom with hesitating steps.

293   INT JOSIANA'S BEDROOM - MED CLOSE SHOT

Of Josiana's bed. Josiana looks at him and smiles
invitingly. His eyes look into hers as though he were
hypnotized by her lure. As he nears her side, she reaches
out and grasps his hand. Gwynplaine is startled, but makes
no resistance as she draws him down until he sits beside
her upon the bed.

294   INT JOSIANA'S BEDROOM - CLOSEUP

Of Gwynplaine's face and head. Shot as if seen from
Josiana's position in the bed. He still has his mask
over the lower part of his face. Josiana's hands come up
into picture and take the mask from Gwynplaine's horrible
laugh is again disclosed. His eyes and expression register
the terrific temptation under which he is struggling.
Josiana's hands drop around his neck. Still he looks down
at her out of picture with a fascinated stare.

295   INT JOSIANA'S BEDROOM - CLOSEUP

Of Josiana's head and shoulders. She lifts her head
toward camera as if pulling herself up by her hands which
are clasped around Gwynplaine's neck out of picture. Her
face registers a violent emotion. Her eyes are swimming
with passion and her lips are parted in anticipation of her
desire to feel Gwynplaine's horrible mouth against hers.
She talks:

TITLE: "In India you would be a God. What a
                          wonderful monster you are! How beautifully
                          hideous."

BACK: She finishes title as she draws herself into a
large closeup.

296   INT JOSIANA'S BEDROOM - CLOSEUP

Of Gwynplaine's head and shoulders. He is looking down at
Josiana out of picture. Her arms extend into picture
and her hands are clasped around his neck. The strain
him toward her. Gwynplaine is suffering under the throes
of his first grate passion for a woman. He bends over at
the insistence of her grasp, as though yielding. Then
he stiffens up and pulls back in sudden resistance. He
tries to look away from the sight of this woman out of
picture; tries to pull his eyes from the maddening beauty of
her. But his gaze returns to her lure. He yields a bit
and leans forward. PAN CAMERA HE LEANS FORWARD TO A
CLOSE SHOT OF JOSIANA'S HEAD AND SHOULDERS. STOP PAN WITH
BOTH IN PICTURE. As pan stops, Josiana slowly pulls
Gwynplaine's face toward hers. He is like a hypnotized man.
His soul tells him to break from this siren's grasp, but his
flesh cries out for him to yield. Slowly, he nears her
face.

297   EXT. TADCASTER COURTYARD - SEMI CLOSEUP

Of Dea. She is asleep as she sits on the ground beside
the wagon wheel as before. Homo is lying beside her. She
stirs restlessly and Homo moves closer to her.

296   INT JOSIANA'S BEDROOM - MED CLOSE SHOT

Of Gwynplaine and Josiana. As scene cuts in, he is
about to succumb to his emotion. He grasps Josiana in
a fierce embrace as she yields to him. As his lips near
hers, he stops short and then he releases her, pushing her
from him. She takes this sudden change of attitude with
a start of displeasure.

299   INT. JOSIANA'S BEDROOM - CLOSEUP

Of the little bell in the wall compartment used for
messages in royal households. It rings, indicating that
a message from the Queen is at hand, and continues to
ring insistently.

300   INT. JOSIANA'S BEDROOM - SEMI CLOSE SHOT

Of Gwynplaine and Josiana. As scene cuts in, Gwynplaine
looks off with a startled look as though the ringing of
the bell has fully wakened him from a bad dream. Her
displeasure at the cooling of his ardor is accentuated
by this interruption. The terrible emotion stamped upon
her face changes to anger and hysterical impatience.

301   INT. JOSIANA'S BEDROOM - CLOSEUP

Of the exterior of the wall compartment in the wall of
Josiana's bedroom. It is next to Josiana's bed. As scene
cuts in, a little panel opens in the wall. On this panel
is a gilded crown. A plush lined compartment is seen.
In this compartment, a little silver tray is lying, and the
little bell still rings above it, insistently. On the tray
is an important document; a folded parchment stamped with the
Queen's great seal. Then the Duchess' hand and arm enter
picture and takes the note with an impatient grasp. The
panel in wall compartment closes again.

Of bed, in scene, the little wall compartment is registered
beside the bed. As scene cuts in, Josiana rips open the
Queen's message, almost tearing it in her reactive anger
at its effect upon the situation. The psychology of the
interruption has caused a complete awakening to normal on
Gwynplaine's part. He rises to his feet and looks around

(continued)

dazedly. The depths of his emotion have left him weak
and shaken for the moment.

303   INT JOSIANA'S BEDROOM - CLOSEUP

Of Josiana. She reads the message with a startled expression, almost unable to believe her eyes. Then she reads
it again to make sure.

INSERT: CLOSEUP of message in the Queen's handwriting.
                        It is addressed to Her Grace the Duchess Josiana
                        and sealed with the Queen's great seal. It is
                        attended by the seal and name of William Cooper.
                        Lord Chancellor of England. It reads to the effect
                        as follows.

                                    We are graciously compelled to inform you
                                  that the legitimate son of Linnacous Lord
                                  Clancharlie has just been discovered in the
                                  person of Gwynplaine, the laughing mountebank.

                                    Therefore his property and estates of you
                                  Peerage revert to him. Thus having regard to
                                  your welfare, we will and command, as sister
                                and Tween that the said person Lord
                                  Clancharlie, hitherto called Gwynplaine, shall
                                  be your husband in the place of Lord David
                                  Dirry-Moir, whose betrothal to you is hereby
                                  annulled. Such is our royal pleasure.

                                                    ANNE R.

BACK: She looks up as a transition comes over her. Her
emotion disappears under the storm of anger that floods her
face. Then she rises, reaching for a robe and quickly
starting to slip into it.

304   INT JOSIANA'S BEDROOM - CLOSE SHOT

Of Gwynplaine and Josiana. As scene cuts in, she finishes
slipping into her robe and draws it around her. Gwynplaine
looks toward her and she turns on him like a tigress and
shakes the vellum message in his face, crumpling it together
in her hands. Of course, Gwynplaine knows nothing of the
contents of the message as Josiana supposes, and he only
looks at her in a puzzled stare, wondering at the change
in her, and yet relieved. Josiana's rage changes to cold

(continued)

(304 continued)

anger and she draws herself to her full height. She
points to the door and talks in a regal manner and with a
nasty sneer upon her beautiful lips.

TITLE: "Begone thou fool! And do not forget,
                          My Lord Gwynplaine, that this room is for
                          my lovers - not my husband."

BACK: She finishes title. Gwynplaine take it with a
puzzled expression. Then as her violent anger returns
and mounts hysterically, he turns and exits from picture,
glad of the chance to get away gracefully. She stops,
remembering his mask. He picks it up from the bed, puts
it on and quickly exits again as Josiana glares after him.

305   INT JOSIANA'S HALLWAY - MED CLOSE SHOT

Of Josiana's boudoir door. As scene cuts in Barkilphedro
enters picture. He listens at the door and beckons in
a servile manner. Lord David enters picture behind him.
Barkilphedro points to the door, registering that this man,
Gwynplaine, is surely within. Lord David reaches for the
doorknob. It opens and he enters quickly. Barkilphedro
remains in the hall and pulls the door shut after Lord David.
He listens with a diabolical grin of cunning. Then with a
satanic peal of laughter, he sits exits down the hall out of
picture.

306   INT JOSIANA'S BOUDOIR - MED. SHOT

As scene cuts in, Lord David approaches. Gwynplaine as he
is on his way to the hall door. They stop confronting
each other, and Lord David looks in anger at this unknown
person in his betrothed, Josiana's apartment. He talks
and starts to draw his sword.

TITLE: "Who dares insult my honor in the
                          chamber of my betrothed?"

(continued)

(306 continued)

BACK: He finishes title and without giving Gwynplaine
time to answer, he pulls his sword from its scabbard and
like lightning, flings the edge of Gwynplaine's mask with
its point. The mask drops down as Gwynplaine steps back
and the lower half of his face is disclosed. Lord David
stares in wonder, at first, as he sees this laughing man,
who he saw in the Green Box show. Then he drops the point
of his sword and puts it back in the scabbard with an expert
motion. He throws back his head and laughs heartily, taking
the whole situation as a huge joke. Gwynplaine turns from
him and passes him quickly. He walks to the door and
exits as Lord David looks after him and holds his sides with
laughter. Then Josiana enters picture from direction of
the bedroom. There is a venomous look of malice upon her
face. She walks to hurt Lord David as she has been hurt.

307   INT JOSIANA'S BOUDOIR - SEMI CLOSE SHOT

Of Lord David. He turns and bows to Duchess Josiana as
she enters picture to him. He tries to control his laughter
and pantomimes to Josiana that he thought this man was her
lover. That it was very clever of her to play such a
joke on him. Without answering, Josiana hands the crumpled
vellum to Lord David. He takes it with a puzzled air and
manages to control his laughter as he reads it. Slowly
the laughter fades from his face as he absorbs the contents
and is replaced by a hurt look of wonder. Josiana talks with
a sneer:

TITLE: "That grinning mountebank is Lord Clancharlie's
                          son. A clown has become a Peer of England."

BACK: She finishes with a majestic shrug of her shoulders.
Lord David's jaw drops and he just stares in open-mouthed
wonder from Josiana to the vellum and back again to Josiana

                                              FADE OUT

308. FADE IN.
      EXT. SOUTHWARK FAIR.. DAY SEQUENCE.

      MED. LONG SHOT. As scene fades in, the Fair grounds is
      deserted. It is early morning, shortly after down. Nobody
      is astir at this early hour. Everywhere, the ground is
      littered with the debris left by the multitude of the night
      before. The muddy ground is trampled into a pulpy mess.
      The banners advertising the various shows flap listlessly.
      Several stray dogs wander around seeking food. Then, in
      background, the figure of Gwynplaine enters picture. He
      hurries along toward camera, paying no attention to any-
      thing but his progress. He passes close to camera as he
      turns into the entrance of the Tadcaster Inn. He is wear-
      ing his mask and has his cloak wrapped around him tightly
      in the chilly air.

309. EXT. TADCASTER COURTYARD.

      SEMI CLOSEUP of Dea. She sits on the ground as she was
      last seen in the preceding night sequence. She is sleep-
      ing with her head leaning back against the spokes of the
      rear wheel of the Green Box. Her hand rests in her lap
      and holds the crumpled note sent to Gwynplaine by the
      Duchess Josiana. Homo is lying close to her, with his head
      in her lap. He has kept her warm during the night. As
      scene cuts in, Homo lifts his head and gets to his feet
      with a joyful little growl as though he sensed Gwynplaine's
      approach.

310. EXT. TADCASTER COURTYARD.

      MED. SHOT of courtyard entrance-way. Gwynplaine enters
      the entrance-way as scene cuts in. His head is bent for-
      ward as he walks along and from over the flagstone court-
      yard. He stops in medium foreground and looks toward
      camera upon hearing Homo's growl. A startled exclamation
      escapes him as he sees Dea asleep in the courtyard. He
      hurries past camera, quickening his step.

311   EXT. TADCASTER COURTYARD.

MED. CLOSE SHOT of Dea as she sleeps restlessly. Gwynplaine enters picture. Homo jumps up at him and Gwynplaine pushes him gently aside as he kneels down beside
Dea. Instinctively he realizes that he is the cause of
her being there; that she is waiting for his return. He
looks at her sweet purity of countenance and bows his
head shame-facedly, as he realizes how nearly he for-
feited all rights to gaze into her blind eyes. Then he
sees the crumpled note in Dea's hand. With a start, he
takes it from her. He looks at it and toward her in sudden fear that she knows the contents. Then he realizes
how foolish is this thought; that she could not read it.
He tears the note up into small bits and throws them out
of picture, scattering them to the winds. At this moment, the first shaft of sunlight from the morning sun
strikes Dea's face, illuminating it brightly. Slowly she
wakes up and Gwynplaine bends toward her.

312   EXT. TADCASTER COURTYARD.

SEMI CLOSEUP of Dea and Gwynplaine. She lifts her head
with a startled air as though she were just emerging from
a bad dream. Then she reaches out and touches Gwynplaine.
She clings to him in wild relief at the contact which
proves that he is really there. She talks:

TITLE: "Gwynplaine! I dreamed that you
                          had gone away..."

BACK: She pauses, a bit bewildered as she realizes that
she is not in her bed. She reaches out around her and
feels the wagon wheel. Then memory floods her mind and
she continues a bit excitedly..

TITLE: "... It was not a dream! But you have come
                          back. Everything is light again!"

312 (con'd)

BACK: She finishes the title and turns her face full
into the sunlight. Gwynplaine looks at her with a tender
air, thankful that she is all right. A happy smile replaces the anxiety upon Dea's face. She feels approval of
her strength and in her great joy, she gropes toward
Gwynplaine's hand and grasps it. He looks at her with a
tender expression. She is so pure, so beautiful in com-
parison to the woman of fire, when he has held in his
arms, that his gaze of reverent and worshiping. Dea
talks as she pours out her love for him:

TITLE:

"My beautiful Gwynplaine! God gave you to
me instead of sight. Without you, my heart
would die within me."

CUT FROM TITLE FOLLOWING SCENE

313   EXT. TADCASTER COURTYARD.

CLOSEUP of Gwynplaine. He looks at her with an expression of utter love. As a great determination comes
over him, and slowly he reaches up and pulls his mask
from his face. Then he lifts her hand into picture and
talks quietly,

TITLE:

"Feel my face. My hideous lips.. see for
yourself how horrible I am.. how your heart
is deceiving you!"

BACK: He finishes title and places her hand against his
horrible laugh. He forces her to feel it contour in an
effort to impress her how ugly he really is. He loosens
his hold upon her hand and she withdraws it from picture. Then he waits with an agonized expression, bowing
his head before the reaction he is sure will come from
her lips.

314   EXT. TADCASTER COURTYARD

CLOSEUP of Dea. She lifts the hand from Gywnplaine's grasp toward her face. Then, with a tender motion, she kisses the fingers where they have touched his horrible mouth. She talks with a tender expression:

TITLE: "To me you are beautiful... no matter how ugly you may be to others. I love you.

CUT FROM TITLE TO FOLLOWING SCENE

315   EXT. TADCASTER COURTYARD

SEMI CLOSE SHOT of Dea and Gwynplaine. As she finishes title Gwynplaine looks up at her in unbelief. Then he questions her excitedly, asking her whether it does not make any difference in her love for him. She shakes her head that nothing could make any difference. With a tender motion, Gwynplaine reaches out and takes her into his arms. His embrace is not fiery and passionate, like the embrace in which he folded the Duchess Josiana. This is an embrace of love and not of desire. He holds her to him, and with her head upon his shoulder, they lean back against the wagon wheel. She nestles her hand in one of his and they are lost to the world in this great love which has discovered them. The sunlight bathes them in its full brilliancy, as the sun rises higher.

316   EXT. TADCASTER COURTYARD.

CLOSEUP of a morning blue bird on the bough of a tree that projects over the courtyard wall. The bird sings forth a cheery carol of happiness

317.   EXT. TADCASTER COURTYARD..

MED. CLOSE SHOT, of the Green Box. Gwynplaine and Dea
are sitting on the flagstone beside the rear wheel as
before. They are oblivious to everything but themselves
and their great love. The two lovers alone in the world. Her
hand rests upon his shoulder as she lies in the circle of
his arms. He bends over her and kisses her hair tenderly.
Then they are silent again. Homo is lying near them. Seem-
ing to sense the situation, he is turned away from them
with his head between his paws. The door of the Green Box
which was left open by Dea on her wait during the night,
is pushed completely open and the two gypsies come out.
One has a pail for water and the other a basket. They
are on their way for water and bread from the Inn. They
descend the steps and see Gwynplaine and Dea with looks
of surprise. They giggle together as they pass them out
of picture. But Gwynplaine and Dea do not even notice
them. Then, Ursus sticks his head out of the door. He
sees Gwynplaine and Dea with a start.

318.   EXT. TADCASTER COURTYARD.

CLOSE SHOT of Ursus as he looks out the door. A quizzical
smile is registered upon his face, Then he talks in grave
disapproval, purposely appearing very stern.

TITLE: "It is too early for such billing and cooing.
                    Dea is frail and must have her sleep."

BACK: He finishes title, and beckons the two cul-
prits into the Green Box. He , of course, does not know
that Dea has been in the courtyard all night and that Gwynplaine has been out of the Inn.

319.   EXT. TADCASTER INN COURTYARD

MED. CLOSE SHOT of Gwynplaine and Dea, shooting the group,
Dea doorway beside them in background. Gwynplaine turns
as he hears Ursus' voice, he jumps up, a bit embarrassed
As this is the first time he has ever made love to Dea. It
is the first time Ursus has caught him at it. He helps Dea
                                        (cont'd)

319. (con'd)

        to her feet. But she is stiff and weak from her all-
        night vigil. In sudden realization of her condition,
        Gwynplaine picks her up lightly in his arms and carries
        her into the Green Box.

320   INT. GREEN BOX

        MED. SHOT of rear compartment. Ursus is busying himself
        straightening up his bed and getting the room in order
        for the day, as Gwynplaine carries Dea into the compart-
        ment thru the doorway. He and Dea are laughing and talk-
        ing together like kids. They pay no attention to Ursus
        and Gwynplaine carries her through the curtained partition
        toward her compartment. Ursus looks after them with a wry
        grimace of disgust and mutters to himself as he walks over
        and shuts the door, putting his coat around his bony frame
        in the chilly morning air.

321.   INT. GREEN BOX

        MED. SHOT of Dea's compartment. Gwynplaine enters through
        the curtained partition and places her upon her couch.
        She sits up with a happy smile. Her cheeks are glowing at
        this unusual and tender attention of Gwynplaine's. He
        looks at her and tells her how beautiful she is. He reaches
        out and lifts the strand of her long hair in his hand. He
        bends his head and kisses it. Then he kneals beside her and
        looks up at her with an expression of tender worship.
        All his pent-up Love for her is duly finding expression
        in his heart. He bends down and kisses her head and arm
        with a gentle tenderness and she reaches out and touches
        his hand. She holds his to her and they are motionless
        in the ecstasy of their happiness.

322.   INT. GREEN BOX

MED. SHOT of rear compartment. As scene comes in, Ursus
looks up from his work and with a sharp look toward the
door as if someone was knocking. He starts for the door
with a puzzled expression at such an early caller.

323.   EXT. TADCASTER COURTYARD.

SEMI CLOSE SHOT of the Green Box doorway. As scene cuts
in, an official in a black coat and long white wig, is
knocking upon the door. It is the Wapentake and he knocks
with his staff of office, the iron weapon. The door opens
and Ursus looks out with a startled expression. As he starts
to talk the Wapentake silences him and speaks ponderously.

TITLE: "Silence! I am the Wapentake and come for the
                            laughing montebank called Gwynplaine, in the
                            name of Her Royal Majesty!"

BACK: The Wapentake finishes title and enters the door
past Ursus with a dignified air.

324   INT. GREEN BOX.

MED. SHOT of rear compartment. Ursus stands back and
bows low as the Wapentake looks around him. Then the
Wapentake sees the curtained partition and walks to it.
He flips aside the hanging and exits to explore the
Green Box in search of Gwynplaine. Ursus looks after
him with a look of fear, wondering what terrible thing
Gwynplaine has done to have this high official come after
him.

325.   INT. GREEN BOX

MED. SHOT of Dea's compartment. Gwynplaine is still kneeling beside Dea as she sits upon the couch. He looks at her,
lost in the spell of his tender love. She caresses his
head. Their happiness is complete. Then the curtained hanging parts in the doorway and the Wapentake enters. He sees
Gwynplaine and touches him with his iron weapon upon the
shoulder. Gwynplaine turns with a start, but before he
can say anything the wapentake sternly orders silence
and points out the doorway with his iron weapon, indicating that Gwynplaine shall follow him. Gwynplaine slowly
gets up and looks from Dea to the Wapentake. He does not
understand why he is arrested, but he dare not tell Dea.
He quickly makes an excuse to her as though Ursus had called
him and then follows the Wapentake out of the door. Dea
listens after them with a puzzled expression. She does
not recognize the Wapentake's footsteps, and she is sure
they are not those of Ursus.

326.   INT. GREEN BOX

MED. SHOT of rear compartment. Ursus quickly resumes his
deep bowing position as the Wapentake comes out of the
curtained door. Gwynplaine looks behind him
and approaches the Wapentake in a respectful attitude,
questioning him in a startled whisper so that Dea will
not hear him. He asks the Wapentake what it all means.
The Wapentake shakes his head and silences Gwynplaine.
He points to the door and starts toward it. As he exits
Ursus looks toward Gwynplaine and a questioning look of
fear is on his face. Gwynplaine quickly whispers to
Ursus,

TITLE: "Do not tell Dea. It cannot be any-
                    thing serious, and I will hurry back."

BACK: He finishes title and hurries out the doorway
after the Wapentake. Ursus walks cautiously to the
door and peers out after them.

327.   INT. GREEN BOX

           MED. SHOT of Dea's compartment. She still looks off and
           her gaze is troubled as she watches the curtained door.
           Then she arises and calls off, "Gwynplaine! Where have
           you gone?"

328.   INT GREEN BOX.

           MED. SHOT of rear compartment. Ursus is putting on his
           hat and coat preparatory to following Gwynplaine and
           the Wapentake. Then he looks up as he hears Dea's voice
           from her compartment. He thinks a moment and then hurries
           to the curtained doorway to calm her.

329.   INT. GREEN BOX

           MED. SHOT of Dea's compartment. She starts forward to
           the door upon hearing no response to her call. Then
           Ursus enters and walks to her. There is a little look
           of relief on her face as she recognizes him. He talks
           soothingly:

TITLE: "Gwynplaine and I must go to the Fair
                       on business. Go to sleep and rest now.
                       We will return soon."

           BACK: He finishes title and leads her to her couch.
           She sits down upon it and her happy smile returns at
           Ursus's speech. She has no reason to doubt him; he has
           never lied to her about anything. Ursus looks toward
           her and drops his eyes before her trustful expression.
           He turns and exits as she lies down upon the couch with
           a peaceful air of contentment.

330.   EXT. TADCASTER INN

MED SHOT of the entrance door. As scene cuts in, a
squad of police is waiting. The Wapentake leads Gwynplaine out the door and toward them. The squad of police
closes in around Gwynplaine and he starts from picture,
a prisoner as the Wapentake leads the way with a dignified step. Then the innkeeper appears at the door. He
looks out as the two gypsy girls appear behind him.

331.   EXT TADCASTER INN

MED. CLOSE SHOT of the entrance doorway. As Master Niclass
and the other peer out. Ursus appears and forces his way
through them, out of the doorway. Master Niclass questions
him severely, but Ursus pays no attention to him as he
looks up the street. He motions to the two gypsy girls
and they come to him in foreground. He talks:

TITLE: "Do not tell Dea of this. The shock might
                    kill her, and there may yet be hope for
                    Gwynplaine."

BACK: He finishes title and the gypsy girls nod. Then
with a look of anxiety upon his face, Ursus then starts
out of picture to follow Gwynplaine.

332.   EXT. SOUTHWARK FAIR GROUND

CLOSE SHOT toward Gwynplaine as he walks along with the
camera trolleying him. He casts a nervous and
fearful glance at the squad of police which guards him
on all sides.

                              FADE OUT........

333.   FADE IN

EXT. PRISON LANE DAY SEQUENCE

MED. SHOT of prison doorway, shooting toward the prison
cross-street that divides the prison lane from the contin-
uation of the lane which leads to the cemetery gate. This
is the same set as described in Victor Hugo's book. As
scene fades in, the Wapentake approaches the prison door,
leading the little procession of police which surrounds
Gwynplaine. The Wapentake steps to the door and lifts the
heavy knocker, as he signals the others to halt, with a motion
of his iron weapon. Gwynplaine stops behind the Wapentake
as the police guard him.

334   EXT. PRISON LANE

MED. CLOSE SHOT of the prison cross street. As scene cuts
in, a few curious people have stopped and are peering up
the prison lane as they watch the Wapentake's procession.
Then, Ursus forces his way through the small crowd from
background. He peers around the corner and up the prison
lane cautiously.

335   EXT PRISON LANE

SEMI CLOSE SHOT of Ursus as he stands beside another man, Ursus
questions the man, pantomiming what the place is. The man
answers Ursus:

TITLE   "It is the door to the torture chamber,
                  Many men go in, but none come out."

BACK: He finishes title and Ursus takes it with a sudden
expression of fear. The man exits from picture and Ursus
steps forward as he gazes out of picture with a look of
anxiety and apprehension upon his face.

336   EXT. PRISON LANE

MED. SHOT toward the prison door as if seen from Ursus'
position at the corner of the cross street. As scene cuts
in, the prison door opens and the Wapentake leads the way
in, through it. Gwynplaine follows him and the police enter
after him. The door closes with an air of finality as if
the prison wall had suddenly yawned and swallowed up
Gwynplaine.

337   EXT PRISON LANE

MED, CLOSE SHOT OF URSUS. The small crowd turns away and exit
from picture in the various directions of their interest.
The procession is over and they are no longer interested.
Ursus is left all alone. He is stunned and horror stricken.
Everyone knows that this is the door of the torture chambers,
and that very few come forth from it alive. Ursus steps
toward the wall at the corner of the prison lane and leans
against it to wait. He can only hope that Gwynplaine will soon
reappear. He watches up the prison lane with a steady watchful gaze, never taking his eyes from the door.

338   INT PRISON CORRIDOR

MED. CLOSE SHOT of Gwynplaine as he is led along the corridor
with the camera trolleying ahead of him. This corridor is as
described in Victor Hugo's book. It is a dark and narrow
passage between damp walls of stone. It is torturous, low
and winding. The flickering light of a torch carried out of
picture by a prison attendant, lights Gwynplaine's progress.
A terrible fear has started to grip him. He knows where he is
and yet he does not know why he is here. Everywhere is only
ominous and menacing silence. He feels like a man walking to
his doom with closed eyes and not knowing where he is being
led, nor to what terrible end. He walks along as the fear
takes more definite shape within him. He is becoming terror
stricken and looks around him as he follows round the winding
turns. Then the iron weapon of the wapentake enters picture
from in front of him. It touches Gwynplaine's shoulder and
he stops.

339   INT. PRISON CORRIDOR

MED. CLOSE SHOT of doorway in a solid wall. It is a sheet of
iron without a knob or hinge. The Wapentake steps into picture
and raps upon the door with his iron weapon. Then the sheet of
iron raises like a portcullis and the Wapentake steps through
the cavernous opening, motioning Gwynplaine to follow. Gwynplaine enters picture past camera and follow through the door.
The iron doorway closes after him, leaving the police behind.
TROLLEY CAMERA QUICKLY BACK. The police wait silently for a
moment and then walk out of picture, back along the corridor
as if their duty were finialized and the prisoner delivered to
his fate.

340   INT. TORTURE CHAMBER

MED. FULL SHOT. This is the torture cell as described in
Victor Hugo's book. The doorway seen in the last scene is at
the top of a narrow flight of stone steps. These are almost
perpendicular and have no balustrade. At the bottom of this
dungeon-like stone tomb is the torture chamber. Four columns
support a mitre-like vaulted stone canopy in one corner. From
the center of this, a lantern is hanging. This is the only
source of light. A raised stone platform faces one side of
this pillared enclosure. On this platform the sheriff of the
County of Surrey is seated beside an ancient table. Behind
him, the Sergeant is standing with an ancient book
of the law in his hands. Beneath the stone canopy lies a man in
the position of being tortured. His back is upon the bare ground
and his arms and legs are outstretched so that he is in the
form of the letter Y, each member being stretched and attached
by heavy chains to a pillar. Upon his chest is an iron plate.
Upon this plate, several huge stones are placed. Other stones
lie on the ground beside him. An executioner, in black tights
and hood, stand silently by the pitiful figure. In this long
shot, the man's face is not seen, only his naked body, which is
clothed with only a breech-cloth. The man is Hardquanonne.

As scene curs in, the Wapentake is leading Gwynplaine down
the stairway. Gwynplaine follows him and they cross the chamber
toward the pillared enclosure. Gwynplaine looks around him fear-
fully, and at the figure under the stone canopy with a feeling
of terror.

341   INT. TORTURE CHAMBER

MED. SHOT of the pillared enclosure, shooting through the
pillars and toward the stone platform. The Wapentake leads
Gwynplaine into picture and bows respectfully to the Sheriff,
indicating that he has brought this man and that he is here.
We see now, in this closer shot, that the tortured man on
the ground is Hardquanonne. The Sheriff nods and the Sergeant
steps closer to him. The Wapentake steps back and
leaves Gwynplaine standing alone before the Sheriff and the
tortured Hardquanonne.

342   INT. TORTURE CHAMBER

CLOSEUP of Gwynplaine. He looks around him in a terrified
manner. Then, with a quick bolstering up of his courage, he
talks questioningly to the Sheriff out of picture.

TITLE   "I am but a poor strolling player, why
                         have you brought me to this awful dungeon?"

CUT FROM TITLE TO FOLLOWING SCENE:

343   INT. TORTURE CHAMBER

MED. CLOSE SHOT of Gwynplaine as he stands near Hardquanonne
and in front of the Sheriff's platform. As scene cuts in, he
finishes title, pleading his cause to the Sheriff with a
respectful air. The Sheriff picks up the bunch of roses, which
is a sign of his office, and waves them at Gwynplaine ordering
him to silence. Gwynplaine obeys helplessly and the Sheriff
turns his attention to Hardquanonne on the ground. Hardquanonne's
eyes are closed. The Sheriff points his roses at Hardquanonne
and questions him. But Hardquanonne does not open his eyes or
answer. At a motion from the Sheriff, the executioner leans
into picture and places another rock upon Hardquanonne's chest.
Hardquanonne writhes under the pain of it, getting over that
he is not dead. Gwynplaine looks on with horror registered
at the cruelty of this torture.

344   INT. TORTURE CHAMBER

CLOSE SHOT of Sheriff. He leans forward and talks with an
air of grave dignity. He recites the law in such cases, as
the Sergeant repeats the Latin law from the statute book
as he stands behind the Sheriff's chair, The Sheriff finishes
his speech.

TITLE   "Doctor Hardquanonne, Comprachico, this man
                         confronts you. For the last time we adjure
                         you to break your silence."

BACK: He finishes title with an air of finality and waits
silently to give Hardquanonne a chance to speak. The Sergeant
reads the law in a solemn manner as he turns a page of his
book.

345   INT. TORTURE CHAMBER

SEMI CLOSEUP of Doctor Hardquanonne. He grits his teeth with
pain of the added load on his chest. Then he turns his
head so that he is looking in the direction of Gwynplaine
out of picture. He opens his eyes and then he talks:

TITLE   "Tis he - - and I am free from his
                         haunting laugh forever!"

BACK: He finishes title and breaks into a loud laugh as he
looks at Gwynplaine. Then a tremor shakes his body, and he
falls over with his face to the ground. He is dead. The
executioner leans down into picture and feels his heart. Then
he looks up and talks in an unemotional manner

TITLE   "He laughed, and it killed him."

BACK: He finishes title and starts to unchain Hardquanonne
as he lies motionless and limp upon the ground.

346   INT. TORTURE CHAMBER

MED. CLOSE shot of Gwynplaine as he stands in front of the
Sheriff. He is bewildered and takes Hardquanonne's speech
as some kind of admission. He turns toward the Sheriff
and pantomimes that whatever this man says about him is not
true. That he as done nothing. The Sheriff silences him
with a motion of his arms and talks very solemnly.

TITLE: "My Lord Clancharlie, Baron
                          Clancharlie Baskerville, Marquis of
                          Corleone, design to seat yourself.

BACK: He finishes title and arises with a bow toward Gwynplaine
offering him his chair upon the stone platform. Gwynplaine
is dazed and obeys mechanically as the Sheriff beckons him toward the chair. He casts himself in it and the Sergeant steps
forward and unfolds the document that Barkilphedro took from
Hardquanonne and gave to the Queen in previous sequences.
The Sergeant reads from it as the Sheriff stands beside
Gwynplaine in a respectful attitude.

347   INT. TORTURE CHAMBER

MED. SHOT of the entire pillar enclosure. As scene cuts in,
the executioner and a prison attendant lift the unchained
form of Hardquanonne and carry his limp body out of picture
toward the stairway. The Wapentake follows them, touching
the corpse with his iron weapon and pointing off toward the
stairway. The Sergeant still reads the facts of Gwynplaine's
heritage as Gwynplaine sits dazedly in the chair as before
in background.

348   INT. TORTURE CHAMBER

MED. CLOSE SHOT of a masonry column that supports the roof
of the dungeon. This column is behind the Sheriff's chair.
Beyond this column, the chamber is in utter darkness. As
scene cuts in, the form of Barkilphedro steps out from behind
the column. He is dressed in a gorgeous costume, that carries
official weight in appearance. It is the costume of his
new position as Chief steward to this new Lord Clancharlie.
There is a look of diabolical satisfaction upon his face as
he steps forward. He is no longer a Jester, but a person of
importance.

349   INT. TORTURE CHAMBER

MED. CLOSE SHOT of Gwynplaine. The Sergeant finishes, reading
the document and folds it up with a solemn air. Both he and
the Sheriff await Gwynplaine's pleasure, as they wait beside
him in respectful attitudes. Gwynplaine is bewildered; then
Barkilphedro enters picture and bows before Gwynplaine.

350   INT. TORTURE CHAMBER

CLOSEUP of Barkilphedro. He looks up from his deep bow,
and talks to Gwynplaine out of picture.

TITLE   "I am the Chief Steward of Your Lordship's
                      household, by appointment of Her Royal
                      Majesty, the Queen. Your coach is waiting
                      My Lord."

CUT FROM TITLE TO FOLLOWING SCENE:

351   INT. TORTURE CHAMBER

CLOSEUP of Gwynplaine. He looks off, slowly recovering from
his bewilderment. He looks around him and pinches himself to
be sure it is not all a dream. Then he arises from the chair.

352   INT. TORTURE CHAMBER

MED. FULL SHOT. As scene cuts in, Barkilphedro steps aside
from in front of Gwynplaine and bows as he indicates the stairway. Gwynplaine steps down from the stone platform and walks
from the pillared enclosure. The others follow him at a respectful distance. First, Barkilphedro, then the Sheriff and
finally, the Sergeant with his big book. Gwynplaine's exit
is very different from his entrance. The little procession
mounts the stairway and passes through the door at the top. The
door closes after them and the torture chamber is empty.

353   EXT. PRISON LANE

MED. CLOSE SHOT of Ursus. He still waits as he leans against
the wall, with his untiring and anxious gaze riveted upon
the prison door around the corner in the prison lane.

354   EXT. PRISON COURTYARD

MED. SHOT. This is the prison courtyard on the opposite
side of the prison from the prisoner's door in the little
lane. The Duchess' Coach is waiting, with a body-guard from
the Queen's guard in attendance. The big prison doorway opens
and Gwynplaine comes out. He is followed by Barkilphedro.
The Sheriff and other high prison officials stands in the
doorway and bow in deep respect as Gwynplaine walks toward
the coach, with a bewildered air. As Gwynplaine sees the
coach, he stops with a start of recognition, recognizing this
coach as the one in which he rode to the Duchess' apartment.

355   EXT. PRISON COURTYARD

SEMI CLOSEUP of Gwynplaine. He looks off in a bewildered
manner at this coach. He is dazed and apprehensive. Barkilphedro enters picture and looks up at Gwynplaine with a
respectful and inquiring glance. Gwynplaine talks:

TITLE   "Whose coach is that?"

BACK: He finishes title and Barkilphedro looks off at the
coach out of picture. Then he looks back at Gwynplaine and
answers with a fawning smirk:

TITLE   "It belonged formerly to the Duchess
                         Josiana, but now it is yours, My Lord."

BACK: He finishes title and looks back toward the coach with
an air of satisfaction. Gwynplaine take the title in a
puzzled manner. He cannot understand it all.

356   EXT. PRISON COURTYARD

             MED. SHOT toward coach. As scene cuts in, a footman opens
             the door and Gwynplaine hesitates. Barkilphedro indicates
             the coach and Gwynplaine walks toward it. He enters the
             door and Barkilphedro slides in after him. The door closes.
             The footman jumps to his place. The Queen's Guard forms
             around the coach and the coach drives out of picture.

357   INT. MOVING COACH

             MED. SHOT of Gwynplaine as he looks around the coach's
             interior. He almost shrinks from it, as he remembers the
             former night when he rode in this same coach through London.
             Barkilphedro squats on the opposite seat in a servile attitude.
             Gwynplaine suddenly comes out of his bewildered state long
             enough to remember the Green Box. He talks to Barkilphedro.
             There is an anxious manner to his questioning:

TITLE   "But where are you taking me? I must
                                 return to the Tadcaster Inn - My father
                                 Ursus will worry.

             BACK: He finishes title and Barkilphedro take it. He
             shakes his head in a respectful manner and talks in answer to
             Gwynplaine's question.

TITLE   "That is impossible at present. Her Royal
                                 Majesty commands your presence at Corleone
                                 Lodge, My Lord."

             BACK: He finishes title and Gwynplaine takes it. Then a
             rebellious air is registered under this command of the Queen's.
             Gwynplaine slides toward the door as if to tell the coach to
             stop and let him out. Barkilphedro shrugs his shoulders and
             reaches toward the window. He pulls the curtains aside and
             Gwynplaine looks out of the window. Outside, the weapons of
             the Queen's guards are on a level with the window as they
             ride beside the coach. Gwynplaine settles back in his seat,
             as he realizes that he is virtually a prisoner. Barkilphedro
             draws the curtain shut again, and settles back silently.

358   EXT. PRISON LANE

             CLOSE SHOT of Ursus. He is waiting, as before, watching the
             prisoner doorway out of picture, with a steady gaze. He
             lifts his head and listens, without taking his eyes from his
             vigil.

359   EXT. STEEPLE

             MED. CLOSE SHOT. The clock in the steeple registers the
             hour of nine o'clock DOUBLE EXPOSE OVER THIS SCENE AS BEFORE
             the four other miniature steeples and the five different bells
             of these steeples, as the five parishes of Southwark strike
             the hour of nine.

             LAP DISSOLVE OUT AND INTO:

360   EXT. PRISON BELFRY

             CLOSE SHOT of the Bell. As the other bells slowly
             dissolve out, the ringing of this bell takes their place.
             It tells with measured and funeral strokes. A dirge-like
             melody.

361   EXT. PRISON LAND   DAY SEQUENCE

             CLOSEUP of Ursus. He is listening to the striking of the hour
             as he lifts his head with a weary air. The hours of waiting
             have only increased his anxiety and fear. Then his face
             slowly undergoes a change of expression. This bell has a
             different sound than the others. He slowly recognizes it as
             the Bell in the prison belfry. He looks off quickly,
             with a more intense gaze as his fear increases.

362   EXT. PRISON LANE

MED. SHOT toward the prison door, shooting as if seen from
Ursus' position of the corner of the cross street. The door
opens and the squad of police, as seen before, comes out.
Following the police, is a bier-like coffin, carried upon the
shoulders of four prison attendants. The Wapentake follows
after the coffin, and the grave-diggers with spades, and the
prison chaplain reading his ritual, bring up the rear. It
is the funeral procession of Hardquanonne.

363   EXT. PRISON LANE

MED. SHOT, shooting across the prison lane toward Ursus.
The camera shows a close view of Ursus as he watches up the
prison lane. He is horror-stricken. Of course he naturally
thinks that Gwynplaine is in the coffin and has been tortured
to death. TROLLEY CAMERA BACK QUICKLY SO THAT THE WHOLE
STREET OF THE PRISON LANE IS VISIBLE AS IT CROSSES THIS
CROSS STREET. The procession which makes up the funeral
cortege passes through picture between the camera and Ursus.
The police pass, then the coffin with the white skull and crossbones
upon it. Then the Wapentake and finally the grave
diggers and the shovels. They exit and Ursus turns his
head in the opposite direction and follows their progress with
a stunned gaze of horror.

364   EXT. PRISON LANE

MED. SHOT toward the camera gateway, on the opposite side
of the cross street. As scene cuts in, the funeral procession
enters picture and starts into the cemetery gateway. Then
the cemetery gate closes after the procession.

365   EXT. PRISON LANE

CLOSEUP of Ursus. He is looking off in the direction of the
cemetery gate. His faze is transfixed and he is stunned, as
the thought takes possession of him that Gwynplaine must be
dead. That he will never reappear at the Green Box. A wild
hysteria possesses Ursus and he starts as if to rush out of
picture, calling Gwynplaine. Then he stops as his mind becomes
normal again after this shocking blow. He turns his face away
from the direction of the cemetery gate and the tears father
in his eyes. He leans weakly against the wall. He has suddenly
grown very old and his bony figure hunches down
under the weight of a tremendous load of sorrow.

366   EXT. PRISON BELFRY

CLOSE SHOT of the bell. As scene cuts in, the bell
slowly stops tolling and becomes motionless and silent.

367   EXT. PRISON LANE

MED. SHOT toward Ursus and across the prison lane. As scene
cuts in, Ursus is leaning against the wall as before. He
bows his head under the last strokes of the Bell. Then
he turns slowly and walks away from the camera down the
cross street. His shoulders are bent and his head is bowed
as he walks toward background with faltering steps.

                              FADE OUT.

MED. FULL SHOT. This is the chamber of Corleone Lodge as
described in Victor Hugo's book, Volume II, Chapter 3.
It is a huge room and situated on an upper floor. There is
a large double door to upper hall and a high window reaching
from the ceiling to the floor. A small balcony is outside
this window. This balcony is situated high up against the
palace wall, and far below it is the palace moat, with a
sheer wall of stones between. A large fireplace occupies one
side of the chamber opposite the window. It is furnished
stiffly and regally with much space. A huge feudal bed is
at one end. Near this, is a curtained doorway which covers
a wardrobe and powder closet. A row of armchairs and
ordinary chairs, with two massive tables complete the
furniture. The ceiling is domed and the room is lighted by
two candelabras which are placed upon the table. The ceiling
is emblazoned with coats-of-arms and gleaming escutcheons.
It is a room fit for a king, in its appointments.

As scene fades in, Gwynplaine is discovered in background.
Barkilphedro is attending him. They are standing near the
bed and wardrobe. Beside the wardrobe, three lackeys are
standing and holding articles of rich wearing apparel.
Another lackey is powdering and adjusting a wig upon
Gwynplaine. Another is kneeling before him and buckling
on his sword. In foreground, three more lackeys are arranging refreshments upon one of the tables; a cold foul, wine
and brandy, served on a silver-gilt server.

369   INT. PALACE CHAMBER

MED. SHOT of Gwynplaine and Barkilphedro. As scene cuts in,
the lackeys finish Gwynplaine's toilet. He is dressed in a
beautiful costume of the period; a costume befitting his
lordly state. Barkilphedro dismisses the two lackeys with
a wave of his hand and they exit. Gwynplaine is bewildered
at all this attention, and can hardly realize that it is
true. Barkilphedro approaches him and hands him a purse of
money, pantomiming that it is his, Gwynplaine takes it as
Barkilphedro steps back from him with a respectful air.

370   INT, PALACE CHAMBER

CLOSEUP of Gwynplaine. He looks at the purse in his hand
and opens it, gazing at the money, as he drops some coins
into his hands. There is a dazed look of wonder at all
his good fortune. He puts the coins back in the purse and
looks around him, his gaze centering toward the wardrobe.

371   INT. PALACE CHAMBER

MED. CLOSE SHOT of wardrobe doorway. The three lackeys are
putting away the articles of clothing not used by Gwynplaine.
In the wardrobe are hanging gorgeous clothes - costumes of
every descriptions. A complete gentleman's outfit of the
period. The lackeys finish and start out of picture. On a
chair, Gwynplaine's old clothes are lying. One lackey stops
to pick up these old clothes and the other two lackeys exit.
Barkilphedro enters picture and stops the lackey, pantomiming
that he will take care of these things for his Lordship.
The lackey exits with a respectful air and Barkilphedro
awaits Gwynplaine's pleasure as he stands beside the chair
upon which are lying his mountebank's garments.

372   INT. PALACE CHAMBER

MED. SHOT toward the hallway door with the tables in foreground. As scene cuts in, the five lackeys who have attended
Gwynplaine are finishing arranging the refreshments upon the
table. They turn and walk toward the others. Then all eight
lackeys bow respectfully in the direction of Gwynplaine and
exit through the hall door, in single file. The door closes
after them.

373   INT. PALACE CHAMBER

MED. CLOSE SHOT of Barkilphedro. He is still standing beside
the chair as before. He is looking off with a shifting gaze
of cunning satisfaction. Then he glances at Gwynplaine's
clothes upon the chair, and an amused smirk appears on his
face. He looks up quickly and resumes his servile attitude
as Gwynplaine enters picture to him. Gwynplaine talks, with
a look around him, and wanting some concrete proof to his
mind that all this is true.

TITLE: "all this belongs to me? It is really true?"

BACK: He finishes title and Barkilphedro nods that most
assuredly such is the case, that Gwynplaine is a Lord and
a Peer of England. He reaches toward the wardrobe doorway
and lifts a gorgeous garment from behind the half-closed
curtain. It is a magnificent velvet robe, trimmed with
ermine. Barkilphedro talks as he indicates it,

                              (Continued)

373 Continued:

TITLE   "Here is your peer's robe of red velvet
                              bordered with ermine, My Lord."

BACK: He finishes title as Gwynplaine looks at the robe
in awe. He reaches out and touches it as though even now
he could hardly believe this thing that has happened to him.
Barkilphedro replaced the robe in the wardrobe and turns again
to Gwynplaine. He talks impressively,

TITLE   "Beside the palace, you own Clancharlie
                              Castle, and nineteen bailiwicks with
                              eighty thousand vassals and tenants."

BACK: He finishes title with an eloquent wave of his hand.
Then he leads the way from picture, indicating the Gwynplaine follow him, with a respectful gesture. Gwynplaine
starts out of picture, carrying his purse gingerly in his
hand.

374   INT. PALACE CHAMBER

MED. FULL SHOT As scene cuts in, Gwynplaine follows
Barkilphedro across the huge room. He looks around him
and walks with light steps upon the velvet carpet. He
shifts his sword around to his side. Being unused to it,
it interferes with his walking. Barkilphedro stops at the
first table. Upon this table is a pile of documents and
patents of Lordly holdings. Gwynplaine approaches the
table at a respectful sign from Barkilphedro.

375   INT. PALACE CHAMBER

MED. CLOSE SHOT of table. Barkilphedro runs thru the various
documents as Gwynplaine enters picture. Barkilphedro talks,
indicating what the various parchments mean.

TITLE   "Here is your patent of peerage, of your
                              Scilion Marguisete, of your eight baronies
                              with an income of forty thousand pounds a year.

BACK: He pauses to let this fact sink in; to let Gwynplaine
realize how rich he is. Then he resumes the cataloging of
Gwynplaine's assets

376   INT. PALACE CHAMBER

           CLOSEUP of Gwynplaine. He is motionless as his mind absorbs
           these wonderful facts. Then a sudden change is registered
           as the memory of Dea and Ursus breaks through his daze.
           He suddenly realizes how they must be worrying about him.
           He holds up his hand, interrupting Barkilphedro out of
           picture, and talks quickly.

TITLE   "Enough! I cannot allow my father Ursus
                             to worry longer. I must return at once
                             and tell him of our good fortune."

           CUT FROM TITLE TO FOLLOWING SCENE.

377   INT. PALACE CHAMBER

           CLOSEUP of Barkilphedro. He takes Gwynplaine's title with
           a servile shrug of his shoulders. He answers respectfully,

TITLE   "Impossible, my Lord! Gwynplaine is dead,
                             at the Queen's command."

           CUT FROM TITLE TO FOLLOWING SCENE

378   INT. PALACE CHAMBER

           MED. SHOT toward the hall doorway. Barkilphedro finishes
           title as he stands in front of Gwynplaine beside table in
           foreground. Gwynplaine resents this command and starts past
           Barkilphedro toward the door. Barkilphedro endeavors to
           stops him in a diplomatic manner, but Gwynplaine pushes past
           him and walks to the hall door in background. Barkilphedro
           shrugs his shoulders and grins to himself

379   PALACE CHAMBER

           MED. CLOSE SHOT of hall doorway. Gwynplaine enters picture
           and strides to the door. He pulls it open and as he starts
           out, two members of the Queen's Guards step forward and
           block his way in the hall. Gwynplaine stops in sudden reali-
           zation that he is virtually a prisoner. He turns and closes
           the door again. Then he looks around as though seeking
           another means of exit. He starts out of picture toward the
           window.

380   INT. PALACE CHAMBER

           MED. CLOSE SHOT toward the room's one window. Gwynplaine
           enters picture and pulls aside the curtains. He opens the
           French window and steps out upon the balcony. He looks
           down over the railing.

381   EXT. CORLEONE LODGE

           MED. SHOT shooting down from his position. A shear
           stone wall descends like a precipice to the waters of
           the palace moat, one hundred and fifty feet below. This
           shot not only serves to indicate definitely the impossibility
           of Gwynplaine's escape.

382   INT. PALACE MOAT

           MED. FULL SHOT shooting toward the balcony window. Through
           the window, the form of Gwynplaine can be seen as he stands
           on the balcony with his back to camera in background.
           Barkilphedro watches him at the table, near foreground.
           Gwynplaine turns and enters the room. He looks around help-
           lessly in realization that there is no escape. Then, angrily,
           at his helplessness, he looks toward Barkilphedro, cross-
           ing the room with quick steps.

383.   INT. PALACE CHAMBER

MED. CLOSE SHOT of Barkilphedro. The cunning grin upon
his face changes to a fawning servility as Gwynplaine
walks into picture. He looks around and tells Barkilphedro that they cannot hold him here against his will.
Barkilphedro shrugs his shoulders, pantomiming that
the Queen's command must be obeyed. Gwynplaine talks impatiently.

TITLE: "You say I am a lord.. yet a Lord is
                          his own master."

BACK: He finishes title and Barkilphedro takes it and
answers in a humble manner of advisor to him:

TITLE: "Tomorrow you accept your peerage in the
                          House of Lords. After that Your Lordship's
                          wish is law.

CUT FROM TITLE TO FOLLOWING SCENE

384.   INT. PALACE CHAMBER

CLOSEUP of Gwynplaine. He takes this title with sudden
enlightenment. A transition comes over him. According to
this, he can do what he wishes after this ceremony tomorrow. He can share his fortune with Dea and Ursus. He
is rich. An idea comes to him as he looks down at the
purse he still holds.

355.

MED. CLOSE SHOT of Barkilphedro and Gwynplaine. Gwynplaine
quickly hands this purse to Barkilphedro and talks with
a commanding air.

(This title omitted from body of scene #325

TITLE: "Take this to my father Ursus and acquaint
                          him of our good fortune and my safety."

BACK: He finishes title and Barkilphedro nods that he
will go at once to London. He withdraws from Gwynplaine's
presence and exits toward the rear of the chamber, there
the wardrobe is situated. Gwynplaine turns from him as
he exits and fingers the costume with a thoughtful air

386.   INT. PALACE CHAMBER

MED. SHOT. toward the wardrobe doorway. Barkilphedro enters
picture. He walks to the chair where Gwynplaine's old
clothes are lying. He puts the purse of money in his picket
and rolls the old clothes into a bundle. He looks off with
a furtive gaze and then quickly starts out of picture in
the direction of the hall door. There is a diabolical grin
upon his face.

387.   INT. PALACE CHAMBER

MED. FULL SHOT as scene cuts in, Barkilphedro walks toward
the hall door. Gwynplaine's back is turned toward him and
he does not see that Barkilphedro is taking his old clothes
with him. Unnoticed, Barkilphedro glides past Gwynplaine
with soft steps. He opens the hall door and slides out with
a backward look toward Gwynplaine. The door
closes after him and Gwynplaine is alone in the huge room.
His back is toward camera and he stands motionless and
lost in the dreams conjured up by this sudden realization
of his new riches and power.

388.   INTO PALACE CHAMBER..

CLOSEUP of Gwynplaine. There is a happy look registered in
the expression of him spreads as he looks toward camera and
visualizes Dea as the lady of this great castle.

389.   INT. PALACE CHAMBER

MED. SHOT toward a beautiful armchair. Scene cuts in to
empty stage. THEN THE SOLID PICTURE OF DEA DISSOLVES INTO
PICTURE AS SHE SITS IN THE CHAIR. She is, of course, a
figment of Gwynplaine's imagination. The great chair
seems to swallow up her frail figure. She is dressed in
an elaborate silken robe of the period, and there are
jewels upon her hands and person.

390.   INT. PALACE CHAMBER

MED. FULL SHOT in background, Dea is seated in the great
chair as before. Gwynplaine walks toward her from the table.
He bows gallantly and takes her arm as she arises with a
happy smile. He escorts her toward the table upon which
the cold repast is spread. He pulls up a chair for her
and seats her in front of the table. Then he walks around
the table and seats himself opposite her.

391.   INT. PALACE CHAMBER

MED. CLOSE SHOT of the table. Gwynplaine looks across
the table at Dea and starts to serve her from the various
dishes. He pauses and as he selects a piece of wild fowl
talks questioningly...

TITLE: "My Lady Clancharlie will have a wing..
                          or mayhap a piece of the breast?"

BACK: She points to the fowl's leg as he finishes title
and he puts it on the plate. Then he hands the plate
across the table as she reaches out her hand to take it.

392   INT. PALACE CHAMBER

CLOSEUP of the plate as Gwynplaine's right hand holds
it out. Dea's left hand enters picture to take it. Upon
her finger is a wedding ring of the period. Instead of
taking the plate, she covers Gwynplaine's hand with hers,
holding him a gentle prisoner. He bends his head down into
picture to kiss her hand THEN DEA'S HAND DISSOLVE OUT OF
PICTURE. Gwynplaine starts a bit as if awakening from a
dream, and nearly kisses his own hand.

393   INT. PALACE CHAMBER

MED. CLOSE SHOT. of Gwynplaine at the table. Dea's
figure is gone and the chair opposite Gwynplaine is
empty. Gwynplaine straightens up wit the plate and puts
it down in front of him. Then he picks up the leg of the
fowl and starts to eat it with enjoyment as he continues
to visualize the happiness he intends to bring Dea and
Ursus, now that he is rich,

FADE OUT

394   FADE IN   EXT. TADCASTER INN   NIGHT SEQUENCE

MED. SHOT. As scene cuts in, a small crowd is already
passing into the Inn. It is early for the real Fair
patronage to begin. Ursus makes his way toward the Inn
doorway, on his return from the prison. His shoulders are
hunched forward and he is a dejected figure as he approaches
the doorway.

395.   EXT. TADCASTER INN

MED. CLOSE SHOT of the Inn doorway. As scene cuts in,
Ursus enters picture. He stops as he sees that his footsteps have led him back to the inn at last. His eyes look
up at the sign of the Laughing Man, as it hangs to the
sign of the Inn. As ursus looks at it, the tears father
again in his eyes. He brushes them aside and reaches up,
pulling down the Laughing Man sign, which advertises
Gwynplaine. Then Ursus puts the sign under his arm and
enters through the doorway.

396   EXT. TADCASTER COURTYARD

MED. CLOSE SHOT of the courtyard entranceway. The gypsy girls
are waiting for Ursus' return. They are dressed for the
performance but have not started to sell tickets on account
of Gwynplaine's absence. They look off as Ursus enters
through the entranceway. They run up to him and he stops. He
silences their questions as Master Niclass follows him into
picture. Ursus shows him the sign and pulls out his purse.
He unties the string and counts out some coins. Then he talks
without looking up.

TITLE   "The play of the Laughing Man is over.
                         Gwynplaine is not coming back."

BACK: He finishes title and pays what he owes. Niclass holds
out his hand and accepts his last farthing. He exits, and the
gypsy girls are paid. Ursus bids them say nothing to anybody
and he walks from picture as they look after him, talking
together in whispers.

397   EXT. TADCASTER COURTYARD

MED. SHOT of the Green Box. It is dark and there is no
light inside of it. Homo is lying beside the rear steps,
chained to the wheel in his accustomed position. He gets
up and wags his tail, awaiting Ursus' approach. Ursus enters
picture and pets Homo. Then he unchains the wolf and enters
the Green Box. Homo follows him inside.

398   INT. GREEN BOX

MED. SHOT of rear compartment. The compartment is dark.
As scene cuts in, Ursus enters with Homo. He strikes a
flint and lights the lantern. Then he places the Laughing
Man placard behind Gwynplaine's makeup table. He passes on,
pauses a minute as he thinking of Dea and wonders how he will
break the news to her. He calls her softly. Then he walks
through the curtained partition. Homo sits down beside
Gwynplaine's makeup table.

399   INT. GREEN BOX

MED SHOT of Dea's compartment. The set is dark. Dea is
lying on her couch asleep. The early evening moonlight
lights the compartment through the front window. Ursus
enters and looks down at Dea's face as she sleeps with a
peaceful and contented smile upon her lips. He shakes his
head and wipes a tear from his eye. He cannot tell her now.
He turns and walks again from the compartment.

400   INT GREEN BOX

MED. SHOT of rear compartment. Ursus enters through the
curtained partition. He sinks into his chair and his
grief overcomes him, now that he is alone. He bows his
head upon his hands and arms upon the table. Homo comes
to him and tries to lick his face as he sits beside him

401   INT. GREEN BOX

MED. CLOSE SHOT of Dea's couch in her compartment. As scene
cuts in, she wakes up. Slowly she sits up, instinctively
feeling the lateness of the hour. She listens. Everything
is very quiet. She wonders how long she has slept. She calls,

TITLE   "Gwynplaine! Where are you. It must
                        be time for the show!"

BACK: She finishes title with an anxious air and a bit
worried at the stillness surrounding her.

402   INT. GREEN BOX

MED. CLOSE SHOT of Ursus. He lifts his head from his hands
as he hears Dea's call. He hesitates and then talks to Homo
in a whisper.

TITLE   "The truth will probably kill her."

BACK: He finishes title and starts to get up, then he
thinks better of it. He has not the courage to tell Dea
the truth now. A sudden idea comes to him and he forces
his mouth into the twisted line apparent when he practises
ventriloquism. He holds his hand in front of his mouth and
imitates Gwynplaine's voice as he talks in answer to Dea's
call.

TITLE   "I am right here, my beautiful Dea.
                        Rest some more and I will call you."

BACK: He finishes title and continues to talk as he imitates
Gwynplaine's voice. Homo lifts his head in a puzzled manner
and walks quickly to Gwynplaine's makeup table. But Gwynplaine is not there, and Homo looks from the makeup table to
Ursus, unable to understand.

403   INT. GREEN BOX

MED. CLOSE SHOT of Dea. She sits on the bed listening.
The worry and anxiety disappear from her face as she hears
this voice which she thinks is Gwynplaine's. Then she lies
down again to wait for him to call her.

404   INT GREEN BOX

           MED. CLOSE SHOT of Ursus. He stops talking and slumps down
           in his chair as Homo again comes to him. Ursus pats Homo
           on the head and whispers to him with a shrug of his shoulders.

TITLE   "For that lie of impulse, many other lies must
                          now be manufactured. It is always the way."

           BACK: He finishes title with a shake of his head as if it
           were a problem he did not care to ponder upon this moment.

405   EXT. TADCASTER INN

           MED. SHOT of the inn doorway. As scene cuts in, a coach
           drives into picture. It is the Duchess's coach. It stops
           and Barkilphedro gets out. Surrounding the coach, is a
           detachment of police and a constable. Barkilphedro is
           carrying Gwynplaine's clothing beneath his cloak. He
           beckoned the constable and enters the inn, as the constable
           and the police follow him.

406   EXT. TADCASTER INN

           MED. SHOT of the Inn doorway. The door opens and
           Barkilphedro points to the Green Box out of picture and the
           constable stalks out of picture toward it. Barkilphedro
           follows him.

407   INT. GREEN BOX

           MED. SHOT of rear compartment. Ursus is on at the table
           with Homo, as before. He looks up as though somebody were
           at the door. He arises as Homo growls. Before Ursus can
           reach the door, the door opens and the constable enters
           followed by Barkilphedro. The constable reads and asks his
           name. Ursus nods that he is Ursus and the constable points
           at Homo and reads again from his official document.

                                              (Continued)

TITLE   "A wolf is against the law. You will leave
England tomorrow or go to prison.

BACK: He finishes title as Ursus takes it with a shocked
start. Homo growls loudly at this intruder, as Barkilphedro
watches it all with a malignant grin.

408   INT. GREEN BOX

MED. SHOT of Dea's compartment. She is listening as she
sits upon her couch. Then she gets up and walks to the
partitioned entrance. She exits to find out who is talking
in the rear compartment and why Homo is growling.

409   INT. GREEN BOX

MED. SHOT of rear compartment. The constable turns and exits
through the door. Then Dea appears in the curtained doorway
opposite. She enters and stops, listening. Ursus does not
see her, as he faces Barkilphedro with his back to her.
Barkilphedro looks toward Dea and approaches Ursus, taking
out Gwynplaine's old clothes from under his cloak.

410   INT. GREEN BOX

SEMI CLOSE SHOT of Ursus. Barkilphedro enters picture and
places Gwynplaine's old clothes upon the table. Ursus looks
at them with a start. At first a wild hope possesses him.
Then he realizes that these old clothes only confirm what he
saw. There is agony in his expression as he looks up at
Barkilphedro with a questioning gaze. Barkilphedro
answers his unspoken question.

TITLE   "Gwynplaine, the laughing mountebank
is dead."

CUT FROM TITLE TO FOLLOWING SCENE

411   INT. GREEN BOX

CLOSEUP of Dea. As scene cuts in, she takes Barkilphedro's
title with a gasp. Then she swoons. Her hand reaches out
instinctively and grasps the cloth of the curtain. She sinks
to the floor of the Green Box as the curtain pulls down with
her, breaking her fall.

412   INT. GREEN BOX

MED. SHOT of rear compartment. As scene cuts in, Ursus
runs to Dea and picks her up in is arms. As he carries
her toward his own bed. Barkilphedro shrugs his shoulders
with a sneer and turns away from them. He walks out the
door, closing it after him. Homo growls after Barkilphedro
and then runs to Ursus and Dea.

413   EXT. TADCASTER COURTYARD

MED. CLOSE SHOT of the Green Box rear entrance. As scene
cuts in, Barkilphedro walks down the steps. He pauses with
a cunning grin and takes the purse, which Gwynplaine gave
him for Ursus, from his pocket. He looks at it, weighs it
with a greedy expression, pouring the coins out in his hand
and counting them as he pours them back into the purse.
He puts the purse back in his tunic and, with a backward look
of diabolical glee toward the Green Box, he exits from
picture.

                                        FADE OUT....

414   FADE IN

EXT. LONDON STREET   DAY SEQUENCE

MED. LONG SHOT As scene fades in, a procession is approaching
camera through the crowded street. It is the coach of
Gwynplaine, carrying him to the ceremony in the House of
Lords. This street should be a replica of the street that
leads to the entrance of the House of Lords. The coach is
attended by a peer's consort, and a guard of honor from Her
Majesty's royal household follow after it, in a galloping
cavalcade. On the low front seat, provided for pages, sits
the Usher of the Black Rod and carrying on a cushion his black
portfolio stamped with the royal crown. The coachmen, and
footmen are in the livery of the house of Clancharlie. A
crier preceeds the entourage, clearing a way
through the crowded streets.

415   EXT. LONDON STREET

CLOSE SHOT of the crier as he rides his horse and clears
the way for the procession with an air of great dignity
as he calls out, to clear the path.

TITLE   "Make way for a peer of England!
                         Clear the path! Make way in the
                         name of His Lordship and Her
                         Royal Majesty, the Queen!"

BACK: He continues to all out his warning, clearing the
street to the right and to the left of him.

416   INT. MOVING COACH

MED. SHOT. Gwynplaine is seated all alone in the interior.
He wears no sword and is dressed in a gorgeous silken costume of the period. Over his face is his mask which covers
his terrible laugh. The curtains of the coach are closed and
Gwynplaine leans back against the cushions, visualizing the
happiness he will bring to Dea and Ursus when he is a Lord.

417   EXT. LONDON STREET

MED. CLOSE SHOT of the gentlemen attendants from the royal
household. In f.g. of this cavalcade, is Lord David Dirry-
Moir. He wears a scowl as he follows after the coach of
this man who has come to life to take away from him everything that he desires.

418   EXT. LONDON STREET

MED. LONG SHOT Shooting in the opposite direction and
toward a curve in the street. As scene cuts in, the Green
Box is coming toward camera on its way to the docks, to leave
England as ordered by the constable. Ursus is driving the
two horses with bent head, letting them pick their own way.
The crier from Gwynplaine's entourage rides into picture from
the opposite direction past camera, as he clears the street
ahead of the approaching procession.

419   EXT. LONDON STREET

MED. SHOT of the Green Box, as it drives along with Ursus
taking little heed of its course. The crier rides into
picture and shouts to Ursus. Ursus pulls in his horses and
the crier reins in his horse and rides Ursus off to the side
of the road, with an angry gesture to get out of the way.

420   INT. GREEN BOX

MED. SHOT of rear compartment. Dea is lying on Ursus' bed.
She is weak and the life seems gone from her face. She lies
motionless and ill to the point of death. Beside her, Homo
is lying as if on guard over her. She moves restlessly, and
Homo licks her hand. She pats his head with a weak gesture.

421   EXT. LONDON STREET

MED. LONG SHOT, shooting in the opposite direction, in reverse of the last shot. The Green Box is in f.g. as Ursus pulls
his horses to the side of the street. In b.g. the outriders
of Gwynplaine's coach are approaching. Then they pass through
picture as the crier rides on ahead out of picture. The coach
rumbles past the Green Box. But of course, the curtains at
the window of the coach are closed. Inside the coach, Gwynplaine has no way of knowing he is passing Ursus and Ursus
has no way of knowing Gwynplaine is passing him. Neither
thinks to meet the other, as Gwynplaine does not know Ursus
has been ordered from England, and Ursus thinks Gwynplaine is
dead. The coach drives past the Green Box.

422   INT. GREEN BOX

MED. SHOT of rear compartment. As scene cuts in Homo gets
up and sniffs the air as though he scented the nearness of
Gwynplaine. Dea seems to catch the wolf's attitude and sit
up on the bed; prompted by that sixth sense of the blind, she
calls out the name of Gwynplaine. She gets to her feet,
holding weakly to the wall, and calls again, "Gwynplaine!"

423   INT. MOVING COACH

MED. CLOSE SHOT of Gwynplaine in the coach. He is dreaming
happily as he thinks of the future happiness he visualizes
for Dea and himself. Then he lifts his head as though he
thought he heard a call. It is a psychic reaction to Dea's
call. Gwynplaine settles back again in his seat, realizing
that he must be day-dreaming.

424   EXT. LONDON STREET

MED. LONG SHOT shooting on reverse angle. As scene cuts in, the coach of Gwynplaine rumbles away from the Green Box, as the gentlemen in the cavalcade pass the Green Box, following Gwynplaine's procession.

425   EXT. LONDON STREET

MED. CLOSE SHOT of Lord David as he rides on the outer side of the cavalcade. He turns his head as he passes the Green Box, recognizing it. He reins in his horse and wheels out of his position in the procession, looking back as he rides along.

426   EXT. LONDON STREET

MED. CLOSE SHOT of the Green Box. As scene cuts in, the door opens and Dea gropes her way out of the Green Box. She pushes the steps down and descends to the street. Then she calls off for Gwynplaine, and walks with outstretched arms toward camera. Homo follows her from the Green Box door.

427   EXT. LONDON STREET

MED. LONG SHOT toward the curve in the street. As scene cuts in, the procession of Gwynplaine's turns the curve in the street and the coach rumbles around in out of picture, followed by the cavalcade of gentlemen. Lord David is now in the rear of this cavalcade and watching back along the street. The crowds in the street surge, forward, filling the street again after the passing of the procession.

428   EXT. LONDON STREET

MED. SHOT of the corner of the street where it makes the
curve. As scene cuts in, the last of the gentlemen gallop
around the corner. Lord David reins in his horse and drops
from the procession as he looks back toward camera with a
watchful gaze of interest.

429   EXT. LONDON STREET

MED. SHOT of the crowded street toward the Green Box. Through
the crowd, Dea is trying to make her way with outstretched
hands. She is buffeted back and forth by the rough crowd
and walks in a bewildered manner as she calls Gwynplaine.
Homo walks beside her.

430   EXT. LONDON STREET

MED. SHOT of the Green Box. Ursus looks around from his
seat with a shocked expression as he sees Dea running through
the crowd. He calls to her and then reins his horses, deliberately turning them around in the street. The crowd
curses and swears at him, and Ursus continues in his efforts
to turn the Green Box around and drive back to Dea. He is
unable to climb down from the seat as he is hemmed in by
the crowd, and cannot leave the Green Box alone in the middle
of the street.

431   EXT. LONDON STREET

MED. SHOT of Dea as she makes her hazardous way through the
crowd, calling for Gwynplaine at each step. Vehicles just
miss hitting her and the crowd pushes her to and fro. But
still she goes forward with outstretched hands. Her face is
flushed and feverish, but the thought that Gwynplaine is
surely near, holds her up and gives her strength. Homo growls
at the passer-by as he tries to protect her. TROLLEY
CAMERA WITH HER THROUGH THE CROWD AS SHE WALKS ALONG.

432   EXT. HOUSE OF LORDS

MED. SHOT under the arched way of the King's Gate. As scene
cuts in, Gwynplaine's coach enters picture and stops. The
attendants form a semi-circle around the carriage. The footmen jump down and stand at attention. The USHER OF THE BLACK
ROD alights and waits for Gwynplaine's appearance. Then
Barkilphedro enters picture. He is in a gorgeous costume,
as Chief Steward of Gwynplaine's household. With proud step,
he walks to the door of the coach and opens it. Gwynplaine
alights from the coach. The camera shifts, as the Usher of
the Black Rod leads the way, and Gwynplaine follows toward
the small side door above the roadway. They enter the door
and it closes behind them. Gwynplaine is the last to enter.
Two guards are standing beside the door. They are pike-men.

433   EXT. LONDON STREET

MED. SHOT of Dea. She makes her way through the crowd with
difficulty, still calling Gwynplaine, with Homo beside her.
She is becoming desperate and whirls around and round in a
circle. In her confusion, she is jostled and falls to the
ground, as if smothered under the weight of the crowd.

434   EXT. LONDON STREET

MED. CLOSE SHOT of Lord David. He is looking off as he rides
toward camera through the crowd and watching Dea's progress.
Of course, he recognizes her from the Green Box show. With
an exclamation, he reins in his horse and dismounts as he
sees Dea fall beneath the crowd. Then he starts from picture
leading his horse.

435   EXT. LONDON STREET

MED. CLOSE SHOT of Dea. She lies motionless upon the street
where she has fallen beneath the crowd. Homo is standing
over her, on guard, and shows his teeth as he holds the crowd
back from trampling her under foot. Some try to help her,
but Homo drives them back, keeping the space clear around
her. Then Lord David enters picture. He shows no fear at
Homo's growl and bends down, lifting Dea up to a sitting
position on the pavement. The people fall back, leaving
them alone. Lord David's action has brought Dea to, slightly
and she murmurs faintly in her semi-conscious state, calling
for Gwynplaine. Lord David smiles sarcastically at the name
as he repeats it after her. Then, he looks out of picture
with a shrewd narrowing of his eyes and talks as he voices
his thoughts aloud.

TITLE   "So this clown left his lady love to
                         become a Lord! How like a nobleman."

BACK: He finishes title and turns his attention to Dea again
as she still continues to murmur Gwynplaine's name plaintively.
Lord David lifts her to her feet. He starts from picture
with her, half carrying her along, as she still murmurs and
calls for Gwynplaine. Homo runs back out of picture to bring
Ursus.

436   INT. HOUSE OF LORDS GALLERY

MED. FULL SHOT This is the gallery that extends from the Gothic State
Chamber and the Painted Chamber to the threshold of the
House of Lords during this period of history. There are tows
of pilasters and between the spaces, alternate sentinels,
pike-men of England, and halberdiers of Scotland in magnificent kilts. At the end of the gallery, is a circular space in
front of a magnificent door. A large armchair is under the
have window. The Lord Chancellor is seated in this chair in
his robes. Gwynplaine's procession enters the door from the
Painted Chamber, as scene cuts in. The brilliant costumes
make a gorgeous picture. The Usher of the Black Rod comes
first, then the Principal King-at-arms next. The mace-
bearer of the peers of England precedes Gwynplaine. Two
ancient lords, and Gwynplaine's sponsors follow through
the gallery as the Camera TROLLEYS WITH THE PROCESSION
TOWARD THE WINDOW

437   INT. HOUSE OF LORDS GALLERY

MED. SHOT toward the huge window and the Lord Chancellor's
chair beneath it. Gwynplaine's procession enters picture
and groups around the Lord Chancellor of England in the
proper manner. The oath is administered to Gwynplaine by
the Lord Chancellor, with closeups ad lib. The ceremony of
investiture commences after the proper manner

438   EXT. HOUSE OF LORDS

MED. CLOSE SHOT of the little door under the arched way
of the King's gate. Lord David enters picture with Dea.
He supports her and looks the way to the door. The guards
recognize Lord Dirry-Moir as a Lord, and bow before him
admitting him. Lord Dirry-Moir enters with Dea and the door
closes after them.

439   EXT. HOUSE OF LORDS

MED. CLOSE SHOT of Gwynplaine's coach. Barkilphedro is standing beside the coach door. His faces shows the surprise and
consternation that he feels as he sees Lord David Dirry-
Moir taking Dea into the House of Lords. Quickly, Barkilphedro walks from picture.

440   EXT. HOUSE OF LORDS

MED. CLOSE SHOT of the little door. Barkilphedro enters
picture. He talks to the guard, indicating that he is Lord
Clancharlie's Chief Steward. They allow him to pass and he
enters the door quickly, closing it after him.

441 EXT. ANTECHAMBER ROOM

MED. SHOT. This is a small stone room. It is a small
vestibule-like room which lords from the outer door
of the first chamber of the House of Lords. Barkilphedro enters through the outer door, closing it after
him as scene cuts in. He takes a step forward, but
hesitates to go farther. He peers off, hoping to catch
a glimpse of where Lord Dirry-Moir took Dea. Curiosity
and a shrewd watchfulness are apparent as he looks around
him.

442 EXT. HOUSE OF LORDS

MED. SHOT shooting along the wall of the House of Lords
toward a quiet portion of the roadway. As scene cuts in,
Homo runs into picture, followed by the Green Box with
Ursus driving. Homo has led the way. Ursus stops his
horses and climbs down with a bewildered look as he real-
zes that Dea has been taken into the House of Lords. He
follows Homo out of picture.

443 EXT. HOUSE OF LORDS

MED. CLOSE SHOT of the little door under the arched way.
Ursus follows Homo into picture. He steps before the door
and hesitates. Then he knocks upon the door cautiously.
The door opens and the guard looks out at Ursus in surprise.
Ursus questions him about Dea. The guard shakes his head
and tells Ursus to get away, that this is the House of Lords.
Ursus takes a step as though to push past the guard. But the
guard gives him a rough push and throws him violently away
from the door. Then the door closes. Ursus picks himself
up from the pavement and Homo jumps at the door with fierce
growls. Then Ursus pulls Homo and walks out of picture to
wait developments in a safer spot, as Homo follows him.

444   INT. HOUSE OF LORDS GALLERY

MED. SHOT toward the Lord Chancellor's chair. The
ceremony of Gwynplaine's investiture is finished.
THE-KING-AT-ARMS buckles the golden sword around
Gwynplaine's waist. His peer's robe is placed upon
him, and he is presented with the Red Book. The two
clerks beside the Lord Chancellor's chair write in the
register of the CROWN and in the register of the HOUSE.
The Lord Chancellor signs both books, as the clerks bring
them to him. Then the Lord Chancellor arises and greets
Gwynplaine.

445   INT. HOUSE OF LORDS GALLERY

CLOSE SHOT of the Lord Chancellor of England. He talks
with great dignity:

TITLE: "Lord Clancharlie, Baron
                        Clancharlie, Baron Baskerville,
                        Marquis of Corleone in Sicily, be
                        you welcome among your peers, the
                        lords spirtual and temporal, of
                        Great Britain."

BACK: As he finishes title and lapses into silence.

446   INT. HOUSE OF LORDS GALLERY

CLOSEUP of Gwynplaine. He stands before the Lord Chancellor's chair in his red velvet peer's robe, bordered
with ermine and with his golden sword buckled around him.
His mask still covers the lower part of his face. The
hands of Gwynplaine's two sponsors, the ancient lords
enter the picture and touch his shoulder. He turns around

447   INT HOUSE OF LORDS GALLERY

MED. SHOT toward the door of the House of Lords.
As scene cuts in, it swings open, and Gwynplaine
starts toward it. The ceremony is over and he is
an invested peer of England. He starts through the
door to take his seat in the House of Lords.

448   INT. HOUSE OF LORDS

MED. FULL SHOT. This is the room of the House of
Lords as described in Victor Hugo's book and is the
room used in this period of England's history. A
gorgeous assembly is present. The Lords are occupying
their places as they sit in their magnificent robes on
this tier-like seats that extend around three sides of
the vast room. The usual clerks of the House are kneeling. Queen Anne is seated in her throne chair at one
end of the room. There is a gallery-
like partitioned enclosure, the Duchess Josiana is sitting
all alone. As scene cuts in to the registering of the
foregoing atmosphere and personages, Gwynplaine enters
from the gallery courtway. There is an expectant clapping
of hands in his direction as he walks first to the throne
chair, followed by his two sponsors.

449   INT. HOUSE OF LORDS

MED. CLOSE SHOT of the Duchess Josiana as she sits all
alone in the partitioned enclosure. She is here at the
command of the Queen and is nervous and extremely angry.
She lifts her head in a haughty manner as she sees this
man whom she sent from her apartment and to whom the Queen
has betrothed her. This clown who has become a lord.

450   INT. HOUSE OF LORDS

MED. CLOSE SHOT of the throne chair. As seen cuts
in, Gwynplaine enters picture and greets the Queen
in the proper manner for his station. She bids him
rise, and talks with a commanding air.

TITLE   "You will remove your mask, My Lord-
                         so that your peers may see the Duchess
                         Josiana's future husband."

CUT FROM TITLE TO FOLLOWING SCENE

451   INT. HOUSE OF LORDS

CLOSEUP of Gwynplaine. As scene cuts in, he slowly takes
off his mask. There is a confusion in his attitude and
he is bewildered, not understand the Queen's reference
to the Duchess and her future husband. His figure and poise
is lordly as he stands before the Queen in his peer's robe.
But his terrible laugh ridicules the whole effect, now that
his mask is removed.

452   INT. HOUSE OF LORDS

MED. SHOT of the other lords as they sit in their tier-like
benches along the walls. They lean forward and one by one,
they burst into hilarious laughter at the sight of Gwynplaine's
face. The camera runs along the line of seats with closeups
ad lib, so the various lords and peers of England succumb to
the contagious merriment.

453   INT. HOUSE OF LORDS

CLOSE SHOT of the Duchess Josiana as she sits alone
in the partitioned enclosure. The laughter is like
the stab of a sword to her. The Queen has deliberately
belittled her and she must sit through it and stand the
terrible insults. She stiffens up and attempts to brazen
it out as her eyes blaze forth with hatred at her torment-
tor.

454   INT HOUSE OF LORDS

CLOSE SHOT of the Queen. She is well pleased with her
revenge upon this sister whom she hates. She smiles
acidly as her eyes glance out of picture toward the Duchess
Josiana with a triumphant gaze of malice.

455   INT. HOUSE OF LORDS

MED. FULL SHOT. The House is reeking with merriment.
The peers and lords have lost their dignity completely,
and are nudging each other and giving vent to their mirth.
The Duchess Josiana is like one upon the rack, while the
Queen watches the scene, gloating over her torture. Gwynplaine looks around him and bows his head a bit before the
laughter and he realizes that he is being ridiculed.

456   INT. HOUSE OF LORDS GALLERY

MED. SHOT toward the door to the House of Lords. As scene
cuts in, Lord David is leading Dea along the gallery toward
the door to the House of Lords. He stops as he hears the
laughter inside, and speaks to Dea:

                             CONT'D

466   CONT'D

TITLE: "We have found your noble Gwynplaine -
                          you can plainly hear for yourself."

BACK: He finishes title and the emotion that Gwynplaine
is near at last, giving Dea new strength. Lord David has
brought her here, thinking to embarrass Gwynplaine.
He steps toward the door to open it as Dea walks toward it
with outstretched hands and a feverish look of hope upon
her face. It may be that Gwynplaine is not dead; her heart
has told her that he is near ever since she walked from
the Green Box into the streets.

467   INT. HOUSE OF LORDS

MED. CLOSE SHOT of Gwynplaine before the Queen. He lifts
his head and asks permission of the Queen to speak. She
inclines her head, and Gwynplaine talks:

TITLE: "My betrothal to this Duchess Josiana
                          is impossible, Your Royal Majesty -
                          I am already betrothed and love another.

BACK: He finishes title as the Queen takes it with a look
of displeasure at his insolence.

458   INT. HOUSE OF LORDS

MED. SHOT of the door that leads into the House of Lords
from the gallery. The door is open and Dea is standing
alone in the doorway. The two doormen have not noticed
her, as they are doubled up with laughter at this funny
looking Lord. Dea has heard Gwynplaine's voice, and with
a happy cry of "Gwynplaine" she runs from picture with outstretched arms toward camera and the direction of the voice.

459   INT. HOUSE OF LORDS

MED. CLOSE SHOT of Gwynplaine, as he stands with his back
to camera and in front of the Queen. As scene cuts in,
he turns around, facing camera and an exclamation of wonder
escapes him as he sees Dea. He starts out of picture
quickly toward her. The Queen forgets her displeasure
for the moment, in the amazement and curiosity this scene
affords her.

460   INT. HOUSE OF LORDS.

MED. FULL SHOT. As the Lords and peers continue to laugh
in their enjoyment and acting as though they were attending
a show of some kind. Gwynplaine rushes across the vast
chamber toward Dea, as she rushes toward him. As he reaches
her, her strength fails her and he grasps her quickly before
she falls to the floor.

461   INT. HOUSE OF LORDS.

MED. CLOSE SHOT of Gwynplaine and Dea. She slings to him and
touches him with her hands, asking him whether it is really he.
Gwynplaine forgets his surroundings, everything, as she tells
him how she thought he was dead, and how they have been ordered
from England. Gwynplaine holds her to him and walks with her
from picture toward the Queen's throne.

462   INT. HOUSE OF LORDS

MED. CLOSE SHOT of the Queen's throne chair. The Queen watches
Gwynplaine as he leads Dea into picture. He tells the
Queen that this is the girl he loves and the girl he must
marry - that nothing else matters to him. The Queen holds
up her hand and bids him be quiet.

463   INT. HOUSE OF LORDS

CLOSE SHOT of the Queen. She looks off with a displeased
expression and talks:

TITLE

> "It is our pleasure that you wed Her Grace
> the Duchess - and a lord can but obey his
> Queen's command.

BACK: She finishes title with an air of finality and a
shrewd narrowing of her eyes as though she were enjoying
the unusual situation.

464   INT. HOUSE OF LORDS

        SEMI CLOSE SHOT of Gwynplaine as he holds Dea to him protest-
        ingly. He looks off around him with a lordly attitude.
        But his grin belies the serious look in his eyes. He talks:

TITLE   "I am a lord - yet you laugh at me! I must
                         act as a lord - yet a lordly hand stamped
                         this laugh upon my face!"

        BACK: He finishes title and continues. He is so serious
        that for a moment his mouth draws down so that his face is
        more terrible in its look of denunciation.

465   INT. HOUSE OF LORDS

        MED. SHOT of a section of the lords as they sit in their
        tiers of seats. The camera pans over them, getting their
        expressions. The laughter is fading from some of their
        faces. Others lean forward interestedly. Some old man wake
        up with a start as their neighbors nudge them. There is an
        air of anticipation and amazement at this man's speech.

466   INT. HOUSE OF LORDS

        CLOSEUP of Gwynplaine. He talks as he looks off, his mouth
        still held down into a terrible seriousness by sheer
        will power.

TITLE: "What is my laugh?"

        BACK: He finishes title and again his laugh breaks beyond his
        control and he grins more horribly than ever. He does not
        heed it as he pauses and looks around, stirred to the
        depths by his thoughts.

467   INT. HOUSE OF LORDS

             MED. CLOSE SHOT of two cordial characters in the lords'
             seats. The are fat and registered as high livers. They
             have their arms around each other and are rocking with
             laughter as they see again the laugh on Gwynplaine's face.
             One manages to shout an answer to Gwynplaine's question.

TITLE   "Tis a cure for my spleen, thou funny
                           fellow!"

             BACK: He finishes title and wipes his eyes, coughing
             violently as the other slaps him on the back.

468   INT. HOUSE OF LORDS

             CLOSEUP of Gwynplaine. He looks around and his gaze
             centers on the two who answered him. He talks, as he
             continues:

TITLE   "My laugh is a symbol of your lordly cries and
                           the cruelty of these times.

             CUT FROM TITLE TO FOLLOWING SCENE

469   INT. HOUSE OF LORDS

             MED. FULL SHOT. The Queen is looking at Gwynplaine in a
             curious manner. A sight like this is so unusual that it
             amuses her. The lords are in a turmoil. Some start to
             stand up, waving their arms at Gwynplaine as if to stop him.
             Others pull them back into their seats and tell them to
             let him go on. Others shout ridicule at him. Others are
             threatening in their attitude. Still others take it all as
             a part of a show, and laugh at him as though he were a clown.

470   INT. HOUSE OF LORDS.

         MED. CLOSE SHOT of an old peer. He is deaf and carries an
         ear trumpet. He leans toward his neighbor and talks:

TITLE   "How did he vote?"

         BACK: The other lord looks at the old peer in a disgusted
         manner and yells through the horn at him.

TITLE   "against everything!"

         BACK: The old peer nods his head and adjust his glasses
         as he peers off at Gwynplaine. He talks to his neighbor
         with conviction.

TITLE   "I can well understand it, with a face like his."

         BACK: He finishes title and promptly closes his eyes to go
         to sleep again, now that his curiosity is satisfied.

471   INT. HOUSE OF LORDS

         CLOSE SHOT of Gwynplaine. He looks around and continues
         his speech through the turmoil.

TITLE   "At whom am I laughing? At you - at myself -
                         at everything!"

         CUT FROM TITLE TO FOLLOWING SCENE

472   INT. HOUSE OF LORDS

            MED. CLOSE SHOT of an incensed peer of the House. He
            shouts off.

TITLE   "The House of Lords returns thanks to the
                             Green Box for the wisdom of a buffoon!"

            BACK: He finishes title, continuing to hurl ridicule at
            Gwynplaine.

473   INT. HOUSE OF LORDS

            CLOSE SHOT of Gwynplaine. Dea stirs nervously as she
            listens to his fiery words. She cannot understand it all
            and nestles close to him, feeling the turmoil around them.
            Gwynplaine finishes his speech in an outburst of de-
            nunciation.

TITLE   "Behind this laugh are the tortured cries
                             of the poor - the tears of the suffering, the
                             beggars, the hungry, the human worms beneath
                             your heals!"

            BACK: He finishes title and turns with Dea. He picks her
            up in his arms and turns in the direction of the Queen's
            chair.

474   INT. HOUSE OF LORDS.

            MED. CLOSE SHOT of the Queen's chair. Gwynplaine stands
            before the Queen as he holds Dea in his arms. He talks with
            a determined air,

TITLE   "A king made me a clown. Your Royal Majesty has
                             made me a lord. But God first made me a man -
                             and Dea a woman."

            BACK: Gwynplaine finishes title and instinctively holds Dea
            closer to him, as Dea nestles against him in the circle of
            his protecting arms.

475   INT. HOUSE OF LORDS

     MED. FULL SHOT. Without another word, Gwynplaine bows
     before the Queen and backs away from the throne. Then
     he turns and carries Dea across the vast chamber, on
     his way to the gallery door. The lords watch his progress,
     talking together, nudging each other and laughing at this
     wonderfully funny fellow.

476   INT. HOUSE OF LORDS

     CLOSE SHOT of the Duchess Josiana. She arises in her seat.
     There is a look of fury in her face at this added insult.
     This laughing mountebank has scorned her in front of the
     Court, and in front of the Queen, who seeks to belittle
     her dignity. Unable to hold her rage in check any longer
     the Duchess blurts out angrily:

TITLE   "Seize him! Seize this laughing mountebank,
        who dares insult the Queen of England!"

     BACK: She finishes title in an effort to wreak vengeance
     upon the only person she is able to hurt.

477   INT. HOUSE OF LORDS

     CLOSE SHOT of the Queen. She looks off with a shrewd

              (continued)

477   (Continued)

glance toward her sister and does not raise her hand
against Gwynplaine. He has unknowingly capped the
climax of her revenge against this sister she hates.
Nothing could have caused this Queen greater satisfaction.

478   INT. HOUSE OF LORDS

MED. CLOSE SHOT of the gallery door; as scene cuts in,
Gwynplaine enters picture on his way from the House of
Lords. In uncertain response to the Duchess Josiana's
plea, the two guards stop in front of Gwynplaine and
block his path in a threatening manner, as if awaiting
the Queen's command. Gwynplaine looks at them and
talks with great dignity.

TITLE   "Make way for a Peer of England."

BACK: He finishes title. The guards hesitate a moment
and then step aside from Gwynplaine's path. He opens the
door and through it, the long gallery can be seen extending toward background. Gwynplaine enters doorway
and starts down the gallery with Dea in his arms.

479   INT HOUSE OF LORDS

MED. FULL SHOT - shooting from the gallery door toward
the Queen. The Queen is motionless and pays no attention to the pandemonium that has broken loose in the
chamber. The lords and dignified peers of England shout
and hold their sides with laughter. It has been a great
performance - and they laugh and wipe the tears from
their eyes - in their hilarious mirth.

480   INT HOUSE OF LORDS - GALLERY

MED SHOT toward Gwynplaine, as he walks toward camera
along the gallery. He passes the silent figures of the
pike-men and the guards in their Scotch kilts. He
walks into f.g. and stops, as Dea moves weakly in his
arms. He stops and looks down at her. She talks
weakly:

TITLE   "Hold me closer, my Gwynplaine - it
                         is cold - and the darkness is creeping
                         around me - "

BACK: She finishes title, and Gwynplaine slips his
Peer's robe from his shoulders. Then he wraps her
warmly in it. The ermine border frames her pale face.
She snuggles closer to Gwynplaine, and he holds her tenderly to him - soothing her and telling her that now
everything will be all right. A sudden anxious look is
dawning in his face. Dea looks so pale. Maybe he has
come back too late. He pushes the thought from him and
starts from picture quickly. But there is a look of
anxiety in his eyes. But his laugh contradicts this
look.

481   INT HOUSE OF LORDS - GALLERY

MED CLOSE SHOT - with the camera moving along the gallery wall, as Gwynplaine walks along. The pike-men are
seen as the camera passes them. Some laugh outright at
Gwynplaine's face - while others stifle their laughs
with difficulty. All are laughing in the face of this
funny peer of England.

482   INT HOUSE OF LORDS - GALLERY

CLOSE SHOT of Gwynplaine's face. He looks off with a
steady gaze as he walks along. But the terrible laugh
upon his face contradicts the agony in his eyes. He
slowly bends his head so that his laugh is hidden from
the camera. His eyes are now seen to be full of tears.
They are tears of anxiety. They drop out of picture.

483   INT. HOUSE OF LORDS - GALLERY

           CLOSE UP of the ermine border of the Peer's robe,
           as it covers Dea in Gwynplaine's arms. As scene
           cuts in, Gwynplaine's tears drop down upon the ermine
           that signifies his lordly estate.

484   INT HOUSE OF LORDS - GALLERY

           CLOSE SHOT of Gwynplaine's feet. As he walks along
           the end of the Peer's robe is dragging along the
           floor, as it hangs down.

485   INT HOUSE OF LORDS - ENTRANCE ROOM

           MED SHOT. As scene transposes in, Gwynplaine is walking
           toward the outer door as he carries Dea. Barkilphedro is
           waiting for him, with a look of annoyed amazement as he
           sees him carrying Dea. Gwynplaine does not even notice
           Barkilphedro as he makes for the outer door. Barkilphedro's
           face quickly masks his annoyance by a look of servility.
           He hurries ahead of Gwynplaine and opens the door for him.
           Then he follows him out as the door closes after them.

486   EXT. HOUSE OF LORDS

           MED CLOSE SHOT of Gwynplaine's coach. As scene cuts in,
           Barkilphedro runs into picture, ahead of Gwynplaine and
           opens the door of the coach with a flourish. The lackeys
           stand at attention, but Gwynplaine does not enter picture.

487   EXT HOUSE OF LORDS

MED CLOSE SHOT of the little door of the King's
Gate. Gwynplaine is standing in picture. The
guards pay no attention to him as they stand in
stiff attitudes of attention, but having a hard
time to keep smiles from their faces. He holds
Dea closer to him - with an anxious look at her
face - and looks off around - wondering where
the Green Box can be. Of course, Dea has told
him that it was near.

488   EXT LONDON STREET

MED CLOSE SHOT of Ursus and Homo - as they wait
for Dea's reappearance. In picture, the end of
the Green Box projects into scene. It is around
the corner from the House of Lords' entrance. Suddenly, Homo barks and runs around the corner and
out of picture. Ursus takes a step forward toward
the corner - and peeks around it cautiously - to
see what has caused Homo's excitement.

489   EXT LONDON STREET

CLOSE SHOT of a street corner. As scene cuts in,
Ursus looks around corner toward camera. A startled
gaze of amazement appears on his face - as he sees
Gwynplaine - out of picture. He rubs his eyes in
unbelief. He looks - motionless - but careful not to
show himself to any of the guards that may be watching.

490   EXT HOUSE OF LORDS

MED CLOSE SHOT of Gwynplaine - as he stands before
the little door under the archway. He is looking
down at Dea - as he holds her in his arms. There
is a worried expression upon his face - as he watches
her. Then he holds her against him - and looks up as
Homo runs into picture. Gwynplaine sees him and Homo
jumps up at him. Then Gwynplaine starts from picture,
pulling the door closed behind him. Homo leads the
way with joyful barks.

491   EXT HOUSE OF LORDS

MED SHOT of Gwynplaine's coach. The footman wait
as before. Barkilphedro stands beside the open
coach door. They bow more deeply as Gwynplaine
enters picture - following Homo. Barkilphedro steps
aside - with a bow -as if he expected Gwynplaine to
get into the coach. But Gwynplaine walks on past -
without a look at Barkilphedro or the coach. As he
exits - Barkilphedro looks after him. Then he starts
out of picture, to ascertain what it is all about.

492   EXT LONDON STREET

MED CLOSE SHOT of the Green Box. Gwynplaine rounds
the corner into picture - following Homo. Ursus is
on. He looks at Gwynplaine - in wonder - then rushes
to him. He touches him and talks in hysterical joy;
asking whether it is really he - and whether he is
really alive. Gwynplaine nods and turns Ursus' attention to Dea. He quickly carries her into the Green
Box. Ursus follows him up the steps - and Homo jumps
through the door after them.

493   EXT LONDON STREET

MED CLOSE SHOT. A reverse shot toward the corner,
As scene cuts in, Barkilphedro is seen as he watches
around the corner - with a shrewd gaze of displeasure.
He starts around the corner, toward camera.

494   INT GREEN BOX

MED CLOSE SHOT of bed - in rear compartment. Dea
is lying upon the bed where Gwynplaine has placed
her. She seem brighter and smiles up toward Gwynplaine - as he and Ursus stand beside the bed.
Gwynplaine looks down at her anxiously - and feels
her head - in a worried manner. Homo sits upon the
floor silently. Ursus looks Gwynplaine up and down -
and talks:

TITLE   "To think - that you are a Lord -
                         and rich!"

BACK. He finishes title - and Gwynplaine looks up
at him with a tragic expression. He talks in answer:

TITLE   "My riches are here. I never knew
                         how rich I really was - before."

BACK. He finishes title and then looks quickly out
of picture - as though he heard someone at the door.
Ursus looks off also - and Homo gets to his feet -
and growls.

495   EXT. LONDON STREET

               MED. CLOSE SHOT of the Green Box. Barkilphedro is on at
               the door knocking. He knocks again with a respectful
               attitude. But there is a shrewd glance upon his face as
               he watches the door.

496   INT. GREEN BOX

               MED. SHOT toward the door. Gwynplaine walks to the door and
               opens it. Ursus and Homo watch beside the bed as Barkilphedro
               enters. He bows respectfully to Gwynplaine and tells him that
               his coach is waiting. Without a word, Gwynplaine walks to the
               bed and picks up the ermine bordered Peer's robe. He unbuckles
               the sword from around his waist and walks back to Barkilphedro;
               he hands the Peer's robe and the sword to him. Barkilphedro
               takes them with a look of awe, and Gwynplaine reaches in his
               costume and takes out his purse. He weighs it in his hand and
               drops it in Barkilphedro's waiting palm. Then he indicates
               the door, telling Barkilphedro to leave. Barkilphedro argues
               respectfully against such foolishness, but Gwynplaine ushers
               him to the door.

497   INT. GREEN BOX

               MED. CLOSE SHOT of rear door. As scene cuts in, Barkilphedro
               backs into picture and Gwynplaine follows him in. Gwynplaine
               talks, interrupting Barkilphedro's arguments.

TITLE   "Once you informed us that Gwynplaine the clown
                         was dead. I now inform you of the death of a
                         peer of England."

               BACK: He finishes title and opens the door. Barkilphedro
               backs out with a look of awe.

498   EXT. LONDON STREET

MED. CLOSE SHOT of the Green Box. Barkilphedro backs out the
door and Gwynplaine shuts it after him. Barkilphedro forgets
the step and walks backwards, doing a comedy roll to the pavement. He sits on the pavement as the Green Box starts away
from him down the street. He forgets everything but his loss,
and shakes his fist after the Green Box as it drives away toward
background.

FADE OUT

FADE IN

499   EXT. THAMES WHARF   NIGHT SEQUENCE

MED. SHOT. As scene fades in, a two-masted vessel is seen
against the wharf. In background, a heavy mist hangs over the
River Thames. Little lights pass back and forth through the
mist. Upon the deck of the vessel, the Green Box is seen as
it stands silently beneath the shadow of a mast. The ship starts
away from the wharf, catches the tide of the river and floats
away into the mist.

LAP DISSOLVE OUT AND INTO:

500   EXT. BACK OF SHIP

MED. CLOSE SHOT of Gwynplaine and Dea as they stand beside the
steps of the Green Box. Ursus is watching them from the door
above. The little lantern is shining over the doorway, and
lights up the group upon the deck. Dea nestles against Gwynplaine as he holds her protectingly in his arms. Ursus descends
to them and Homo appears in the entrance and lies down, watching
the group with a happy air. Ursus walks to Gwynplaine and
Gwynplaine reaches out his hand and grips the old man's shoulder.
Ursus grasps Gwynplaine's arm and shakes with emotion as he
drops his old, weary head upon it.

501   EXT. BACK OF SHIP

CLOSEUP of Ursus. He raises his head. There are tears of
joy in his eyes. He talks brokenly:

TITLE   "My son! You have saved Dea's life -
                         and mended the broken heart of a weary
                         old man."

BACK: He finishes title and turns his head away to hide the
flood of tears that fall down his cheeks.

225

502   EXT. DECK OF SHIP

MED. CLOSE SHOT of group. Ursus turns away from Gwynplaine
and Dea. As he starts from them, Gwynplaine grips his shoulder
with a last affectionate grip. Then he returns his arms around
the form of Dea. Ursus walks from picture. Gwynplaine leans
down and whispers his love to Dea, as she lays her head against
his shoulder, Slowly, he walks from picture with her, away
from camera, in the opposite direction to that taken by Ursus.

503   INT. CASTLE ROOM

MED. CLOSE SHOT of a corner. It is a stone, tower-like room
and only a corner of it is necessary. Barkilphedro is on. A
chair is in picture. Upon the chair is lying his gorgeous
costume, as Gwynplaine's Chief Steward. His jester's stick
also lies upon a chair. Barkilphedro is in the act of finishing
dressing, in his old jester's suit. He looks at it with a
grimace of hatred, and lifts up the other suit and shakes his
head sadly. He puts it back and picks up his jester's stick.
He looks at the jester's stick with a nasty sneer, and talks
to it.

504   EXT. RIVER THAMES

LONG SHOT. Ursus' ship is sailing away from camera. The mist
hangs over the river in background. At one point, the moon
breaks through the mist, partially silhouetting the ship, as
it recedes into the distance. Upon the deck, two forms are
visible in the moonlight. They are Dea and Gwynplaine, as they
stand beside the rail of the ship, journeying toward the path
of happiness over the moonlight. The mist closes in about the
ship, and it disappears into the distance as the fog swallows
it up.

FADE OUT

FINIS

Greta Garbo gets a visit from Lon Chaney (in his "Road to Mandalay" makeup) on her set - Behind Chaney is Clarence Brown who was set to direct him in "The Man Who Laughs" in 1924

Following is an article written by Adela Rogers St. Johns, which appeared in *Liberty Magazine* in May of 1931, about 9 months after Lon Chaney's death. This is the first time a detailed first hand account of Chaney's marriage to his first wife Cleva, as well as family members and co-workers memories.

Lon

A Portrait of the Man Behind a Thousand Faces

By
ADELA ROGERS
ST. JOHNS

who has won note as a writer for the screen and about the men and women who animate it, and whose life stories of motion-picture stars, several of which have appeared in Liberty, have stood out as vivid and searching portraits painted from first-hand acquaintance. She was born in Los Angeles, grew up there, and still lives near by.

Picture by Dan Sayre Groesbeck

"Maybe you'd like to hear me sing," said Cleva.

(*Reading time: 31 minutes 12 seconds.*)

PART ONE—"LAUGH, CLOWN!" AND LOVE

THIS is the first time that the story of Lon Chaney has ever been told.

For many years he lived in the world's spotlight. His famous characterizations seemed in some magic way to hide the man himself.

He was the man of a thousand faces and of no face, the man who earned millions in the picture industry and for it, yet whose doorstep had never been crossed by a motion-picture star or a motion-picture executive.

He was the greatest make-up artist the world has ever known, but even when his cherished make-up box had been laid aside, the slight figure in the old blue suit, with the inevitable red necktie, the inevitable old cap pulled down on the right side of the lean, lined face, revealed little. He fought for silence on the screen to the bitter end and he kept complete silence concerning himself.

It was part of his great showmanship to destroy Lon Chaney as a man. Unlike any other star who has ever been before the camera, he sold not one iota of his own personality. Instead, he touched it with some gray alchemy and it vanished, past, present, future. No one must be conscious that behind those faces, which were his Rembrandts, lived and moved Lon Chaney, the man.

But there was a man.

Against the glitter of Hollywood's background he moves, the symbolic figure of the common man—the average two-fisted, hard-drinking, hard-fighting, self-made American, clean but hot-blooded, square-shooting and simple, loving his friends and hating his enemies, never forgetting a good turn or forgiving a bad one. A man of one idea, without culture but with a shrewd, dogged determination.

It is a type that belonged more to the last generation than to this.

His is the poignant epic of the man in the streets, who fought his way up alone and single-handed. Within it are all those common heartbreaks and tragedies, those joys and sorrows, defeats and victories which make of every human life a drama, which go on beneath the smooth surface existence of your next-door neighbor, which are buried in the forgotten past of every family.

As the marines in full dress stood at attention beside the casket of Lon Chaney, an old studio organ and a trembling violin began to play the melody of that great song associated always with his name, "Laugh, Clown, Laugh."

It was his last request, spoken almost with his last words.

"I want Sam and Jack to play 'Laugh, Clown, Laugh' for me—if the time comes," he whispered, and tried to smile as the mysterious hand of death began to close about his tired throat.

So Sam and Jack Feinberg, two boys who had played for him on every picture since The Hunchback of Notre Dame, bravely played for ears that could not hear the music Chaney had loved so well.

Perhaps Lon knew best.

Perhaps in death he chose for himself the theme song of his life, as it had been in some measure the theme of every picture he ever played.

I wonder what was in Lon's mind as he chose that song in those last short minutes when a man's unalterable life passes before his blurring vision.

Did he remember the young wife he had divorced on April Fool's Day so many years before? The girl with the golden voice who passed out of the picture before the world knew or cared about Lon Chaney, but who left him a son and indelible things written on his soul?

Chaney

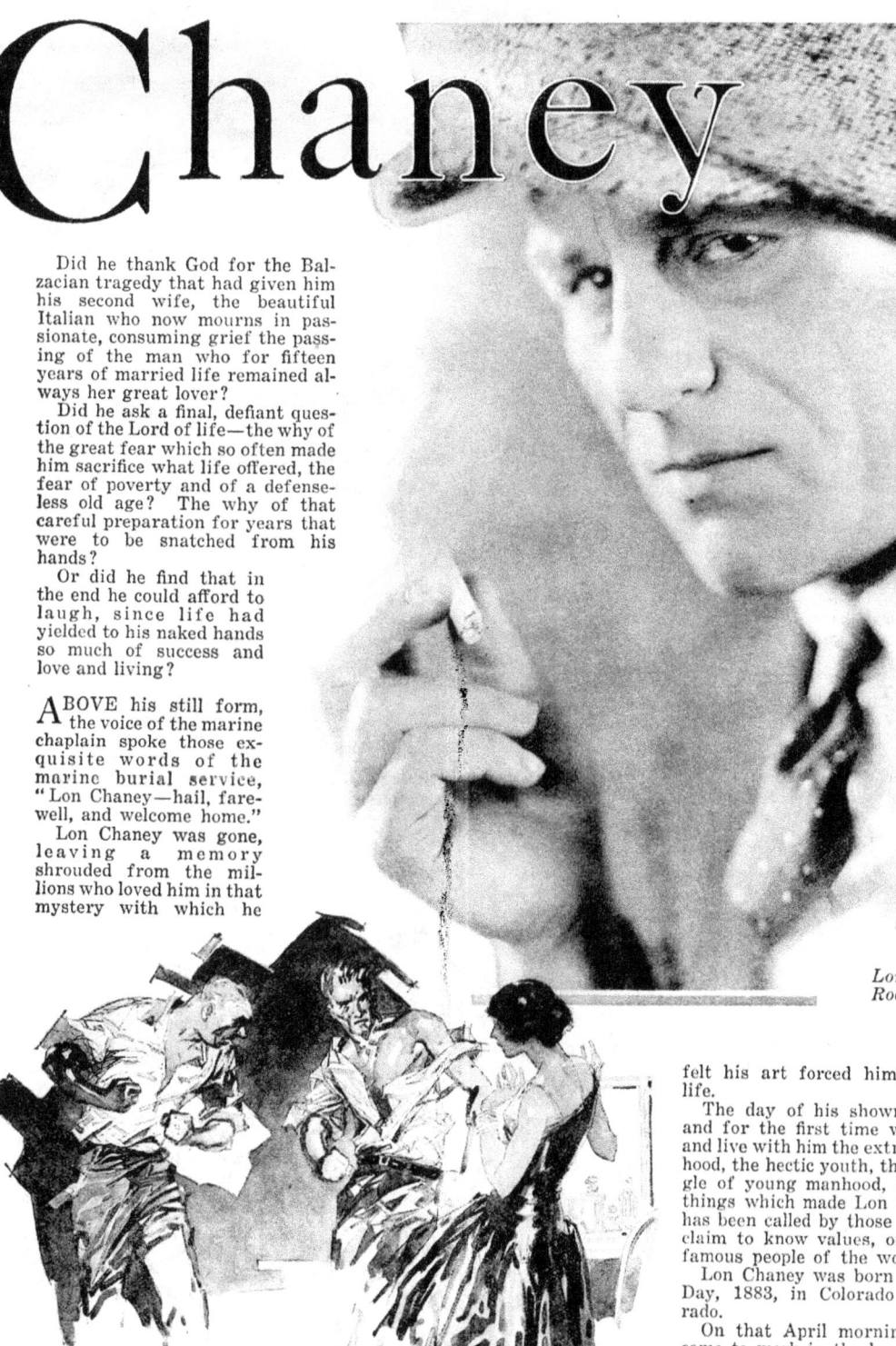

Did he thank God for the Balzacian tragedy that had given him his second wife, the beautiful Italian who now mourns in passionate, consuming grief the passing of the man who for fifteen years of married life remained always her great lover?

Did he ask a final, defiant question of the Lord of life—the why of the great fear which so often made him sacrifice what life offered, the fear of poverty and of a defenseless old age? The why of that careful preparation for years that were to be snatched from his hands?

Or did he find that in the end he could afford to laugh, since life had yielded to his naked hands so much of success and love and living?

ABOVE his still form, the voice of the marine chaplain spoke those exquisite words of the marine burial service, "Lon Chaney—hail, farewell, and welcome home."

Lon Chaney was gone, leaving a memory shrouded from the millions who loved him in that mystery with which he

Lon Chaney in The Road to Mandalay.

Picture by Dan Sayre Groesbeck

The fight was violent and bloody. Lon's young wife ran down, only to faint.

felt his art forced him to conceal his life.

The day of his showmanship is over and for the first time we may go back and live with him the extraordinary childhood, the hectic youth, the upward struggle of young manhood, and know those things which made Lon Chaney what he has been called by those authorities who claim to know values, one of the seven famous people of the world.

Lon Chaney was born on April Fool's Day, 1883, in Colorado Springs, Colorado.

On that April morning, Pop Chaney came to work in the barber shop of the famous Antlers Hotel beaming with delight. Another boy. Such a fine, healthy boy. He couldn't tell his customers about it, though some of them said to him, "Well, Pop, who left you a fortune today?" Pop read the movements of their lips with his keen eyes, but he could not

[CONTINUED ON NEXT PAGE]

[LON CHANEY
Continued from page seventeen]

answer. Lon's father was not born deaf and dumb. When he was a baby he was terribly poisoned, and could neither speak nor hear from that time on.

He had married a deaf-and-dumb girl, Clara Hennesey, whose mother was head of the first deaf-and-dumb school in Colorado. Back of them were Irish and Scotch, English and French ancestors, who had melted into the great farming and industrial population of the Middle West. People of strong sinews and high courage. The best blood of the land for stamina and grit and progression.

They had handed down that heritage to these two who were to become the mother and father of Lon Chaney.

It has been said that every great man had a great mother. Lon's mother was an astounding woman. A tiny little person, with a bright, round face and expressive black eyes that twinkled appreciation and admonition to her strong, unruly brood of youngsters. As a cook and housekeeper she had no equal.

When the San Francisco earthquake came, all her children had left the nest and were in California. John, the eldest, a stage hand at the old Burbank Theater. Lon, trying to find a foothold in the theatrical world. Carrie, the only girl, married and living in Oakland. George, the baby, following wherever Lon led.

NO use telling Mrs. Chaney that all was well, no use showing her telegrams which said that Carrie and her children were safe in Los Angeles with John. She couldn't speak or hear, but her mind and heart were equal to any journey. Little Mrs. Chaney got on a train and went to California, to see that her "babies" were all safe.

"She would have gone if oceans and continents had divided us," said John Chaney. "There never was such a mother."

When she had ascertained that all was well, and looked over her fine grandchildren, she kissed them all good-by and went back alone to her home and her husband.

If she had a fault, it was that she spoiled them all. Many a time she drew herself up to her four feet ten inches and silently defied teachers who complained of John's wildness and Lon's truancy. She even defied Pop himself, who was a genial, round little man very popular with the customers of the barber shop. Still, Pop would have used the rod now and again upon his riotous sons. He would have had to use it on their mother first.

The Chaney home wasn't a rich one. Pop Chaney, for twenty-seven years behind that one chair, made a good salary, but the needs of a family of six were large and Mrs. Chaney was determined that her kids should have everything that other kids had.

No matter what the cost or the sacrifice, on Christmas morning the clean front room, with its enormous stove blazing against the snow without, was centered about a great Christmas tree. Little Mrs. Chaney strung popcorn and cranberries for ornaments. She made red paper streamers for the cut-glass chandelier, she wove wreaths of holly and evergreen, which the boys had gathered, for the long lace curtains at the windows.

The gifts were not rich, but they were those which through the year her children's hands, in fluent sign language, had told the mother they wanted. Lon's first set of tools, his first bicycle. Clay for modeling.

A closed family circle. Mrs. Chaney didn't like and didn't want outsiders. A great love of homelike things, of a home as the center of life, was born in Lon in those early days.

IT was a Puritan home. Pop Chaney, in the free-and-easy atmosphere of the Antlers Barber Shop, had gained a wider, more tolerant view of life. But Lon's mother had no time and no patience with all that. There it was, set down in the Book, just as it came from the hand of God to Moses on Mount Sinai. All the rest was just weak-willed, self-indulgent quibbling. Nothing could be plainer than the thou-shalt-nots, and the fact that if you were good you went to heaven and if you weren't you went to hell.

The most indelible memory of the whole Chaney family—John, Carrie, and George still live with their families in California—is of the deep devotion between Lon and his mother. He was her favorite and they accepted it without question. Long before the older brother, John, could teach him to speak in words, the baby Lon talked with his mother on his fingers. Expressive hands that were to serve him well later.

He had then, and always, a rare aptitude about the house. The close association with his mother gave him some feminine quality, some almost maternal tenderness, that he never lost. Lon Chaney could cook, could sew, could always fix anything that went wrong, whether it was a door squeak or a blown-out fuse.

Came a day when he made clothes for his baby son, when Cleva Creighton Chaney stood before wildly applauding audiences in dashing evening gowns made for her from odds and ends by her husband's quick, canny fingers.

A born nurse. When his mother was ill with the rheumatism that sometimes quenched her fiery spirit, Lon stayed home from school to take care of her—and loved it. A little fellow who could just reach up to her on the tall, old-fashioned bed, he shifted her pain-racked body, smoothed the sheets, prepared her meals and medicine.

But that wasn't enough. There could be nothing in that room but silence. It was necessary for him to lighten the hours of pain.

Into that spotless quiet, for he was neat as a pin, he brought the world as he knew it for his mother to see. The teachers at school. Mimicking. His playmates at their games. The neighbors and their children and the gossip of the street.

Thus began the pantomime of Lon Chaney. There, for his deaf-and-dumb mother, he developed that genius which was to find its perfect medium on the silent screen.

It is too bad that she didn't live to see his great

Motion Picture
Publications photo

Lon Chaney and his second wife saying a word at the première of a picture.

The wizard of false face: first, as he appeared in The Penalty; and, second, in A Blind Bargain.

In the third picture Chaney makes a quick shift as a blind beggar, and in the fourth he's the sport of The Big City.

Lon Chaney's magic box of make-up, material for a thousand faces.

days, for she knew, she was the only one who believed or guessed, that they were coming. But in 1914 and 1915, when he first made pictures, westerns at Universal, extra bits, heavies, little Mrs. Chaney was the first one to enter the picture house when they played Colorado Springs. Bright as a little sparrow, she would arrive before the doors opened. Everyone knew her. She had the best seat. There she would sit, proud and smiling, through as many shows as there were.

For all her limitations, the art of her favorite son belonged to her completely.

Perhaps that is one reason that Lon had such a deep, violent feeling for silent pictures, why he fought against the talkies to the bitter end and was the last star save Chaplin to yield the great art of pantomime to the lesser art of the mechanical word.

Except in his devotion to his mother, Lon was no model child. Indeed, he was a thoroughgoing little devil. His only record in the grammar school at Colorado Springs is that he played hooky oftener in one term than any other boy.

The magnificent mountains that surround Colorado Springs grew to be part of his being. Their silence, their majesty, their infinite color, gave him a joy that nothing else in all his life was to give him. The mountains always called him. He never got beyond them. The moment he was free of work, he went to them, as a seaman returns to the sea. No man in California ever knew the high Sierras better than Lon Chaney. The far places where man seldom went were his delight.

The one home that will always remain to Lon Chaney's memory is a cabin in the Sierras.

Lon spent the last happy days of his life there, when he returned from the doctors' fatal failure in New York.

Sick unto death, suffering silently, clinging to his wife like a child as he faced shadows deeper than those of mountain twilight among which he must soon walk, he found peace with those last days in the mountain cabin. Too weak to fish for trout, the sport always nearest his

heart, he watched them glimmer by in the little stream before his doorway, watched the sunshine patched among the great trees, watched the sunrise bring light to a waiting world. There the fear of death, which he had acknowledged to but one soul on earth, left him.

To his devoted friend and servant, John Jeske, he said, "There is a line in the Bible that my mother used to love. 'I will lift up mine eyes unto the hills, from whence cometh my help.' That is a good line, John."

When he vanished from Hollywood, when people wondered what Lon Chaney—who didn't go to Europe, to New York, to Agua Caliente—did with himself, he was in the hills, fishing, riding, camping for months on end.

All the Chaney boys had the wanderlust. Their father had it before them, but he was chained. They were not. The pleadings of their mother, the commands of their father, who wanted them fitted for life with a good education, could never control this one thing. They were born with the itching foot.

None of them would finish grammar school.

John left the classroom early and became a stage hand at the opera house in Colorado Springs. It was he who finally brought Lon into the world of the theater.

[CONTINUED ON NEXT PAGE]

LON CHANEY
[Continued from page nineteen]

Each year Lon went back to school more and more reluctantly. He loathed it. He never became a student or a reader. Experience developed him, but his tastes were always those that he had when he left home.

It may be, too, that with his young eyes sharpened by love for his mother, he felt that he should take the burden of his support from his father as soon as might be. Unconsciously, he understood in those early days the ceaseless struggle of the workingman to meet his financial obligations. Perhaps there was planted the seed of his fear and hatred of poverty.

During the summer months he acted as a guide around the Pike's Peak country. He dug souvenirs out of the mountain sides and sold them to tourists. Most of the boys in that locality spent their vacations that way. Lon, according to the man who ran the place then, was best of them all because he loved it so. His face grew so eager, he was so anxious that others should love it.

Sometimes John got him a job as prop boy or scene shifter at the opera house. The boy's keen young emotions were stirred, his curiosity awakened. Through dressing-room doors he peered at the great Mansfield, made up as Jekyll and Hyde, as hump-backed Richard. Saw Robert Mantell, Frederick Warde, Louis Mann, Maude Adams as they held their audiences spellbound.

"How do they fix themselves up like that?" he would whisper to John. "Gee, that's wonderful."

Once, many years later, he met Frederick Warde.

"I don't expect you remember me, Mr. Warde," said the great Lon Chaney.

Mr. Warde paid him some graceful compliment upon his work, but admitted that he did not remember meeting him.

"Do you remember, once when you played Colorado Springs, a scene shifter who got so excited watching you he stayed on the stage holding a big blue jardinière while the curtain was up? That was me."

He went to school less and less. Finally not at all. Worked as errand boy, helped in a bicycle shop. Eventually he ran away. Not far. But he wanted new places, wanted a look at "city life," above all wanted to be on his own. So he departed, A. W. O. L., for Denver.

"My first job was laying carpets and cutting window shades," Lon told me once. "Don't believe that business they print about interior decorating. Boloney. We hadn't got that snooty in Denver in those days. It was a carpet-laying and window-shade store, that's what it was. If the talkies put me out of business, I can still lay linoleum and hang window shades. Man's got to have a job."

LON never forgot the things from which he came. Rather, in every act, he flaunted them. The self-made man. Of, by, and for "the common people," was Chaney. His tastes, habits, principles were theirs. Perhaps the story that is best known about him, the one that he allowed to be publicized most frequently, was the fact that he carried his card in the stage hands' union to the day of his death.

With all his soul, he believed in the rights of labor against capital. He lived up to that principle when he became the big shot at the Metro-Goldwyn-Mayer studio. Many the battles he fought for the under dog.

No other star who has ever been in pictures has been the open, avowed champion of the laboring man. Most of the stars give mere friendliness and courtesy. But Lon Chaney was a leader who belonged to those for whom he fought.

The great tide of gold and glory swept Reid and Valentino away. It swept by Chaney, leaving him what he had always been, a simple, common man. Kipling has said:

If you can walk with crowds and keep your virtue,
And talk with kings nor lose the common touch.

Lon Chaney did that—and turned the studios upside down, as I will show you.

For his job with the carpets and linoleum Lon got seven dollars a week. He paid three dollars a week for his room and the rest was his. If he spent it in riotous living, he jolly well went hungry. If he ate all his young stomach would hold, he stayed in his room nights. It was swell. It was life. There was always free lunch.

Motion Picture Publications photo

The Chaney home in Beverly Hills, California.

HIS father had told him, in their last sign-language talk, that if he wanted to drink, to drink beer. Beer was five cents for a big glass in those days, good, healthful, harmless stuff, which a fellow could enjoy and at the same time grab a ham sandwich and a slab of roast beef to plaster an empty belly. Puppies cut their teeth legitimately instead of upon bootleg poison. Thus they might grow up to be men, not morons.

Young Chaney, slim, quick, hot-headed, full of vim, vigor, and vitality, bummed, fought, laughed, and loved like any normal boy under twenty. He stood in barrooms and listened to men talk—and since in Denver barrooms sang such poets as Eugene Field, spouted such tale-tellers as Van Loan and Runyon and Floto, he may well have heard great conversation.

Wherever there were men, Chaney forgathered. He was no lily, but his code was sound—never double-cross a pal, never do a girl dirt, earn your own living, and be honest.

His quick smile got him out of some tough places, his quick fists out of others. When the going got too tough, he could always write home and Pop Chaney would manage a few dollars.

While he labored long daily hours and enjoyed free nights, destiny, in the hands of brother John, was shaping his unexpected ends.

John was a wild youth who had caused many a sleepless night to his father and mother, but he was a worker. With a flair for stage management, he had put himself in a position to strike out for himself. With a young actor named Holmes he had got backing for a small musical-comedy troupe to tour the sticks.

He sent for Lon to come and help.

Now somewhere, in those days backstage, no one seems to know exactly where or when, Lon had learned to dance. Rumor to the contrary, he was never a contortionist. He was an amazing eccentric dancer. A virile grace and suppleness belonged to him. When he was a big star, I have often loitered on his set to watch him tap-dance for hours at a time. It was one of his ways of keeping fit and of relaxing.

Lon left the floors and windows of Denver to get along as best they could and entered the world of make-believe for good and all.

In the new company he did dance numbers, he shifted scenery, he was head property man. All his theatrical days, Lon Chaney doubled in brass. They let him do his stuff before the footlights to save a salary or two, and because he was such a great man backstage. Until he had been some time in pictures, no one took Lon seriously as an actor. He belonged behind the scenes.

In spite of the presence in the cast of the great Lon Chaney, who made no impression of any kind as far as I can discover, the troupe didn't do so well. John was a

[CONTINUED ON PAGE TWENTY-TWO]

[CONTINUED FROM PAGE TWENTY]

good stage director, but the day came—as it has come to thousands of theatrical managers—when he couldn't pay salaries. One of the chief causes of the disaster appears to have been a show called The Little Tycoon, which the Chaney brothers wrote in their spare time when they weren't acting or shifting scenery. When all seemed darkest, an angel—a theatrical angel—appeared upon the horizon. A Denver manager suggested that he take over the scenery, the repertoire, and the company and allow them to fill an engagement in the Southwest. John maintained his dignity—but sold quickly.

The new manager wanted to keep Lon. His dancing act wasn't bad, and he had begun to develop a talent that kept him going through many lean years. As a trainer of choruses he was okey. He could take a bunch of green girls and make them into pretty fair chorines.

"What'll I do?" Lon asked his brother.

"If I were you," said John, "I'd go. You're young. You'll be learning all the time. A good stage manager can always make a living and you might get to be one."

Thus, in the early spring of 1905, when Lon was twenty-one, the Columbia Musical Comedy Repertoire Company landed in Oklahoma City, Oklahoma, and prepared to knock the inhabitants out of their seats.

By that time, as usual, Lon Chaney was doing three jobs of his own and half of several others.

The day after their arrival, he inserted an ad in the local paper: "Chorus Girls Wanted."

In the background you might have heard a tiny click, when the rails of his future shifted, as a tiny switch shifts a whole railroad system.

THE little troupe couldn't afford to carry a complete chorus. So in each town they picked up girls with theatrical ambitions, daughters of their fair city, who not only cut down expenses but helped to fill the house with admiring friends and relations.

The paper containing the ad drifted into the telephone office and fell into the hands of a fat girl who knew that the chorus wasn't for her. But next to her on the switchboard was a girl who everyone said should be on the stage.

Her name was Cleva Creighton and she was only fifteen. Her mother held a unique position in the town. They called her a practical nurse, but she was really a first-class trouble-shooter. When anybody had a baby, Mrs. Creighton went in, took care of the mother and the new arrival and the house and saw that the other kids got to school and had their meals. She mothered sick kiddies, took care of troublesome old people, filled the gap as cook, nurse, washerwoman, comforter in every family where there was trouble. A drunken husband had left her with four kids to raise and she was doing an excellent job of it.

Cleva was a tall, dark-haired young thing, with the wide, changing-blue eyes of her pure Irish ancestry. Not beautiful, but with a warm, soft appeal that is sometimes as effective as beauty. There was something so vivid, so eager, so breathless about her—and a peculiar sweetness. There are remnants of it now, when life has used her with tragic hands.

Picture by
Dan Sayre Groesbeck

It was the girl with the golden voice. "Come here," said Chaney. "Let me show you."

Above all, she had a natural singing voice that swelled out of her girl's throat with all the free ecstasy of a bird.

Between calls the girl friend said: "You ought to go try out for that, Cleva. Gee, with a voice like yours! Look what you might do. Get to be an actress."

That night Cleva asked her mother.

"You stay away from there," said Mrs. Creighton. "I don't hold with girls going on the stage. It's not your class. You've got a good job. Stay where you are."

Too late. The girl's Irish imagination had been stirred. Visions, the same ones that have glittered before every stage-struck girl for centuries, danced before her. She did have a voice. She might become famous, make a lot of money, help ma and the kids.

EVEN now, there is a warm, appealing sweetness about this woman. Even now, when she is middle-aged, worn by years of hard work as a waitress, as a cook, as anything to keep soul and body together.

Sitting with her in her clean, poor little living room where she was preparing to go out the next day to cook for forty-five ranch hands, I found in her graciousness, tolerance, a lack of bitterness, that made me ache over the terrible price she has paid for folly, for ignorance, for wild blood.

Nothing can separate her story from the life of Lon Chaney. He could shut the doors of memory and never mention her name. But her name was there, part of his character, his viewpoint. He could cut her off in his will with a dollar "because he owed her no obligation." But she repaid his stern justice by taking the dollar to buy a little bouquet of flowers to scatter before the door of his last resting place. No obligation. But he owed her his son. And the pictures upon the walls of that tiny brown house write a story of years that cannot be removed from Lon Chaney's span of existence.

You see, little Cleva Creighton, crying that night into her pillow because her mother wouldn't let her be a chorus girl, didn't know that within her was a terrible weakness which was to undo her, which was to make waste all her loyalty, her sweetness, her great talent.

For at that time Cleva Creighton had never had a drink.

So her dreams were the dreams of any young girl, who believes that the world is kind.

The next day she talked her mother around and Cleva Creighton, her blue eyes round as dollar chips, applied for a job.

A young man came out from behind some scenery. Unconsciously, she felt the impact of his nervous, vibrant force. He wore a pair of overalls and an old sweater, but he looked clean and strong. His black eyes moved swiftly over her thin, childish body, noted with the dancer's eye the awkwardness of her movements. He took the cigarette out of his mouth, smiled, and said, "Nope."

That smile undid her. She had never been in love. The warmth that crept over her, the throbbing of her heart, were new and nameless. She didn't want to go away.

The young man forgot her instantly. He hammered away blithely, whistling, his swift hands moving surely.

When he turned around, the girl was still there, watching him.

[CONTINUED ON PAGE TWENTY-FOUR]

233

LON CHANEY
[Continued from page twenty-two]

"Maybe you'd like to hear me sing," said Cleva Creighton.

"Sure," said Lon Chaney, "but I'm awful busy this morning."

"I can sing," said the girl wistfully.

He stared at her a minute, brows down over his eyes. Then he laughed. She looked such an absurd young thing, standing there in her plain, childish dress.

"Shoot," he said.

Through the empty dark theater, without even a piano, rose a clear young voice. People who heard her later in the cabarets of San Francisco and Los Angeles tell me they never heard another voice like it until Helen Morgan sat on top of a piano.

Chaney loved music with a blind idolatry. Not good music. He knew nothing about it. But the sob ballads, the waltzes, the folk songs moved him deeply. That morning he listened and was lost.

"You're hired," he said.

He remembered the voice but forgot the girl until a few days later at rehearsal. Something was wrong. Someone in the back row was always out of step. With a yelp, he called the girl out.

It was the girl with the golden voice.

"You others get out," said Chaney. "Come here, you. Let me show you."

After that he worked with her every day. He couldn't understand how one with music like that in her throat should lack rhythm in her feet.

She never did learn to dance. She wasn't built for dancing. The Irish-American stock of the Southwest had built her strongly for hard work, for motherhood, for endurance, and at the last moment had slipped in that voice. But dance she could not.

"I was always in the back row, until I got songs to sing by myself," she told me, her eyes gazing back through dark years to those days of youth and hope. "Lon was so kind, trying to help me. I never knew anyone with such patience. Never would admit he couldn't lick anything. Then, too, I made him laugh. He was such a clown. When he found he couldn't make me graceful, he tried to make me funny. My, I used to sit and watch him and laugh till the tears ran down my face. I was a fool kid. Skinny as a rail. When the chorus wore tights they always had to hide me behind a table or something. I—I've put on weight since. A woman does."

The fantastic fortunes of the theater overtook the company. Oklahoma City didn't support them. They took to the road. One-night stands, through sparsely populated towns. Lon Chaney keeping up their courage, making them laugh, trying to make life endurable.

AFTER a bitter struggle with her mother, Cleva Creighton had gone with the show.

When they came back to Oklahoma City, she was just sixteen. Two days later, on May 31, 1905, she and Lon Chaney were married by the mayor at his home. Mrs. Creighton had always taken care of the mayor's wife.

Mrs. Creighton wasn't there.

"Probably you better marry him," she had told her daughter. "I can see you're too friendly with him now. But I can't come to the wedding. Mrs. Smith is sick and her baby's got croup."

So, with no member of either family present, the bride of sixteen and the bridegroom of twenty-two took the majestic vows, "for better for worse, for richer for poorer, in sickness and in health, to love and to cherish, till death us do part."

NEXT WEEK—

An extraordinary short story

A Doll for
the Maharanee

By

GUY GILPATRIC

——AND——

What a golf champion thinks
about women who play golf

The Fair on
the Fairway

BY

GLENNA COLLETT

Their tenure of office was to be far shorter than that. But they didn't suspect it then.

It was Chaney's first romance. He was never a man who cared for women just as women. A one-woman man. A man's man. He loved man companionship, bull sessions, drinking bouts. No women. Great friendships with men came into his life. I have never in my life seen as many men—hard-looking, weather-beaten, middle-aged men, too—weep as I saw at Chaney's funeral.

There were only three women in his life. All of them bore the name of Chaney. His mother, Cleva Creighton Chaney, and Hazel Hastings Chaney. Very few women for an actor and a picture star. Their rôles were big.

Cleva left her home and her mother and followed her man into the strange, upside-down, mad life of a theatrical road company.

SHE had never had a drink, never slept outside her mother's home, until she met Lon Chaney.

In September of that year, from Dallas, Texas, where they were playing, Cleva Chaney wired frantically for her mother. She was going to have a baby. She was frightened and her young husband was nearly as bad. The "almost inevitable consequences" hadn't been in their gay young plans. Lon's cocky worldliness was mostly pose. They were a couple of ignorant kids. What in the world could they do with a baby in their gypsy life? How could they take care of a baby in cheap hotel rooms, in drafty theater dressing rooms? How could they carry a baby about from one town to another on cheap trains at impossible hours? They found out.

Mrs. Creighton arrived and soon had the situation well in hand. She was a pioneer woman who had raised children in any and all conditions. Babies, in her opinion, survived anything—and so did women.

"Of course you'll have your baby," said she. "It'll be a fine baby, too. Don't you worry, child. I don't hold with all this foolishness about babies. It's nature and nature takes care of it. It's been going on a long time and a lot of us are still here."

Cleva stayed with the show until December. In those months she learned many things about her husband. His tenderness to her was so beautiful that it has given a glow to all the after years. But she saw in him, too, that hard streak which never forgave an injury and which believed in the righteousness of revenge.

There was a quarrel with a man in the company. Something about a shirt. The man said it was his, when it came back from the laundry. Lon said it was his. The feud grew. Lon said little, smoldering. One night the man came into Lon's dressing room. One word led to another and the last word led to a blow. The fight was violent and bloody. Lon fought then, as he did later, very silently and with the swift menace of a panther.

The noise reached the women's dressing rooms and Lon's young wife ran downstairs, only to faint at the sight of the blood that flowed from two young faces.

Lon cared for her tenderly. Then he sought the other man.

"I'm telling you something," he said. "If my baby is marked because of what you've done, I'll kill you, no matter where you are. Remember that, because it's the truth."

Two days later the man left the company. But Lon kept track of him, without comment, until the day when he could release him from that declared vengeance.

The Chaneys left the show in December and went back to Oklahoma City. Mrs. Creighton had prepared a little house for them near her own, and it was the only home Lon and Cleva Creighton Chaney ever had.

Lon got a job at fifteen dollars a week in the local furniture store. He could still lay carpets and he did. Fifteen dollars a week wasn't much and Lon resented the fact that there was so little he could do to prepare for the great event. But they managed to be happy.

On a terribly cold night in February, a son was born.

The girl-mother bore her long struggle well. There was joy in it for her because beside her every minute, his hands holding hers, was the man she loved and whose only child she was bringing into the world. It is the memory of those moments that has kept Cleva Creighton sweet through the years, while she watched Lon Chaney climb the heights without her.

In the dawn, she lay back in his arms, her face white and drawn, and together they looked down upon their son.

They called the boy Creighton Tull Chaney, Creighton for his mother and grandmother, Tull for the kindly old family friend who owned the furniture store and had given Lon his life-saving job.

THE happy, peaceful days soon ended. Taking their baby with them, the young Chaneys went back to the theater. They landed in Chicago broke, and they stayed broke. A week or two with small musical companies that played the suburbs was all they managed to get.

It wasn't just gay, gypsy poverty now, wasn't a question of laughing it off any more. Cold and hunger became real things to the Chaneys and they left scars that wealth itself did not heal.

At last he wired his father for money enough to go to California. The promised land. The land of sunshine and plenty. Motion pictures? They had heard of motion pictures, of course. But Lon Chaney didn't travel west with any idea of motion pictures. Hollywood meant nothing to him. The future was veiled. The dark days ahead were veiled.

And it was well they were.

From those coming years emerged the man Lon Chaney was to be. Darkness and chaos lay between him and the heights.

There may be a greater love in a man's life than his first love. There may be a higher love than he knows for the woman whom he first calls wife, who lays in his arms his firstborn son.

No love holds the intensity, the hopelessness, the disillusion.

The next six years were to prove both those things to the serious, dark-eyed young man who in 1906 got aboard a train for California with his wife and baby.

Lon Chaney was bound for Hollywood, but he didn't know it.

The gags and the grief that mingled in the life of Lon Chaney until his first love came to wreck in divorce will be told by Adela Rogers St. Johns in next week's Liberty.

Drink your own health
in the Saline Cocktail

GO right on drinking your own health in tomato juice, clam juice, sauerkraut juice, fruit juice. These "health-cocktails" are a fine idea.

But for those 7 A.M.'s who climb out of bed half-sick, dull as Old Man Gloom —the best cocktail is the Saline Cocktail!

Today—get a bottle of Sal Hepatica from your druggist. And tomorrow morning, if you wake up sluggish, headachey, depressed, pour a teaspoon or so of Sal Hepatica into a glass of cool, fresh water.

Drink it down—this bubbling, sparkling cocktail!

For Sal Hepatica cleanses the whole system. It combats acids, rids the intestinal tract of toxic wastes, and purifies the bloodstream. Constipation, headaches, colds, rheumatism, digestive disorders—all yield promptly to its saline action.

In Europe, year in and year out, the great spas are crowded with people of wealth and position, come to regain their health by drinking the saline waters. And Sal Hepatica is the efficient American equivalent of the famous European spas.

From your doctor, learn more about the saline method. Ask him about Sal Hepatica. And when your system is sluggish and toxic, try a saline cocktail each morning for a week. You will find your general tone rising with every day; your skin will clear; and you'll have a more optimistic view of life and humanity.

Sal Hepatica

At your druggist's   30¢, 60¢, and $1.20

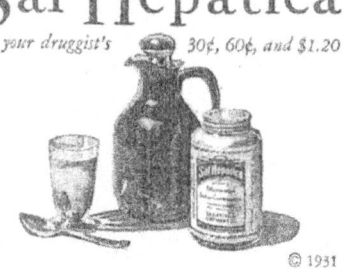

© 1931

Lon CHA

*L*ON looked at him
steadily. "I'm not
high-hat," he said quietly.
"But I don't like you, and
I don't like the things
you do."

A Portrait of the Man Behind a Thousand Faces

By
ADELA ROGERS ST. JOHNS

(Reading time: 26 minutes.)

*T*HE first installment of this story of the life of Lon
Chaney, printed last week, told of his boyhood in Colorado Springs as the son of a barber; of his first job in the
theater as a prop boy and his subsequent employment in a
dancing act and as a stage hand with road shows; of his
meeting the girl he later married, and of the beginning of
their struggles in the life of the theater.

PART TWO—IN MUSICAL-COMEDY STOCK

*L*ON CHANEY—hoofer.

Slim, neat little man with quick black eyes and
nimble feet. Hard body, hard mouth. Busier than
a daily columnist. Ready for anything. Taking the
bumps with that quick smile that changed his serious face.

There were plenty of bumps.

Lon Chaney didn't amount to a darn in the general
scheme of things. Sometimes he had a job, sometimes
he didn't. If he didn't, upon his shoulders rode the stark
fear of not being able to buy milk for the kid. When he
did, it meant twenty hours' work a day and no sense of
security.

What was one hoofer, one stage hand, more or less?

If Cleva was working too, he got up at dawn with the
baby. The wife hadn't been too well ever since the baby
was born. Then there were day-long rehearsals in cold,
dim theaters with rows of empty seats staring across the
dim footlights. Nothing tougher in the theatrical game
anywhere than musical-comedy stock, putting on a show
a week, sometimes two.

In his shirt sleeves, cigarette between his lips, cap over
one eye, Chaney rehearsed dance numbers hour after

hour. One, two, three, four. Come on, snap
into it! Hey, you, there on the end! Come
around quicker on that turn! This is no funeral
march! All together! Let's take it a little faster!

Hoofer, second comedian, stage hand, property man, scene shifter, stage manager, transportation handler—buying tickets and getting
hotel accommodations for everybody when they
went on the road.

At night playing two or three small parts
with changes of make-up, dashing about backstage to see that the lighting was right, helping
to change the scenery, yelping at the girls to
hurry into their costumes and get back on the
stage, giving orders to prop boys.

*M*ONEY was always short. The kid had to be
looked after. Good kid. But kids compli-
cated existence. Cleva worked most of the time.
Because of her voice, she got a chance at some
fairly good parts. Later she sang in cabarets.

Lon made a cradle out of string, a woven hammock, and
they hung that in the dressing room during the performance for Creighton to sleep in. Between scenes Lon
would dash in and heat his milk over the little gas jet he
used to melt his cosmetics. When the show was over, Lon
would pick him up, very tenderly so as not to awaken the
little fellow, and back they'd go to the hotel.

It was always a hotel or a cheap apartment house.

They fixed up one gag, he and Cleva, that saved money.
Every nickel was precious in those days. Salaries were
never big and if they did manage to save a few dollars the
out-of-work periods soon ate them up.

They got a big, cheap suitcase and packed it full of
groceries and an alcohol lamp. The improvised kitchen
was a bureau drawer turned upside down on the bed.
Cleva managed many a meal out of a couple of cans and a
cheap cut of steak. She made the baby's mush at night
and set it on the window sill. When he awoke in those
hours which every actor considers sacred to Morpheus,
Lon would get up and warm it for him.

As he grew older, the kid used to tag Lon around behind
the scenes like a small shadow. A dark, solemn-eyed
youngster who regarded his dad as the center of a very
hectic universe. The girls in the chorus were all fond of
the youngster and on the train jumps they helped take
care of him. His favorite nurse was the belle of the show,
a pretty, blue-eyed girl named Fay Parkes. Many of the
old gang in San Francisco will remember Fay Parkes.

Fay had a beau in San Francisco who wasn't in the
show business. When they went on the road, Lon always
saw to it that Fay had the room next to his and Cleva's.
Later she married the San Franciscan, Phil Epstein, and

NEY

for years he has handled all the Chaney business details. Lon never forgot how good Fay was to the little boy in those tough days. When he was up in the world, he sent for her and her husband.

Lon never forgot a favor—nor an injury.

No time for the boy's schooling. Cleva taught him his letters. Neither she nor Lon had better than a grammar-school education. But they did what they could.

Lon made his clothes. There was one little blue suit, with an Eton jacket, contrived from a last winter's coat of Cleva's. The young gentleman admired himself

While filming The Big City Chaney used the derby he wore, and no other aids to disguise, to portray a series of characters. Here he is as the Sport.

Picture by Dan Sayre Groesbeck

Behind his comic mask his face went white. He snatched her up in his arms.

very much in this creation. The first night he wore it backstage somebody complimented him, and little Creighton said solemnly, " My dad made it for me." Poor Lon took an awful razzing on that one.

Those were good old days, remembered by every Cali-

fornian. There was Pop Fischer's show. Will King. The Ferris-Hartman troupe. The Columbia Opera Company. The Princess Theater in San Francisco and Idora Park in Oakland. The Grand Opera House and the Lyceum in Los Angeles.

Walter Catlett, Fatty Arbuckle, Texas Guinan, Blossom Seeley, Frances White, May Boley, Robert Z. Leonard, Walter de Leon, and Muggins Davis—all rotated around them. Texas Guinan wore her all-over white tights with the ostrich-feather headdress. Frances White first sang

[CONTINUED ON NEXT PAGE]

Alexander's Rag Time Band. Blossom Seeley crooned Barbary Coast blues. The great Catlett hoofed and sang and pulled gags he was later to use before the royal family of England.

It was in that same Princess company that a little girl named Hazel Hastings, just out of the convent, made her first appearance on any stage. No one noticed her much. Just one of the chorus. In time she was to play the most important rôle in the life of the man who of all that group was to become the most famous.

You could have gotten a thousand to one at that time that Lon Chaney would never rise above the ranks.

He showed nothing out of the ordinary. They didn't realize that his shrewd, practical mind was absorbing every detail of stagecraft, every trick of showmanship, all the technique of comedy which anyone in any of those companies knew. He was studying the stage methods of the enormously popular Kolb and Dill, ranked for years as the Weber and Fields of the west. When he wasn't busy he was hanging around Catlett's dressing room, watching Catlett make up.

With Kolb and Dill he made his first make-up experiment. It didn't do so well, either.

Chaney was playing a small comedy bit which called for a beard. But the finances of the company were low, as usual, and Kolb and Dill laughed heartily at the idea of spending any money to buy a beard for a bum second comic.

THE man who was to become the great make-up artist of the screen refused to be stumped. The Chaneys had a very small, very cheap apartment out near Larkin Street and one of the ornaments was an Angora rug. It was already slightly the worse for wear, but when Lon got through with it a severe attack of mange might best have explained its aspect. Having constructed a beard from the pluckings, Lon bought some drugstore dye and dipped it. But while he was a good hoofer and a pretty fair dressmaker, as a dyer he was a flop.

He appeared that night before the footlights with a slightly demented sunset hanging to his lower jaw.

Kolb, who was on the stage at the time of Lon's entrance, let out a squawk of mingled rage and amazement, while the paid customers whooped. That beard nearly cost Lon his job.

Lon always looked down on people in pictures who knew nothing of the arts which the theater has been developing for centuries.

One day, after the talkies arrived, a big musical revue was in production on the Metro-Goldwyn-Mayer lot. The director was holding up a lot of extras and wasting expensive hours trying to figure out a gag. The idea was to have the silk hats of the chorus men leave their heads by several inches without visible support. Camera experts had been summoned. Mechanical geniuses who could devise means for photographing the parting of the Red Sea were giving their best. Expense was no object. They couldn't seem to figure it out.

A two-gun Chaney in While the City Sleeps.

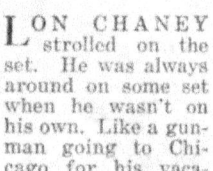

LON CHANEY strolled on the set. He was always around on some set when he wasn't on his own. Like a gunman going to Chicago for his vacation. Lon stood around bulling with the stage hands, watching pictures in the making. No one ever noticed him; visitors never recognized him.

The terrible dilemma was explained to him.

"Get a series of flats," said Lon wearily to the assistant director.

They got the big square canvas frames which are called flats.

"Attach invisible wires to them and tie those through the hats. When you're ready have your men up above lift the flats. Hell, any bum stage hand in vaudeville could have told you that!" And he strolled off.

As time went on in those early days, Cleva Creighton had more success than her husband. Lon yearned to act. He adored comedy. A clown at heart and at home. Little Creighton would sit up in the middle of the bed and beat time on the covers while Lon invented gags and eccentric steps.

But he was held back by the fact that he was more valuable backstage than anywhere else. A handy man. Anybody could play bum comics.

Cleva's real success was in the cabarets, the famous old cafés of San Francisco.

I find a lot of people remember her when she sang at the Portola, at

Techau's Tavern, at Tait's. There was one evening gown she wore in which she looked particularly stunning. Nobody dreamed that her young husband had made it for her out of an old stage wrap, a lace table cover, and the black velvet from a winter hat. There was another one she wore later at the Bristol in Los Angeles, where I heard her sing. Lon did some hoofing on that same bill. The gown was a white princesse with a turquoise blue lining. A Lon Chaney creation.

The whole thing was somehow like a cheap carnival. Merry, mad, and perilous. Grease paint and footlights. Night turned into day, day into night. Laughter and applause. Trains caught at all hours. Nothing permanent. Swift intimacies and sudden partings. Changing backgrounds. Stone-broke one week, flush the next.

How few of the marriages of that day lasted! Bob Leonard, later the husband of Mae Murray and now of Gertrude Olmstead, was married to a quiet girl named Lillian Leighton. Fatty was married to Minta Durfee. During a run at the Princess Walter Catlett married a pretty chorus girl, who has been separated from him for years. Dill and his wife are divorced. Texas, Frances White— they've changed husbands.

And for the young Chaneys a dark tide began to flow beneath the funny tinsel of the carnival setting.

The heavy in that little family of three, who lived so swiftly, laughed so much, worked so hard, was the heavy who has appeared on the divorce bill of many a family disaster. Old John Barleycorn himself.

"DON'T be hard on Cleva," said John Chaney, the older brother, when we talked of it. "The whole set-up was wrong for domestic happiness. Cleva had just one fault. Except for that she was a good girl. Why, they brought our kid brother, George, out from Colorado Springs and she looked after him like a mother. He thought the world of her and still does.

"You know, Lon wasn't an angel in those days himself. Nervous, high-strung, worried half to death all the time about money, with a pretty nasty temper. Time hadn't softened him yet. He had strength. Strength that came from his mother and father, who were the salt of the earth. Only, Lon never did develop any tolerance for or understanding of the weaknesses of others. It's a fault strong people often have."

Cleva Creighton was a girl who should never have taken a drink. I have known a lot of them. Perhaps you have. As far as I can find out, since prohibition there seem to be one or two in every family and nine or ten in every social group. There may be women who can drink with dignity and self-control. This big Irish girl from Oklahoma wasn't one of them.

If there is such a thing as an inherited thirst, Cleva Creighton was a victim of it.

There was a fever in her blood.

[CONTINUED ON NEXT PAGE]

TOUGH BEARD?

MENNEN
IS MADE *specially* FOR YOU!

ARE *YOU* one, too? One of those morning martyrs who has to shave a tough beard over a tender skin?

All right—now listen! There's one shaving cream specifically made for you: that cream is Mennen.

It contains specially processed *tristearin* $(C_{18}H_{35}O_2)_3 C_3H_5$. That's the ingredient which builds "tough beard" lather—lather that can wilt the wiriest whiskers and tame the spikiest stubble. Your razor has less work to do. Your blade cuts clean.

You get *comfort* with your shave.

While You Shave — A Cleansing Treatment! Mennen lather penetrates into the pores and there softens the embedded dirt and grease deposits. As you wash away the lather, you flush out the pores. Thus, Mennen lather helps **you to** keep your skin free from pimples, blackheads and other skin ailments.

• • •

P. S. *After the shave — Mennen Talcum for Men. Doesn't show. Protects the skin. Removes face shine. Great after a bath, too.*

A NEW TUBE
A NEW PRICE 35c
GIANT TUBE 50c

2 KINDS · ORIGINAL AND MENTHOL-ICED

Albert Davis Photo Collection

Universal City, where Lon Chaney worked as an extra for three dollars a day—when he could get it—at the beginning of his career in the movies.

LON CHANEY
[Continued from page thirty-one]

Cleva Creighton admits it. She never drinks now. You cannot drink and carry heavily loaded trays in the dining room of a Pasadena hotel. You cannot drink and cook three meals a day for forty-five ranch hands.

But then she was hail fellow well met with the gang around the theater. Not the best atmosphere for a girl who couldn't handle her liquor.

She tried. Fought many a battle and lost. When she was herself, she was a devoted mother. Everyone in those old days remembers her adoration for the little boy and his for her. When she wasn't herself, Lon worked and took care of the kid, and grew hard and bitter.

As Cleva booted chance after chance in her work, his fury grew. He'd come home from his stage clowning to find the old tragedy waiting for him.

In its train drink brought the things it always brings to those who can't handle it. Terrible quarrels, with unforgivable things said on both sides. Jealousies. Raw nerves. Days of melancholy. Passionate reconciliations that were worse than the quarrels.

Tied together in one room, the storms beat them down, and Lon went back to his work white and exhausted, to clown once more before an audience who saw only a little man with a bulbous nose and a funny hat, or a hoofer twinkling his toes in time to gay music.

At heart Lon was and always remained a puritan. A tough guy with a hard-boiled surface, his moral color sense was limited to black and white. He could cuss like a marine and scrap like one, too. Take a quart of whisky at a sitting and never show it. But like most men of his type he believed in custom, convention, and inherent decency. The easy modern viewpoint disgusted him. Dirty stories were absolutely taboo.

When he had become a great star, he happened to be in the Western Costuming Company one day picking out some wardrobe. Across the room was a man whom he had been with in a musical show when Lon was a prop boy.

The actor had made good on Broadway in a big way.

He spoke to Chaney heartily, and got a cold chill that was nobody's business.

Burning up, he ramped across and said, "Hey, listen, Chaney, how do you get like that? I know you're a big star now, but you needn't put on any tiaras for me. I'm a big shot myself and I knew you when you were on the goof squad. What's the idea of the Byrd expedition you're giving me?"

Lon looked at him steadily.

"I'm not high-hat," he said quietly. "But I don't like you, and I don't like the things you do. You're rotten. You're not a man who lives decently and I don't want anything to

Picture by
Dan Sayre Groesbeck

Chaney as a stage clown in his younger days.

do with you. Get that straight."

The stage star had a reputation as a rough-and-tumble fighter of no mean ability and Chaney knew it. They eyed each other a moment. There was no scrap.

His yearning for a good, respectable, middle-class home survived everything. He never had it with Cleva. They lived on a merry-go-round.

The wife was madly jealous. Most women are when they love a man. Probably she was wrong. But the theater was full of pretty girls, young girls, girls who could dance. They liked the quick-moving, good-looking, hard-boiled stage manager who yelled at them when they were wrong and grinned approvingly when they were right. They clustered about him and there was much of that free-and-easy kidding which goes on in a theatrical troupe.

A girl wrote him a mash note. Cleva found it. The uproar was appalling.

In the cabarets where she sang there were men, men, men, who drank and cheered and expected the handsome young singer to sit at the tables and "crack a bottle of wine" with them. To be a favorite, you were expected to play up to the customers. Kid them along.

The April stars must have been wrong for Chaney.

April always made plenty of showers for Lon.

On April 29, 1913, the Los Angeles Herald carried a picture of Cleva Creighton and a story which said:

Cleva Creighton has returned from San Francisco, where she has been the furor of the cabaret shows, and only comes to Los Angeles because of the fact that her husband, Lon Chaney, comedian, is here with Kolb and Dill for a short engagement.

The truth was that Lon had been out of work for some time, and Cleva had gone first to Porterville to sing in a picture house, later back to San Francisco. Finally Lon caught on as stage manager for Kolb and Dill.

When she arrived, he expected soon to go on the road with the show and leave her and the boy in Los Angeles, where she could go on singing at Brink's. There was a girl in that show of whom Cleva was wildly jealous. While she was away, Lon had taken the girl out to dinner. Nothing could make Cleva's green eyes see that he had taken her only because she was kind to little Creighton.

"You're crazy," said Lon briefly. "Behave yourself. She was decent to me and helped with the kid. We can't afford to give up a couple of good jobs because you've got bats in your belfry."

ON the night of April 30 Cleva Creighton finished her dinnertime show at the old Brink's Café where the night life of Los Angeles congregated. Above the clatter of dishes, the hum of laughter, the golden voice rose in the cheap sentiment of that old song, The Curse of an Aching Heart. Somehow the crowd stilled before a passion that lifted the trash into real music.

Then she walked over to the Majestic Theater, where Kolb and Dill were playing. Brooding, jealous, utterly bewildered, she stood in the wings and watched Lon.

Lon laughed and clowned and kicked somebody in the stomach and got knocked down by a paddle on the seat of his pants. The audience roared. Cleva Chaney threw back her head and swallowed the little tablets that were to take her away forever from the welter and horror of living. I think a woman has to be pretty unhappy, pretty well licked by life, before she desires to leave it. Right or wrong, your heart must ache beyond bearing before you try to stop it with your own hand.

The clown rushed off. Laughter pelted him. A soft body rolled at his feet. Behind his comic mask his face went white.

He snatched her up in his arms. Someone phoned for an ambulance.

All night long the doctors fought for her life, while she—so the newspaper men wrote the next day—"called continually for her little boy."

Sordid, tawdry little tragedy. No class. Common as—as Street Scene. Cabaret singer and clown. The hoofer

[CONTINUED ON NEXT PAGE]

LON CHANEY
[Continued from page thirty-three]

and the entertainer. The Curse of an Aching Heart—and a kick in the pants. Just another fool woman for the doctor to battle over wearily. Just another story to flame its cheap tale across the last edition and go to molder in the morgue of newspaper files where so many tragedies and scandals and heroisms lie buried.

Who could know that this man would one day play his rôle of the tragic clown for millions of people to see and applaud?

Cleva got well, but it was the end. Lon had had enough. He was fed to the teeth with the whole business. Her attempted suicide had wakened in him no sympathy. The weak gesture of a quitter. That was the way Chaney saw it.

Besides, he had found a letter, a silly, characteristic letter, which poor Cleva had written to a man in Porterville:

MY DEAREST BOY: Creighton is in the bathtub. I am in my nightgown. Going to play at Clune's, 5th and Main. Gee, honey, you don't know how sick I am of work. I don't know what is the matter with me. The doctor says I have lost control of my nerves. I am taking medicine all the time. Well, Don, I must close and wash the baby. Yours all the time with love, CLEVA.

A pitiful letter. But a terrible one for Lon Chaney.

They separated, and she took the boy with her when she went to sing in a ten-cent movie house in San Bernardino. But once there the real consequences of her mad moment caught up with her. The poison had burned her vocal chords beyond redemption. She tried and tried, but she was never to sing again.

She sent for Lon and gave little Creighton into his father's keeping.

What else could she do? She had no money, no job, no friends. A woman alone, under a curse. Gangrene set in in the injured throat, but death refused her pleas. She was to fight it out here.

ON December 19, 1913, Lon Chaney filed suit for divorce from Cleva Creighton Chaney in the Superior Court of Los Angeles County.

He struck hard, ruthlessly, for all time. He wanted custody of that boy, for always. He was through. He'd given Cleva chance after chance. Now he'd use the surgeon's knife, cut his life loose and the boy's life, too.

The complaint alleged habitual intemperance and named another man, a bartender. The woman was paying a price to drown her sorrows.

No cross complaint was filed and the suit went undefended.

From the day in May when she and Lon separated, from the day when she gave the boy to his father, Cleva Chaney had gone her own way.

"I knew he would be better with his father," she told me. "I couldn't earn a living for him. Lon was a good man. Hard, but good. I knew he could do better for the boy's future than I could. I was—very unhappy. I didn't know much about

Acme photo

The old Majestic Theater in Los Angeles, where Chaney's first wife attempted suicide.

anything when I married Lon. Things came too fast. I don't think I realized then that my boy was gone for good. I was so ill and miserable and I hated myself so. Perhaps it's all better as it is. Look at what Lon has done for my boy. He's happy, he's a fine man, respected by everyone. I —I'd like to see Creighton's little boys. I've never seen them. But I manage to go on. Lon meant well, but he shouldn't have hated me like he did. I've paid for being an ignorant fool."

SHE smoothed down her clean gingham dress and looked at me with clear blue eyes.

"Life can be pretty cruel, can't it? I never envied Lon his success. He worked hard for it. Harder than most. I never felt bitter about what I'd thrown away in my youth, all his success and money. Only I miss my boy. I pray for him every morning and every night. Sometimes when I'm so tired I think I can't take another step, I think about him and how glad I am life has been kind to him. Maybe some day he'll know I let him go because I thought it was best for him. A woman can stand almost anything when she knows her child is all right. He was—a cunning little fellow, wasn't he?"

She held out a picture of the three of them. A clean-cut young man, Lon Chaney without the deep lines which identified him later. A young woman with happy eyes. A handsome little boy. Her fingers touched the little face in the picture. Then she began to cry so softly—so *accustomedly*—as though tears were her daily bread.

I got up and went away. I am not wise enough to judge people. I have sons of my own. The farthest I ever get when I try to think out things like that is something *about*

"Judge not," and "The greatest of these is charity," and "There but for the grace of God goes—any one of us."

Probably I'm a fool. But some women get tough breaks and suffering isn't any easier to bear because you brought it on yourself. It's harder.

On April 1, 1914, Lon's thirty-first birthday, the divorce suit was heard. On April 2 the decree was granted and Lon Chaney given custody of his son. A divorce decree which dissolved the marriage of Lon Chaney and Cleva Creighton and freed them "from each and all obligations thereof."

It wasn't as simple as that. It never is. Human justice doesn't yet work miracles.

Lon never saw his first wife again.

But in that hour of divorce he wrenched himself free of his youth. And of all that youth means.

HE went through some pretty bad days. Sometime a great psychologist will write a book about the effects of a first marriage which fails. In Lon's generation, a broken marriage meant a great deal. It left behind fears which were never overcome, strange fears of being hurt, humiliated, strange complexes and inhibitions for protection.

Lon Chaney from that day to the day of his death never mentioned the name of his first wife except when he came to make his will. The people he met in later years, and who saw his second wife and handsome young son, never even knew that he had been married before. It was taboo. The locked door.

Once the blackness of hate which he felt in those days had passed under the control of his will, once his hurt pride and wounded ideals had been buried deep enough so that no casual word could uncover them, he ceased to dwell upon it.

But from that day Lon saw life through different eyes. He wanted only peace, security, safety.

A new chapter began in everything. His married life was over.

He had lost his job with Kolb and Dill.

He didn't have a dollar in the world.

Figuratively speaking, he marched out into the middle of Hollywood Boulevard, holding Creighton's small, trusting hand in his, and said, "Hollywood, here I come."

There wasn't much joy in it. No great hope. He was past thirty. His belief that life was something wonderful, something a young man could bend to his will, was gone. He was afraid of life. From that day forward, he kept his guard up. No more unexpected socks on the chin for Chaney.

All he asked or hoped was to make a living for himself and his son. To have, some day, a decent little home. Maybe to have some money soaked away in the bank, so the first of the month wouldn't be a peril, so the landlord wouldn't look like Shylock.

[CONTINUED ON NEXT PAGE]

LON CHANEY
[Continued from page thirty-five]

When a man starts at thirty with such a fixed desire, it doesn't alter much, even if a gold mine opens at his feet. Lon never desired much more, nor took much more.

Pictures had begun to dawn upon his horizon only through the medium of picture shows. They didn't amount to much in those days—back in nineteen twelve, thirteen, fourteen. There were no great superproductions, no enormous theaters, no fabulous salaries.

Some of the boys around the theaters told Lon that there was a chance in the directing end for a man with stage experience. Lon was sick of the uncertainty, the impermanence of his footlight existence. Now that he was both father and mother to his boy, something had to be done about it. With his background of all angles in the theater maybe he could click in pictures.

With cold determination he set out to wrest a living from the movies. At least he could stay in one place and not have to cart the boy around with show people. The southern California climate was good for kids.

He put the boy in a private home, run by a Mrs. Coots, where the children of divorce and disaster found food and care for a small sum per week. The house was somewhere out near Slauson and Moneta, now the heart of the industrial district.

LON looked at the boy a long moment. " Be a man, kid," he said.

Today the road to Universal City, five miles beyond Hollywood, is paved as wide as Michigan Boulevard. Busses carry extras along its smooth surfaces to the Universal Studios and to First National, just around a corner of the Hollywood hills.

In nineteen fourteen things were different.

The first time Lon Chaney went to Universal City he walked.

If he had known that a few years later he was to travel that road for twenty-five hundred dollars a week, the walk might not have been so long

and trying. The bright future was veiled and it seemed plenty long. Nor did it grow shorter as the weeks went by.

Many times he walked it twice a day. Three dollars a day as an extra—when you get it—isn't a great deal if there is board and room to pay for a youngster. A man must eat if he is to work. Every nickel counted. Every nickel counted with Lon for so long that he never got over it.

He could give away money, but he never learned to spend it as spending goes nowadays. In Hollywood they called him the star who lived like a clerk. He died worth over a million dollars. Some of those who used to laugh at his frugality, his simple habits and conservative living, will probably die broke. Not that it matters much either way to them after they are gone.

IF, as many who watched him from the side lines used to say, Lon Chaney never got but a dollar's worth of fun out of every thousand he earned, it was due to the impress of those early struggles. He was building a fortress for an old age he was never to enjoy.

There is a thing never to be forgotten about Chaney. He was a workman. He came of working people. He loved work. The great majority of picture stars—Mary Pickford is the one exception I would make—work toward leisure. They all intend to buy islands in the Pacific or yachts on the Mediterranean. In fact, if all goes well, the Mediterranean will be populated exclusively by retired motion-picture stars in another ten years.

Chaney wasn't having any of that, ever.

He had bred in him the conviction that work was an essential part of existence, not a means to an end. A conviction that seems to be fast dying out. Without work, he wouldn't have had the faintest notion what to do with his life.

The story of Chaney as a director, the birth of his " great idea," and his second marriage will be told next week.

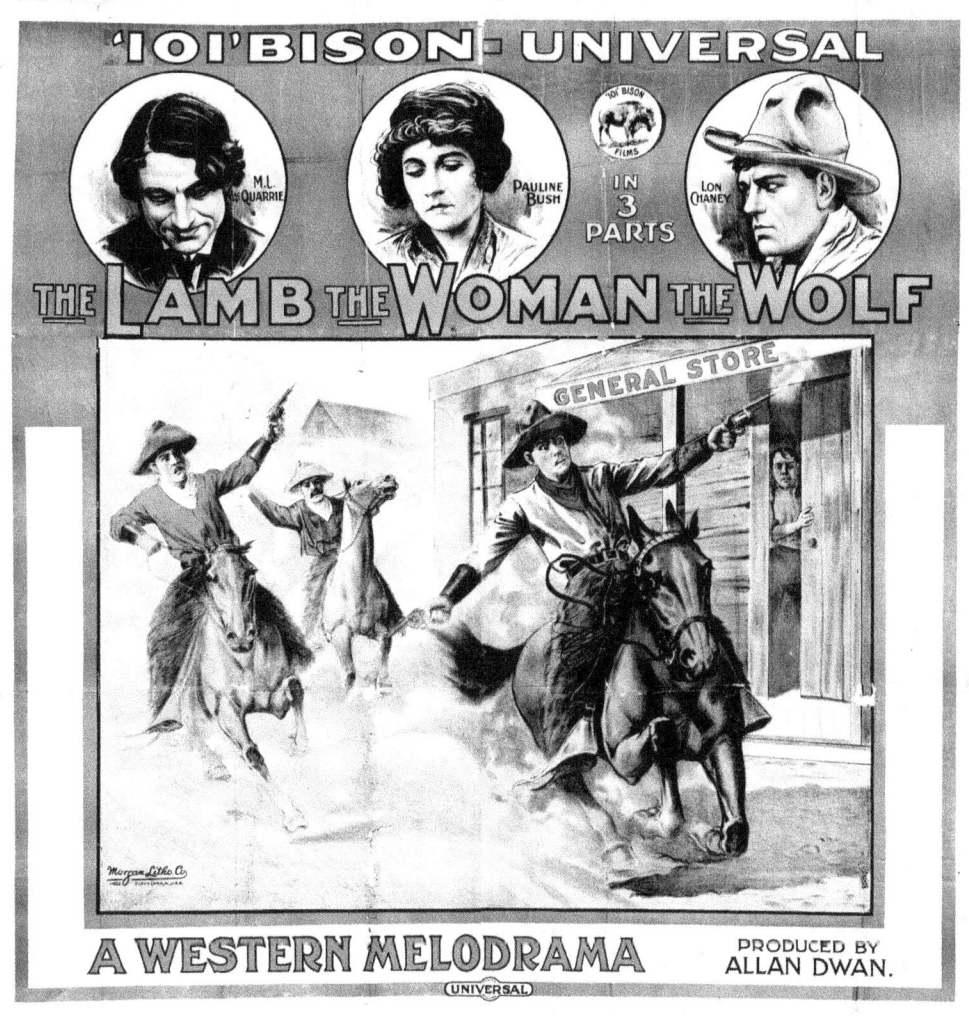

Lon Chaney was already getting poster billing by 1914 as seen in this Universal 6 sheet

*A characterization from the
early teens - "The Maverick",
DeGrasse/Universal Production*

Lon

A Portrait of the Man Behind a Thousand Faces

Laugh, clown, laugh— the Chaney formula. It was real to Lon and he made it real to the world.

(Reading time: 28 minutes 5 seconds.)

THE hard knocks Lon Chaney took in his early days as a hoofer and general handy man about the theater; his wife, Cleva Creighton, and their turbulent life together, finally ending in divorce; and his try at the movies as an extra were described in this series last week.

PART THREE—THE CHANEY FORMULA

WHEN I first met Lon Chaney at Universal about the time he did Hell Morgan's Girl, which gave him his first screen recognition, he had a dynamic flair of some kind. Difficult to define. Like a prize fighter the day before a big bout or a football player before the big game.

Perfect condition, tons of pent-up energy, taut as a wire. All his movements were quick, as though he had no time to waste. Nervous, high-strung, slightly grim. Very attractive.

There was a beautiful widow who—but that is another story, because I don't think Lon ever suspected why she hung around the set all the time and went out on long, dirty locations. His mind was on his work.

Fortunately, sex appeal hadn't been discovered as a screen commodity or the history of Chaney might have been different. No, I don't think so. He would have starved first.

Lon Chaney got his first chance, not by any cometlike fluke, by any sweep of personality, by any one part, but by making himself generally useful.

When he was an extra on westerns, he was always around making himself useful. He slipped the director gags. He did odd jobs and chores in general. If anything came up that nobody else wanted to do, Chaney was your man.

When he was working in the studio, he helped shift scenery, he aided with the props, he carted lights for electricians. Opportunity had no chance to sneak by him in any guise.

He was out for a permanent job and he didn't care what it was so long as it paid a living wage.

The boy spurred him on.

ON Sundays he rode clear across Los Angeles—and the Chamber of Commerce will tell you that is some ride—to see little Creighton. The boy was still a solemn youngster. He wasn't happy. Torn up by even such shallow roots as life had permitted him, he hated the separation from his father.

Lon saw it and said nothing, but it hurt. The kid had a right to a home, a father—and a mother.

The best friend of Lon's beginnings was Tod Browning, who in the big years directed most of Lon's great pictures. Tod did underworld stuff and he found something in that hard, intense young face, already marked with lines, that fitted into his stories. Tod used him in so many pictures, for small parts, that Papa Laemmle, the grand old man of Universal, finally complained.

"That face looks like it's a trade-mark in your pictures, Tod," he said.

Not a bad trade-mark, as it turned out.

As usual, Lon doubled in brass. He talked himself, by sheer dogged persistence and nagging, into a chance to direct J. Warren Kerrigan in seven westerns. In these he played parts, cast the stories, helped write them, was location man and transportation manager, general stage hand, and everything but the horses. Carl Laemmle must have saved a lot of salaries on Lon in those days. He paid for it later through the nose.

A woman saved Lon's job for him the first time.

A very fine scenario writer named Ida May Parks was given a chance to direct at Universal. There have been few women motion-picture directors. Lois Weber, Ida May Parks, Jane Murfin, June Mathis, Frances Marion, and Dorothy Arzner all tried it. They knew pictures, stories, values as well as any man. But there seems to be a nervous or nerve-racking quality to direction which the feminine physique cannot stand. Dorothy Arzner, however, is still successful at it.

The enormous bulk of harrowing details and physical

Chaney

By
ADELA ROGERS
ST. JOHNS

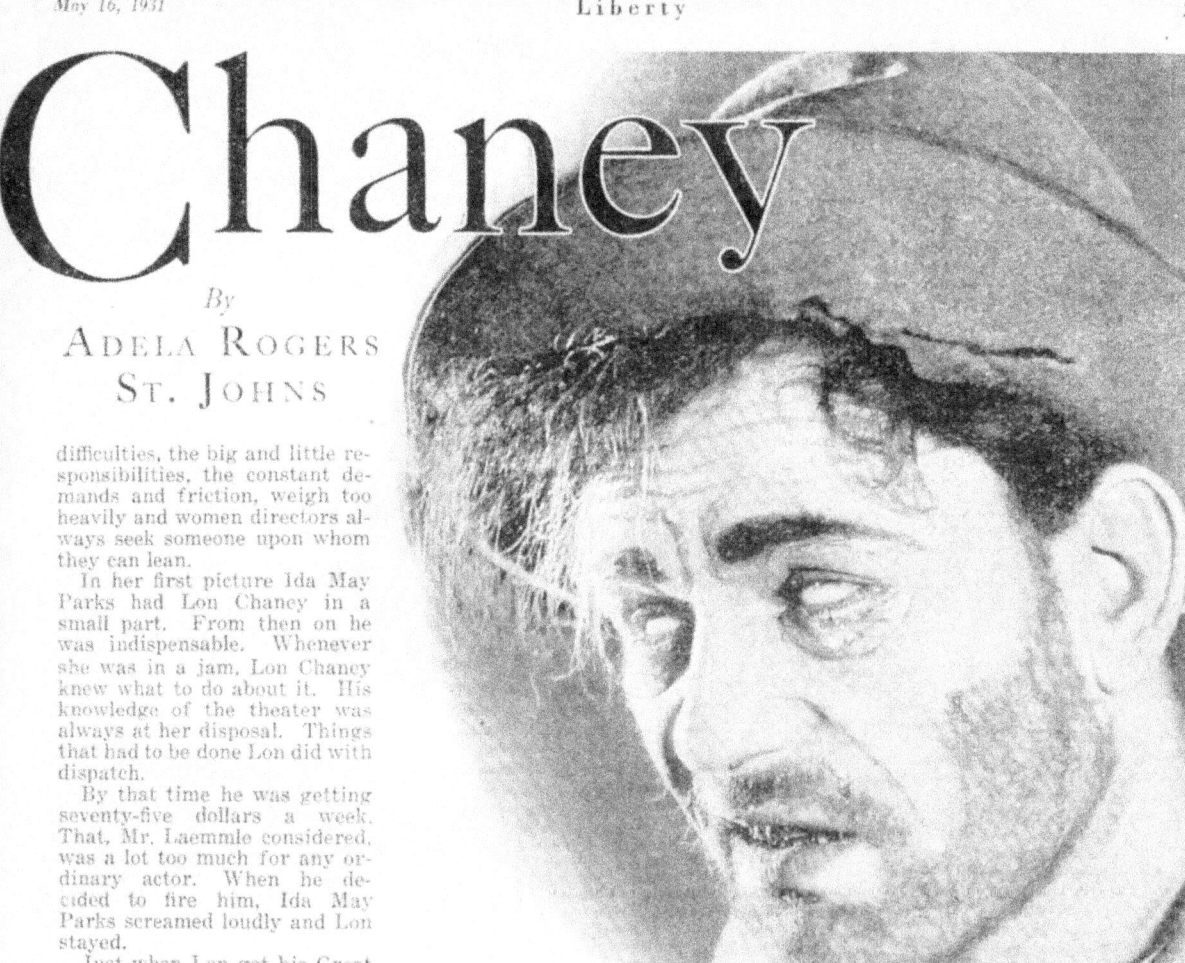

Chaney in The Miracle Man, the play which enabled him to "sell" his Great Idea to the producers.

difficulties, the big and little responsibilities, the constant demands and friction, weigh too heavily and women directors always seek someone upon whom they can lean.

In her first picture Ida May Parks had Lon Chaney in a small part. From then on he was indispensable. Whenever she was in a jam, Lon Chaney knew what to do about it. His knowledge of the theater was always at her disposal. Things that had to be done Lon did with dispatch.

By that time he was getting seventy-five dollars a week. That, Mr. Laemmle considered, was a lot too much for any ordinary actor. When he decided to fire him, Ida May Parks screamed loudly and Lon stayed.

Just when Lon got his Great Idea, I am not sure. Sometime during that long uphill pull at Universal.

It *was* a great idea, it was deliberate, and it was wholly his own. Gradually, as he watched, studied, worked, it sneaked up on him. A compound of his early years, of an inner sympathy that may have been prenatal.

Make-up had always fascinated him.

Deformity had for him some morbid appeal, which was at once sympathetic and curious. The vessels marred by the potter in the making aroused in him a deep interest and a real pity. Those who entered the battle of life already handicapped were always objects of his keen study.

From a crippled beggar who had his stand in front of a saloon in Chicago where Lon used to go for beer and free lunch he got a lasting impression that served as the basis for the Frog in The Miracle Man.

After one or two small parts in strange guise, Chaney began to experiment, as quietly as an inventor working in a laboratory. A nebulous idea was taking shape in his mind.

THERE were great stories—or one great story which could be clothed in many garments—around those queer mistakes of nature.

Trying to explain to me once how the idea was born, Chaney paraphrased the great Shakespearean speech of Shylock.

"I felt this way about them," said Chaney. "As Shakespeare said—I know my Shakespeare, like every good stage hand—well, Shakespeare said something that I didn't forget, though he was talking about something a little different: 'Have they not eyes? Hands, organs, dimensions, senses, affections, passions? Are they not fed with the same food, hurt with the same weapons, subject to the same diseases, healed by the same means, warmed and cooled by the same winter and summer, as an ordinary man? If you prick them do they not bleed? If you tickle them, do they not laugh? If you poison them, do they not die?'"

So Chaney saw them. And he saw, too, that tragedy and comedy and drama were utterly inseparable from such men, since nature had created them outside the normal, outside the ordinary round, in their physical aspect.

The poor clown, laughing behind his funny face, might often have a bleeding heart.

The man who seemed a monster might be pure gold within.

One of the oldest formulas in the world. Every great motion-picture star has had a formula. There are dozens. The Cinderella formula of Mary Pickford. The ugly-duckling formula. The good bad man—that made Bill Hart. The good bad woman. The Robin Hood formula of Fairbanks. The guy in wrong of Harold Lloyd. The Great Lover formula of Valentino.

Laugh, clown, laugh. The Chaney formula. It was real to Lon and he made it real to the world.

Tod Browning told me that in story conferences, when they were making great pictures, Lon always had one comment to make. "Don't you think he might get the girl in the end?" he would say wistfully. He never did get the girl—not once. It wasn't in the formula.

I remember one day around 1916 when he hailed me as

[CONTINUED ON NEXT PAGE]

[LON CHANEY
Continued from page twenty-nine]

I crossed the little street along which the dressing rooms of Universal City are built, on my way to do an interview with Priscilla Dean.

"Want to show you something," he said.

In his small dressing room he had a little black make-up box. Nothing to compare with the one which is being presented to the Los Angeles Museum by Mrs. Lon Chaney. But it was a lot more elaborate than those I usually saw. Most screen folks in those days were content with two sticks of grease paint, some black cosmetic, and a lip stick. The art of screen make-up was also in its infancy.

With all the seriousness of the discoverer of King Tut's tomb, he displayed some gobs of putty, several sets of false teeth, and some small celluloid tubes. His hands trembled with excitement.

Eagerly he demonstrated how the teeth fitted into his mouth, how the putty could be put on under grease paint to change the entire face, how the little tubes could be inserted in his nostrils and under his lips. A fanatical light burned in his black eyes. I realized that I was looking at a man with an Idea. You can always tell. It happens so seldom.

At home at night he used to sit until two and three o'clock putting on one make-up after another.

For he had a home by that time.

Strange coincidence that Chaney met both the women he married in the same way.

He was putting on a chorus number of a show at the Lyceum in Los Angeles. One of the girls was taken ill on the afternoon of the opening; a hurry call went out. Lon waited alone on the darkened stage.

A girl came in timidly. A very little girl, with a smooth, oval, Italian face.

Lon taught her the steps. Her tiny feet—she wore a twelve-and-a-half shoe—twinkled through them, and in an hour she had the routine.

During the run of the show they met occasionally. Later, in San Francisco, Hazel Hastings was in a show with Lon and Cleva. She was also in the chorus of the last Kolb and Dill comedy, the one Lon abandoned to go into pictures.

THEN he didn't see her for some time. She went back to her home in San Francisco. He stayed in Hollywood. But during 1914 and 1915 she came back to sing at Jahnke's Tavern, on Spring Street, only a block from the old Brink's Café. A sweet, gentle little thing, with a small, sweet voice and tiny hands that fluttered like butterflies. Great soft dark eyes. The face of an early Italian Madonna.

Lon began to see something of her, to take her out to dinner.

When they first met, both were married. Now both were divorced.

He had been through one kind of hell.

Picture by
Dan Sayre Groesbeck

*There was a rich old lady who
was a great Chaney fan.*

She had been through another.

I have always wondered if she first stirred Lon to some amazing pity when he found that she was married to a man who had no legs.

II

LON CHANEY first asked Hazel Hastings to marry him in the summer of 1915.

But it wasn't until November 26 of that year that a minister in Santa Ana—the Greenwich of California—made them one.

Those months held the secret of much of his "mysterious" later life.

The woman who ruled Lon's existence for fifteen years surrendered only at discretion. She didn't want to marry an actor.

Before she would say yes, Lon entered into an agreement that, in so far as his personal life was concerned, he wouldn't be an actor.

For fifteen years Hazel Chaney was to live in Hollywood, many of those years as the wife of the most consistently popular of all male stars. Yet no one knew her. Outside the little social circle which she formed around herself there were not ten people in Hollywood who had ever spoken to her. None of the officials of the Metro-Goldwyn-Mayer studio knew her even by sight. She had been on the lot where Lon worked as a star only twice.

Yet she was in all things the power behind the throne, the final court of appeal, the last word in every decision.

The enormous fortune which on Lon's death went to her without strings of any kind, to do with exactly as she pleased during her lifetime and at her death, was as much hers as his. Her shrewd business judgment, her careful handling of expenses, had doubled, tripled his earnings.

She spent ninety thousand dollars on doctors, radium treatment, possible cures for him during his last illness. Yet for fifteen years Lon had only a small weekly allowance for his own use. The rest went to Mrs. Chaney, who controlled every dollar and every business move that was made.

First mortgages were her favorite form of investment. Real estate, even in southern California, she didn't believe in, with the exception of quick turnovers on houses which she designed and built herself.

One of these, in Beverly Hills, she sold at an enormous profit completely furnished to a rich old lady who was a great Chaney fan and desired to sit in the very chair which the famous star was wont to use. But when the craze for Hollywood and Beverly Hills real estate struck the picture industry and Tod Browning suggested that he and Lon make some buys together, Mrs. Chaney quietly vetoed the idea. She was right. For most of his friends bought at the peak and have carried a load of soil around ever since.

Of all the people I have met in Hollywood, no more amazing figure has dawned upon my startled eyes than that of Hazel Hastings Chaney. "My beloved wife," as Lon always called her.

Unknown, unphotographed, getting no glory and no pleasure from the fact that her husband's name was familiar to every nation in the world, this little Italian woman dictated, inspired, protected with an almost uncanny intuition and mental vision the steps that the great Lon Chaney took up the steep pinnacle to success, and regulated his conduct when he reached it.

As you study her, she seems to belong to another age—an old-fashioned age when women accomplished through their men and were content with the power and the profits, without demanding the credit as well.

Quietly, competently, on November 26, 1915, Hazel Bennett Hastings took over the chaos of Lon's personal life, the management of his son, his finances, and his home.

Their prenuptial bargain was based upon their own experiences. They were mature people. Lon was thirty-two and Hazel Hastings was twenty-eight when they married.

Both were deeply scarred by unhappy first marriages. Neither wanted to make another mistake. Their aims and desires were the same—peace, security, confidence, the commonplace.

LON insisted first of all that she give up for all time any notion of a career for herself. He had been burned once at that fire. The new Mrs. Chaney was pretty as a picture, she had a sweet little voice, and danced like a fairy. But Lon insisted that they should bind themselves to a policy whereby, no matter what happened, no matter if they starved, she should never again appear before the public in any capacity.

The woman agreed without argument. Naturally domestic, she had always hated the stage. She had no ambition. Work had been for her an economic necessity. Ten years in show business had convinced her of the perils when two people attempted separate successes. The dangers of separation, of a wife with a divided heart and a divided duty—such was not her ideal of the married state. Her Italian blood, which dominated her in both appearance and temperament, gave her an old-world conception of the rightful place of woman.

But on her side she made certain demands.

Always she had sworn she would never marry an actor. She definitely disliked and distrusted them.

It was her set conviction, almost an obsession, that no actor could make a good husband. The irregular hours, the lack of home life, the continual demands of the public if one was successful, the outside pressure of many people who cluster about the actor for reflected glory, the temptations brought by flattering women, the over-development of ego which results from all that—these spelled to her certain disaster.

[CONTINUED ON NEXT PAGE]

The coolest and Fascist shave by the 2 INGRAM barbers

(JERRY JAR AND TERRY TUBE)

ANYONE who goes in for direct action in shaving can't avoid coming straight to the 2 Ingram barbers!

Il Duce himself couldn't deny that Ingram's is hot stuff—for it gives you the coolest and Fascist shave you ever had. Il Duce! Il Certainly Duce!—which, freely translated, means, it does!

It's cool, It's Cool, It's COOL

We reiterate, Ingram's Shaving Cream is cool, COOL, *COOL!* The sooner you take *that* fact to heart and *this* cream to your chin, the sooner you'll know what shaving comfort really is!

You'll get a chill from your first shave by the 2 Ingram barbers—(Terry Tube or Jerry Jar)—for both boys carry the same fine cream, and give you the same fine shave!

INGRAM'S

Shaving Cream

Here are the facts—the cold, chilly truth!

Ingram's is the coolest shaving cream ever devised by the hand of man. It's cool because we set out to make it cool. You'll recognize its difference as soon as the first dab of lather nestles on your cheek.

You need no lotion with either kind of Ingram's. It's shaving cream, lotion and face tonic combined—the three-in-one benediction to the faces of men.

We know Ingram's is good—good. To show you how good we think it is we're offering you 10 cool shaves—FREE. We lose if you don't like them (small chance, that) but we make a dime a year if you do.

10 COOL SHAVES—FREE

BRISTOL-MYERS CO., DEPT. B-51
110 Washington St.
New York, N.Y.
I'd like to try 10 cool Ingram shaves

Name————————————————

Street———————————————

City———————————State————

[LON CHANEY
Continued from page thirty-one]

Her years as a chorus girl had soured her forever upon all that had to do with the theater.

None of that should enter her life if she could help it.

She loved Lon. But she was wise beyond her years. That first nightmare marriage to a man without legs she had borne with dignity, with kindliness, as long as her body and spirit could endure. This time she meant to do everything possible to insure peace and sanity before they started.

To marry Lon she had to abandon the church under whose laws she had been born, whose dictates had been taught her through many years of convent education, and she was willing to take that chance only if Lon agreed to her way of living.

Years later the omnipotent Irving Thalberg, who rules Metro-Goldwyn-Mayer with a mere word, was to be defeated for the only time in his life by a woman he had never seen.

Lon Chaney refused, on any pretext, plea, or condition, to work after five o'clock.

At the very stroke of the hour appeared one John Jeske, chauffeur extraordinary and prime minister for the unseen Mrs. Chaney. At one minute after five Lon walked off the set. It didn't matter if he was in the middle of an important scene. It didn't matter that if they finished that scene an expensive set might be struck. It didn't matter if in another five minutes they might finish with two thousand extra people.

Lon Chaney quit at five o'clock. No other star in the business ever attempted such a thing.

Thalberg, who is under thirty, a slim, vital, nervous young genius in the forefront of the producers, sent for Chaney. They faced each other across Thalberg's desk. And Thalberg, who liked Lon, explained what a lot of money he was costing the company.

He put it well. Lon couldn't regard working time as it was regarded in other businesses. The motion picture could not possibly be confined within the routine of strictly business procedure. If Lon was called upon to work overtime one day, there were many days for which he was liberally paid when he didn't work at all. It was only fair that he should be reasonable with the firm which paid him five thousand dollars a week.

LON, standing at ease, his cap in his hand, his black eyes smiling faintly, shook his head.

"Can't be done," he said briefly. "I'm sorry, but I have a date with my wife at six o'clock. I promised to be home every night at six, because we have dinner at six thirty, and my wife likes me to have time to relax and get comfortable."

The great executive looked at him in amazement. Married himself to Norma Shearer, who worked on the same lot and understood the exigencies of this mad business, he couldn't figure Lon Chaney. Night after night he himself didn't leave the studio until eight, nine, ten o'clock.

"But, Lon," he said, "today you have two thousand extra people on your set. They get from five to ten dollars a day. If you work fifteen minutes more—one more shot—we can let them go. Otherwise, we'll have to call them in the morning and pay them for a whole day. It'll cost the company fifteen thousand dollars."

Lon Chaney in The Hunchback of Notre Dame.

Chaney's face grew stubborn. He was, as a matter of fact, as stubborn as a mule.

"Well," he said, "what's fifteen thousand dollars to this company? Five or ten dollars a day means a lot to those guys working out there. It means bread and butter for them and their kids. They need it and this company doesn't. I'm glad I'm in a spot where I can make you give them an extra day's pay. Anyway, I told my wife I'd stop at five o'clock. I've never been one minute late on the set since I've worked for you. I'm always on the set on time. Even if I have to get here at six o'clock to get on my make-up. I'm never late. Any director will tell you that. I'm a workingman. I start on time and I quit on time. Five o'clock's quitting time for me."

HE went on quitting at five o'clock. He was home at six. At six thirty Mr. and Mrs. Lon Chaney sat down to dinner, a dinner cooked often by her own hands even when Lon was up in the biggest kind of money.

When they were married Lon was getting forty-five dollars a week at Universal.

"It's not much," he said rather wistfully.

"It's enough," said the new Mrs. Chaney.

She made it enough.

There was never a week from the time he married her that, if he had a pay check, they didn't save something out of it.

When you find a small, soft woman with power, look out for her.

On the day of their wedding in the Santa Ana courthouse, Mrs. Lon Chaney weighed considerably less than a hundred pounds and was four feet nine and a half inches tall. Her eyes were large and dark. Her hands were exquisite—still are. Perhaps the most beautiful hands I have ever seen. Men always turned around to stare at her unbelievably tiny feet.

But every inch of her was pure steel.

They took a small flat on Edgemont Street just south of Hollywood Boulevard, facing the Mount of Olives, the famous estate of Aline Barnsdale. The rent, furnished, was thirty dollars a month. Near by was a good public school.

Creighton Chaney came home from his boarding place. The Chaney household began to run on well oiled, methodical wheels.

Creighton, clean, brushed, properly clothed, went to school on time. He came home at noon for a hot lunch. At six thirty the three of them sat down to dinner, an abundant meal prepared with all the art and economy of the Italian, who knows so well how to make a little go a long way.

On forty-five dollars a week, Hazel Chaney ran a perfect home and saved money. She sewed, she washed, she cooked, she kept the little flat spotless.

But she announced quite definitely that she didn't intend to do it always.

She hated to sew and wash and clean, though she loved to cook. The woman in her wanted pretty things, a nicer home, comfort, a bank account. Not the extravagant waste of the average American home, but good living, easy surroundings, freedom of mind. There was, she said, no reason why she shouldn't have them. It was Lon's business to give them to her. She expected him to succeed.

While they were climbing she was perfectly willing to do her share, to conserve what they had. But they must aim at financial independence. He must make sufficient income so that they could, in time, live on their savings if necessary. Middle age, old age, must be reckoned with. They must have something with which to educate Creighton and—their other children.

But Lon Chaney was never to have an old age or another child, though both of them prayed to whatever gods ruled the little household.

When Lon had been getting seventy-five a week at Universal for some time, Mrs. Chaney quietly informed him that he was worth more.

"You are to ask for a raise," she said sweetly, one night after she had cooked him a very special spaghetti which he liked.

"Why, I can't do that, honey," he said. "I'm getting a good salary now. We're all right."

"You are worth more," said Mrs. Chaney. "You've worked there like a slave for years. We have saved. You need not fear. It is right to make them pay you what you are worth."

For three days she hammered at him. Lon loathed talking money always. Finally she lost her temper. Probably it was a bluff, that temper, but it was a red-hot Italian bluff, and it did the work.

The fourth day Lon asked for a raise, and Carl Laemmle offered him ninety dollars.

"A hundred and fifty," said Hazel Chaney.

When they refused, with laughter, she told him to quit, and he quit.

"You must not work for anybody now unless they give you one hundred and fifty dollars a week," said Mrs. Chaney. "You are worth it. Now is the important time. You will get it. You are a wonderful actor and you have ideas. Otherwise we may stay just where we are forever."

WEEKS crawled into months. Lon didn't get it. Panic grew in him. The old terrible fear of poverty. He wanted to take extra work, to do anything he'd get paid for. They had a couple of battles that shook the little flat, because Lon had a temper of his own. But the steel in Hazel Chaney held against this emergency. It was as much her fight as his. They could always go back. She meant to gamble for something bigger. It was her only gamble, and it was a big one.

They lived on almost nothing. They denied themselves everything. Lon yielded because always he had a mystic, blind faith in his wife. She could do no wrong.

There was in him an almost pathetic gratitude for those things from which she had rescued him. Here was a woman he could trust— trust entirely. If he went away on location, he didn't have to worry about what *she* was doing. His son

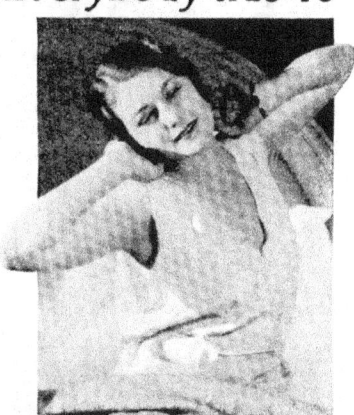

was safe in her hands, given all the tender, efficient care of a mother. He came home at night to warmth and comfort and good food.

After a weary wait, Lon Chaney got his hundred and fifty dollars a week from Bill Hart.

"That is the first step," said little Mrs. Chaney.

Every raise, every big salary, every big and bigger contract that Lon Chaney got, his wife made him ask for, forced him to demand. There was a modest streak in Lon, modest in outlook, narrow in scope. He couldn't figure that he was worth all that money. Always he would have taken less.

Mrs. Hazel Chaney, the actor's widow.

BUT Mrs. Chaney had no modesty for him. Little as the picture industry knew her, she kept a shrewd eye on the box office and considered it wisdom and economy to hire one of the best lawyers in Los Angeles to protect Lon's interests.

Lon knew very little about the contract for five more years which he signed with Metro-Goldwyn-Mayer in January, 1930. The contract he was never to fulfill, a fortune he could never earn. It was arranged entirely by Milton M. Cohen, acting with Mrs. Chaney.

He did a few unimportant pictures after the one with Bill Hart, and then, in 1918, came The Miracle Man.

The Frog—Lon Chaney.

The fake cripple, the fake healing by the Miracle Man. The wonderful scenes between the crook and the old saint, the death scene itself. They made screen history.

They made Lon Chaney.

It was a great performance; it was the proof of Lon's Great Idea, and it established him not only with the public but with the producers of Hollywood. At last he was able to sell them his Great Idea.

When he went back to Universal to play The Hunchback of Notre Dame, Lon Chaney didn't ask for a hundred and fifty dollars a week. He asked for twenty-five hundred. There was uproar. Ridicule and sarcasm. There was denial and days of waiting. But Lon Chaney, like many another man, was more afraid to come home and tell his wife he had failed than he was to stand up to the whole Universal Company.

"It is your great chance," said Hazel Chaney. "No one else can do it. I *know* they'll give it to you."

Creighton Chaney, now a young gentleman who overflows any room with his six feet three and his two hundred and ten pounds and who adores the only mother he has ever known, told me that when "mother" said she *knew* there was no more dispute.

"It's uncanny," he said. "Why, she can read people by just looking at them. I remember one friend I

[CONTINUED ON NEXT PAGE]

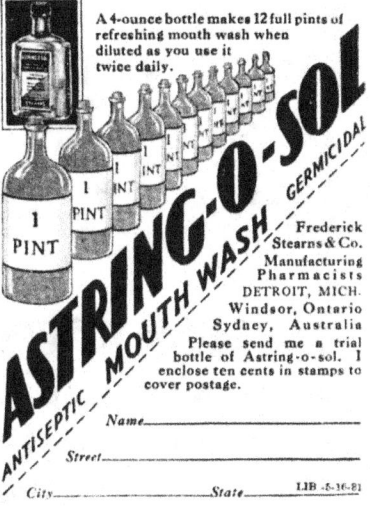

LON CHANEY
[Continued from page thirty-three]

had in high school. After meeting
him once, she told me he was no good
and to stay away from him. Sixteen
months later he was in jail. That
tickled dad. He laughed like anything and said, 'You can't beat her,
son. She's always right.'"

In the matter of the Hunchback
she was right.

Lon got his twenty-five hundred.
They built a little home, almost next
door to their first flat. The bank
account grew by leaps and bounds,
since they spent little more. The one
extravagance was Lon's first car, a
big Cadillac roadster—not new, but
in good condition. In it he rode
triumphantly over the old road to
Universal City.

So we come to the man of a thousand faces.

While Hazel Chaney ran his home
and his business and guided his deci-
sions, Lon was free to concentrate
upon the two things of which he was
master—make-up and showmanship.

For his great idea, Lon Chaney
suffered tortures unbelievable. The
public did not guess—Lon did not
wish them to guess—what he suffered in some of his rôles. He had
only a passionate determination to
convince them of the reality of the
character he was playing.

Personal publicity was bad showmanship for Chaney. He had less of
it than any other star, by his own request. That mystery was the height
of salesmanship for him.

HE ruined his health and crucified
his flesh in a sort of morbid
obsession. As his fame grew, his
desire for weird rôles increased.

When the famous wise crack, repeated with laughter from one end of
the country to the other, came out—
"Don't step on it, it might be Lon
Chaney"—Lon laughed delightedly.
Perhaps he knew he was being im-
mortalized in a jest. "You can't
fool me, I know you, you're Lon
Chaney." Quips like that tickled the
little man, who peeped out from behind his thousand faces and studied
the great public as it poured wealth
and glory in upon him.

They didn't know him. Had never
seen him. But, oh, how well he knew
them! The dear public, so fickle,
so omnipotent! How easily, how
swiftly, they tired! How brutally
were old favorites dethroned for new
faces! They shouldn't grow tired of

him! He'd give them new faces—
thousands of them.

It would never do for them to know
Lon Chaney, an ordinary man without any great flair, without any great
personality. For, literally, his personality, his flair, seemed to fade beneath his success. What did he care
that when he moved among them in
some theater lobby they shoved him
aside, just another rather hard-
boiled-looking bird in an old cap and
dark glasses?

The laugh was his, for they had
gathered there to see Lon Chaney.

Keep interviewers away. Keep
personal appearances away. Keep
away from stories about Lon Chaney.
The others could have that food for
vanity. Chaney couldn't afford it.

OVER a quart of Scotch on a Sunday
morning he would sit and chuckle
about it all with his great friend,
Fritz Tidden, for years a great newspaper reporter, then a publicity man
for Von Stroheim.

At eleven o'clock every Sunday
morning he would appear at Fritz'
house. The bottle would be set between them. They would empty it
and start on another. That was the
way Lon liked to talk. Man to man.
Then he need not fear to betray himself by the limitations of his education and his knowledge of the world.

His mind would unfold about those
subjects of which he knew much:
Labor and labor unions. The public
and its reactions. Politics. The theater and the screen. Prisons and
prison reform. Great men and their
deeds. He talked well, in blunt, con-
vincing phrases. Opinionated, rabid
on the rights of the workingman, red-
hot against injustice in any form.
Direct and sound in argument.

Only in matters of art and literature did he betray his lack of culture.
His taste in art was unbelievable. He
adored old-fashioned pictures in huge
gilt frames. Was always discovering
them, buying them, and exhibiting
them with glee.

When, about two o'clock on Sundays, the rest of Fritz' friends
dropped in for the afternoon, Lon
Chaney would get up and go home.

*The story of Chaney's meeting for-
mer President and Mrs. Coolidge, his
make-up for the Hunchback—most
difficult and painful of all his imper-
sonations—and his battles for those
under him will be told in Liberty next
week.*

ANSWERS TO TWENTY QUESTIONS ON PAGE 22

1—Emerald.
2—One who attacks cherished beliefs
as impositions or shams; a radical.
3—A period during which a debtor
may legally defer the payment of a debt.
4—In central Asia, mostly in Mongolia.
5—Any broad sheet of water inter-
spersed with many islands or with a
group of islands; also such a group of
islands.
6—Tegucigalpa.
7—A rhymed verse of four lines.
8—Essay on Criticism by Alexander
Pope.
9—The rupee.
10—A mock serenade; a medley of
discordant noises.
11—Ninety feet.
12—At Hanover, New Hampshire.
13—Delaware.
14—Republican.
15—Arrows.
16—Zero.
17—A leading ballet dancer.
18—Malachi.
19—One having two chambers or
branches.
20—The Netherlands.

Publicity Photo from "Thunder" 1929

Lon

A Portrait of the Man Behind a Thousand Faces

By
ADELA
ROGERS
ST. JOHNS

Lon Chaney and Lila Lee in The Unholy Three.

(Reading time: 27 minutes 25 seconds.)

CHANEY'S *first venture into the movies as a director and his experimenting with make-ups for the impersonation of the unusual characters with which he was so successful later were described in last week's installment. It also told of the events leading up to the meeting of the woman whom he afterward married, and who was destined to be such an inspiration to him in his climb to fame and fortune.*

PART FOUR—MYSTERIES OF MAKE-UP

LON CHANEY hid his secrets of make-up as carefully as a gambler hides a fifth ace. While he lived it would have broken his heart to have any publicity concerning them.

Not even the director on the picture knew what was coming off.

The first day of a new Chaney picture was a ceremonial. At five o'clock, just as the cold dawn was breaking over the studio, the gateman on duty would see the familiar roadster drive up, with John Jeske, silent and impenetrable, at the wheel, and Chaney, as silent, beside him. The gates would swing back upon the empty silence of the tremendous plant. Chaney would park his car in the most select spot—it always gave him a secret glee to put it in exactly the spot where the great executives could most conveniently descend to go up to their offices—and proceed to his dressing room.

No dressing bungalows for Chaney. No valets.

Basil Rathbone once stopped Chaney on the lot to ask him if a valet who had once been with Ramon Novarro—Ramon was in Europe—was a good man.

"I mean," said Rathbone with his careful English accent, "does he understand all the duties of a first-class valet?"

"How the hell should I know?" said Chaney. "I don't know what the duties of a first-class valet or any other kind of a valet are."

Chaney and Jeske would enter the dressing room. At nine o'clock on the second, Chaney would appear on the set as the character he was supposed to portray. No one knew how he had turned the slim, wiry body, the lean, haggard face of Lon Chaney into the one-eyed man of The Road to Mandalay, the armless man of The Unknown, the menacing figure of London After Midnight.

No one could casually drop into Lon's dressing room as they did into the others on the lot. It was a holy of holies, a sanctum, a magician's cell. Dirty, disorderly, as ordinary as that of any second-rate leading man on the lot, it was inviolate. Louis B. Mayer himself couldn't get by that door.

A sacred few were admitted. They knew somewhat of the mysteries. It was an added joy to Chaney to have a small, intimate audience to watch the rites. It gave him the thrill he denied his vanity so often and he knew that in their hands he was safe.

His intimates included none of the "big names" on the lot. He liked to flaunt his independence.

John Jeske, to whom he left five thousand dollars in his

Chaney

will. His servant, friend, constant companion. How often we find some such figure in the life of a famous man or woman—a sort of shock absorber and equalizer! John had been a mechanic in a garage where Lon used to take his car. Lon loved fine automobiles. They were his one extravagance. An extravagance he always alibied by the time he used them.

WHEN necessity forced Lon to have someone to help him in his many activities, Lon hired John Jeske, a German born. From that day forward the two men were seldom apart. John was like a second self. Oddly enough, there was a striking resemblance between the two. Jeske had the same build, the same deep lines in his face, the same quick black eyes. They went to the fights together, seated every Friday night in those same seats in the Hollywood American Legion Stadium. They went to football games together. On Lon's long fishing trips. And it was John Jeske who drove Mrs. Chaney to the hospital on that last fatal midnight and stood beside her, her comforter and sustaining friend.

John Jeske was always in Lon's dressing room.

Creighton Chaney was allowed to go there and sit perfectly quiet while the master sculptured his strange masterpieces.

The two Feinbergs, Jack and Sam, his set musicians.

Perhaps no one knew Lon better than Jack and Sam. In the long, long hours that he put in at the studio they were his constant companions. They

[CONTINUED ON PAGE FORTY]

ONE of Chaney's greatest rôles— Quasimodo in The Hunchback of Notre Dame.

[LON CHANEY
Continued from page thirty-seven]

were his playmates and his relaxation. He liked to rough-house with them, cuss them, pull their ears, and knock them about.

They had a game which all three loved.

Jack and Sam would get out the violin and the old organ. Lon would stand beside them. Lon would name any song—going back mostly to the old musical shows. The boys would play it. If he named a tune they couldn't play, they lost. Then they would play songs, and if he couldn't name them, he lost. The repertoire on both sides was enormous. Mostly the old musical comedies, which Lon adored—The Prince of Pilsen, Robin Hood, The Merry Widow, Babes in Toyland, It Happened in Nordland, Mlle. Modiste, The Wizard of the Nile, The Rose of Algeria, The Fortune Teller, Dolly Varden, The Red Mill, The Stubborn Cinderella, The Time, the Place, and the Girl, Forty-five Minutes from Broadway, The Pink Lady. Literally, there were hundreds and the game went on for hours.

The loser had to buy lunch in the commissary.

The terribly sentimental streak in Chaney came out where music was concerned. When they wanted to make him cry on the set, Sam and Jack played Dear Old Girl. Two bars, and Lon was weeping.

One day in his own hand he scrawled out a list of the songs he loved best and wanted played every day on the set—The Rosary; Oh, How I Miss You, Dear Old Pal of Mine; Let the Rest of the World Go By; Laugh, Clown, Laugh; Buddy; Dear Old Girl; Just a-Wearyin' for You.

Chaney as the old lady in his first all-talking picture, The Unholy Three.

That was Lon Chaney's idea of great music. He always hated jazz. It was never allowed on his set.

It was for Jack and Sam that Chaney braved Calvin Coolidge himself.

When the former President and Mrs. Coolidge were in California, they paid a visit to the Metro-Goldwyn-Mayer studio. Stars, executives, directors, and a mob of studio workers turned out to cheer their arrival. Every other star was there, but Chaney was nowhere to be seen. One by one the celebrities of the screen shook hands with the silent ex-President and his charming lady. Still no Chaney.

Probably no one would ever have seen him, hidden among the mass, if it hadn't been for Jack and Sam Feinberg. For himself, Chaney would never have allowed himself to be seen by the exalted visitors.

The most treasured possession of the Feinbergs is a violin upon which are the autographs of all the famous ones in moviedom. Right in the middle, the boys had saved a little space for just such an emergency as the arrival of Coolidge.

THEY didn't have the nerve to ask for it themselves. Where, oh, where was their pal, Lon? They peered about. No Lon. But there was a way. Among themselves they had a code whistle. It called for immediate action. Jack whistled above the crowd. Two minutes later, Lon appeared beside them.

"What in hell do you want?" he demanded.

They held up the violin and pointed at the vacant space, then at the famous man who was the occasion for all this vast celebration.

Lon gave them a dirty look, took the fiddle, and went through the crowd like a football player. Once in the front row, eager hands grabbed him and presented him to Mr. and Mrs. Coolidge, who smiled with delight. They had inquired about Mr. Chaney.

Chaney smiled, bowed, and immediately asked them to sign his violin. Coolidge's name appeared at once in the vacant space. Lon bowed again and vanished.

"Here's your so-and-so fiddle, you blankety-blank nui-sances!" he said as he handed it back to Jack and Sam.

"He was the finest man that ever lived," Jack Feinberg said to me, the tears streaming down his face. "There will never be anybody like him. He was so kind. He loved us boys and he did everything for us. When he died, we felt like everything was ended."

Clinton Lyle was the fifth man who had seen Chaney make up. In the old San Francisco days Lyle had been the leading man in a company where Lon was property man. They were friends and Lyle was very good to Chaney. Lon never forgot. A few years ago Mr. and Mrs. Lon Chaney were in a small town in northern California. On the vaudeville bill they saw the names Clinton Lyle and Flo Emerson. Their vacation plans were abandoned. They followed the act around over the circuit and Lon had a wonderful time.

And at last he persuaded Clinton Lyle to come to Hollywood and go into pictures. Lyle had refused Lon's letters and telegrams, but he could not refuse Lon personally. The Lyles came home with the Chaneys, and the quartette had been inseparable ever since.

JOHN JESKE. Creighton Chaney. The Feinbergs. Clinton Lyle. Friends of many years' standing, all of them. Friendships between men that had endured. It didn't make any difference who they were, what they were. Didn't make any difference that Lon Chaney was now a great star. They were his *friends*. They alone knew his secrets.

The Hunchback of Notre Dame was without question the most difficult and the most painful of all Chaney's make-ups.

The call on the set for that picture was nine o'clock.

At four thirty in the morning Lon Chaney arrived and went to his dressing room. It took him a full four hours and a half to put on that amazing disguise. To become, in all truth, a hunchback.

First of all, he took the putty and built the outside of his face into a gruesome mask. Later he came to use mortician's wax because it gave better results. Then he still used putty.

When he had completed the new putty face that transformed his own, he inserted the false teeth, the tubes in his nose, and built carefully, hair by hair, the false eyebrows that gave such a menacing, weird expression to the face. Eyebrows were always important to him. He'd spend half an hour on them.

Then, over it all, he applied a grease-paint make-up with a delicate, careful hand.

Inside his eyelid he inserted a small piece of fish-skin, and held it in place with collodion. That in itself was a nervous torment, for it continually irritated all the hypersensitive nerves of the eye. Everyone knows how a mere eyelash can annoy you past bearing.

The harness which transformed him into a hunchback Lon Chaney designed himself. In the Middle Ages they might well have used it for an instrument of torture.

It was made of thin leather. Shoulder pads, such as a football player wears, fitted tightly about his neck and across his back and over the shoulders themselves. Across the front was a heavy breastplate. From front to back, between his legs, ran a strap of heavy leather, which was hooked into the shoulder pads and laced on to the breastplate with heavy leather thongs.

Lon put it on. Then he pulled the thongs tighter—tighter—tighter, until gradually his spine bent into a curve. The thongs were tied tight, and Lon Chaney could not straighten his back a fraction of an inch.

Over this he wore a complete suit of heavy rubber which concealed the harness and to which monkeylike hair was attached.

Twenty minutes was the longest time he was supposed to endure this position. Then he was supposed to take off the rubber suit, loosen the straps, and rest for at least an hour. Not Chaney!

"I'm okey," he'd say. "Let's get on with it. I can stand another shot."

The muscles of his back screamed and protested. His poor spine ached so that he couldn't sleep at night for pain. His flesh crawled under the heavy binding rubber. The nerves in his eyes and nose twitched and jumped. But he never said a word. It was almost as though he gloried in the torture, gloried in doing something no actor had ever done before.

He had guts, plenty of them. Too many.

I remember one terribly hot day when I went out to watch them work on this great picture. Interest in Hollywood was terribly keen. Weird tales of the make-up drifted about.

When I arrived, Chaney was having a battle with the director. There was some argument about the story, about the authenticity of a scene. Bound in his harness, hopping about like something in a nightmare, his eyes snapping and his hands clenched half in anger, half in pain, Chaney was calling down denunciations upon the head of the scenario writer who had dared to question or take liberties with the immortal Victor Hugo.

"Hugo knew, didn't he?" he yelled. "He knew about Paris. He'd been there, hadn't he? I guess we can take Victor Hugo's word for it, can't we? We don't need any blankety-blank, half-witted, cockeyed so-and-so to tell *Victor Hugo* how to write his own stuff, do we? By God, I say we'll make it the way Victor Hugo wrote it and to hell with the scenario writer, whoever he is!"

Ten minutes later, as they finished a scene, he fainted from pain and exhaustion and had to be carried off on a stretcher. That happened not once but many times.

IT seemed to me more than any public would demand or had the right to demand for its entertainment. It was as though we had gone back to the days of the Roman arena for our amusement. Such self-torture made me a little ill.

I told Lon so. If you had seen him, the lines carved deep in his face, his eyes haggard with pain, you would have agreed with me.

But he only stared stubbornly, and again I saw in his eyes the blazing light of the fanatic.

"You're wrong," he said. "This is truth, not acting. I'm not playing a hunchback with a bundle of straw on my back. I am a hunchback. I know how it feels. I've only got one eye with that make-up, to show them the torments of that poor deformed soul and body. Well, that eye will show it because I feel it. I'll show 'em. I can do it."

Lon Chaney never fully recovered from The Hunchback of Notre Dame. To be sure, he became more famous. Was a star. Little by little, though, the flair died. The marks of pain grew. The spirit and body lost fire, though he was always in fine physical shape. He was never quite the man—quite the vital, dynamic person—he had been before he put on that ghastly harness.

You can't give the human spine the beatings Lon gave it and get away with it. Nothing could convince him of that. His stubborn, dogged pride never faltered. *He* could do it. When he left the studio for the last time, he was talking about another great hunchback part.

The hunchback was only one of the many beatings Chaney inflicted upon himself.

The legless man of The Penalty was a thing no one should have to go through. There were tricks suggested to Chaney—cover-ups, lighting, chairs, and all that sort of thing. He only snorted.

Try it yourself. Get on your knees and bend your lower legs back and up until they are parallel with your thighs. Strap them together as tight as human flesh can bear. Place your bent knees in a tight leather stump shoe. Try walking around for hours, working hard, in great emotional stress, in that position. No wonder Lon used to weep when he collapsed after those great scenes.

To me, that was the greatest thing he ever did. For he was a great actor.

It is not strange that little Mrs. Chaney hated these parts. They must have called up the tortured past when in real life she had been wife to a legless man. And now

[CONTINUED ON NEXT PAGE]

[LON CHANEY
Continued from page forty-one]

again she was watching a nightmare imitation of that tragedy in her husband's unreal rôles. More than that, they distressed her because of the pain they caused Lon.

But in that one thing and that one thing only she could do nothing with her husband. Even a beloved wife cannot alter a man who is fanatically pursuing a Great Idea. After Tell It to the Marines—an enormous success which was almost a straight rôle for Chaney—the studio suggested that he do a few of those parts. He was furious. Wouldn't ·consider it. Was wounded that they thought the public would stand for the disappearance of the man of a thousand faces.

Lon had never been satisfied with the fishskin he used in The Hunchback. When he played the one-eyed man in The Road to Mandalay, he went to one of the finest opticians in Los Angeles and had a glass shield made which exactly resembled a sightless eye. This he inserted over his own eyeball, under the eyelid. The pain grew terrible after a time. For hours after he removed it, Chaney couldn't see out of that eye at all. Not even his family knew that in that picture he injured that eye beyond repair and could never see out of it as well as he did out of the other.

Another painful make-up, though perhaps it didn't show it, was in London After Midnight.

Do you remember those strange eyes, those inhuman eyes, that peered from beneath the tall black hat? The eyes with the pouches underneath?

To achieve those eyes, Chaney had two gold rings made. These he fitted into the flesh below the eye and against the bone at the top, almost as a man wears a monocle, only much more tightly, so that the whole lower and upper lids were distended. Over these he put a layer of mortician's wax and then applied grease paint. The rings cut deep grooves in the tender flesh beneath the eyes. The irritation made water run from the eyeballs and helped the strange effect.

Do you remember the weird, distended nose whose wide nostrils flared back from the face in The Phantom of the Opera? It wasn't only critics and audiences who were puzzled by that one. Actors watched and tried to figure out how he had done it.

IN a way, it was simple. Lon found one more use for the old-fashioned hairpin.

Taking a wire hairpin, Lon made the ends into small sharp hooks, which he inserted inside the nostrils. At the upper curve of the pin he tied a piece of string, which went straight up the bridge of his nose and tied tightly around his head, pulling the hooks inside and pulling back the nostrils. Before the picture was finished, he had two deep, bleeding holes in the sensitive flesh at the end of his nose.

The armless man of The Unknown was another torture chamber for Chaney. To conceal his arms he wore a strait-jacket so tight that it broke the veins in his legs by the pressure of the blood pumping down from the strapped-up part of his body. Chaney put it on day after day and worked for hours. Sweat poured down his face and he had to have John Jeske always at hand to help renew his grease paint. At night when he removed the jacket his arms and back were a mass of black-and-blue bruises.

Yet Lon's own favorite make-ups were often the simpler ones. The old lady in The Unholy Three. The Blackbird. Things where, without tricks or sensational changes, he yet changed his whole face. He believed that his clown make-up in Laugh, Clown, Laugh, was the best clown make-up ever put on. So worked the man of a thousand faces and the spotlight could not penetrate his disguises.

People came from all over the earth to interview Chaney. He was hopeless. Even if they got to see him, they learned nothing of the man or his past. Celebrities desired his acquaintance. No one could find Chaney.

He kept his mystery to the last.

II

THERE is only one unfailing power in Hollywood. They call it box-office draw.

Lon Chaney had it. Knew it. Used it.

Yet no star ever lived in Hollywood who made so little impression upon the motion-picture industry itself.

On the afternoon of the day the morning papers announced that Lon Chaney must submit to a blood transfusion in a last effort to save his life, the switchboard at the Metro-Goldwyn-Mayer studio had to be closed for the first time in its history. It was impossible, even with three extra girls, to handle the thousands of calls that came in from strangers, fans, rich and poor, young and old, begging to be allowed to give their blood for Chaney. No one in motion pictures remembers another such public reaction. Even the newspapers were swamped with calls.

In view of his immense popularity with the public, his enormous fan mail, the crowds that always filled theaters where his pictures played, it is astounding to realize how he ignored and was ignored by the people of his own profession.

Even in discussions about box office his name never came up. The wise ones would speak of Colman, Gary Cooper, Haines, and Powell, and speculate as to whether they would ever reach the great heights of the old-timers like Fairbanks, Barthelmess, Valentino, and Gilbert. A star's gross over the year would be told, compared with that of somebody else.

As the Phantom of the Opera in the play of that title.

Maybe, at the very end, somebody would say, " What about Chaney? " A surprised silence and then, " That's right. We forgot Chaney."

More or less naturally, they always forgot Chaney.

Great artist as he undoubtedly was, he never belonged to Hollywood.

His way lay far apart from the beaten paths of studio politics, social intrigue, the deadly battle for place and power which is carried on in office and drawing-room. How he despised it all! His contempt became almost a pose.

And all the time he was playing his rôle of the common man in life's drama a shadow walked with him.

Did you ever happen to read Rebecca McCann's little verse?

> When I consider Time and Space,
> It fills me with quiet mirth
> To see a human fencing off
> A tiny portion of the earth.

Chaney was busy fencing off his portion of the earth. Walling it round and round with gold. Shutting out the dangers of wealth and fame. Tightening the bonds that held the little family securely together. Barring the doors against any new thought, any newcomer, any new thing that might derange the well ordered plan of his safe existence.

As I think of it I hear again the sad little melody of his last music, Laugh, Clown, Laugh, and the agony of that shriek which rent the reverent silence in the little chapel when his wife cried out the question that was in every heart, " Why? Why? Why? "

Of himself Napoleon said, " I am the man of the people: its pulse beats in unison with my own."

It can be said in all truth of Lon Chaney.

In a land where snobbery is rampant and ambition makes strange bedfellows and the newly elected favorites of fortune forget overnight what manner of men they were, Chaney remained what he had always been. A simple, sentimental, hard-boiled guy who gloried in the fact that he was often mistaken for a stage hand.

They called him the man nobody knew. I thought no

one knew Chaney. When I talked to the higher-ups, I got nowhere. They didn't know Chaney. The wise guys that know everything about everybody knew nothing about Chaney. There were no stories current at the Embassy, to which he did not belong, nor the Mayfair, to which he had never been, nor in the Brown Derby.

But there were plenty of people who knew him.

He was no mystery to the hundreds of men and women who worked in the rank and file of the Metro-Goldwyn-Mayer army. No mystery to the old gang who shifted scenery and moved lights at Universal.

Like our great admiral, Farragut, Chaney rose from the ranks and the ranks worshiped him. Probably, at the test, Chaney controlled more votes in the motion-picture industry than any other man who ever stepped on a set. That was because, as the great English public looked upon the royal household of Victoria and saw reflected their own ways of living, so the thousands in the movie business whose names never appear on any title sheet saw in Chaney one of themselves lifted up.

WHEN he used his power, he made it stick. Always for his own gang. There was in his heart not the slightest understanding of or sympathy for the man with the money bag. As long as the do-re-mi continued to roll into the box office for Lon Chaney, so long Chaney would delight in defying authority and fighting for his own kind.

If a man in the ranks got a raw deal, he came to Lon. Called him Lon. Told his story. Then, with glee, Lon took up the cudgels. He never got the complex of believing that he knew more about stories than the writer, more about directing than the director, more about producing than the producer. That was their job. Let 'em do it. But they couldn't pick on the workingman.

Things that busy executives knew absolutely nothing about and with which they had no personal connection were brought forcibly to their attention by Chaney.

In the carpenter shop was an old man who had been there since Thomas H. Ince first built the great white studio at Culver City. The efficiency expert drew a line through his name. His best days were past.

Chaney went into action.

" I don't give a damn for efficiency experts," he said. " Let 'em fire a lot of these high moguls that sit around all day talking to New York on the telephone. Let them get rid of some of these playwrights that talk about backgrounds and motivation and wouldn't know a plot if it crawled into bed with them. But tell them to keep their hands off a good honest workingman. Hell, they can fire one supervisor and his salary will pay a hundred good men and they'll never miss him! "

The man stayed.

[CONTINUED ON NEXT PAGE]

LON CHANEY
[Continued from page forty-three]

An electrician had been made the goat for a big director in a sequence which cost a lot of money. It wasn't Chaney's picture, but the electrician went to the "Little Corporal" and spoke his piece.

Chaney went at once to W. W. Greenwood. Greenwood was his one real friend in the powers that be at the studio. He was crazy about Greenwood. When nobody else could handle Chaney, they sent for Greenwood.

He is, in truth, one of the most interesting men in the picture industry. One-time gambler, gold-miner in the bonanza days of Nevada, a man who could speak Chaney's language. His position is an unusual one. He is really the trouble shooter. Everyone trusts him because he always speaks the truth.

He and Chaney grew very close in the years they spent on the same lot. Yet even Greenwood was never inside Chaney's home.

"I want this thing fixed up," Chaney said to him. "This boy's okey. I don't want him made the patsy. The boy's got a wife and two kids. He's a good citizen and a first-class workman."

The electrician went back on salary.

There is no place on earth where the caste lines are drawn tighter than in Hollywood. Many tears are shed over failing invitations. I have heard hour-long discussions over whether a producer who produced a picture "ranked" the star who starred in it at a dinner table. Somebody should get out a Hollywood Peerage.

Chaney knew nothing about such things and actually cared less.

The tide of his rise in pictures had been slow, steady, sure. No flaming comet. He was forty before he became the great Chaney. His ideals and ideas were set. His morals were convictions. His ways unalterable.

He was in the thing. But he regarded Hollywood as mad, bad, and dangerous. He disapproved of it almost as much as he disliked it. From loyalty to the hand that fed him, and because he believed in motion pictures themselves if he didn't believe in the people who made them, he kept quiet. With one exception.

Creighton Chaney, when he left Hollywood High School, wanted to go into pictures. A tall, handsome youth, dark and very appealing, he might easily have been another Gary Cooper. After all, he was all but born in the theater.

Lon Chaney stared his own fairy godmother in the face and said, "I'd rather see a son of mine dead than in Hollywood."

HE had raised the boy sternly, severely, without indulgence. From the time he was fourteen, young Chaney worked summers to earn his own spending money. His father refused to buy him a car when he was in high school.

"Kids have no business with cars," he said. "They only get into trouble. Besides, he's no rich man's son. He'll earn what he gets, the same as I did. Most boys that are brought up with too much don't amount to a damn."

When Creighton wanted to get in the movies, Lon said "No." But the boy persisted.

So Chaney went to his great friend Greenwood.

"I'm going to send the kid out to you," he said. "You talk to him. You talk better than I do, anyway. He may have a secret notion that I don't want him in pictures because I don't want the public to know I've got a son six feet

tall. What the hell do I care for that? I just don't want my son in this business. Maybe he'd survive. Most of them don't. It's a crazy racket. You know that. I'd been through hell and back before I got into it, so it didn't upset me much. Besides, I could afford to stay away from most of it. The kid's different. I want to keep him out of Hollywood. I'm not afraid he'd be a failure. I'm afraid he'd be a success. I'd rather he'd be a good plumber than a movie star."

Greenwood did talk to him.

"But that wasn't what kept me out," Creighton Chaney told me. "I wouldn't for the world have done anything dad didn't want me to. He might have known that."

Creighton Chaney married a lovely girl, Dorothy Hinckley, before he was of age. Strangely enough, he is in the plumbing supply business with his father-in-law. They knew few picture people. Young Mrs. Chaney went to the University of Southern California and her brothers were prominent at Stanford. Their friends are mostly young married couples not long out of college.

LON was tickled to death with Creighton's marriage, with his quiet, sane way of life.

He hadn't wanted him to go to college.

"I'm not sure I hold with this college business," he said. "I guess a man can use those four years better if he gets to work. Unless maybe he wants to be a doctor or a lawyer or something. The Chaneys don't run to that sort of thing. He'd better go to work and make a man out of himself. I'd like him to play football, but I guess he can't take four years out of his life just to play football, though I notice a lot of boys are doing it."

No bigger football bug than Lon Chaney ever fluttered about a gridiron. He didn't only go to the big college games staged at the Los Angeles Coliseum. He never missed a Friday afternoon high-school game if he wasn't working. He and Fritz Tidden would sit up on the top row and Chaney would yell himself hoarse while the kids fought and scrambled on the turf.

Nobody ever recognized him. The boys whose idol he doubtless was up there rooting his head off for the under dog and the little fellows.

His pet football idol was a Stanford half back who weighed a hundred and fifty pounds and was apt to be a bit unconventional in his tactics. The newspapers occasionally mentioned his differences with his coach, and that enlisted Lon—who read all sporting sheets from headline to the final period—on his side.

"That's the way to do it!" he'd yell, when the half back carried the ball. "Those kids ought to fight on their own, use their own brains, not just do what some hired coach says. To hell with the coaches!"

That was Chaney. To hell with the coaches. To hell with the man in authority if you could get away with it.

It was the same at the fights. The greatest thing that could happen, in Lon's eyes, was for the under dog to win. He always picked the little fellow, and would stand up and yell frantic advice, direction, encouragement.

Chaney's charities and the things that made him the "idol of the ranks," the closed circle of his home life, and his last hours are told in next week's concluding installment.

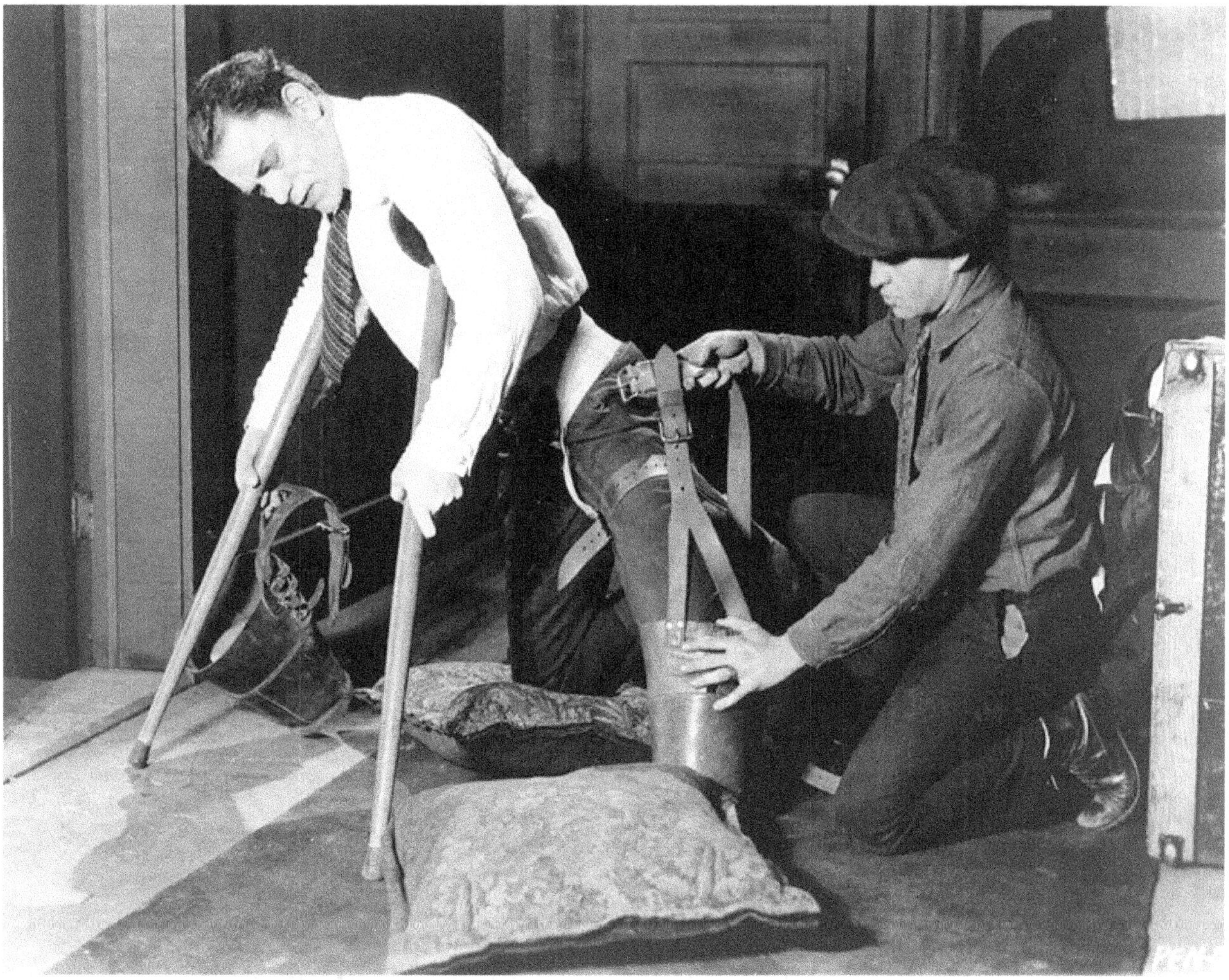

Lon Chaney is assisted with his
costume for *The Penalty*, 1922.
The leather harness gave him the
appearance of a legless man.

This costume can be seen, along
with his makeup cases at the
Museum of Natural History in
Los Angeles.

Lon Chaney

A Portrait of the Man Behind a Thousand Faces

By
ADELA ROGERS ST. JOHNS

The hard-boiled Sergeant in Tell It to the Marines.

Motion Picture Publications photo

(Reading time: 25 minutes.)

SECRETS of some of the make-ups with which Lon Chaney amazed Hollywood as well as the public; the torture he inflicted on himself in his efforts at realism; his readiness always to aid those with whom he worked; and how, despite the fame that was his, he remained the simple, sentimental, hard-boiled guy who gloried in the fact that he was often mistaken for a stage hand, were told last week.

PART FIVE—CONCLUSION

LON CHANEY'S charities were his own. Based on sentiment, on something he could see and understand. The abstract didn't appeal to him.

The Community Chest of Los Angeles, which is the official organized charity supplying funds through a central outlet to the needy of all creeds and races, calls heavily upon the motion-picture industry for funds and workers. Each studio has a quota and the amount is proportioned out by the heads. So much to be given by each big star, so much by actors and directors getting certain salaries, so much to be raised by smaller contributions among the less highly paid employees.

During the last drive Chaney's name, with those of Norma Shearer, William Haines, Joan Crawford, Greta Garbo, was down on the list for five thousand dollars. It was a fair "tithe" of the salary earnings of these people to be given to public charity.

Lon refused absolutely.

Greenwood sent for him to talk it over.

"What's the matter, Lon?" he said. "You can afford that."

"Sure," said Chaney, with his quick grin, "but I'm not going to. I've got my own gang to look after, and they aren't the kind the Community Chest could ever help. They need somebody they can get in touch with in emergencies. There are plenty of folks that need a helping hand in the tough spots. I know what that means and that's where my charity goes. You can't tell me where to give my money, you nor the Community Chest nor anybody else. I know what's right and I'll do it."

There was a swift gesture, a ripping noise.

What he said was true. The little girl up in the accounting department whose kid brother had to be sent to Arizona for a year or die. He went, and Chaney footed the bills. The wife of an electrician who had to have an expensive operation. The famous doctor received a check signed Lon Chaney. The mother of an assistant cameraman who needed X-rays and treatments. Lon saw that she got them. Young men with families who had been out of work and couldn't make the payments on their little homes. Lon, with a slap on the back, gave the money and usually refused to take it back.

When a new baby was expected in a family where the income was small, it was Chaney who paid the hospital bills and sent out the new crib and the clothes for the expected arrival.

When a clean, honest young chap had a chance to buy into a small business with a future, it was Chaney who put up the money.

There is a girl studying music in Paris on a bank account arranged for her by Mrs. Chaney. She was a waitress in the M.-G.-M. commissary, a girl with a beautiful voice. Lon told his wife about it and they gave her the chance she had ceased to hope for.

I know two boys who are going through engineering college at Chaney's expense. He approved of engineers.

[CONTINUED ON NEXT PAGE]

[LON CHANEY
Continued from page thirty-nine]

After he was gone, they found in his dressing room all his charity accounts, kept in separate bank books and so arranged that they could be carried on after his death.

His greatest interest in his fan mail was in that which came from prisons all over the world. No secretary handled the mass of letters which arrived every day. He took time to check it himself and with his own hand answered the messages that came to him from behind the bars.

"If they are interested enough to write me, I guess I can manage to answer them," he said.

His ideas on prison reform were definite and active. For the Island Lantern, a magazine issued at the United States Penitentiary at McNeil Island, Chaney wrote a splendid article on the correction of faults in our present system of imprisonment. Its literary merits weren't great, but it was pervaded by sound sense and constructive suggestions.

Among other things, he said:

"To sum up my ideas as an observer, effective prison work leading to better observance of the laws would embrace the following points:

"Segregation of prisoners and corrective education.

"Indeterminate sentences, coupled with an effective scheme for state rehabilitation, furnishing a goal toward which each man should work.

"Education work in prisons: trade instruction and interesting labor.

"Administration of prisons by specialists trained for this important work and not fettered by politics. Like our schools, our prisons should be entirely removed from the influence of politicians.

"And don't class any man as a permanent danger to society until all efforts at rehabilitation have failed—and then, I think, you'll find the 'failure' is a case for the psychiatrist rather than a penologist.

"Underlying it all is just one thing—a square deal.

"The Golden Rule is still a splendid old idea and doesn't get old-fashioned. And man is still his brother's keeper."

THERE you have Chaney. Simple, a little trite, honest and direct. The champion of the under dog. Jobs for men out of prison were part of his charity.

"They're supposed to have paid their debt, aren't they?" he said once to a man whom he asked to give employment to an ex-convict, "Are we going to keep nagging at them the rest of their lives and force them back into crime? If we do, we're just as guilty of it as they are."

Above the mirror in his dressing room was a verse which he told Clinton Lyle summed up all his ideas of religion:

Do what thy manhood bids thee do.
    From none but self expect applause.
He noblest lives and noblest dies
    Who makes and keeps his self-made laws.

He tore up a bunch of fan mail, and yelled across at the gateman, "There's my high-priced secretary!"

Picture by Garrett Price

Yet, with it all, Chaney was rabidly unforgiving of small injuries.

He loved to flaunt his pose, loved to make fun of the "aristocrats."

One day another famous male star drove through the front gate with his valet and secretary in attendance. After all, such service is almost essential to a hard-driven screen star. Chaney watched him with something like a sneer and as the car passed he tore up a huge bunch of fan mail, threw it in a near-by ash can, and yelled across at the gateman, "There's my high-priced secretary!" The ash can.

Once he started to take some friends on a set where a certain man star was working. The star refused to allow the party to watch him work. The reason, which he couldn't at the moment explain, was that his leading lady, a New York actress now dead, was very drunk. It wasn't wise to allow outsiders to see her in that condition. Later he told Chaney about it. But Chaney never forgave him and never missed an opportunity to show his contempt.

AT the Metro-Goldwyn-Mayer studio the big commissary is divided into two rooms. A big main dining room with a lunch counter at one side, where the majority of people who work on the lot eat. At one side is a charming porch, with screened windows looking out on the grass. There the stars, directors, executives, and important players have their meals.

The caste line is drawn, invisible but sure.

Lon Chaney never ate on that porch in his life. He was the only star who ever ate anywhere else.

His table was just inside the main doors. There he sat daily and the gang stopped to have a word with him as they came in.

Eating was a favorite pastime with him and he had his favorite dishes and got better service and more special attention than any other star.

But always in the main dining room.

A few days after Lon's death I was eating there myself with a couple of men who knew Lon well. The place was crowded and two girls, evidently stenographers, came and sat at the same table. One of them ordered a "Lon Chaney sandwich," a concoction of bacon, tomatoes, and cheese which Lon had invented.

The waitress, a big middle-aged woman, stood perfectly still. The girl looked up, startled. Then they both began to cry.

"Oh," said the girl, "I'm sorry. I forgot. I don't want any lunch." And she flew out of the dining room. The waitress openly wiped her eyes on her apron and went on to another table.

At Christmas time he always arrived at the studio with carloads of presents. For Ruth and Rosie. For Clara and Peggy. For Jane and Bess. Not a girl was forgotten and not one but found a Christmas card with her name and a little message in the box of stockings or gloves or the merchandise order from some big store.

Yet Lon's name was never connected even momentarily with that of any girl to whom he was kind.

Clinton Lyle told me a little story that explains Lon's

ideas on this subject and probably put him definitely out of the class of men who are "on the make," as the saying goes.

They were in Fresno on location. About eleven o'clock they were standing on the curb getting a last breath of air before they went to bed. A

Chaney at the throttle in Thunder.

swell big roadster drew up to the curb; a man got out and hurried into the hotel, leaving a woman alone in the car. Lyle noticed that she was very beautiful, wrapped in a big fur coat and wearing a smart little hat. Peeping out of the door, she recognized Chaney. After a moment she called to him. Lon went over.

The girl smiled up at him, talking rapidly.

Then Lyle heard Chaney say, "It's very kind of you; but, you see, Mrs. Chaney is waiting for me, so I couldn't very well."

Mrs. CHANEY being some hundreds of miles away in Hollywood, Lyle asked Lon afterward what he meant by that one.

"Well," said Lon, "she is waiting for me, isn't she? She's always waited for me. She doesn't have to be right around the corner to know I'm on the level with her. As long as she's in the world at all she's with me. Hell, if I was a woman I'd hate to be married to one of these guys you couldn't trust unless you were looking right at him. I suppose those guys'd think it was all right to commit a murder if they weren't going to get caught."

I asked Tod Browning how Lon was to direct. No one, perhaps, knows a star so well as his director.

"Never said anything to me on the set except, 'Yes, boss,'" said Tod. "We used to—argue a bit before and after hours. But on the set he was a good soldier."

Argue! They fought like a couple of sea lions. They yelled and cussed each other out plenty. But just let

anyone else interfere. Let any executive or writer attempt to take advantage of the apparent friction. They soon found out it was a very private fight. Tod and Lon instantly ganged on the intruder, who decided that he would be better occupied elsewhere.

The idol of the ranks was Chaney.

But the opinion in front offices was different. The big bosses mourned little save financially over the passing of Lon Chaney. They didn't even go to the cemetery for the last sacred rites. They arrived twenty-five minutes late at the services in the chapel of a downtown undertaking parlor. When the last word had been said, they departed in haste, their car shooting out from the long line that followed the casket where lay the man who had earned as much money for his company as any man who ever worked for it.

A BOLSHEVIK he lived and a bolshevik he died.

I happen to know that a six-foot-four stage carpenter, who stood bareheaded in the crowd, had to be held back from assault and battery when he found that the bosses weren't going to pay Lon that last earthly courtesy.

Lon wouldn't have cared. He would have understood. He had worked for them, given his best, earned enormous sums for them. But they had paid him for it beyond his greatest dreams. He didn't like them and they didn't know him. It was fifty-fifty. As long as he lived they had treated him well. He had been grateful for Louis B. Mayer's last visit to the hospital and his kind offer of help in Lon's extremity. Let it go at that. They never spoke the same language. How could they be friends?

At home? The mysterious home life about which the newspapers and magazines said so much? There wasn't anything mysterious about it except that it was so different from that of other screen luminaries. The Chaneys built, lived in, and sold several charming, unpretentious houses.

They gave little parties for their own group of friends—the Clinton Lyles, Phil Epstein and his wife, Fay Parkes, the girl who had helped take care of little Creighton; Mr. and Mrs. M. K. Wilson, another actor from the old days. A closed circle. They were comfortable with those people. No frills. No pretentions. No effort.

A story that Clinton Lyle told me is typical of Chaney's attitude in all things social. The Chaneys were having a little anniversary party. About fifteen of these close friends had been invited. One of the guests, an actor once well known with the Kolb and Dill show, didn't have a good blue suit. Things hadn't been breaking very well. He had a gray suit, not too new, and a dinner jacket. The proper thing to wear at the Chaneys' was a blue suit.

"I'll have to wear my dinner
[CONTINUED ON NEXT PAGE]

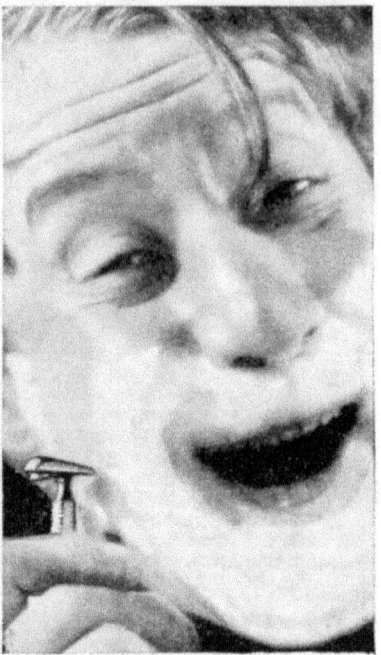

LON CHANEY
[Continued from page forty-one]

clothes," he told Lyle. "I won't go unless you wear yours, too."

After some argument, Lyle yielded and they appeared at the Chaney front door attired in evening garb.

Lon himself opened the door. He took one look. "Waiters go round to the back," he said, and tried to shut the door.

After some parleying they were admitted. Lon regarded them with the severest disapproval.

"Gone Hollywood or something?" he demanded. "What you made up for, the Hall-room Boys?"

He sauntered about, still keeping his eye on them. Finally he called them over in a close little circle, putting down his head as though he had a secret to impart. They bent toward him. There was a swift gesture, a ripping noise—and the two dressy guests stood divested of their collars and most of their shirts.

"That'll teach you two," said Chaney, with infinite satisfaction.

Later in the evening Lyle felt merry and tuneful, so he got Jack and Sam Feinberg to play some of his old music from The Rose of Algeria. He was singing his head off when a brutal comment from Chaney stopped him. "Listen to our constipated Caruso," said Chaney.

He still loved to putter around the house. His hands were never idle. When his first grandchild, Lon Chaney II, arrived, he was wild with delight. He carved little wooden animals, molded little clay figures, played with the child for hours on end.

"I'm grandpop now," he used to say. "Guess I can spoil this one. Creighton'll have to look after him. I can have some fun."

ONE of the last things he did was to make a bird house.

Lon and Hazel and Clinton and Flo Lyle were sitting on the patio in the sunshine one Sunday afternoon admiring the pretty garden.

"Lon promised me a bird house," said Hazel Chaney. "He hasn't made it, though. Wouldn't a bird house be pretty over there by the rosebushes?"

Clinton Lyle grinned. "Why, Hazel," he said, "you couldn't expect the great Lon Chaney to make you a bird house, could you? Maybe he made things for you in the old days. Now he's a great movie star. Surely you don't think he'd make a bird house with his own hands?"

Lon pretended slumber.

The following Sunday, when the Lyles arrived, there was the new bird house.

"Now you take it back," said Chaney. "I suppose you thought I'd gone soft. Suppose you thought I couldn't use

my hands any more. Take a look at that. I guess you never saw a better bird house. I guess nobody could make a better one."

There was only one servant in that house. However, like every other house Hazel Chaney entered, it ran like clockwork.

Their amusements were inexpensive, simple. Mrs. Chaney had nice clothes, but she knew how and where and when to buy them.

THE real passion of Chaney's life, outside his work and his wife, was fishing. He was a sworn disciple of Izaak Walton. In the early days he and his wife, and some friends perhaps, or young Creighton, would go to Bishop, hire horses, and pack in from there. Later he built his own cabin.

The men of the mountains around there tell me that Lon Chaney was the finest trout fisherman who ever cast a line. There are two brothers who for a quarter of a century have been taking men to fish the trout streams of the Sierras. Men from San Francisco, men from the east, men from Los Angeles, are guided by them into the beauties and the sports of these wonderful mountains.

They will talk you blue in the face, hour after hour, about the things Lon Chaney could do with a fishing pole and a trout fly. Tireless, enthusiastic, he would fish from half an hour before sunrise to half an hour after sundown. Jeske might tire, Creighton might collapse. Lon was indefatigable.

One of the proudest moments of his life was when Hazel Chaney caught her first trout. Patiently, carefully, he had instructed her in the sacred art as he had instructed Creighton.

Between Lon Chaney and Hazel, his wife, had grown up a love that made them completely one, as people become one who have lived together for many years in unity and devotion. It was a love beyond the romance of youth, the hectic passions that make drama. A union that needed little expression. Husband and wife. A real marriage—and they grow rarer daily, it seems.

"He used to laugh and get embarrassed when I told him I thought he was the handsomest man in the world," she told me quietly. "And he would laugh, too, when I told him he was a great lover, far beyond any they had on the screen. But it was true. I cannot tell you how wonderful he was. Nor all the little things he did for me always. He would say, 'Let me show you, mama'—" She couldn't go on. Because it swept over her suddenly that he would never do those things or say those things again.

Sometimes Lon would read of scandals, disasters, disgrace that happened to other stars in the business.

Then he would say, "You see, mama, we're better off as we are."

When Bill Haines made Tell It to the Marines with Chaney, the older man gave him every bit of help and advice he could.

"I never worked with anyone who gave so much," Bill said. "He was wonderful to me. He taught me more about acting and the camera than anyone else in the business. But he was always giving me hell, too. He'd say, 'Look here, Bill, you must learn to conserve yourself. Save your money. Take care of your health. Why, I'll be able to work

Taps for a comrade. The marines at Lon Chaney's funeral.

Motion Picture
Publications photo

when I'm a hundred. I've taken care of myself. I've never wasted my money. I'll never know want. Always remember you've got to think about the future. You can't live just for today.'"

The wife of a famous director, who knew Lon when he worked with her husband, told me that every conversation ended with that thought.

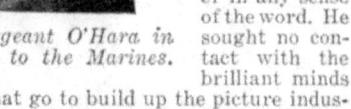

Save. Save money. The fear of poverty, of old age, at the world's mercy, never left him.

His life was a narrow one, judged by modern standards. He never traveled. His few trips to New York were on business. He never went to Europe, or Honolulu. He was not a reader in any sense of the word. He sought no contact with the brilliant minds that go to build up the picture industry. Great writers who came to Hollywood and would have enjoyed knowing Chaney were never invited to his house.

As Sergeant O'Hara in Tell It to the Marines.

Many believed that Mrs. Chaney was responsible for this, that she was afraid to let him widen his circle for fear she couldn't hold her own. That wasn't true. She didn't want to go, but she would have gone if Lon had desired it. Her thought was always to please him. There wasn't anything she hated as much as outdoor life. Horseback riding was torture to her. Camping filled her with horror. But she went on horseback into the mountains and camped for weeks and Lon never dreamed that she didn't enjoy it as much as he did.

SHE wasn't the woman to force intellectual growth upon him. Her home. Her friends. Her visits to the beauty parlor. Little trips to buy clothes. Marketing. Going into the kitchen to cook Lon's favorite dishes. Sitting at night by the fireside, listening to the radio, planning the long years ahead—together. Having Creighton and his wife and little Lon, and finally the second grandchild, Ronald, at the house. That was enough for her. That was peace, security.

As far as anything that ever happened to them was concerned, Lon Chaney might have been a successful contractor or a business man. They never took advantage of the door which Lon's name would have opened to them automatically.

She was terribly proud of him, but she would have been just as proud if he'd been an automobile manufacturer. It touched her—the love people had for him—but she would have been just as touched if he'd been elected president of the Rotarians or head of the Elks.

Against a flaming background they moved—a strange little couple. It is the background that makes them stand out. All the gaud and glitter and genius and uproar of Hollywood as a setting for an existence that might just as well have been lived on Main Street. Personal fame and popularity ignored. Money used without imagination and without vision.

ON September 14, 1929, Chaney had an operation to remove his tonsils.

His health hadn't been good for some time. Pains in his spine. Low vitality. Headaches.

The talkies had worried him. He put up his last fight to avoid them. All that was artist in him rose to condemn the death of pantomime, of which he knew himself master. Silence was the golden mean of his work. To him, a great art, the universal art of the world, was lost when the talkies came.

"I won't make the damn' noisy, squeaky things," he said.

Talkies had come to stay. At last he had to give in. He was the last star save Chaplin, who now holds the silent fort alone, to speak.

"Anyway," he said to Fritz Tidden, "it was good showmanship, even if they licked me. I stood out. I wasn't one of the mob. It was news when Lon Chaney finally consented to talk."

It was poor consolation. The talkies hadn't hurt him financially, since he signed a new five-year contract to make them at an even larger salary. But they broke his heart. They had killed his art, taken the soul out of his work.

He never made but one, and he was sorry he did that. Since his career was to end so soon, he wished passionately that he might have gone out, as he came in, in silence.

A few weeks after his tonsils were out he started a picture called Thunder. He started it too soon, but he had all the old trouper's horror of holding the curtain. "Mustn't hold up production," he said. Even when Mayer assured him that it was okey, his pride made him start on schedule. He hated being ill, as though it were a weakness that robbed him of manhood.

In Thunder was a great storm scene where Chaney drove an engine through clouds of snow. They made the snow of gypsum and asbestos. Great clouds of it were hurled by five wind machines upon the engine where Chaney rode at the throttle. The big flakes beat upon his face with terrific force.

One of those flakes lodged in his throat and was buried in the unhealed flesh. That started the infection which caused his death.

Without that, the sentence was written on the wall. His body had rebelled against abuse. The lungs and heart had been weakened beyond repair. It was only a matter of time.

[CONCLUDED ON NEXT PAGE]

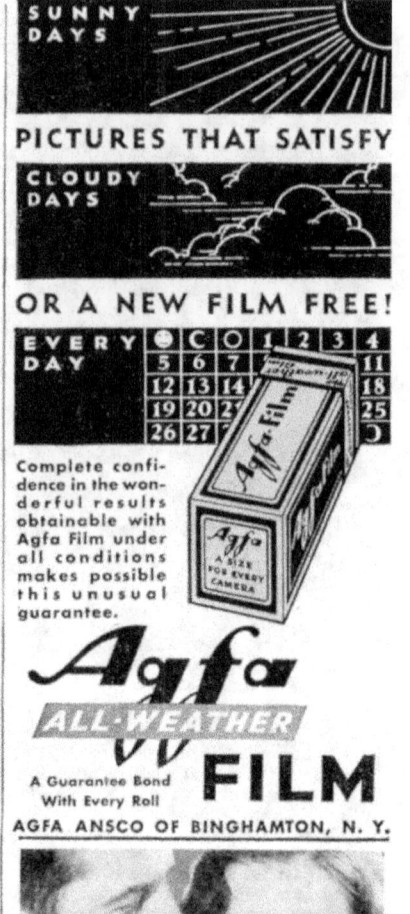

[LON CHANEY
Continued from page forty-three]

Lon Chaney went through those last six months of agony with a smile. To the end his wife and son believed that he did not know he was dying.

He did know.

For a time he was overpowered by a fear of death that shook his manhood to its foundations.

Just before he went to New York for those last treatments that they thought might save him, Lon went to his great friend Greenwood. He had just finished The Unholy Three, his first and last talking picture.

"I've shot my last scene," he said. "I'm through."

Greenwood said the usual things that a man says to his friend in a spot like that.

Lon shook his head. His face was white and there were beads of sweat on his forehead.

"I don't want to die," he said. "I hate going into that unknown darkness. But I can lick that. I don't want to leave my wife and my son and the babies. I love them so. What will I do without Hazel? What will she do without me? I don't want to die. I'm not ready."

There was a silence in the room while Greenwood's wise eyes, that had looked upon so much of life and death, saw the uselessness of deception.

"The last enemy," he said quietly. "A man must face it as he has faced all other enemies. You are fortunate, Lon. Your wife and family are provided for. You must be unafraid. You must be a man."

THERE was an hour-long struggle in that office while the clatter of the studio swept by outside. Lon Chaney went out with steady hands and smiling eyes, facing that enemy. In the end he found peace among his mountains, on the last trip to his cabin, and he played the game to the very end and in the last hours protected those around him by letting them think he didn't know.

On their return from New York, the Chaneys had gone to the beautiful Beverly Wilshire. The new home in Beverly Hills wasn't ready for occupancy. It stood awaiting the finishing touches from hands that had grown too feeble. It was the thing toward which they had worked, the setting for their long years of peace and contentment. Their income was adequate now to support it. But the great clown was never to sleep beneath that safe roof.

In August they took him to a Los Angeles hospital.

"Don't you worry, mama," he said. "I'll be out of there before long and we'll be in the new house. Won't that be nice?"

Hazel Chaney smiled. A woman has courage to smile when it is to comfort the man she loves.

On the morning of August 24, 1930, the papers carried the news of the blood transfusion and of the seriousness of Lon's condition.

Beneath the blow his studio faltered. The men

---

would not, could not, work. The telephone switchboard had to be closed. Outside the doors of the executives stood long lines of men and women begging for a chance to help Lon.

A wave of grief that was like a desert wind swept the place.

Bravely Lon fought.

In his eyes was a great question: Why? He had worked, he had sacrificed, he had saved. Were the fruits to be snatched from him now?

We appear on the scene without asking
And we leave without wanting to go.

Pray for the strength to go out— in character.

"My mask is all worn out with tear drops"—Laugh, clown, laugh!

SUNDAY afternoon. The sensitive soul of this son of a mother and father who could not hear the world nor speak to it felt the presence in that room of his last enemy.

He smiled. The radio played. Ravaged, fighting, his hands clenched until the nails cut his palms, Lon Chaney acted his last part.

His last speech was spoken as his first had been. When his voice failed him, he talked with brother John upon his hands as he had first talked with his beloved mother.

Before midnight he begged his wife to go home. He was all right. Much better. She needed sleep. He was fine.

No matter how much it may hurt,
I must keep on acting, acting, acting—

He knew. His last thought was to save his wife the sight of his final exit from the stage where he had played so brave a part.

A kiss was his farewell. He had never thought much of words.

At midnight the nurse saw him struggling for breath. Above the mask of his face, white as any clown's now without make-up, his eyes were blazing in a tragic smile.

She rushed to him.

Saw, on the white counterpane, two fingers raised. The deaf-mute's signal of distress.

It was Chaney's last gesture.

They laid him to rest at Forest Lawn.

Ahead of him rode a picked guard of motorcycle policemen, all of them his friends. His friends the marines stood about him. The lawns were black with the common people who had loved and honored him, their best friend. The prayers of a wife to whom for fifteen years he had given happiness rose like incense about him. A stalwart son, grandsons to carry on the name of Chaney. Sorrowing hearts in every land.

Out in the vaults still lay the moving, breathing, immortal thousand faces.

"Lon Chaney, hail, farewell—and welcome home!"

I think if he laughed it must have been for joy that life, after all, had given him so much.

THE END

ANSWERS TO TWENTY QUESTIONS
ON PAGE 23

1—Asunción.
2—One that can be seen by the naked eye.
3—After-dinner.
4—A number from which another number is to be subtracted.
5—The bone which forms the posterior part of the skull.
6—Macedon.
7—A meeting for athletic contests, mainly of a racing kind.
8—The mother's side.

9—Strait of Messina.
10—Ten thousand dollars.
11—Twenty-one.
12—A cat, especially a she-cat.
13—Portugal.
14—Stephen C. Foster.
15—Six.
16—Sleight of hand.
17—A voracious sea bird.
18—A warrant issued by the judge of a superior court.
19—In Washington, D. C.
20—Massachusetts.

LON CHANEY RESIDENCE

Beverly Hills

THE ECLECTIC TASTES OF MOVIE STARS AL-
LOWED WILLIAMS THE DESIGN FREEDOM HE
CHERISHED, AND HE OFTEN BUILT BOTH CITY
AND COUNTRY HOUSES FOR THESE CLIENTS.
LON CHANEY CHOSE A MONTEREY COLONIAL
FOR HIS BEVERLY HILLS HOME AND A "ROCK
HOUSE" FOR HIS WEEKEND GETAWAY.

Lon and Hazel Chaney never got to live in their new home in 1930, designed by Architect Paul R. Williams

268

"PHANTOM of the OPERA" with Talking-Singing-Dancing Scenes in Technicolor MADE IN U S

www.ingramcontent.com/pod-product-compliance
Lightning Source LLC
Chambersburg PA
CBHW081147020726
47504CB00009B/2025